CRITICAL ACCLAIM S0-BDL-334

"ALL IN ALL, *JUMP* IS A TAUT AND INTERESTING READ WHICH WILL MAKE YOU RETHINK OUR WORSHIP OF PROFESSIONAL ATHLETES!"

—*South Bend Tribune*

"LUPICA'S *JUMP* FAST BREAKS BEYOND THE GLORY OF THE GAME!"

—*The Providence Sunday Journal*

"THIS GUY CAN WRITE! . . . SPORTS GUYS WILL LIKE THIS BOOK. AND SO WILL ANYBODY ELSE LOOKING FOR A GOOD READ!"

—*Sun Sentinel,* Fort Lauderdale

"SHARPLY WRITTEN!"

—*Arizona Republic*

"*[JUMP]* COMBINES LUPICA'S KNOWLEDGE OF PROFESSIONAL SPORTS AND ALL ITS TRAPPINGS WITH A RIVETING WRITING STYLE THAT WEAVES THE BEST ELEMENTS OF A SUSPENSE THROUGHOUT!"

—*Times Record News,* Wichita Falls, TX

"RIPPED FROM THE HEADLINES . . . UNPREDICTABLE . . . *JUMP* MOVES!"

—*Detroit News and Free Press*

BOOK YOUR PLACE ON OUR WEBSITE AND MAKE THE READING CONNECTION!

We've created a customized website just for our very special readers, where you can get the inside scoop on everything that's going on with Zebra, Pinnacle and Kensington books.

When you come online, you'll have the exciting opportunity to:

- View covers of upcoming books
- Read sample chapters
- Learn about our future publishing schedule (listed by publication month *and author*)
- Find out when your favorite authors will be visiting a city near you
- Search for and order backlist books from our online catalog
- Check out author bios and background information
- Send e-mail to your favorite authors
- Meet the Kensington staff online
- Join us in weekly chats with authors, readers and other guests
- Get writing guidelines
- AND MUCH MORE!

Visit our website at
http://www.kensingtonbooks.com

JUMP

MIKE LUPICA

PINNACLE BOOKS
Kensington Publishing Corp.
http://www.kensingtonbooks.com

This book is for
William Goldman
and Pete Hamill.

Acknowledgments

Nothing important in my life ever gets done without the love and support of Taylor McKelvy Lupica.

And special thanks this time to Detective Tony Giunta, Westport (Conn.) Police Department.

1

Hannah had acted the scene out a thousand times. Played both parts, trying it different ways, just to see how it sounded. She would wake up early, four o'clock, five o'clock, and sometimes be halfway into the scene already, as though it had started in a dream and just kept going. Turned into a movie without her even knowing it.

"I'd like to report a rape."

The cop would look up. It was always a different cop, sometimes young, sometimes older, always in uniform.

Sometimes black, sometimes white.

He'd look up from what he was doing, anyway.

"I beg your pardon?"

"I said, 'I'd like to report a rape.'"

Hannah was always very relaxed, very sure of herself. If she lost it in imagination, what would the real thing be like? She wasn't an analytical person. She'd never seen herself as any great brain. But she had a sense of how things should look.

She could tell you what was wrong with this picture, basically.

So she'd be standing there in front of the cop and finally he would look up, take a closer look at her. He would look at her the way men had always looked at her. Hannah never thought

of herself as beautiful, either. She would look in the mirror sometimes, trying to figure out what the big deal was. Men always
had a different idea, as far back as she could remember.

The cop would say, "Why don't you take a seat, so we can talk
about this. Rape, you said?"

"Yes."

"Where?"

"Right here in Fulton."

Now would come the hard part, as the cop started to write
everything down.

"When did this alleged rape occur?"

Sometimes they said alleged, sometimes they didn't.

"What?"

"The rape, when did it occur?"

Shit.

"Last year."

The cop stops writing and looks up at her, skeptical.

"Last year?"

"Almost a year ago exactly. The first week of October. October fourth, to be exact. The night of October fourth."

"I see." He writes that down and then he says, "The person
who raped you—"

"Per*sons.*" Hannah would lean on the second part of the word,
making sure he knew it was more than one.

"Persons. Do you know these persons?"

And that's when she would tell him, giving one name and then
the other. This was the easy part; now she would have his attention. The cop, white or black or young or old or handsome,
never liked the part about everything happening a year ago. But
the names always made him change his attitude.

Even imagining things, Hannah went out of her way to please
people.

"You're kidding," the cop would say.

"I wish," Hannah would say, or something along those lines.

Sometimes, imagining in the dark, only a slash of light coming from the bathroom, she didn't like it to be completely dark anymore, she had to make sure not to get snippy here. She wanted the cop on her side, not thinking she was some kind of cold fish. Jimmy, her brother, called her that all the time.

She wished Jimmy was with her now, standing in front of a real police station finally, not a made-up one. The sign, sitting there in the middle of the little village green, said POLICE DEPARTMENT, FULTON, CONNECTICUT. The building looked more like a frame house than some police station. Where was she, Mayberry? She was always comparing things in real life to television. If she walked in, who was she going to find in there, Sheriff Andy and Deputy Barney? Across the street was the Fulton Market, and an ice-cream parlor called Scoops, and a movie theater with one of those old-fashioned marquees in front, like you saw in movies about the fifties. And across the green, to the right, was the library. There was a little girl in a pink dress, pink ribbon in her hair, on the steps of the library, waiting for her mother, the mother in a man's white shirt with rolled-up sleeves and blue jeans and Keds, straight blond hair, looking like Martha Stewart on the cover of one of her books, one of those books that told you how to have a perfect house and perfect food and a perfect life. Hannah took it all in: the library, the mother, the little girl, all the cute stores, everything looking like a library, really. The police station, looking different, built in some kind of cream-colored brick, sat right there, across the green.

This was as far as Hannah had ever made it.

Do I go in or not?

Okay, what's it going to be?

She knew if she didn't go in now, she was never going in. She would lose her nerve forever, get back into the car, go back to Manhattan, play it out inside her head for the rest of her life, or with Beth, her therapist. What she'd told Beth, anyway. Because she hadn't ever come close to telling her everything.

What's it going to be?

After all this time, after a thousand dreams, Hannah walked out of her own head and across the green toward the police station.

Inside, it looked more like a bank. They had a receptionist just inside the front door, behind a glass partition.

She said to the receptionist, "I'd like to speak to Detective Hyland, please."

The woman's nameplate said SCHNEIDER. She had short gray hair and a broad nose and glasses with lenses so thick you couldn't make out the color of her eyes. She was smoking.

Schneider said, "What's this in reference to?"

"He'll know what it's about when you give him my name."

"Which is?"

"Hannah Carey."

"Take a seat, Miss Carey. I'll see if he's free."

She sat down across from Schneider. There were two chairs and a little glass table in between with newspapers on top of some magazines. She noticed the New Haven *Register*. The *New York Times*.

"So you finally came," he said.

Hannah knew the voice from all the times on the telephone.

"I finally came."

Hyland said, "Good," then smiled and put out his hand. "Brian Hyland," he said. "Why don't we go back to my office?"

She had wondered what he would look like, whether he would look like any of the cops she had imagined. Or would he be older than his voice sounded on the phone? It turned out he was a little taller than she was, which made him slightly over six feet, with short black hair going to gray on the sides and a mustache the same color, maybe a little grayer. A good tan, cornflower-blue eyes. Straight nose. Probably had a Martha Stewart wife of his own at home. He was wearing a blue button-down polo shirt with a striped tie, khaki slacks, and Bass Weejuns loafers. She thought of him as a television series: *Brian Hyland, Preppie Cop.* He didn't look like he was forty yet. Maybe this wouldn't be so bad.

"Do I pass inspection?"

Hannah said, "What?"

"I feel like you just picked me out of a lineup." He smiled at her with straight white teeth. The smile seemed genuine. Hannah knew phony come-on smiles by now, men looking at her as if she was the most fascinating person they would ever meet in their lives.

"I just always wondered what you'd look like," she said, and Hyland said, "Me, too."

He led her through a big, sunny room, filled with cubicles, and back to his office. He let her go in first, closed the door behind her, then went around his desk and sat down, motioning for her to take the seat across from him.

"So," he said.

"So."

"I haven't talked to you for a while."

"September eighth."

"You have the date?"

"I write it down in this book I've been keeping. Beth . . . my therapist . . . thought it would be a good idea." Hannah cleared her throat.

"Would you like something to drink?"

"I'm fine."

"Why did you finally come in, if you don't mind my asking?"

"It was time for us to have this talk in person."

"We've talked before."

"It was time for me to come here and make an official statement and sign it. Get on with things once and for all."

"You didn't bring a lawyer with you?"

Hannah cleared her throat again. "I don't need a lawyer to tell me what it was like."

It was very quiet in Hyland's office. Out the back window, there was a small parking lot, and then a few more buildings in this tiny shopping plaza.

Detective Brian Hyland said, "Let's get a stenographer in here, and the videotape guy. Okay?"

Hannah said, "Okay."

She told him as much of it as she could remember.

About driving up to her mother's house in Litchfield. The traffic jam on the Merritt Parkway right before New Canaan. Stopping in at the first place, Gates, hoping to see her friend Bobby, who used to bartend there. Then running into them and going along to the next place . . .

Every once in a while, he would stop her.

"About what time did you leave Gates?"

"I don't remember."

"Your friend didn't work there anymore, but you decided to eat at the bar?"

"Yes."

"They came in?"

"Yes."

"You recognized them?"

"The bartender told somebody sitting next to me. So when I looked up, I knew."

"But you *knew* who they were?"

"Yes."

"And that's why you went along with them?"

"You mean, like as a groupie?"

Detective Hyland put his hands up. "Just because it seemed exciting?"

"I guess so. What was in my head before . . . I'm not even sure anymore."

Then about the next place in New Canaan, Mulligan's, and how crowded it was. And having a few drinks. Then one of them, she couldn't even remember *which* one anymore, saying they were moving the party back to their place.

Hannah told him the rest of it and finally looked up at the clock above Hyland's desk. She had been talking for forty-five minutes. It felt like five.

Hyland said, "There are a lot of gaps. Time gaps and so forth."

"I know. I'm sorry."

Hyland said, "When it was over, you don't remember what time it was?"

"I'm sorry, I didn't check my watch."

Hyland let it go, said, "How did you finally get out of the house?"

"I thought I mentioned that before. Collins fell asleep."

"And the other—"

"He went out."

"When?"

"I heard a door at some point, I just can't remember when exactly—"

"And you went to your car then?"

"Yes."

"You were able to drive back to the city."

"After a while."

"After a while?"

"I sat in my car awhile. I don't know for how long. Then I realized my keys were inside. They must've fallen out of my purse."

"So you went back inside to get them?"

"Yes. Hoping he was still asleep."

"Was he?"

"Collins wasn't."

"Where was Mr. Collins?"

"He was in the living room, drinking a beer, watching some kind of pornographic movie on television." Hannah cleared her throat. "He was watching this movie, naked, and masturbating."

"Did he speak to you?"

"Yes."

"What did he say?"

Hannah said, "He looked up at me, smiling, and said, 'You want some more?' I just backed away from him, started to scream—"

"Did Mr. Collins do anything to stop you from leaving after you found your keys?"

"No. He just told me to relax, I was going to wake up his neighbors."

"Did he say anything else to you?"

"Yes."

"What did he say, Miss Carey?"

"He said I'd been such a good sport up until then, why was I trying to spoil a perfect evening."

"Anything else?"

"He said, 'Why couldn't you moan like that when I asked you to?' "

2

Ellis Adair had to slow up as he crossed the half-court line. A couple of minutes to go in practice now, everybody tired, tongues hanging out like dogs. Everybody except him. Ellis never got tired.

Jordan told him one time, right before he up and retired, "I'm already starting to feel it, Fresh. Fans might not know yet, other players might not know. But I know, babe. End of games especially. I tell my legs to do something, you know what they say sometimes? 'Fuck you, Michael,' that's what they say."

He said it would happen to Ellis, too, it happened to everybody eventually, then Ellis'd be looking for the door. It just hadn't happened yet. Couple of minutes to go in practice, in a game, didn't matter, Ellis was what he'd always been.

Fresh.

Ellis "Fresh" Adair.

Freshest boy out there, like fresh was cruise control for him, all the way back to Jersey City, to the playground at the Booker T. Washington projects. He smiled now to himself, seeing himself, all legs then, legs and big jug ears, getting up there so high he felt like he could see the big city there across the river, like he could reach over and touch it. Palm it in his right hand as easy as he could palm a basketball.

Ellis kept going down the right side, feeling the play come to him.

Richie had the ball in the middle, and A.J. was on the left and there were two of them from the Blue Team, scrubs, Boyzie and Riordan, waiting for them at the foul line. Ellis could see Richie looking left the whole time, leaning that way even off the dribble, tilting everything toward A.J., like he was trying to tilt the whole damn court. Now Boyzie went that way, too, and as he did, Richie showed him his left hand, his left hand out anyway, like he was making a shovel pass. Then Riordan committed, dumb shit, going with the pass. Only there wasn't a pass, there was nothing in Richie's left hand, the ball was in his right hand, and now Richie was lobbing the ball toward the basket, even as he kept looking at A. J. Fine.

Ellis flew. Feeling himself smile as he did. The pictures of himself he liked best always caught him smiling.

Fresh boy.

They always wanted to know what it felt like, being able to fly that way, the way he could and Jordan could, and a few others in the past, David Thompson and Doctor J, they had flown. And Ellis would look at them, tell them how it felt, tell them it felt very, very fresh.

Richie always said, you get a good line, stay with it.

They gave him the nickname in the projects, even before he got into Lincoln High and everybody started to come around, because it was close enough to Fresh Air, and Fresh Air was close enough to Air Jordan.

Now in the gym at Fulton College, third day of training camp, everybody's legs shot, fucked-up, except his, he was up there again, taking the ball with his left hand, moving it over to his right. Ellis held it over his head now, the way he always did be-

fore his cleanest dunk, the one that was so smooth, Richie called
it his Fred Astaire.

Who, Richie said, was some dead dancer.

Showtime now, anyways.

Ellis covered his eyes with his left hand.

He could hear Richie, from down below, saying, "Give to me,
baby. Give it to me hard."

The basket was right there now, shit, right under his chin. Ellis
hesitated. He was always amazed when he watched himself on
the news, how fast everything seemed to go, up there, doing his
deal, then down. When he did it on the court, it all seemed to last
much longer, slow motion almost, like he was floating on top of
the whole thing, like the noise and the other players and the
games were some cloud, and Ellis was even above that.

Ellis pulled his hand away from his eyes.

Only he didn't dunk.

Just dropped the ball in. Like he was putting a quarter in the
meter.

They all screamed now at Fulton College.

"I demand a refund!" Richie yelled.

Ellis came limping up to him now, all hunched over like the
old rummies and pipeheads back at Booker T. Washington, head
bobbing all over the place, giving Richie that wheezy old voice.

"Jes' an ol' man, tryin' to get by, legs shot, cain't get up no
way no mo'," Ellis said, going into this fake rheumy cough now.

Gary Lenz, the coach, blew his whistle. He was a pushy dude
from the Lower East Side, in his second year now with the
Knicks. He had started out at Iona, then moved up to St. John's,
now he was in the big leagues, just thirty-two years old, looking
twenty-two. He had all this curly red hair and wore snappy
double-breasted suits. Richie said he looked like he'd grown up
sleeping with Bugsy Siegel's picture under his pillow. Who was
another dead guy, a gangster, who Richie'd read up on in a book

even before there was a movie about him Richie dragged him to
see, with Warren Beatty in it.

Richie had seen more movies than Ellis, and read more books.

Gary Lenz was saying now, "Ellis doesn't want to dunk, I
don't want to coach anymore today."

Ellis was over with Lenz now. Ellis, at six feet eight inches
and change, was nearly a foot taller than the little dude coach.
Ellis ran his hand through Lenz's curls. He knew Lenz hated that.

"Aren't you always telling me to fill the moment with surprise,
Gary? Shit, that's what you say in your new coaching video,
nineteen ninety-five plus tax, available at video stores everywhere."

Lenz grabbed his crotch.

"Surprise this," he said, and walked toward the locker room.
They all knew the real reason he was cutting practice short, even
on the third day of camp; he had to go shoot some BMW commercial in the city. Gary Lenz didn't have as many endorsements
as Ellis. Shit, no one did. But Gary was doing pretty good for a
midget who never got off the bench at Boston College when it
was his turn to fucking play.

The gym emptied out fast. Ellis stayed. He took a ball out of
the rack and motioned for one of the Fulton kids who ball-boyed
during camp to come with him. Ellis shot a hundred free throws
after every practice, everybody knew that. So he was always the
last one out. He looked up at the windows above the court. Gary
would have the windows taped up if this were the regular season, but it was the first week of training camp, so he didn't mind
if people came and watched practice. Ellis waved at the kids
watching him. The reporters were already in the locker room,
wanting to get out of there as soon as they could, the New York
guys pissed they had to drive up to Connecticut to watch fast-
break drills. The kids, though, they just wanted to see Ellis,

they'd stay up there until he shot all hundred free throws. They'd watch him as long as he was out there.

Ellis couldn't remember a time when he hadn't been watched this way.

He made the first ten shots in a row, lost in the routine, when he noticed Frank Crittendon standing next to the ball boy.

Crittendon said, "You got a minute?"

He was the general manager of the Knicks. Crittendon hadn't been around the first two days of camp, so this was the first time Ellis saw he'd gotten even fatter during the summer. He was wearing this faded pink polo shirt that rode up out of his pants, and now when he threw a little bounce pass to Ellis at the line, you could see about half his fat white belly.

Could you get whiter as you got older? Frank Crittendon looked to Ellis sometimes like he'd been washed too many times, something like that, until he was just all washed out.

"This can't wait until I finish, Frank?"

Crittendon said, almost apologizing, "It's kind of important, Ellis." Ellis heard him tell the ball boy to run along, he needed to have a private conversation with Mr. Adair, and motioned Ellis over to the side of the court, where there were still a couple of folding chairs set up. Crittendon sat down. Ellis stretched out on the rubber mat in front of the chairs, started doing some light stomach curls.

"I'm not going to beat around the bush," he said.

Ellis smiled.

"That's a shame, Frank. Nobody ever beat around a bush better than you."

"I just got a call from a Detective Hyland. Fulton police."

"He the crossing guard?" Ellis came up, hands behind his head, held the curl. "Or the one who sets up for the bingo games?"

Crittendon took off the clear glasses he'd always worn and

rubbed his eyes. He'd just turned sixty years old, they'd had a birthday cake for him last spring one night before the last Knicks-Bulls game at the Garden, but Frank Crittendon looked older than sixty because of the drinking. Richie always said the only thing you wondered about with him was what time of day the boy got started.

"A woman showed up today at the police station and has made, um, an accusation of rape."

Ellis said, "Rape."

"She's accused you and Richie of raping her."

Ellis sat up, stayed up, just a little bit out of breath. There was a towel next to the mat. He wiped his face with it.

"Bullshit," he said.

"That's not what she says."

"What else she say, besides rape?"

"She says that during training camp last year, at your house over there at Fulton Crest, you and Richie raped her."

Ellis lay back down now, staring at the ceiling, wishing Richie was there.

Trying to act cool, like he was in charge of the general situation.

"Bullshit," he said.

Frank Crittendon pulled a pipe from out of his slacks, stuck it in his mouth, unlit.

"Her name is Hannah Carey. Do you know her?"

Richie had always said you don't volunteer shit to the man, whoever the man was. Richie was white, but didn't think that way.

"I don't know."

"She sure seems to know you."

"Everybody knows me."

Frank Crittendon stood up, pipe in his teeth, looking like some little Fulton professor out of uniform.

"I just want you to be aware of the situation, Ellis."

"If it's a situation, it's a bullshit situation." Now Ellis stood.

Ellis said, "You read the papers, Frank?"

"Of course."

"I read 'em, too. Not that I'd ever tell a fucking sportswriter that. Know what I find out, the more I read? I find out I can't keep count anymore of the women coming forward, saying that this athlete raped them, that athlete raped them. The beauty-contest girl from Rhode Island stepped forward and got Mike Tyson and now they're all doing it."

Crittendon looked around. Ellis had noticed it before, Frank Crittendon went through life scared of his own shadow, like he was afraid somebody was listening to every single word he said, ready to hear the one bad thing that was going to cost him his job. Or his house.

Ellis said, "Know what Richie says? He says all of a sudden rape ain't a crime, it's a career."

Crittendon said, "You're saying it didn't happen."

Ellis said, "How long have I played for you?"

"Five years."

"Feel like you know me pretty well?"

This part was bullshit. No one knew Ellis, except for Richie, and not even him half the time. Even Richie didn't know everything.

"I like to think so."

"Let me turn it around. Ask you the question: You think I have to force somebody to have sex with me?"

Crittendon shook his head.

Ellis said, "Shit, half the time I got to force them *not* to." Which was the truth.

He walked toward the door. He'd shoot two hundred free throws tomorrow, get back up to speed. He left Frank Crittendon standing there, like he was waiting for the whole gym to fall down on him.

Ellis turned at the door, trying to act cool on this shit, wondering if Richie had left yet. Richie would know what to do.

"Frank," Ellis said, "don't bother me with this again. You feel the urge, you know the drill."

"Call your agent."

Ellis said, "There you go."

3

The little bastard from the *Chronicle* show, WCBS, said on the phone, "The best we can do for the time being is once a week. Which means the same deal as before, we pay you by the appearance."

Coño, Marty thought. Shit, damn, and fuck.

Marty Perez, sitting in his office at the *Daily News,* said, "We talked all summer about three. I come on full-time eventually and give up the column once and for all, if the money's right."

The little bastard's name was Randy Houghton. Marty could never remember whether he was a Houghton from Houghton Mifflin, the publishing company, or not. He was from Boston, Marty knew that. Three years out of Harvard, twenty-five years old, already producing his own tabloid show. *Chronicle* had caught on in New York, even started beating *Wheel of Fortune* in its time slot. Now they were talking about taking it national, moving it up in weight class, putting it into the next gear, primed to go up against all the others: *Inside Edition, Hard Copy, A Current Affair.*

Marty Perez wanted to go national with them.

Randy Houghton said, "I'm glad you brought up the column, babe."

Babe. Back home, you saw little punks like this—*títeres*—looking at you with their attitudes from street corners, like they knew every goddamn thing. In New York they made them television producers.

"The column is one of the problems right now. The plan here, all along, not just with me but with the big bosses, was for you to just take your column and put it on the air. My Gahd"—Houghton still put on the rich-boy Harvard Yard accent sometimes, usually when he was bullshitting you—"nobody knows New York the way Marty Perez does."

Marty just waited, cigar in his free hand, playing with it. Looking at his computer terminal, which only had PEREZ COLUMN at the top, and then a paragraph mark underneath that, and then an empty screen underneath that, which felt like it went all the way down to Forty-second Street, seven floors.

He was pretty sure what was coming.

"Frankly, no one here minded if the TV pieces were expanded versions of the column. Just to give our show that rich New York texture we're shooting for."

Madre de Dios, Marty Perez thought.

Mother of freaking God.

"Texture," he said. "Yeah, I'm full of it."

Among other things.

Randy Houghton wasn't even listening to him. "I'm not telling you anything you don't know already, I've heard you say it yourself, but the column has gotten a little tired lately, babe. My Gahd"—again—"how many times do we have to read about another high school sophomore with a fucking automatic weapon? Do you understand what I'm trying to say here?"

Marty sighed. "I write off the news."

"We know. We know. But we want more than that. We want you back *ahead* of the news, the way you used to be. We want Marty Perez's name back up in lights. I'm not telling you anything you don't know. You're the king, babe. You're Marty Perez. We want people to turn on *Chronicle* the way they used to pick up the *News*. To see what the hell you're going to say next."

"I need a story is what you're saying."

"It would be nice, Marty. I'm not going to lie to you, we know each other too well. I need to be able to sell the big boys here on the idea that you're going to be able to bring in some numbers."

Before Marty could say anything, Houghton said, "Look, there's a call here I've got to take. We'll talk again on Friday, see what you're thinking about for next week."

"I'm ready to make the move to television full-time," Marty said. "I think if I didn't have to work the column and the show, if I could just concentrate on *Chronicle,* the pieces would have the kind of juice you're talking about." Hating the sound of his own voice, begging this punk.

"I hear you, I really do," Randy Houghton said. "Talk to you Friday."

He put down the phone, softly, got his matches off the desk, and relit the cigar. If the little television punk knew it, if he could see what the column had turned into, then everybody knew, maybe even the spics uptown who'd always treated him like the real mayor of New York. The whole thing was getting away from him, in the last year of his contract with the *News,* with people getting laid off all around him in the city room. It was why he was begging for the television job. Marty Perez was still writing three columns a week, he was still a major character in town, with the column and *Chronicle* and the radio commentaries on WOR. But they had taken to running the Sunday column on the Op-Ed page.

In tabloids, that was where they laid you to fucking rest.

Hijo de puta.

All their mothers were whores.

It was three o'clock, he hadn't written a word, and already he wanted a drink.

"Hijo de la gran puta," Marty Perez said out loud.

He was forty-two years old, and he should have been in the clear by now, thirty years in the States, twenty years in the newspaper business, a star for half of that. His father had made his money in the tourist boom that hit San Juan right at the start of the sixties, the one that happened after Cuba closed. His father: running the casino at the El San Juan, then moving across the island to Palmas, but wanting his only son to get out, sending him up to New Rochelle to live with his aunt and uncle.

Martin Perez, Sr., never saying it, but sending his son to New Rochelle and the Horace Mann School because he wanted him to be something more than another spic on the make in New York.

And now, all this time later, that is what he still was. He sat there in his office, wanting to do anything but think about the empty screen, trying to figure out where it all started to get away from him.

Marty Perez had been the boy wonder at first, covering the Yankees right out of Columbia, then moving into a sports column at the *Post* when he was Randy Houghton's age. Then over to the *News* in sports, and finally out front. Pretty soon it was Marty Perez's picture on the side of the *News* trucks, cigar in his hand. Tough guy. It was Marty Perez in the television commercials. Marty Perez as the first Latino to do the big crossover, win just about every award you could win except the Pulitzer, with everybody saying the Pulitzer was just a matter of time.

Pretty soon it was Marty Perez making more than anybody in newspapers in New York City.

They said he was the only one putting names and faces, giving voices, to the forgotten New York. Somebody had written that about him in the *Village Voice*. As if he ever cared about shit like that.

About being King of the Spics.

He just wanted to ride high, and if assholes like the *Voice* guy wrote about his style, that was just part of the deal. Style? It always made him laugh. He had stolen from everybody, from the best, Runyon and Cannon and Hamill and Breslin, especially Breslin, and somehow made it sound as if it all came out the side of his own mouth. Marty's second wife, Madeline, told him he'd stolen everything from those other guys except their talent. That was right before Madeline sued him for divorce and skinned him clean. His first wife, Allie, daughter of one of the hotshots from Condé Nast, the one Marty had used to get into New York society, she hadn't wanted any money, she just wanted out after she caught Marty cheating on her with Madeline.

Madeline, the soap opera actress. She used him the way he used Allie. And ended up with the apartment and most of the big newspaper money, when that was still coming in, before they sold the paper and everybody had to take a cut to keep it alive, Marty Perez taking the biggest cut of all.

Now Madeline was remarried, and so Marty was off the hook with alimony, looking to get out of newspapers and make some real money again.

Looking for a story to get him *out*.

The best part was when these television guys told him that one of the reasons they liked him was because he didn't look like the other blow-dried guys you found all over the dial, that his face had character.

Marty Perez thought, at least his face still had character, right? He put his head back and closed his eyes. Jesus, he was tired.

His secretary, Ann-Marie, woke him up.

"Phone call for you, Mr. Peters."

She always called him that when they were alone because she

knew it pissed him off. Drunk one night, he had made the mistake of telling her that he had been Marty Peters on the school paper at Columbia. He had never legally changed his name, that was a pain in the ass, and besides Marty always liked to keep his options open. But Marty Peters had been the college byline. It wasn't until his senior year that he realized Perez could work a lot better for him, more doors could open for him by being ethnic, especially in newspapers. It was funny, when he thought about it. He had spent most of his life trying to get as far away from Palmas as he could, and now all of a sudden, the last name was like a credit card. It helped him with the ballplayers, that was for sure. It seemed that every season, baseball was importing about one hundred more guys from the Dominican or some goddamn place. It was even better when he moved up to the front of the paper, not just the *Daily News* realizing that New York had become like some suburb of San Juan, but all the other papers, too.

Marty Peters was dead and buried, anyway, except with Ann-Marie, who had some Madeline in her. Pissing him off seemed like a hobby with her.

Now he sat up and said to her, "Phone call from who, it was worth waking me up?"

"Whom. A man. He wouldn't tell me his name. But he said he had a quote scoop unquote."

Perez said, "Stop it, you're making me hot."

"He sounded legitimate, the guy. You want me to tell him you're still taking your nappie?"

She came around the desk and nodded at the empty screen. "Or I could tell him you're writing."

She walked out, shutting the door behind her. He jabbed at the blinking light on his phone.

"Perez."

"I have a story for you, Mr. Perez." Deep voice. He could have been reading radio copy. Or telling people which baggage carousel had their luggage. "A real big story."

"My favorite."

"I thought about giving it to one of the sports guys. But this is a story that will end up on the front page, anyway. So I figured, why waste time? I'll call my old friend Marty Perez."

"I know you?"

"We met in a bar one time."

Shit, that narrowed it down.

"What's your name?"

"Jimmy Carey. I'm an actor?"

Making it sound like a question.

"Jimmy Carey the *actor*," Marty said. "I do remember you, as a matter of fact. Where the hell were we? Elaine's?" Taking a shot. "I was shit-faced, right?"

"We both were. It was Kennedy's."

Marty waited. They always had to do this at their own pace, the way they'd rehearsed it. Jimmy Carey the actor was just getting to it, by way of Kennedy's.

"Are you there?"

"Present."

"You're not saying anything."

"No, you're not saying anything. You didn't call to talk about old times."

Jimmy Carey finally said, "I called to tell you about a rape."

"I'm waiting."

"You're the first person in the media to hear what I'm about to tell you."

"I'm still waiting."

"I'm serious. A rape was reported this morning in Fulton, Connecticut. Do you know where that is?"

"Up near Westport. The Knicks train there, right?"

"The Knicks train there."

Perez said, "Is this about the Knicks?"

"Yes."

He reached into a side drawer of his desk, grabbed one of those long reporter's notebooks, took a pen out of his pocket.

"Which Knick?"

"The cops won't release the names, you know."

"Names," Perez said. "There's more than one?"

"Two."

"But you will."

"What?"

"You're going to give me the names."

"Yes."

"How do you know?"

"I know the victim."

"Who are they?"

"Richie Collins." The guy paused, for effect, and Marty Perez knew.

Marty said, "Richie Collins and Ellis Adair."

His door opened and Michael Cantor, the editor of the *News,* poked his head in. Marty waved him all the way in. Now he said into the phone, "You're telling me that Ellis Adair and this other guy have been charged with rape?"

Cantor went back and shut the door. Then he sat down on the little sofa next to the door, picked up Marty's other extension, and hit some numbers.

"Not charged. Accused."

"Right," Marty said. "You want to give me the woman's name?" He wrote that down, and kept writing. He could hear Cantor talking to Burke, who did the front pages, telling him to forget about some subway train crashing into the station at Eighty-sixth Street, he wanted to see him in Perez's office right away.

Marty heard Cantor say, "Why? Because I got myself a story

all of a sudden that is going to singe your friggin' eyeballs, that's why."

It was seven-fifteen when Cantor came back.

Cantor, looking happy, said, "You close?"

"Five minutes."

"What'd the cops say?"

"I talked to some guy named Hyland. No comment, no names, no nothing."

"But you said you got a confirmation?"

Marty stared at his screen. He deleted something, typed something in its place. Casual, not looking up at Cantor, but nodding.

"A guy I know at the Garden. The Japs brought him in when :hey bought the place."

"Who?"

"You know I can't tell you that."

"What did he say?"

Marty Perez shrugged. "What could he say? The greatest basketball player in the world, who works for them, might end up indicted in a rape case. Let's just say the Japs aren't breaking out the fucking champagne."

"It's Adair and Collins?"

"Yes."

"The guy on the phone, he's really her brother?"

"He's the victim's brother."

"Alleged victim."

Marty shrugged again. "He gave me his home number and his agent's number. They both check out."

"Agent?"

"He's a struggling actor type. Says I met him one time at Kennedy's, over on Second."

Cantor said, "It's a helluva good story."

"A clean fucking hit." Marty tapped the Send button.

Cantor slapped him on the shoulder, walked out the door, leaving it open, and back through the city room to his own office. Marty could hear him whistling.

He waited until Cantor disappeared, called the number at the Garden again. The secretary said, "I know it's important, Mr. Perez, you've made that quite clear. I've been trying to reach him since the first time you called. His plane must have been delayed."

Marty gave her all his numbers again, hung up the phone. He would've liked to have had the confirmation. But the guy was her brother. Somebody's going to make up one like this about his own sister? Fuck that. It wasn't just a good story, he was sure of it. It was a *big* story. If he waited a day, the whole world was going to have it. And he needed it. Needed it to show the whole world, to show the Harvard punk at WCBS. Needed it to show he was still Marty Perez.

Marty Perez stuck his head out the door, saw Burke standing over by the rim, looking at some page proofs. Marty walked over there to see what the front page would look like.

4

It was always a mistake to drive to practice with Richie, sometimes you couldn't find his ass when you were ready to leave.
Or needed to talk to him about something. God*damn,* Ellis
needed to talk to Richie about all of this, but by the time he finished with Frank Crittendon, the old windbag looking like he
might break down and cry right there in the gym, Richie was already gone from the locker room.

Probably off doing what he liked to do best after practice,
which was walk around campus a little bit, casting for strange.

Which was Richie's expression for strange pussy.

Richie liked to say, "The less you know about them, the better sports they tend to be."

Ellis wished Crittendon had done it the other way around, the
more he got to thinking about their conversation, told Richie and
then let Richie come tell him about this fucked-up rape shit. It
always worked best when Richie did the thinking for both of
them.

That's what Ellis should have done, just said to Frank Crittendon, "Deal with Richie." It usually happened this way for
Ellis, he'd get these brilliant ideas afterward, get around to understanding what he *should* have said. Richie didn't ever have

to wait, it always amazed Ellis. Richie had instincts, moves, even talking. He could see shit developing, even when you thought he wasn't paying attention.

Other people thought they had juice with Ellis, but didn't, not Crittendon, not even Donnie Fuchs, their agent, who thought he invented fucking juice. Richie said one time that Donnie was the closest thing to a real Sammy Glick, explaining right away that wasn't a player, but some little Jew character from a play. Richie could explain things like that and not make Ellis feel like an asshole. It was another reason why Richie had always been the one, going all the way back, who had juice with Ellis Adair. Ellis got through Seton Hall because Richie got him through. Same as Richie got him through Lincoln High before that. Richie always said he should have gotten two high school diplomas and two for college.

Ellis's and his own.

But Ellis always came right back at him with "You take the degrees, I'll keep the money from those commercials I always make them put you in with me."

And Richie would come back at him with something like, "Fresh, I'm the only one understands what a cagey motherfucker you are. Only one who *ever* understood."

Ellis smiled now as he came out of the locker-room door and into the parking lot. Richie would know how to handle this, soon as Ellis could talk to him. It had always been him and Richie, Richie not just giving him the ball, but always giving him whatever else he needed. If it was sneakers when they were kids, Richie would figure out a way. A grade. A paper. Assists? Shit. Richie had *always* assisted Ellis Adair. That was the trade-off. The deal. Ellis got him into the games at Booker T. Washington—-all those black faces looking at him like he should have a sheet on at first—and in exchange Richie got him the ball. And after that, the ball and everything else.

"Richie Collins got into the game and dunks for Fresh Adair resulted immediately," that was the way some guy had written it up in the *Times*. The two of them just went on from there, a team, the way they had always dreamed it up. There were a lot of point guards bigger than Richie, faster, better shooters, prettier games. But they didn't have what Richie Collins had.

They didn't have Fresh Adair.

"Remember me, Ellis?"

He'd been walking with his head down, remembering on things, so the girl's voice made him jump a little bit. Richie Collins wasn't around anywhere he could see, but here was this girl leaning against Richie's black Jeep Cherokee in the parking lot reserved for the Knicks behind the gym. Cute with a body on her. Pink shorts, pink-and-white running shoes. Tight Knicks T-shirt, gray, with sweat showing between her breasts. Red hair in a ponytail coming out from the back of a white Knicks cap. Freckles and green eyes.

Remember me?

Richie would know her name right away, remember something about her, even if it was a birthmark. He could do that. There was always something Richie could use to mark them. Like he had some kind of filing system for strange. He would remember the one was saying they raped her, Ellis was sure of it.

Ellis had no idea, of course. How was he supposed to remember names when he couldn't remember faces?

"You remember me, don't you, Ellis?" she said, her voice sounding like this tiny growl.

He put his gym bag down, put his hand to his forehead, grinning, like he was trying to come up with a question on *Jeopardy,* which Richie liked to watch, show off how smart he was, after *Love Connection.* Ellis knew she had come by looking for Richie, waiting here like this by his Jeep, probably as surprised to see

Ellis as he was to see her. Richie had either gone walking around or gotten a ride with someone. If he did, the keys were in the car, once Ellis got through dealing with Miss Whoever This Was.

"You waitin' on Richie?" he asked.

She took off her cap now and reached behind her head, undid the ponytail and shook her head slowly from side to side, letting all this red hair, straight and smooth, fall to her shoulders.

"Waiting to see my two old friends from the Knicks," she said. "You *and* Richie." She tried to look hurt. "You really don't remember me, do you?"

Ellis wasn't in the mood for this. He looked around. All the other players were gone, there was just him, the Jeep, and this girl looking for it big-time. He said to the pouty girl, "You're going to have to help me out. Coach beat us up today, and I'm still out of shape."

"You weren't out of shape last time I saw you."

"Tell me your name at least." He ducked his head a little, like he was embarrassed, giving her some of his Cosby-kid look. Looked up at her, trying to give her big, sad eyes. He didn't want to piss her off in case she was special to Richie. Top-rated strange of some kind. Ellis said, "Tell me your name and we'll go for ice cream."

"No. Not till you remember."

"What grade you in, you can tell me that, huh? You go to school here?"

She sighed. "Maybe a clue will help. I'm a sophomore now. University of Miami. Which is where we met, clue clue, Miami." She went back into her pout. "My feelings are getting hurt now, you don't remember with a clue like Miami."

"I remember, though," they both heard Richie say. Ellis turned around, saw him there, grinning, finishing the ice-cream cone he must have gone for after practice. Ellis wanted to talk to him right away about this rape shit, but knew there was no chance now, not with Whoever She Was leaning against the car.

Not with strange right there in front of them, wearing everything except a fuck-me sign.

Richie Collins liked to talk about their bangability.

"Amanda," Richie said, giving her a bad-boy smile, looking like he was still sixteen, in a T-shirt of his own and baggy jeans and high-top leather sneaks with no socks, with his crew-cut deal, the sides shaved clean, trying to nigger up his hair, as Ellis told him, the way he'd spent his whole life trying to nigger up his whole outlook on things.

"Amanda of Amanda and Chelsea," Richie said. "Am I right or am I right?"

"Long time no see, Richie Collins," she smiled, sliding into the growl again.

"Need to talk at you, won't take more than a minute, Rich, swear," Ellis said. But Richie was on a roll now with Amanda, saying, "Last game of the regular season."

"Pool of the Grand Bay Hotel," Amanda said back. She waved a waggly scolding finger at the two of them. "You both seemed real uptight about the game, and there we were to relax you."

Richie said, "I'm not sure relax is the word you're looking for here, am I right, Fresh?"

Always bringing him into it. "Am I on it, Fresh, or what?"

"What word are we looking for then?" She leaned across the front right fender of the Jeep, put her hands inside the pink shorts, and pulled her T-shirt out of them, giving it a little shake. Cooling herself off.

Ellis, trying to sound interested, said, "Whatever happened to Chelsea?"

Amanda said, "She should be waiting for us at the hotel right now. The Marriott, over on Route 7." Now she walked back to the door on the passenger side, talking to them over the roof.

"The last thing Richie said to us that day in Miami, do you remember what it was?" Not waiting for an answer, she said, "The last thing was, 'Come see us if you ever want some more.' So here we are before we have to go back to school next week." Tilting her head. "Couple of little Super Savers, looking for a fun-filled Connecticut vacation."

Ellis put a hand on Richie's shoulder, leaned down, and said, "No shit, before we get to the general situation here, we got some trouble we need to discuss, I just been with Frank," but Richie shrugged him off. "You drive, Fresh," he said, walking around, opening the back door, nodding in there to Amanda, then following her in, smiling all the way, not worried about whatever trouble Ellis wanted to talk about, just looking like the whole day was shaping up all of a sudden.

"We'll pick up Chelsea at the Marriott, then go have a reunion back at the house," Richie announced.

Ellis pulled his seat belt across him, clicked it in, put the key in the ignition, pissed now, wondering if the whole afternoon was shot because Richie had a hard-on. When Ellis adjusted the rearview mirror, he could see Amanda already working on the zipper to Richie's jeans.

"You can go now, driver," Richie said.

Ellis was driving the car, but he sure as shit knew he was really just along for the ride.

5

She had finally told Jimmy the night before. He thought she was kidding at first. When he realized she wasn't, he started yelling at her, as though by keeping the secret all this time, she had turned him into the injured party.

"How could you keep something like this from your own *brother?*" Jimmy demanded.

"You know I've always been the secret-keeper in the family," she said. "You're the one who always had to tell everything."

"You've got me there," Jimmy said, knowing she was right. He'd come home from school, or from just being out, and go through his whole day for her, whether she wanted to hear or not. It was the same way when he smoked his first cigarette or when he got to first base with his first girl, and when he finally—Jimmy's words—did the dirty deed. He was an open book. Partly because he truly thought that whatever happened to him was interesting enough to repeat to someone, partly because that act of telling somehow made things real, and partly because he just liked to talk and talking about himself was a lot easier than talking about anything else.

Hannah had always been different. Even when they were kids, Jimmy had always called her a woman of mystery.

"Who else knows?" he'd said then, ready to get mad all over again if she'd confided in somebody ahead of him.

"You're the first," Hannah said. "Besides Beth . . ."

Jimmy said, "The world-famous therapist."

He asked if she wanted company going up to Fulton. Hannah said no, this was something she wanted to do alone. When she got back, though, he was ready to take over. It was his idea to call Marty Perez. We've got to go on the attack, he said, making his voice go a little deeper, the way he did when he wanted to look like Mr. In Charge. He told Hannah he'd been giving it a lot of thought, the whole time she was up there with the cops. That one actually got a smile out of her. She loved her brother, still thought of him as this dear, sweet boy, but one thing he had never done in his life was give things a lot of thought.

Jimmy said he'd considered the *Post,* they could probably sex up the story a lot better, but he decided on the *News* finally, which meant Perez, who he said he'd met in a bar one time. It turned out that Jimmy had gone out with Perez's ex-wife, some soap actress. Jimmy remembered a good line he got off that night, when Perez asked him what he thought of Madeline, which was the ex-wife's name.

"I told him I thought she had all the qualities of a dog, except loyalty," Jimmy was telling Hannah now.

According to Jimmy, they got a load on after that, and Perez said he was going to write a column about struggling actors like Jimmy, but never did.

Jimmy had met a lot of people in bars, and she could never remember one of them actually delivering for him. But it never seemed to bother him. She had watched him tell the story about Perez, fascinated as always at the way he threw himself into it, dragging everything out, more interested in playing the roles than getting to whatever the point was supposed to be. He hadn't worked in six months, since the play about the Irish at that off-Broadway theater on Forty-second Street, right after you came out of the Lincoln Tunnel. Maybe this was a way of staying in some kind of shape, acting-wise; she'd never asked him.

Sometimes she liked him better in these roles he played. He seemed brighter, happier, like acting turned on some light inside him that wasn't there in his real life.

Hannah said, "This Perez guy said he was going to write you up and didn't, so why do you trust him?"

Jimmy was pacing, drinking a Diet Coke out of a can. Now he stopped.

"You don't read the papers, do you?" he said. Knowing she really didn't. She might read *Newsday* when she was riding the exercise bike at the Vertical Club to see what Liz Smith had to say. She liked reading the reviews in the *Times*. But Hannah wasn't someone who read all the papers; she just wasn't that interested in everything.

"If you mean Marty Perez, no, I don't read him."

"What I mean is, you obviously didn't read enough when the William Kennedy Smith trial was going on, or the Mike Tyson trial," Jimmy said. "The fighter who got convicted of rape."

Hannah said, "I know who Mike Tyson is."

"Did you read about the woman in Florida who accused the three ballplayers of raping her that time?"

"Brian—Detective Hyland—reminded me of that one today. Apparently, she waited almost as long as I did to come forward and file an official complaint."

"I don't blame that on you. I blame that on the world-famous therapist, Beth."

"Can we bumper-sticker this, Jim?" It was an expression she'd heard one of the other trainers use at the Vertical, meaning get to the point. On her best day, Jimmy could wear her out sometimes talking. It never worked out that he was the audience for her, even when it was supposed to.

"You've got to get your side out before they get their side out, that's what I'm talking about," he said. "You're up against Ellis Adair, remember."

Jimmy made it sound as if she was going up against Jesus Christ. Any kind of celebrity had always gotten her brother worked up.

Jimmy said, "People love this guy so much you'd think he was white."

Hannah let that one go.

"You know what I mean," Jimmy said. "He's a god around here, for chrissakes. People in New York treat him like he's Peter Pan in his two-hundred-dollar basketball shoes." Jimmy made some kind of motion like he had a basketball in his hand, tried to make his deep voice sound black and said, "Looks at me, Ah's can fly." Hannah'd never thought too much about it, maybe Jimmy wasn't kidding around, maybe he really was a racist. He was standing at the counter that separated the kitchen from the living room. He finished the Diet Coke and slammed it down for emphasis. Even before he had thought about acting, when he was still going to make everybody forget McEnroe, when he was a junior tennis player out at Port Washington Tennis Academy, he had always been dramatic.

"I'm telling you, Sis, we've got to hit him before he hits us."

Now it was "we" all of a sudden.

"Brian said that Adair and Collins probably wouldn't talk, even to him."

"They'll get their story out anyway, that's the point. They'll say you're a groupie. Or some kind of bimbette. They won't say it themselves, oh no. But somebody will, so then it'll be out there. Or someone will say you're in it for the money, that this is some kind of setup. Everybody's sure as hell going to want to know why it took you a year to come forward. You can count on that." He went into a slouch, like he was some kind of New York tough guy, with an accent. "What, the rape slipped her mind?"

Hannah bit.

"That's not the way it is," she said, not wanting to have this conversation anymore.

Jimmy said, "The way it *is,* the *fact* of things, that hardly ever matters in cases like this. It's the way it's *covered.* Geez, don't you get it? It's all in the *presentation.*"

"Presentation," Hannah said.

Jimmy said, "Exactly! We need to set the tone. Let them start denying their shit before we have to start denying our shit. Like I said, hit them good before they hit us."

"They already hit us, believe me," Hannah said.

He came around the counter, over to where she was sitting. He knelt down in front of the couch, put his big hands on her shoulders, put his forehead gently on hers, then pulled back and smiled. As usual, Hannah felt like she was looking into a mirror. Jimmy was fourteen months older, but people had been mistaking them for twins for as long as Hannah could remember. Jimmy was hetero—pathologically heterosexual, that's the way he described himself—but gays were hitting on him all the time. It didn't surprise Hannah. She'd always thought he was the prettier one.

"I'm on your side, Sis."

She said, "I know that."

"If you don't want me to call the paper, I don't call the paper. But that means it's out of our control, somebody else gets to call the play."

She didn't say anything, just closed her eyes.

Jimmy said, "The bastards raped you. Let them start denying it."

That's when Hannah finally said, "Go ahead and make the call." She didn't go to the Vertical. She decided against going to an AA meeting. She had started to go less and less. They had seemed like off-off-off Broadway plays to her at first, like something you'd see at some little place down in the Village, one of those coffee-shop productions she'd had parts in once, when she was going to be the next Meryl. But now AA was beginning to bore her. Lately she couldn't even get into talking herself, when somebody finally got around to calling on her. And more and more, she was tired of listening to the other drunks and all their pain. Over the past year she had lost a lot of interest in other people's pain.

Hannah went into Jimmy's guest room, closed her eyes, and slept for fourteen hours, slept until she was on the front page of the *Daily News*.

She had stayed inside Jimmy's apartment all day yesterday. Jimmy had asked her what she wanted to do after they'd both read the paper, and Hannah said, "Hide under the bed." He told her to be his guest, just don't answer the phone. He'd gone out for some auditions, come back with Chinese food; they'd watched all the local news channels try to catch up with Marty Perez's story. Hannah went to bed at eight-thirty and slept like a dead person again.

Now it was the second day. "Hannah Carey held hostage, day two," Jimmy'd said before going out for more auditions and a call-back on a part in a CBS movie they were going to shoot in New York. He left Hannah in the living room, reading Perez's follow-up story.

It was pretty much a rehash of what he had written yesterday, with a statement from the Knicks thrown in, the statement saying they were looking into the matter. There were some quotes from Jimmy that Perez seemed to have saved up, Jimmy still being identified as "the brother of the alleged victim." Hannah read it all the way through, then read the stories in the other papers, trying to take a step back today, imagining the whole thing was about somebody else. After all the times when it had just been inside her head, or inside Beth's little office down in the Village, now it was in front of her, on the page. If it's not on the page, it's not on the page, that's what Jimmy Carey always said. So there she was finally, out there for everybody to see.

See and not see, Hannah thought.

There was no name to go with the story.

There was no face.

This part even Hannah knew from all the other cases. This was the big joke, that this all was a way of protecting the victim's privacy. Oh sure, Hannah thought. The truth was, they didn't protect your privacy at all; Hannah had figured that one out already. Privacy didn't enter into it. They just kept your name out of the paper and off television most of the time, unless they really wanted to screw around with you. They put your age in there, and your height, how much you weighed—which was high, by the way; she hadn't been as high as one-forty in years. They put in there what street you lived on and your occupation. What color your hair was.

Lift weights? They put that in, too.

Just no name. And no face.

Every reporter in town probably had her name already. But the papers didn't tell the reader and acted like they were being more noble than the Queen of England.

Hannah thought it was a bunch of shit. It was like saying there was this city, millions of people, just across from New Jersey, lots of tall buildings.

You just couldn't tell people it was New York.

"She is thirty-one years old," Perez wrote today. "She had all these dreams about being a great actress. But she has not dreamed much lately, certainly not since that night last October, in a quiet little Connecticut town where a lot changed and her nightmare began."

Jesus H. Christ.

Perez didn't put in there that she'd been waiting tables lately. Maybe it was hard for him to get worked up about waitresses.

"She is nearly six feet tall. She tries to work out every day. Her brother is a struggling actor, maybe you'd even recognize the face, if not the name. But this is real life now, for brother and sister. They want justice for what happened to the sister last October in Fulton, Connecticut."

Hannah put the paper down again. She had been putting it down all day, sometimes covering it up on the coffee table with some of Jimmy's trade papers, but then picking it up again, starting to read in different places. And every time she would start to get worked up, she would think to herself, What did you expect?

She went over to Jimmy's phone, the one shaped like a Giants helmet he'd gotten for subscribing to some magazine, and punched out the phone number at her apartment.

Jimmy told her not to be surprised when the whole world had the number. Hannah had said to him, "But it's unlisted." Jimmy just gave her one of those looks, like she was still twelve years old, like he was the smart one, and told her they could get *Madonna*'s number if they needed it.

It was always "they" with Jimmy. Or "them." Him against them, them being agents, or directors, or casting directors, or other actors.

Hannah had stayed away from the phone yesterday, but now

she was curious, punching out her code, listening to the tape rewinding, stopping finally, the first loud beep.

"Miss Carey." Male voice. "I'm from *Fox News at 10 . . .*"

Beep.

"Hannah, my name is Carly Wilson from the television show *Inside Edition . . .*"

Beep.

"Page Six of the New York *Post* calling for Hannah Carey, it's nine o'clock in the morning, what day is this? . . ."

She picked up a pen and Jimmy's message pad off the counter and kept track, making four lines, then drawing a line through them, until she was up to sixteen calls and the tape on her machine finally ran out, for the first time in history. The *National Enquirer*. Beep. Liz Smith's assistant. Beep. Geraldo Rivera's show. Beep. Thirteen from the press in all, two from friends, one from Bobby, her trainer at the Vertical Club, telling her to get her fine ass over there, he'd beat up anyone who came near her.

She went into the guest room and put on black tights and a black T-shirt and an old U.S. Open tennis sweatshirt and her high-top Reebok cross-trainers and the black *Guys and Dolls* cap Jimmy had bought her when they went to see the revival. Then she threw a change of clothes into a gym bag. Get over there and sweat, she told herself, and don't think too hard on where all this was going.

If the messages were like this, what was the rest of it going to be like?

She went downstairs, past the door to the acupuncturist's office, which always had somebody waiting outside, and then out of the great old brownstone and into the sun on West Seventy-first, between Amsterdam and Broadway. Her brother had had one real part, one piece of steady work, playing a doctor for two years on *One Life to Live* before finally being killed in a tragic car accident. It was long enough to buy the apartment. Jimmy still bitched that if the character had lived another year he could've bought a bigger apartment, but Hannah didn't see why he would've needed anything bigger than what he had, which was two bedrooms, a huge living room with a fireplace, and a lot of sun.

Hannah had been living up on West End Avenue the last two years, a cute studio with a partial view of the Hudson. She stood in front of Jimmy's brownstone, wondering if she should go up there, just out of curiosity, to see if "they" really were staking her out already. The hell with it, she decided. If they were staking her out, let them wait until hell freezes over. She could beat the after-work crowd if she went over to the Vertical right now. She could do some bike and some Stairmaster if her legs could take it, then go through her upper-body Nautilus program, sweat, and get out of there.

She couldn't hide under the bed forever.

She walked over to Broadway and up to Seventy-second, hailed a cab. The Vertical Club was on Sixty-first between First and Second. If you ran laps upstairs, you could look out a window and the Queensboro Bridge was right there in front of you. She started working out at the Vertical when it was still trendy, before there were about a hundred clubs just like it. She was walking around with her portfolio during the day, getting nowhere, waitressing nights at Jim McMullen's. She had a tiny apartment on East Fifty-fifth, this one without a view of anything except Fifty-fifth, and even when she moved to the West Side, she decided to keep her membership. Most of her friends on the West Side had joined the Equinox Club, that was the hot new place, up on Amsterdam, with the sculpture of the girl rock-climbing in the big front window. But Hannah was comfortable at the Vertical.

She had always been shitty with change.

Hannah was crossing the street that cuts Sixty-first in half, feeding up into the bridge, when she heard the first shout.

"There she is!"

Hannah looked up and saw them coming for her.

Somebody else said, "It's her!"

The light had changed behind her, and there was already some early rush-hour traffic, so there was a steady stream of cars feeding up into the bridge, on their way home to Queens. Hannah couldn't retreat. She just stood there, seeing the television cameras mostly, the guys pointing them at her like they were guns.

"Hannah!"

"Hannah Carey?"

"Can we get a comment?"

She made herself move, not knowing what she could do, just knowing she had to do *something*. She couldn't make it inside the Vertical without going right through them, so she crossed the street, nearly getting hit by some blue van, the van having a horn that sounded more like a siren, looking behind her to see some of them cutting in front of cars, so there were more horns now, as she got back to the north side of Sixty-first, and started running now, toward Second.

Over the horns, some shrill woman's voice: "Hannah, wait!"

Then it was just the horns behind her, traffic stopped completely going to the bridge and some kind of black town car limo, nearly coming up onto the sidewalk after her, blowing its horn at her as a guy stuck his head out the back window of the town car and said, "You probably ought to get in. The bad guys are gaining on you."

The car stayed on her pace as she ran at a pretty good clip toward Second. Hannah started to tell the guy to get the hell away from her, but there was something about him, casually opening the back door as the crowd closed on her, offering her a way out.

"Who are you?" she said.

He smiled at her, holding the door open, still casual, like he did this all the time, played the cavalry. "My name's DiMaggio," he said. "I'm the good guys."

6

DiMaggio sat across the street from the Vertical Club and waited. He knew how to do it. DiMaggio learned young, all the times he waited for his father, Tony DiMaggio, to come back from the road with Ralph Flanagan's band, bringing him tacky gifts from places like Miami Beach. DiMaggio always wondered what his old man was thinking. Did he think he had a son who wanted to lead the league in plastic pink flamingos? To be able to put his collection up against anybody's in Commack, Long Island? Tony DiMaggio, with his pompadour hair and gangster suits, would spend a couple of days at home, sleeping all day, saying he couldn't get out of the habit. Then he would take off again, on his way to Baltimore and Washington and Atlanta. Then DiMaggio would wait some more, watching his mother hit the Four Roses, until there was the big tour through the southwest, after which Tony DiMaggio never came back.

DiMaggio didn't even have a sample of his father's handwriting, just the fucking flamingos.

Then there was all the waiting as a ballplayer, too, in the game or on the bench or in the clubhouse. Mostly on the bench, even in all those bust-out rookie-league towns in the South, the redneck fools yelling out jokes about his last name, asking where his Uncle Joe was. "Uncle Joe *DiMaggio,* get it?" they'd yell. As if he didn't. They were the kinds of places writers romanticized into the Vatican. It always gave DiMaggio a real thrill, reading about baseball. Every ballpark was a cathedral, and everything associated with the game was a sacrament. Even the waiting.

The Greeks didn't have as much bullshit mythology as baseball did.

DiMaggio had just the one summer with the Yankees. It wasn't even a summer, that was bullshit, he sounded like some asshole spin doctor touching up his career. DiMaggio got twelve weeks, four starts when Thurman Munson got hurt, a total of fifty innings, batting average of .202, only getting up there above .200 because of two hits off Rick Wise the last day of the regular season. DiMaggio didn't remember much about the baseball, remembering much more clearly the phone call telling him he'd been released. He remembered more about living in New York the first time, in this apartment he found, cheap enough, on Ninety-fourth, east of Fifth. A stewardess he'd dated had it. Then she quit it all of a sudden to get married, to some rich guy she met on the red-eye from Los Angeles. DiMaggio grabbed it. The stewardess knew DiMaggio played the piano and told him some old piano player lived next door. DiMaggio did a little investigating and found out it was Vladimir Horowitz. DiMaggio smiled now, his head resting against the window on the right side of the backseat, the other window down, so he could watch the entrance to the Vertical. Some old piano player, he thought. Playing for the Yankees, all those stars, and he'd watch the street in the afternoons until it was time to go to the ballpark, waiting for a look at Horowitz. Mostly he'd just listen in the afternoons, when the old man would open the windows and play, laying the music over all the New York noise, the cabs, the whole shout of the place.

DiMaggio started playing piano again that year, even with every no-good thing catching had done to his hands, catching and the arthritis that had gotten worse every year. After the Yankees released him at the end of October, he traveled around Europe for six months, alone, without any real itinerary, starting in London and finally ending up in Barcelona, living in a small apartment that looked out on the statue of Christopher Columbus, studying for the law boards and playing the piano nights in the little bar downstairs. He came home and passed and started going to Fordham Law the next September. He also took piano lessons from this crazy Polish woman who lived down at Sheridan Square. DiMaggio remembered how after they'd finish on Thursday afternoons she'd pour them glasses of vodka, and they'd drink it and listen to tapes of Horszowski, the woman crying sometimes as if DiMaggio wasn't there.

His first job, the dirty low lawyering job of the world, the rookie league of lawyering, was in New York, at Valerio and Cowen. One of the big shots there was a big Yankee fan and a friend of George Steinbrenner, the owner. The big shot, named DeLuca, acted like he was doing DiMaggio a favor by getting him in there with the other drones, all those young Ivy League dickheads who came to work half asleep because that was the time in New York when cocaine started showing up everywhere and the Ivy Leaguers had been out all night. DiMaggio lasted seventeen fun-filled months, then it was down to Washington, ending up on John Dowd's staff. One of the lawyers at the Players Association knew DiMaggio was looking to make a move. He also knew Dowd was going to be handling the Pete Rose investigation for baseball. He got DiMaggio an interview, and Dowd jumped at the chance of having an ex-player on his staff.

Suddenly, lawyering wasn't just sitting behind a desk. Suddenly, he wasn't waiting anymore. Waiting for his father. Waiting for the big leagues. Waiting for a chance to get into the game. Waiting for real cases. This *was* a real case, with real action. Some of the other guys on the case were in awe of Rose, felt sorry for him because they'd grown up watching him play his ass off and get all those hits. They wanted to buy into the bullshit mythology, too. Shit, he's Charlie Hustle, he can't be betting on baseball! They were like everybody on the outside, amazed that their heroes could fuck up.

DiMaggio came at it all differently, after all the years on the inside. DiMaggio was long past thinking line drives made you smart or noble or good. There'd always been drunks, there'd always been guys taking dope, there'd always been gambling going on. Guys beating their wives. Now it just happened to be the guy who ended up with more hits than anybody in history.

"You're not trying to make a case against Pete Rose," Dowd would tell them. "You're just trying to make a case against some guy who may have broken the baseball law." Sometimes DiMaggio thought he was the only one who got it, all the way up until Dowd got Rose.

Dowd offered him a permanent job in D.C., and DiMaggio thought about taking it. He had an apartment he liked in Georgetown, he had drifted into an affair with a producer from National Public Radio, he felt settled for the first time since he'd left Commack to play ball. Then Dowd got the call from Jupiter that changed everything.

The man's name was Ness Florescu. DiMaggio was vaguely aware of him from watching gymnastics at the Olympics. He had been coaching the Romanian women for years, and the Romanian women had won a pile of medals, and finally Florescu had moved to the United States and opened his own academy in Jupiter, Florida, about a half hour north of Palm Beach. Parents brought girls from all over the country to Florescu because he was supposed to be a kid's best shot at a gold medal. His best shot at a medal that year, 1992, was a sixteen-year-old named

Kim Cassidy. But a few weeks before, Cassidy had been mugged and nearly raped outside one of Florescu's dormitories. In the process, the attacker had ruined the kid's knee to the point where she needed surgery.

It turned out Florescu was a baseball fan, so he knew all about the Rose investigation. Florescu called John Dowd and said he didn't think what happened to Kim Cassidy was an accident. He didn't want to press charges if he was wrong because he figured that would finish him in gymnastics. But the Olympic trials were coming up and now that Cassidy couldn't compete, the favorite for the gold medal was another kid from Houston who'd been Cassidy's rival from the time they started competing against each other when they were eight.

Florescu sat in Dowd's office with Dowd and DiMaggio and told them he thought the attack on Kim Cassidy might have been arranged.

"I don't want to be the official sports snoop," Dowd said after Florescu left. "Besides, this guy sounds crazy. Nobody's been whacking out the competition since they used to do it in boxing back in the fifties."

"What if it's true, though?" DiMaggio said.

"You want him, he's yours," Dowd said.

It took him six weeks in Jupiter and Houston, most of the time spent in Houston. It wasn't a mugging, and it wasn't an attempted rape. It was a hit on the Cassidy girl, ordered by the stepfather of the Houston gymnast, an ex-con named Verne Maywood. There was finally a night in one of Maywood's favorite honky-tonks. DiMaggio had been drinking there a week, watching Maywood get shit-faced, even buying him a couple of rounds of drinks. This night he followed him out and got into the parking lot in time to watch a guy step out from behind Maywood's pickup and start beating him with a tire iron.

"You owe me sixty-five hundred, boy," Tire Iron said. "And

as you have probably guessed, you've officially worn my ass out with your excuses."

Maywood was rolling on the ground, whimpering, still covering up against blows that had stopped for the time being. He said something DiMaggio couldn't hear.

"*Yes,* right here," Tire Iron said. "Right here and right now, goddamnit."

"I promise you," Maywood groaned. "A check tomorrow."

Tire Iron got into a beat-up Grand Prix and drove off. DiMaggio was able to get the license plate. The car belonged to another ex-con, this one named Bobby Ray Bonner. It was easy enough to find out he and Maywood had been in prison together. DiMaggio called the Jupiter police in the morning, Jupiter called Houston. By the next day, Bobby Ray had given up Verne Maywood, and that night there was some wonderful television footage of the two dumb asses screaming at each other in front of a Houston courthouse.

The next Sunday night, *60 Minutes* devoted a whole show to the attack on Kim Cassidy, built around DiMaggio's investigation. Now he was the sports snoop. He was the one you called when you had the kind of problem the Knicks had now with Ellis Adair and Richie Collins.

So Ted Salter, the president of Madison Square Garden, had called. And now DiMaggio was in New York trying to catch a glimpse of a rape victim, feeling like some shitheel reporter himself, all because he'd let Salter talk him into it.

Salter was the Yankee's vice president in charge of broadcasting the one year DiMaggio played there. When the Madison Square Garden cable network bought Yankee games, Salter moved over there, finally ending up president of the network. DiMaggio was vaguely aware that the Garden once belonged to Paramount Communications, along with Paramount's movie and television companies and publishing houses. Then there were takeovers and sales and finally the last company to buy everything kept the movie and television companies but sold the Garden, the Knicks, and the New York Rangers hockey team to the Fukiko Corporation of Tokyo. DiMaggio seemed to recall that Fukiko was the product of some big Japanese merger. Salter went with Fukiko and became president of the Garden.

He called DiMaggio in Jupiter the night he found out about the charges against Adair and Collins. He was moving fast, he told DiMaggio. "Remember?" he said. "I always liked to move fast."

"Find somebody else," DiMaggio said. "Fukiko must have people who do this sort of thing."

"I don't really know the Japs yet," Salter said. "I'm not saying I don't trust them. Hell, what they're paying me, I'd do the geisha thing, walk on their backs if they asked. But I don't *know* them. And I certainly don't know their lawyers. I've got to have somebody I can trust here, so I make sure I look like I'm on top of this fucking thing. I'm not asking for a lot of your time here. Remember that time in Florida, that woman saying those three Mets jumped her booty? I don't remember the exact dates, but it seems to me it started in spring training and the whole thing was wrapped up before Opening Day."

"Cops did that."

"I'm not putting the Garden and my basketball team in the hands of the Fulton Fucking Connecticut Police Department."

"Then hire yourself a private investigator."

"Going with a private investigator I don't know is the same as going with lawyers I don't know," Salter said. "I know you. And I know I can trust you. You were a schmuck when you were a player. You were with the Yankees ten minutes and you were running all that union shit in the clubhouse like you were Jimmy Hoffa. But everybody said you were an honest schmuck."

"Honest has nothing to do with it," DiMaggio said. "It's all juice. *Jurisdiction.* You're not listening here. When I was with Dowd on the Pete Rose thing, we *were* the cops. Baseball commissioners used to run baseball like the commies ran Russia. People had to talk to me. You talk about the Mets thing? The ballplayers that girl accused, they *still* haven't talked to the cops. Your guys aren't going to help the cops, and they're sure as shit not going to help me."

"They work for me," Salter said. "I'm old-fashioned enough to think that still counts for something."

DiMaggio said, "That's not the way these assholes look at it. They think you're just another rich guy put on this earth to take care of them."

They went around and around, Salter saying he wasn't going to hire a private investigator, he didn't trust goddamn lawyers, he wanted a pro. Salter saying he'd want DiMaggio to work alone, he didn't want the whole thing turning into the leak-a-thon—Salter's expression—the O. J. Simpson case had been from the start. And Salter finally saying he'd overpay if he had to, at least fly up from Florida and talk to him in person. Which DiMaggio finally said he'd do. Salter had been out in California when he called; he flew back on the Fukiko jet. DiMaggio caught the early Delta out of West Palm. They met in DiMaggio's suite at the Sherry-Netherland. DiMaggio always stayed there. There were flashier New York hotels, but he liked the suite they always gave him at the Sherry, one of the two they had with a piano. Sometimes DiMaggio had to travel with his little pack-up baby Yamaha keyboard if he wanted to play, but he didn't like to use it if he didn't have to, it always made him feel like some dufus accordion player with Lawrence Welk.

Salter sat at the dining table and sold him on taking the case.

Salter said, "I'm not looking for you to acquit or convict. I don't need something from you that will stand up in court or in front of a jury or as some kind of show on Court TV. I want to know what happened that night. If Adair and Collins did it, I want to be able to hand them your report at the end and say, 'Here it is.' And I want to make sure that my Japs are prepared in the event this woman brings some kind of civil action against us down the road. If they didn't do it and you can prove it to my satisfaction, I want as much ammo as possible."

Salter moved his coffee cup out of the way, leaning forward, cuff links making clicking noises on the glass tabletop, like he'd had this sudden rush of being earnest, the big guy playing the big guy now in the Sherry. He had blond hair slicked back and tiny round tortoiseshell glasses and what looked to DiMaggio to be a tanning-salon tan.

DiMaggio thought: another one of the yuppie gangsters who had taken over sports.

Salter said, "Adair is as much a representative of Fukiko as the star of any television series. He has a cartoon show of his own on Saturday mornings, for chrissakes. NBC did a prime-time special last season built around his goddamn birthday. So you have my backing on this, and the parent company's. Richie Collins is just a sideman here, believe me. A nobody. We're worried about Adair. If you can prove he raped this woman to our satisfaction, he's out of here. We'll get somebody else to dunk the fucking ball."

"There's something you ought to know," DiMaggio said. "They probably don't think of it as rape, even now."

"Then what the hell do they think it was?"

"One Thursday night with laughs last October. Something to break up the monotony of training camp."

Salter reached down, snapped open a thin Vuitton briefcase, took out a manila envelope, handed it to DiMaggio. "There's a picture of her in there."

DiMaggio said, "Where'd you get this?"

"We got it," Salter answered. "Hannah Carey, age thirty-one.

Didn't make it as an actress. Waitressed for a while, then went to work as a trainer for the Vertical Club. Her mother was a professional tennis player. Brother's an actor, too. Jimmy Carey. Did a soap one time. Does commercials. No one seems to know whether Hannah Carey's working right now, but she still works out at the Vertical almost every afternoon. We talked to the guy who runs the place."

DiMaggio looked at the old black-and-white publicity picture of Hannah Carey. Short blond hair, huge eyes, great smile. Classic features all around, nose and cheekbones and jaw. Hannah Carey looked the way beautiful models used to look, before the famine.

Salter clapped his hands. "You're supposed to be the best," he said. "So go be the best." Then he told DiMaggio to use his town car for the rest of the day if he wanted. Salter said he was going to walk back to the Garden, it would give him an hour when nobody could find him.

When DiMaggio got downstairs fifteen minutes later, the car was at the front door, next to the Sherry's big clock. He told the driver, Rudy, to take him to the Vertical Club. Now they had been sitting in front of the Vertical since two o'clock, watching the media crowd grow on Sixty-first Street: photographers, mini-cams, kids with press cards clipped to the breast pockets of their blazers, most of the kids in jeans, DiMaggio surprised there seemed to be as many women as men.

He was starting to think about giving up on Hannah Carey, taking a ride up to Fulton instead, when everything started to happen across the street. The media crowd started to move, and then he saw Hannah Carey running toward Second Avenue.

"Go!" DiMaggio snapped at Rudy.

"Where?" Rudy said, pulling his cap down as if by reflex, half turning to DiMaggio as he did.

DiMaggio pointed to Hannah. "Get up alongside her before the dinks catch up."

DiMaggio opened the door to the backseat when they started to catch up to her. Told her he was the good guys.

Hannah Carey, feeling dizzy and disoriented, hesitated.

"What is that supposed to mean?" she said. "You're the good guys?" Still not making any move to get into the backseat.

The guy nodded past her, at the crowd. "You sure you don't want to talk about this in the car?" Then he made some room for her.

Hannah looked over her shoulder, made up her mind, jumped into the backseat next to him, slammed the door behind her. The light was changing up ahead. The driver gunned the car and beat it. Now they were heading toward Third. Hannah twisted around in her seat, taking one last look. They were back on the other side of Second, pointing the minicams at the car like they wanted to open fire.

The guy smiled. "We should be able to make it over the mountains and into Switzerland from here."

"This isn't funny," she said. "How do I know . . . ?"

"You're safe? You don't. But you are. I'll drop you at the next corner if you want."

Hannah, still catching her breath, got herself turned around on the seat so she was facing him. Her dark-haired rescuer. Not bad-looking in his blue suit.

"Who *are* you?" she said.

"I told you," he said. "My name's DiMaggio."

"I mean, what are you *doing* here?"

"Don't get out of the car at the next corner and I'll tell you."

"But if I want to . . ."

"All you have to do is tell Rudy here to stop."

Hannah leaned back, away from him, tucking herself into the corner. Maybe she should be as scared of him as she was of the bastards chasing her. But she felt safe all of a sudden in this car, for some reason she couldn't understand.

"I'm listening," she said.

She sat there studying him, seeming to relax a little bit. "I'm listening," she said, and that was it. She had long, elegant fingers, resting on top of the gym bag in her lap. DiMaggio always noticed people's hands.

They were waiting for the light at Lexington Avenue. DiMaggio said, "Where to?"

"That's your idea of an explanation?" She made a halfhearted move for the door handle.

"I just wanted to give Rudy some idea . . ."

"West Side," she said. "Do you have a first name, Mr. DiMaggio?"

"I don't like to make a big thing of it." He smiled at her, then told her his first name. "Do you follow baseball?"

"No."

"No use explaining then."

"I don't follow you."

"Don't try. Usually when people press me, I tell them to look it up in *The Baseball Encyclopedia,* if it's that important."

Giving her a routine, just to keep talking.

Keep her in the car.

"What do you want from me?"

"The Knicks have hired me."

She leaned forward as soon as he said it. "Hey," she said to Rudy. "Hey, you."

"Yes, ma'am," Rudy said.

"Pull over anywhere, please." She leaned back, said, "The Knicks, Jesus."

"Lady, we're in the park," Rudy said.

"I don't care. I'll walk."

DiMaggio said to her, "Just listen to me for one second before you get out. I'm working for the Knicks because they want to know what happened."

"I told the police what happened."

"I know," he said. "I come into this believing *you*. Thinking they did it."

Hannah Carey gave him a sarcastic "Thanks" for his effort.

Rudy hadn't stopped, but she didn't seem too worked up. She had her hands back on top of the bag and was looking out the window. So DiMaggio kept going. "The Knicks aren't necessarily on their side. And I'm not on anybody's side. I just wanted to meet you, talk to you."

"Why?"

"I'm going to be around. I don't want you to think of me as the enemy."

"Why can't the police handle this?"

DiMaggio stared at her. You couldn't help it. Hannah Carey was better-looking in person, blond hair cut even shorter than it had been in the picture Salter had given him. Her blue eyes were so light they seemed to have faded somehow, like old denim. He stared and tried to see her with Adair and Collins, wondering how it came to that.

As if looks ever had anything to do with it. DiMaggio thought: No wonder women think we're such assholes. Now he said, "Because these things are a bitch for the police. Because a lot of time has passed. Because the police may come out of this convinced that it happened just the way you said it happened and still throw up their hands, say, 'We can't make the case.' I don't have to worry about that. The people who run the Knicks, they don't want the case. They want the truth."

"They have it. It's in the report. It's all over the papers now."

DiMaggio said, "I'm going to be the second opinion."

They got to Central Park West. Rudy said, "Do you still want me to stop?"

She said, "Yes."

DiMaggio said, "You don't live here."

"No," she said. "I don't."

"I'd like to talk to you again."

Rudy had come around, giving her the full treatment. He opened the door and Hannah Carey got out, not saying anything. So DiMaggio got out, too.

"What do you say? A cup of coffee sometime. Anything you don't want to tell me, blow me off, don't tell me. I'm easy."

Hannah, studying him now, said, "I don't think so."

DiMaggio shrugged.

"Think it over. I'm at the Sherry-Netherland. Like I said, I'm going to be around."

"I'll think it over." She gave him a quizzical look. "Mr. Second Opinion DiMaggio." She walked north on Central Park West, the park on her right, swinging her bag in her right hand, like a kid. DiMaggio watched her until she was out of sight. He told Rudy to find him a rental car place, he wanted to drive himself up to Connecticut in the morning.

"She seem like an actress to you?" DiMaggio said, and Rudy said, "Don't they all?"

7

DiMaggio took the Fulton College exit off the Merritt Parkway. It put him on Route 7, which didn't look like Connecticut at all to DiMaggio, just some kind of anywhere fast-food drag, Burger King and McDonald's and Taco Bell and Roy Rogers, until everything finally settled down and he got into the town of Fulton, with its small-town movie-set library and all its beige designer brick. DiMaggio thought they just should have called it Town Beautiful.

It didn't take long to go all the way through downtown Fulton. The directions said take a left when he could see the train station. DiMaggio did that and then went up a hill, past a pretty white-frame Congregational church, following signs to a town called Ridgefield, exactly the way Salter's secretary said. He wasn't even a mile out of town and already he felt like he was in the country, with elegant old houses set back from the road and huge fenced-in areas with horses. He took a right off the road to Ridgefield, went down a hill this time, and saw Fulton College spread out below him.

Salter's secretary told him he couldn't miss the huge stone arch that served as the front gate. You went through the arch, and then about a hundred yards down was a security booth. She said his name would be left with the guard there. She promised that the guard could direct him to the gym, all the way in the back of the campus.

It took him almost half an hour to get from the stone arch to the booth with the security guard. DiMaggio counted fifteen cars and vans ahead of him. Most of the vans had spaceship satellite dishes coming out of their tops. The guard was stopping everyone, DiMaggio could see him, busting balls, checking his list, then waving them through.

When DiMaggio got to the front of the line, the guy took him through the same drill, looking at the first page on his clipboard, flipping to the next page, running his finger down the long list, making a small check mark. DiMaggio figured him for about seventy in his blue-and-orange Knicks windbreaker. He was more of a greeter than a private cop. Maybe it was working at the college. He wore a denim shirt and some kind of flashy tie with what looked to be basketball players jumping all over it. His white hair was brushed back and curled down over the collar of the denim shirt.

"DiMaggio?" he said, turning it into a question, leaning forward to take a better look inside the car. DiMaggio just waited with the window down, looking past him at the campus, which looked beautiful, cut out of woods, hills, and sky. Some of the roofs had red tile on them, like Stanford. If you were going to steal, steal from the best.

The white-haired greeter said, "It's a little crowded over there at the gym today, which is straight down to the end of this road and then to the right. My advice is to take the first space you see and then just walk from there or the Knicks'll be all done and—"

The white-haired greeter stopped. A Cherokee, black, was pulling around DiMaggio's rented Taurus, going up on the grass, spitting dirt and rocks, coming so close to DiMaggio on the pas-

.senger side he could feel his car move a little bit. The guard looked up and said, "Hey," then seemed to recognize the black Jeep. He gave a sheepish wave, and the Jeep gunned its way past them.

DiMaggio said, "Who was that?"

"Right there? Right there was Mr. Adair and Mr. Collins. Themselves." He smiled. " 'Course this time of year, that's not what they're known as around here."

DiMaggio could see a couple of the cars ahead of him start chasing after the Jeep. He said to the guard, "What are they known as around here?"

"The Dick Brothers."

Ellis said to Richie, practically screaming, "Take the service road behind the library. Cut back up that little dirt road next to the soccer field." He was turned around in the front seat, looking back at the reporters, somehow feeling like they were chasing them with ropes and torches. "Get me the fuck inside that gym."

Richie slowed down, let two girls pass. The first one, with real short black hair and a nice body on her, waved at Richie like she knew him.

Ellis said, "Not now, man. Shit." He turned around again. There was a TV reporter and his cameraman, on the dead run, maybe a hundred yards behind them. "Fuck it," Ellis said. "I ain't practicing today, I can't deal with this shit. Tell Gary I'm having some of that tendinitis behind my knees again."

Richie didn't say anything back. Sometimes he could position Ellis, they both knew it, get Ellis to do something he didn't want to do. But Richie also knew there were times when you shouldn't push. Richie knew better than anyone: Push too hard and you couldn't move Ellis Adair in a million fucking years.

Richie understood something else along the same lines, dealing with how hard-ass Ellis could get when he had to: Guys didn't get out of Booker T. just because they were some asshole who could jump.

Most white guys, sportswriters especially, made that mistake all the time with black ballplayers. Ellis explained it to Richie one time when they were both still in high school, and Richie never forgot it. Ellis told him there were a lot of guys who could play, play just about as well as him, but who never got out of the projects or off the corner. Never got off the playground. Ellis had said, "I call them Idas."

Richie had said to him, "Now what the fuck is an Ida?"

Ellis smiled and said, "Idas are the bitches always telling you what they *coulda* been if they'd just applied themselves. 'If Ida done this, I could have made the NBA.' 'If Ida done that, I'd be the one making three million dollars a year.' Idas, Rich. Those bitches are on every street corner in Jersey City."

In the front seat now, Richie said, "If Ida done somethin' wrong, I'd listen to you. But we didn't do anything, we're not going to act guilty. And if you don't show at practice today, that's what these little TV cocksuckers are going to say, that Fresh was afraid to show, maybe he's got something to hide."

He was driving through campus now a little slower than he usually did, like he was buying time, trying to settle Ellis down.

"Wasn't talking about guilty or innocent," Ellis said, "just about not being able to deal with this shit yet."

"Listen to me," Richie said. They were passing the registrar's building, coming up alongside the quad, all green in the sun. "It's like I told you yesterday. We don't even *address* any of this shit."

Gary Lenz had fucked the reporters yesterday, giving Ellis and Richie the day off, even though it was the first week of camp. But then Donnie Fuchs, their agent, had thrown a shit fit, saying he didn't want it to look like they were hiding. So now here they

were, Ellis more upset than Richie that they were being chased
to practice by a goddamn posse.

Richie took a right after the quad, going down the tree-lined
street with some of the frat houses on it. He'd lost the reporters,
now there was just this one Taurus behind him, making the same
turns he was making.

"You just let me do all the talking when we get to the gym.
Look at me, Fresh." Richie talked sharp to him sometimes,
cracked the whip, never doing it unless it was something important and he needed for Ellis to listen up. "Just say something
like, 'If you want to talk about anything except basketball, talk
to Mr. Collins.' Don't smile or act like what the woman's saying is just jive because that'll piss off women. Don't come across
like some smiley-boy homey. Just give them that smile of yours
and a little shrug, like you wish you could say more." Richie said,
"I'll take it from there."

"What does that mean, 'take it from there'? You know what
Donnie said."

Fuchs had come up from Washington last night and laid it all
out for them, the way only Donnie could. Ellis had started to explain about that night, saying it wasn't anything like it was coming out in the papers. Donnie had cut him off, "Ellis, *listen* to
me: I don't give a shit." Ellis said, "Don't you want to know what
really happened?" and Donnie had said, "As a matter of fact, I
don't. What happened isn't relevant. What's relevant is how we
handle it from here." This was one of those times that Donnie
said the D.C. after Washington stood for Damage Control.

"I heard what Donnie said," Richie said. "And I'm going to
do what he said. I'm going to tell them I can't talk about this,
and I'm not going to talk about this, but as soon as there's a time
when I can, they won't be able to shut me up." Richie pulled over
and let the Jeep idle for a minute in front of a red-barn-looking
house with a porch in front. "We just got to make sure we don't

act fucked-up about this, Fresh. We can't come off cockylike, but we can't go hide under the bed either, 'cause we didn't do anything."

Ellis said, "But—" and Richie said, "We didn't do anything *criminal.*" Ellis, edgy, not sitting still, turned around again. The Taurus had passed when he pulled over, now it was coming back the other way. There was a guy in a blue suit behind the wheel, acting like he was lost, staring at some of the houses on the other side of the street.

"Trust me," Richie said.

"You think this bitch is setting us up?"

"Donnie does. Donnie thinks the phone will ring any day now, and it'll be the bitch's lawyer, expecting some money to change hands."

Ellis said, "Then what do we do?"

Richie smiled. "It's like Donnie said. We tell her she should've asked for money that night, I would've given her a hundred."

Donnie thought everybody was like him. Richie'd fix Donnie up with strange sometimes, and it made them laugh, he couldn't even enjoy the hand on his dick because he was worrying about the other hand maybe ending up on his wallet.

Richie said, "That's Donnie. The thing that bothers me is, she waits a year. What is that? I understand, maybe she looks at Anita Hill—"

Ellis Adair stopped him right there.

"Anita who?"

Richie just nodded, like it was an obvious question, Anita who?

"You remember her. When they were trying to get that brother nominated for the Supreme Court, then this bitch comes forward and testifies about pubic hairs and that porno movie *Long Dong Silver?* I made you watch on television."

Richie did this, drew pictures for him.

Richie said, "Anyway, this Anita Hill, she goes on to become the queen of the man-haters, even though the brother made the court. Donnie says she makes like ten thousand bucks a pop now, going around giving speeches about women rising up, kicking the shit out of men. The women all cheer, then she goes on to the next city, gets another ten thousand."

"I remember her now," Ellis said. "You think that judge really did it?"

"That's just the point I'm trying to make here. All this time later, people still wonder if he tried to jump her or not. We got to play this better than he did, so when this is all over, people aren't saying, 'You think Ellis Adair gang-banged her?' "

Putting it all on me, Ellis thought. He didn't say anything, not out loud, but to himself he repeated, *Ellis Adair gang-banged her.*

"People didn't know shit about Clarence Thomas. The judge. They know you, though, Fresh. They want to believe you're innocent. They don't want to buy into some woman waited a year to yell rape." Richie put the Jeep into gear and pulled away from the red-barn-looking house.

"You're saying a girl can come out of this the bad guy?" Ellis said.

Richie Collins smiled. "Now you're paying attention," he said.

DiMaggio hated car phones usually, but you could rent them right along with your car now, and he had found that they saved him a lot of time. He called Frank Crittendon, the Knicks' general manager, and told him they needed to talk. Crittendon said come ahead, the team didn't practice until six on Thursdays.

Now DiMaggio was standing there in the back parking lot with everybody else to see Adair and Collins make their entrance for twenty-two television cameras—DiMaggio had counted—and three times that many other people, TV reporters, print reporters, and photographers. If something else happened in the tristate area—something minor like a nuclear attack—all the stations were going to be screwed because the cameras that weren't in Fulton were still back at the Vertical.

DiMaggio wondered how Adair and Collins would play it. He had followed them through the campus for a while until Adair pulled over and then Collins really gave it to Ellis Adair, doing most of the talking, pointing a finger at him sometimes. Looking very much in charge.

When the Jeep pulled in, everybody swarmed it, both sides, barely leaving space for the two Knicks to open the doors. Adair got out first, smiling but acting shy, putting his hands up, as if to say, Don't shoot. DiMaggio couldn't hear what he was saying, but he couldn't have said very much because right away Adair was moving toward the door of the gym. Most of the crowd moved with him. All DiMaggio could see, over all of them, was Ellis Adair shaking his head no, then disappearing. Collins was still there, smiling, looking small compared to Adair but bigger than most of the media people, coming across the way he did the few times DiMaggio had watched him play, like this cute gym rat.

Collins didn't last much longer than Adair. They cleared a path for him, and he started for the gym door and would have made it as easily as Adair just had, except that here came this big, handsome blond guy out of the pack, jogging casually after Collins, catching up to him right before the door. DiMaggio was about twenty feet away from the door, leaning against the wall. He didn't read what was happening right away. But there was something about the blond guy, speeding up now as Collins reached for the door. Now DiMaggio moved, started for the door himself, just as the blond guy's right hand came out of the side pocket of his windbreaker and DiMaggio heard him say to Richie Collins, "This is for what you did to my sister, asshole."

8

Hannah was exhausted when she got back to Jimmy's apartment. She tried to take a nap but couldn't and put on the television instead, one of the eight thousand movie channels you got with Manhattan Cable if you were willing to pay. They were showing some movie with Mary Stuart Masterson, who had become Hannah's spunky favorite after she saw her in *Fried Green Tomatoes* a few years ago. Hannah didn't know the name of this one. Mary Stuart was a teenager and in love with some guy who thought he was in love with somebody else. Hannah stayed with it until she was sure the guy would come to his senses, which he did.

How come life never worked out that way?

Hannah was positive she was going to be a great actress. Jimmy used to joke that they were going to be the new Barrymores. He sat her down one night and made her watch this old newspaper movie, *Deadline U.S.A.,* with Humphrey Bogart and Ethel playing the woman who owned the paper Bogart was trying to save. Hannah thought Ethel Barrymore looked like she was ninety.

"I'm not so sure I want to be Ethel," Hannah said.

She gave it five years, though. Five hard years. When it was all over, she had made a little over four thousand dollars, total. She had done walk-ons in soap operas, including Jimmy's. After what Hannah used to joke was her retirement from show business, she figured out that she had been in restaurant scenes on all three networks. The two stars would be having some earnest conversation and there, behind them, acting like she was talking to some guy, looking a lot more animated than she ever felt, was Hannah. Twice she played a dead body in one of those simulated murders on *Inside Edition*. She was in the toy store in *Home Alone 2* the first time little Kevin went in there to shop. She was an extra in Scorsese movies. She actually got two lines of dialogue in a *Kate & Allie;* she was an admitting room nurse and Susan Saint James—for the life of her, Hannah still couldn't remember whether she was Kate or Allie—had gotten sick on her way to some formal dance.

But it wasn't the shit work that made her give it up finally, even as Jimmy kept going. Jimmy used to tell her to hang in there, he had enough confidence for both of them. Only they both knew that was a lie. What little Hannah had, what little her mother had left her with, was completely gone at the end. She would go to these miniature casting theaters, reading for television movies. The casting people would be there, the director, sometimes the writer. They would hand her the page and she would read what she was supposed to read, and there would always be that moment she dreaded when she was through, when she'd look up at them, see the awkward smiles, and feel like some dog outside the back door, begging.

God, she hated that.

It was one of the things she hated most about the night in Fulton, the way she ended up begging . . .

The movie with Mary Stuart went to six o'clock. Hannah turned to the news. Wednesday night, she had gone crazy with the switcher watching the eleven o'clock news, like Jimmy watching football games on Sunday afternoons. She'd gone from channel to channel to see how they handled Marty Perez's first story.

Hannah didn't even know what channel she had now, but there was Jimmy Carey rolling around in some parking lot with Richie Collins, then being pulled off by DiMaggio, who looked bigger than he had in the backseat of the car, big enough to throw Jimmy inside a door and drag Collins in there, too.

What was Jimmy doing in Fulton?

She hit the display button for the set. It was Channel 2. She didn't recognize the anchorwoman in the studio. There was just a split screen, and the woman was talking to a reporter in the field, and underneath the reporter in the field it said, "Live, Fulton, Connecticut."

The reporter in the field, a kid with a lot of hair, said, "Bryne, one minute we were trying to get a comment from Collins, Ellis Adair having already gone inside, then the accuser's brother seemed to appear out of nowhere. We thought he was trying to get an autograph. Then the other man jumped in."

The kid with the hair said the Knicks were going to make some kind of official statement. Then the anchorwoman said they, meaning the media, were in an awkward position because identifying the attacker would be another way of violating the victim's right to privacy.

The kid with the hair smirked and said, "Accuser, not victim, Bryne."

Hannah said "Screw you" to the television now, wondering what the kid with the hair would think about rape, what any man would think, if it ever happened to them.

The phone rang. Hannah hadn't been answering it when she

was in Jimmy's apartment alone, just letting his machine pick up.

Hannah grabbed for it, thinking it might be Jimmy.

"Hannah, is that you?"

Mother.

Without waiting, she said, "My God, it's you, isn't it? The rape? You couldn't even tell your own mother, all this time? Where is your brother, disgracing me on television that way in front of the whole world."

It was always about her and always about the whole world.

Hannah said, "Is there one question in there you'd like me to address first? Or should I just start anywhere?"

She knew she shouldn't take that attitude, any kind of sarcasm was lost on her mother. But sometimes Hannah couldn't help herself.

"You think people aren't going to recognize your brother on the television?"

"Would you listen to yourself please? What do you think they're saying right now, 'Richie Collins and the other basketball player raped the sister of the guy in the cat food commercial'? It's not like Collins got tackled by Kevin Costner, Mother."

She stood there holding the phone, wondering why she'd picked it up in the first place. I need this right now, Hannah thought. First Jimmy on television and now her mother's review.

Her mother said, "I saw it on Channel Three. Was it on in New York?"

She had moved to Litchfield, Connecticut, when she finally remarried, but she still didn't think the news counted unless New York had it, too. If she'd found out about the Gulf War on a Connecticut channel, she would have called Hannah on West End Avenue to confirm it.

Sheila Carey was about the four silliest women Hannah had ever known. Silly about tennis, thinking she was actually going to be somebody with her boring little baseline game, silly about marriage and men and money.

Silly about everything.

Even Hannah could see that.

Her mother wasn't saying anything now. She always liked to wait Hannah out. It didn't matter because they both knew where this was going: Hannah would end up feeling like shit for getting herself raped and upsetting her mother this way. Hannah had the television remote in her hand. She idly switched channels, the mute button on, finally hitting Jimmy again, and Collins, and DiMaggio in his blue suit, then a different reporter in the field, Asian this time.

"Hannah?"

"I'm here, Mother."

"Is this true?" She ran this little shiver through her voice the way she still could. She seemed to think it made her girlish somehow.

"Is what true?"

"They . . ."

"Raped me. Go ahead and say it."

"On television, they said it was a year ago."

"Almost exactly. They actually get things right sometimes."

"They said on Channel Three that because it took you so long to come forward, people were going to question—"

Hannah cut her off.

"They're already questioning, Mother. You really should try reading a newspaper once in a while."

"Oh, let's not turn this around."

What had they done with Jimmy?

"I was afraid to come forward, in answer to your question. Do you really want to talk about this?"

"I'm your mother, Hannah. If you were raped—"

"I *was* raped."

"You were raped, of course I want to know. You confide in your brother just the way you always did, and now I have to find out about this on television."

"I'm sorry, Mother."

That always worked.

"I want to hear all about it. I want to understand, Hannah."

She wasn't being a mother here. That had always required too much effort. This was like some conversational shorthand, her mother imagining what a mother would say.

Her mother said, "I may not always have been there for you the way you'd hoped, but I'm certainly here for you now."

"I'd rather not talk about it right now. On the phone, I mean."

Hannah could feel the relief in her voice. "I've got to run right this minute, there's a party. We'll talk tomorrow?"

"Call me here, I'm not staying at my apartment right now."

"I love you, Hannah," and then before Hannah could reply, not taking any chances, because she never did, said, "I hope you know what you're doing."

And hung up.

They were watching it again, this time on one of the smaller Connecticut stations, Channel 61, Marty Perez couldn't remember whether the guy had said Hartford or New Haven. They had just switched over from the top of Channel 9's ten o'clock news show, which had led with Jimmy Carey's tackle of Richie Collins. They were at the Marriott Courtyard on Route 7, just down from the Burger King, right off the Merritt Parkway extension. They were in the room Marty had rented there; he figured he might need it, depending on how everything played out. He'd just filed his Jimmy Carey column with the *News*, typing it out on the new Toshiba laptop he'd taken from the wire room, then hooking the phone jack into the back, getting ready to let the Toshiba do its deal. Every time the column got through, Marty Perez felt like he'd performed some microchip miracle.

The laptop even dialed the phone number. Then the column would scroll past him on the screen, and that was that. Just because Marty could do the drill now, it didn't make him feel any less old. Most of the kids coming into the business, hotshots, they'd never used a manual typewriter in their lives.

The column was in, that was what mattered. They'd ask him sometimes at the bar afterward if the column was good, and Marty Perez would say, "Good and done."

Which became the title of his first collection.

First collection. Even Marty Perez had to smile at that shit. As if there were going to be a second collection.

Jimmy Carey, sitting there eating a cheeseburger at the room service tray, said, "What's so funny?"

"Nothing," Marty told him.

"They like the column?"

"Front page again. The headline's going to be something like IN HIS OWN HANDS. Then a nice picture of you trying to choke the bastard."

Jimmy drank some Heineken out of a bottle, eyes full of the scene. "I just thought of it as an acting exercise. Something you'd do in class, like. An expression of rage, but controlling it at the same time. Trying to keep the top on it. The desire to kill losing out, in the end, to common sense. That part of it was real, you know? Two warring sides of the same personality."

Marty came over and got a beer for himself out of the ice bucket, shutting off the television in the little suite. Channel 61 had gone to a game show.

Marty said, "Whatever your motivation was, you were great." He hoped the compliment would shut him up. Marty had called Jimmy Carey Wednesday night, after Hannah was in bed, and said they should meet for a drink. They went for a beer at some place called Iridium.

After a couple of beers, Marty had pitched the idea of a scene to Jimmy Carey, explaining that stories like this usually only had a certain shelf life, and you had to help them along sometimes.

The kid had gone for it right away, the on-the-make actor in him stepping right in front of the brother without any problem. Marty helped him along by telling him more people would see him on the news than ever saw him at some nice off-Broadway theater over by the Lincoln Tunnel.

Now, after the fact, the column in the midst of being edited back in New York, Marty had to say the kid took direction like a dream. But he was like every actress Marty had ever known, the ones he had dated or the one he actually married, you couldn't shut them up afterward, whether it was a performance they were talking about or sex.

Not that there was much of a difference. Everything was a performance for them, if you thought about it.

Not that he should talk.

"The only time I had to improvise," Jimmy said, "was when that guy pulled me off and threw me into the gym."

Marty said, "DiMaggio."

"You said you used to know him, when he played for the Yankees." Jimmy hadn't changed clothes. He was still wearing jeans, a white button-down shirt, and some old Chuck Taylor Converse sneakers, tanned. There was dirt on the front of the shirt and on the shoulder and a tear at the right knee of the jeans, which were so dark-blue, shiny almost, they had to be new.

"He couldn't play much," Marty said. "By the time he got with them his hands were pretty much shot. Arthritis or some fucking thing. He could call a game, though, the bastard, I have to give him that. The pitchers loved his ass. But a real smart-ass in the clubhouse, all these books in his locker. And this big tape player, playing Sinatra and Tony Bennett all the time. He thought he was smarter than everybody. Not just the other players, the writers, too."

Jimmy opened another beer. "Hey, we forgot Channel Five, they've got a ten o'clock news, too. Maybe I'll be in there." He used the remote control, and the picture came back up. There was some blond woman, smiling with a mouthful of teeth that were like some giant headlight.

Jimmy stared at the screen, locked, and said, "This DiMaggio guy, you say he's some kind of big-time investigator?"

"You follow sports at all?"

"Not too much. My mother was a tennis player, I guess I mentioned that."

"It was in the first column." Jimmy Carey didn't stay too interested once the subject got off Jimmy Carey, Marty had noticed.

Jimmy said, "In the end, tennis was about the only thing Hannah hated more than her."

"It started with Pete Rose," Marty said. "You've heard of him, right? They thought he was gambling on his own team when he was managing. That's the one capital crime they've got, worse than dope or rape or anything. Anyway, the baseball commissioner at the time, Giamatti, he's dead now, hired this big Washington lawyer, name of John Dowd, to investigate. Well, it turns out he investigates the nuts right off of Rose, who gets kicked out of baseball. Dowd's a big star, and he handles a couple of other cases for baseball, but he's on his way to bigger and better things." Marty looked at him. "You want to hear this?"

"Sure."

"Dowd ends up defending one of those cheap politicians in that savings-and-loan deal a few years ago, the Keating Five?" Jimmy was staring at him, as if he was speaking Spanish all of a sudden. "Whatever. DiMaggio worked for Dowd on Rose. He was a lawyer by then, ex-jock, perfect. The *Times* did a big piece on him, and all of a sudden he's about two hundred times more a star than he ever was as a player. ¡*Madre de Dios!*" He stopped and explained, "Mother of God, it means. Now he's into business for himself. And now here he is in our mother-of-God business."

Marty got his cigarettes out of his jacket pocket, unfiltered Camels. He smoked them once in a while, just to remember how great they were. He always told people if the big one, the big bomb was going to hit, and Marty knew he had an hour to live before everything went up, he'd go buy a carton of Camels, sit on the curb, and just start smoking.

He said to Jimmy Carey, "Try to remember again. Did he say who he was working for here? It could be the players, it could be the team. Maybe even the league."

Jimmy shook his head. "I told you, he got me inside, he gets both of us inside, then he tells Collins to get the fuck out of there and go practice. Collins says something, like, 'I'm going to nail this asshole'—meaning me—'on a fucking assault rap.' So DiMaggio goes, 'That's what you need right now, a chance to sit down with the cops. Think it over, Rich.' Which is what Collins does, eyeballing me the whole time. Then without saying a word, he gives me a little shove and leaves."

"Just like that?" Marty said.

Jimmy said, "I'm telling you. Then he turns to me, DiMaggio turns, and asks what my name is. I tell him. He goes, 'You're really her brother?' I say, 'No, I made it up, asshole.' To tell you the truth, I didn't say 'asshole.' He asks me then how I got here, and I told him my car was parked off campus. He tells me to go out the side door of the gym, away from the press, and go get in my car and get out of there. Oh yeah, then he said he ran into my sister and that I'd be hearing from him, too. But I'm not quite ready to go. So I say, 'What if I don't want to go anywhere?' You know, just letting the scene play out a little more."

Actors. Marty closed his eyes, saw himself making the sign of the cross, just so he wouldn't scream. He wanted to remind this schmuck that he wasn't being interviewed for *Entertainment Weekly*. Marty was amazed Jimmy Carey'd kept his end of the deal, actually left without holding a press conference, and remembered to meet Marty at the Marriott.

"That was when he told me, I think I mentioned this before, that he was not someone to be fucked with."

Marty said, "He's not."

Then Marty told him they were going to do the *Chronicle* show the next night. Jimmy wanted to know if they were going to do the gray-dot thing, and Marty, with a sigh, explained that they covered the victim's face, not the next of kin.

"Besides," Marty explained, "one of the objects of the game here is to make you a star, right?" He sucked in some Camel, feeling the little burn. "If we play this right, we don't just see that justice gets served. *Everybody* can come up a star."

Jimmy said, "Let's get drunk, what do you say?" and Marty nodded. The room was paid for, and where the hell was he going, anyway? The story was right here. He'd cornered the market, at least for the time being. So what if he had to listen to Jimmy Carey all night?

Get him drunk and keep him away from the opposition.

"Let's go downstairs to the bar," Marty said. "You ever drink Puerto Rican rum?"

9

From one case to the next, DiMaggio forgot what punks they could be.

It didn't matter what sport it was or what color they were. White or black or Hispanic, they had become the celebrity homeboys of American life, looking at you the way the real homeboys looked at you, eyes half closed, bored, like they were almost too exhausted even to show you an attitude. What could you possibly say that could interest them? What did you have to *offer* them? It was like dealing with gang members, except everybody in this gang was rich. DiMaggio had seen it when he was a player, but it had gotten worse now. The only way you could get their attention was to find something they wanted. People had been giving them things their whole lives, from the time when they could hit a ball harder than the next kid, get up closer to the basket, run through the line. Now they thought they deserved it all, and who the fuck were you?

Adair and Collins sat in Frank Crittendon's office. Donnie Fuchs, the bald-headed agent, sat behind Crittendon's desk, trying to look like one of the boys. He wore a paisley silk shirt buttoned all the way up, baggy slacks, brand-new white Reebok sneakers that looked to DiMaggio like nurses' shoes.

Fuchs had done almost all the talking so far.

"There's only downside for me," Fuchs was saying after Crittendon left them with DiMaggio.

Me. He sounded the way fight managers did, talking about his fighter in the first person. I won the fight. They robbed me. It happened to a lot of these guys eventually.

Fuchs probably thought he could dunk if he had to.

And they always thought it was their money. Fuchs probably thought of the money Adair and Collins got to spend as their allowance.

DiMaggio said, "The woman making the charges is the enemy here, not me. They work for the Knicks, I work for the Knicks. We're on the same side."

Fuchs tried to smile and looked like a fish, his lips not so much seeming to open up but pull back.

"Go run that kind of bullshit up somebody else's flagpole. You work for a great American named Ted Salter, who works for the big boys at Fukiko. And the big boys from Fukiko, who are not great Americans, would forget Ellis Adair's name if they thought he jumped some girl who didn't want him to."

Fuchs stole a quick look at Collins. "They'd forget Ellis and Richie existed if they thought they did this thing," he said. It was a way of correcting himself. He couldn't leave the other client's name out, even if they were talking about rape. DiMaggio was impressed. Fuchs was fast. He didn't want Richie Collins mad at him.

Fuchs said, "How long did it take Pepsi to get rid of Michael Jackson after the little boys started to come forward? How many Hertz commercials did you see O.J. in after they threw his ass in jail? You think the same thing couldn't happen to me?"

DiMaggio said, "I could turn up something that might help you."

"Such as?"

"Such as something that would break down her story."

"The cops do that."

"Not as well as I do."

"Point?"

"You're talking about small-town understaffed cops here. They've never had a case this big, they're going to be under a lot of pressure. Is there any physical evidence?"

It couldn't hurt to take a shot.

Fuchs said, "No comment."

DiMaggio said, "Physical evidence can be everything in a case like this. But how much can there be a year later? So say they've got none of that, or very little. They can go look at the crime scene, but what are they going to find there all this time later? Next they go asking questions of people about a night a year ago, and who can remember that? The cops look for somebody to back up her story then. The word they use is 'consistency.' I'm sure you've been reading the papers the last couple of days. Where are all the friends of the victim coming forward to back her up? There's an excellent chance this boils down to Adair's and Collins's word against hers."

"There you go," Fuchs said. He looked down, frowned, noticed a button of the paisley shirt was undone, fixed it. He had small hands, pudgy fingers, like a baby's. Even across the desk, DiMaggio could smell some kind of cologne. Maybe it was the same kind his boys used.

DiMaggio said, "If they give it to the state's attorney, which is how they do it up here, and he says, 'No charges,' people will say the cops rolled over because it's the Knicks, and they'll have the National Organization for Women camping out in front of the Fulton police station. If they bring charges, there's going to be people saying that they're making an example of them because they're ballplayers, and there've been so many cases like this lately. Remember that in Florida, they said that if the kid's

name didn't have Kennedy in it, the case never gets past probable cause. Remember that woman that said half the Cincinnati
Bengals raped her? That should have been much more sensa-
tional, but it wasn't because they didn't have a star in the whole
bunch. This one has stars. Fulton is a small town, but it's close
enough to New York, everybody will be looking over the cops'
shoulders. It might be easier for me to find out what happened,
even working it alone."

Fuchs stood up, walked around to the front of Crittendon's
desk, sat down on it, crossed his legs. DiMaggio wondered why
he'd even brought Adair and Collins in here. So far they were
just props.

"Suppose I am innocent," Fuchs said. "Suppose she made the
whole thing up. Or suppose there was some sort of sexual, ah,
encounter, but she gave it up willingly to either Ellis or Richie
or both of them? Hypothetically speaking. Say those are the
facts as I know them. How does you finding them out all over
again help me?"

"Because it's not you saying those things, it's somebody from
the outside. Somebody without an agenda."

"But you *do* have an agenda, see, that's the thing. If Ted Salter
and Frank Crittendon really think I'm innocent, they don't bring
you in here in the first place." Fuchs shook his head sadly. He
was sweating a little, up where his hairline would have been if
he had any hair left. "No, they have brought you into this because
they think she is telling the truth, which means that in their minds
Ellis and Richie are guilty until you can prove them innocent.
Fuck that."

DiMaggio looked at Collins.

"Do you believe that?"

Collins took a finger to his lips, wet it, and leaned over and
cleaned a smudge off the toe of his own brand-new sneakers.
DiMaggio thought they might be Nikes, but there was so much

design all over them, different colors, he wasn't sure. They looked like they'd come right out of the box. DiMaggio had heard one time that some of these guys wore a new pair every day. Collins was wearing black warm-up slacks, same as Adair, but just an old gray T-shirt that said I WILL WORK FOR FOOD.

Collins finally looked up at DiMaggio, with the attitude, as if DiMaggio were a cop coming into the neighborhood.

"Believe what? Believe you want to help me? Donnie's right, fuck that. There's all different levels of the Man, you understand? You're just some guy on one of the middle floors." He looked at Fuchs. "Yo. How much more of this we need to hear?"

DiMaggio loved it when they tried to sound black.

Fuchs said, "A couple more minutes, then we'll go clean up, I'll buy dinner."

"Let me ask you something," Collins said to DiMaggio. "How does it benefit us to tell you shit? What's the payback? You got nothing Fresh or me want or need."

DiMaggio noticed Collins was acting a lot tougher now in the office than he had in the parking lot.

DiMaggio said, "If I can clear you before the cops do, it will make the people who sign your checks feel a lot better a lot sooner, think of it that way." He smiled at everybody.

Ellis Adair straightened up a little, on the couch next to Collins.

"I'm innocent," he said casually. "That make you feel better?"

"Lose it, Fresh," Fuchs snapped at him.

DiMaggio didn't even look at Fuchs, he wanted to see how Adair went with that, being talked to that way by the bald-headed agent.

"I can't tell this motherfucker I'm innocent?" Adair said.

"We went over this," Fuchs said, realizing he might have stepped over some line some ballplayer had told DiMaggio once was the fucked-up line. "Innocent and guilty," Fuchs continued, "only come into play when there's a *case*. Maybe even innocent and guilty come into play when there's an official investigation. But Mr. DiMaggio here, he is *not* official. The press, *they* are not official. You don't say innocent or guilty to them because you are addressing accusations. Accusations are not charges or indictments. If you don't have to talk to the cops, you don't have to talk to anybody. And even Mr. Ted Salter, a man I respect, would never force you to give up your rights as a citizen. Isn't that right, Mr. DiMaggio?"

"He said he would like them to cooperate. Within reason. But he wasn't going to order anyone to put themselves in jeopardy with the police."

Fuchs said, "Here's how we're going to help you, Mr. DiMaggio. We're not going to get in your way. You want to talk to Ellis and Richie's teammates, be our guest. You want to interview the whole campus, go ahead. But beyond that our response is, We have no response."

"You don't answer any questions about that night?"

"What night is that?" Fuchs said, grinning at Adair and Collins.

DiMaggio hands were starting to hurt, he needed to move them around some, flex them a little. He said, "If I go back and tell Ted Salter I asked them what happened that night, and they told me, 'No comment,' it won't bother you that he might see that as a lack of cooperation?"

Fuchs said, "He's a smart guy, he'll figure that *I* figured out that if you're here, he's not really on our side. So if you think you can make a case for Salter against me, go ahead. Same with the cops. I don't think anybody can." He shrugged. "But I can't go around answering questions like some criminal."

"You're saying they didn't do it."

He made a motion like he was flicking a piece of lint off his shoulder.

"I'm saying something to you I've been saying to Ellis and Richie," he said. "We're dealing with a fly here. You want it, there it is."

DiMaggio stood up, like he was stretching, just so he could put his hands behind him, make a couple of fists. He had to get them in some hot water.

"You ought to keep one thing in mind," DiMaggio said. "Tyson thought he was in the clear, too."

He left them sitting there. Let them practice the pose for each other.

10

Frank Crittendon was sitting in the gym, bottom row of the bleachers. He wore a navy blazer and wrinkled khaki pants with cuffs and beat-up old penny loafers and thick socks that fell in bunches on the tops of the loafers. His hair, what was left of it, looked like it had been blown-dry from the back. He had a long skinny black pipe, with a narrow bowl not much bigger than a thimble, stuck in his teeth. DiMaggio thought he was asleep there at first, even with the pipe in his mouth, arms folded across his fat belly. But he straightened up when he saw DiMaggio coming across the court, turned his wrist around, and checked his watch, like some kind of reflex. DiMaggio saw he had one of those multicolored preppy nylon bands. Crittendon had turned off all the overhead lights except the ones on his side of the court. The rest of the Fulton College gym was dark.

"How'd it go?" Crittendon said.

DiMaggio sat down next to him. He said, "You've probably spent a lot of time with Donnie Fuchs. How do you think it went?"

Crittendon made a weary, half-assed pass at a smile. "You played ball, right?" he said. "Baseball?"

"Not so's too many people noticed."

"What I'm getting at, you saw things from that side. From a ballplayer's perspective." He took the pipe out of his mouth, laid it gently between him and DiMaggio. "So you know that in the ballplayer's mind, it's always us against them. Them being the manager, the general manager, the owner. Whatever. And what you mostly thought, you being the players, is that all of us were out to screw you. Am I right?"

DiMaggio said, "More or less. Theoretically, we were all on the same side, but it really only seemed to feel that way player to player and not so much there sometimes. From the low minors on, I always thought there were all these other games going on that the fans never got to see. Or'd want to see."

Crittendon got up on his bowed legs, the pants too short, and walked out to the middle of the court, where the ref would throw the ball up. He picked up a ball that was sitting out there. "It used to be a game," Crittendon said, his voice echoing some in the empty gym. Here we go, DiMaggio thought. Another guy all set to make sports into church.

"Used to be a game," Crittendon repeated. "Now it's a fight to the death with some parasite like Fuchs." He bounced the ball hard with both hands. "I don't think of people like Donnie Fuchs as working in this business." He slammed the ball down again. "I think of them as *growing* on it. Like things that grow on a leaf."

Crittendon dribbled the ball in a walk toward the basket to DiMaggio's right, and now DiMaggio was surprised because he looked like he knew what he was doing. When Crittendon got to the top of the key, he took a quick look at the basket, threw up a right-handed push shot, his right arm coming up as his knee came up, and the ball floated in this big rainbow arc toward the basket and swished through. The basket was in semidarkness. DiMaggio felt like he was watching some grainy film clip out of the fifties. Frank Crittendon had played a long time ago, but he had played.

Now he walked back toward DiMaggio, saying, "They're not going to help you, are they?"

"I didn't expect them to," DiMaggio said. His hands were starting to scream at him, but Crittendon had waited a long time.

DiMaggio said, "I wouldn't have talked to me. Fuchs was right. There's only downside, whether they did it or not."

"I talked to Ted. You think they did it, don't you?" Crittendon sat down, picked up the pipe. He struck an old wood match to the side of the bleachers, got the pipe going again.

"I see how it could happen, even without knowing any of the particulars, just knowing what's been in Perez's column. I saw what it was like when I played. I saw how it started to change at the end of my time."

"It?" Crittendon said.

"The whole thing. Women. Sex. What you thought they wanted and what they wanted. What they were saying and what you were hearing. What you ended up getting."

"How could it change that much? I'm forty-five years in basketball, if you count high school. I started in this league with the Rochester Royals. I've been a traveling secretary, PR man, scout, assistant coach. I coached in Europe one time, two seasons in Spain, just to stay in, when the ABA closed. I saw the whole thing before the shot clock. I come from when the whole thing was still played on the floor. And there's only one thing I see that hasn't changed, other than most points win: The women were always there."

He needed to relight the pipe again. DiMaggio noticed Crittendon's hands shaking this time. He thought it might be some kind of palsy. Drinkers' hands most likely. He always wondered what it was like watching them get the first cup of coffee to their lips in the morning.

DiMaggio waited for him, the way you waited for somebody

who stuttered, Crittendon finally needing three matches to do the job.

"It used to be simple," DiMaggio said, picking it up for him. "You wanted them, they wanted you. I'm talking about the sixties and seventies. No questions asked. I wasn't ever a star, not for a single day after they started paying me to play. But the women were there for me, too. Even in the low minors. Fort Lauderdale. Jackson, Mississippi. Columbia, South Carolina. Some wanted a ballplayer just for the sex. Some of the young girls, eighteen years old, nineteen, smalltown girls in tight jeans with all these dreams, they looked you over as a potential ticket out of there, a first-class ticket out of Lauderdale or Jackson or wherever. It wasn't just that you were young yourself, a jock, on your way somewhere. You know what I always thought part of the lure was? The thing that made it safe sex for these women before that was even in the language? They could see you work. Some guy they met at a singles bar, or at a party, he could talk about being a lawyer or a cop or working construction or pumping gas. If they didn't know him, they had to take his word. Ballplayers were different. You could come see us. We were safe."

DiMaggio looked out at the empty court. "At least we used to be."

Crittendon said, "You said it changed."

DiMaggio blew some warm air into his hands, as though he were thinking about what he wanted to say next. The air felt good. He tried to picture his hands under a faucet, not just warm water, but hot water, coming out hard.

"Everything got bigger," DiMaggio said. "Everything got louder in sports, the fame and the money, all of it. And these dumb-jock bastards, they got more and more full of themselves, so they didn't have time to notice that the world was changing and women were changing along with it. The jocks thought it was still cut-and-dried, meet them and get them back to the room. The volume was up, remember? They'd never heard anybody say no. It was like some foreign language. Sometimes they couldn't hear it, and sometimes they *did* hear it, but they didn't know what it fucking meant."

"I know what you mean," Crittendon said. "Jesus, Mary, and Joseph do I know. From the time Ellis Adair was a better jumper, had a nicer touch, than some kid from the next project over, things started to come for free. Sneakers first. Then clothes maybe. Somewhere along the line a car. Then, if they're the one in a thousand, whatever the statistics are, and they made the pros, it's whatever the market can bear. There was a piece in the *Wall Street Journal* the other day. Adair made fifteen million dollars in endorsements last year."

DiMaggio said, "And he thinks he deserves every dime."

"Am I answering my own question here?" Crittendon said.

DiMaggio said, "Ellis Adair isn't any bigger than Magic or Bird or Jordan, or Russell and Chamberlain were in the old days. He's just more available. He gives off more heat, gets more. And the one constant in his life, for as far back as he can remember, all the way back to his first hard-on, is this: Women want him. They're one of the perks that go with everything else. Somebody telling him no? What's that?"

"Yes," Frank Crittendon said, making it come out like a sad blues note. "Oh yes," he said, not talking to DiMaggio now, just talking. "I was going to be a priest. You didn't know that, did you? Came out of the Jesuits. Now I am sixty years old, and I deal with these players who look at me like I am some worthless piece of shit. Like I am garbage. I have a teenage daughter. She used to come here to watch practice. I finally asked her to stop. Would you like to know why? Because I do not want her around when this team, these players that *I* assembled, look at me like I am *nothing,* Mr. DiMaggio."

Crittendon got up. "I'll walk you to the parking lot," he said. They made their way across the court, DiMaggio trying not to think too much about his hands, talking more than he ever did. He asked Crittendon if he was any good with the Fulton police. Crittendon told him there'd never been any problems before this, it had always been minor shit, parking tickets, speeding tickets, somebody blowing his horn in the middle of the night after too many beers in one of the neighboring towns. Fulton was a dry town, Crittendon explained, so if the players wanted to have a beer and chase a little bit, they went to Westport or Fairfield, some place called Masters there or the Georgetown Saloon, up Route 7 a couple of miles. Or Gates, in New Canaan.

"The chief of police is retiring at the end of this year," Crittendon said. "The one you want to talk to over there is a detective named Brian Hyland. Good kid. His old man used to be assistant athletic director here at the college. I don't think he'll give you a hard time, especially if he knows you're working for us."

"You've obviously talked to him already."

"He called when she filed her complaint."

"Did he say if there's any physical evidence?"

"Evidence?"

"Panties," DiMaggio said. "A dress maybe. Something with semen on it, or blood, or hair, or skin."

Crittendon chewed on his pipe. "He just told me about the complaint and that he'd be coming around when he decided how he wanted to proceed with this. Then he told me that he appreciated I'd been friends with his old man, but not to expect any favors."

It was all right. You could only work your side of it. Sometimes the cops helped, sometimes they didn't. Big cities or col-

lege towns, it depended on the cop. Most of the time they looked
at him like some hotshot on a retainer, cutting in on their action,
out to make them look bad somehow. It was one thing TV and
the movies always got right, DiMaggio had found that out first-
hand. They got just about everything else wrong about cops and
investigators, but not that. Cops didn't want you around because
they didn't know where they stood with you. They were more
comfortable with bad guys. They knew where they stood with
them, at least.

"Maybe you could give this Hyland a call in the morning before I call him," DiMaggio said. "I have a feeling he's not going
to want to talk to strangers."

They were outside now, leaning against the rented car, summer really over, the air cool.

"Do you think you'll get to talk to the woman?" Crittendon
said.

"I met her this afternoon." What day was it? Thursday?
DiMaggio looked at his watch. Thursday, October seventh. He'd
gotten the call from Salter the night before. He hadn't even been
on this thing twenty-four hours and already it felt like he'd been
here a goddamn week.

Crittendon turned to look at him, surprised. "Where?"

DiMaggio told him about the Vertical Club, and when he finished, Crittendon said, "What's she like?"

"You mean, does she look like someone who got herself raped,
Frank? Yeah, it was written all over her."

"It's not what I meant," Crittendon said.

"I know it's not. I'm sorry—it's been a long day. Donnie
Fuchs and his boys, *your* boys, finally wore my ass out."

"It was a stupid question," Crittendon said, as if he wanted to
out-apologize DiMaggio. "What difference does it make what
she's like?"

DiMaggio said, "It always matters who they are, where they come from. Patty Bowman, the woman in the Kennedy Smith trial in Palm Beach, she had one kind of back story. Unwed mother and so on. So you looked at her one way. Desiree Washington, with Tyson? She was a kid, and her being a kid, National Honor Society, head of her class, you better believe that mattered to the jury. Anita Hill and the jogger in Central Park and the woman with the Mets. Then there was a woman who said she was gang-raped by twenty pro football players. Where'd she come from? How did she get to that night, that place? I don't care what Marty Perez thinks. Or what some loose-cannon brother thinks. We all want the same thing here, we meaning me and you and your boss. We just want to *know.*"

Crittendon said, "Do you think she's got some kind of angle here?"

"She could, Frank. She could. Most people do, I've found."

The GM sighed. DiMaggio couldn't tell if it was a sigh of agreement, exhaustion, or disgust. "If I need to reach you?"

"The Sherry-Netherland when I'm in the city."

DiMaggio got into the rented car, left Crittendon in the parking lot. He wondered about an angle, suddenly wanting to explain that there wouldn't be just one. But why make him feel worse than he already did? DiMaggio would have had to tell him that everyone would have an angle here before they were through, whether they knew it or not, would admit it or not. It could be money, or getting famous, or even getting justice. Getting a story. Getting some *play.* DiMaggio could see it taking shape already, before he was a day into it. Perez here. Jimmy Carey, the brother, over there. Ted Salter worrying about the boys from Fukiko. Adair and Collins. Donnie Fuchs.

Making his way across the campus, hearing music in the cold night air, different music from every dorm, even some classical,

DiMaggio thought: Somebody got jumped here. Smiling to himself, because he was using Donnie Fuchs's word. Somebody *always* got jumped, if you really thought about it. The trick was finding out who.

And, if you were really lucky, why.

11

Ellis stuck his head inside the living room door, careful the way he always was when Richie was in action. Never knowing what to expect, what kind of show might be going on, how many people. But there wasn't much: Richie and the girl were asleep on the floor in front of the television set on the big soft quilt Richie'd pulled off the bed. The porno tape was still playing.

Ellis looked at them, thinking every girl on campus must have their phone number. No, not just that. Ellis shook his head, all the way in the doorway now, looking down at them. Richie had to have some of that mental telepathy shit going for him. Some way he connected to them that Ellis had never been able to understand. Like Richie sounded some kind of dog whistle only the strange could hear. That morning, Ellis had barely noticed this one. All she'd done was walk in front of their car, give them a little smile. The next thing he knew, she was ringing the doorbell during *Love Connection*.

Richie had given him that I-can't-help-it look like he always did, then said, "You remember Jenna?"

Richie had told Ellis he could stay. He was always making fun of Ellis, not in a mean way, because Richie always knew when to stop, just playing with him, because Ellis liked to sleep with something on, a light, the television, the radio. Then it was Richie who acted sometimes like he was afraid to fuck by himself. Ever since they were kids, he was always trying to get Ellis involved in a threesome, or more, thinking Ellis would like it as much as he did, as if anyone could like it the way Richie Collins did.

Ellis would go along sometimes, mostly because it was easier to go along, hating himself every time. Like that time in high school. Shit, it still made him ashamed just thinking about it, Richie doing that poor Spanish girl, or Puerto Rican, whatever she was. Richie doing it right there on the couch and Ellis not wanting to stay, but being afraid to leave because he didn't want to make Richie mad, didn't want to lose Richie, even then. So Ellis'd stayed, trying to pretend like he was watching the ball game. Like he couldn't see. Couldn't hear . . .

He'd always needed Richie.

Donnie'd said for both of them to lay low for a while, there were probably reporters staking out every bar in Fairfield County, trying to put them with some strange. Donnie got all worked up, the way he did, and said finally the one thing nobody needed right now was a picture in the *Post* of Ellis and Richie trying to make some kind of coed sandwich.

But Richie, god*damn,* he thought if you stayed at home, it didn't count. Ellis'd seen guys addicted to shit his whole life, all the way back to the projects, but he'd never seen anybody have a need the way Richie had a need for pussy. Ellis said to him one time, "It's like something chronic. Like you've got some kind of con*dition.*"

Then Ellis said to him, "What's that medicine diabetics take?"

"Insulin," Richie told him.

"Jumping somebody, that's like your insulin then."

Richie smiled at him and said, "Fresh, some people are just born lucky."

He wondered sometimes how Richie had enough strength to play ball the way he went through life all-fucked-out.

Ellis needed some air, he decided just like that. He thought about just staying up here, taking out the blue bike—god*damn* he loved that bike—maybe riding it all the way over to the college and back.

No, he needed to get away from Fulton for a while. Ellis knew where he wanted to go. Who he wanted to see. Just thinking it made him feel better. He went in and found the keys to the Jeep, not wanting to take his own car. Richie'd throw a fucking fit if he wanted to go out later. But Ellis came back, saw him there snoring, still with a hard-on, hand right there on Jenna, ready to go to work when he woke up.

He didn't have to worry about Richie. Ellis could see the two other dirty tapes he'd rented, sitting right there on the VCR.

Ellis needed to get out. Coach Gary'd said they could have tomorrow off, he did that sometimes, even during camp, and then the press would write him up as some master psychologist or whatnot. Say how well he understood the long season. Ellis knew Gary had this girl he flew in sometimes when his wife was out of town with the kids. It was some anchorwoman from the Midwest. They probably just had the one day before the sparrow wife came back.

So Ellis had the whole night. He could feel all the pressure coming right off him all of a sudden, feeling light. He closed the door softly, went downstairs. He got in the Jeep, rolled down the windows, smiling to himself, knowing he'd be cruising down past Central Park by midnight, easy.

The best part was, nobody'd know, not even Richie. Like he was invisible.

All the years they'd all been watching him, when they said he was as good at being watched as he was everything else, they didn't know Ellis Adair's secrets. Even Richie, who thought he knew everything, he didn't know.

They didn't know Ellis really wanted to be invisible, for one damn thing.

Be a ghost.

He found a jazz station on the radio, put it up real loud, not minding the cold air hitting him from all sides, feeling fresh now, feeling very fresh, pretending the wind was some crowd cheering for him.

But cheering for the secret Ellis. Ellis the invisible man.

All of a sudden, Ellis was yelling over the wind, yelling like a crazy man, driving too fast, feeling like he was above the wind.

Like he really could fly.

12

Hannah said to Beth. "I'm thinking about putting myself out there."

Beth gave her that little surprised look, the one that said: Oh? How amusing. Hannah always wanted to tell her how much that look got under her skin, reminded her of her mother, her mother the airhead, acting as if she knew things Hannah didn't, when her mother really didn't have a clue.

But Hannah never said anything.

Beth said, "Out there?"

"My name. My face. I'm not comfortable hiding."

"Maybe we should talk about this."

Hannah tried to make a joke out of it. "Would you like to go first?" she said to Beth. "We could switch chairs."

Beth started scribbling on her long yellow legal pad, making her wait.

That was just part of the game.

It was her Monday morning appointment with Beth, who was her official therapist. The amateurs, the newspaper reporters, they were nearly a full week into analyzing her now. By her count, hers and Jimmy's, they had branched out from him and gotten quotes from eight of her friends, one former boss, two old boyfriends, four neighbors. The newspapers and the *Current Affair* and *Inside Edition* shows and the local television stations were hardly getting anything from the Knicks; no one in the organization was talking, so the media was finding new ways, or at least trying to find new ways, to work Hannah's side.

The media had started showing up at Jimmy's apartment after he attacked Richie Collins. But then Marty Perez had helped out both Hannah and Jimmy, saying they were staying indefinitely with friends in the Hamptons. It didn't stop the camera crews from staking out her apartment on West End, for some reason. On Friday, *Inside Edition* had set up across the street, just showed people walking in and out.

Then they showed the clip of her running away from the Vertical Club. Hannah noticed that television made her butt look fat.

Hannah started to wonder what she was running away from, exactly.

Beth was still scribbling.

Hannah said, "So what do you think?"

Beth looked up. "About switching chairs?"

"About letting people know my name. What I look like. They're going to find out sooner or later. Somebody faxed Jimmy's agent a clip from one of the London tabloids; they're already using my name in the papers over there and some picture of me that looks like they got it from my high school yearbook. Why not have it be, you know, on my terms?" She looked past the cool therapist, lemon-colored overalls over a white T-shirt and Keds so white Hannah wondered how she could keep a straight face when she talked to obsessive people about being obsessive. Hannah looked past her to the tiny garden behind the office, set in there between Tenth Street and Eleventh, near the corner of Sixth Avenue, just a few blocks away from one of Hannah's favorite things in New York, the arch leading into Washington Square Park. Hannah wanted to look at her watch, but felt the way she always did, that Beth would see it as another little victory, one for her side.

"Well," Beth said finally, "you've obviously done some thinking about this since I saw you last." Hannah watched her, trying to wait her out for a change. She was almost pretty, in this miniature way, with short brown hair and small features, everything about her small, really, even her voice. Hannah didn't know how old she was, if she was married, if she was gay. She'd try to picture her sometimes having sex, with either a man or a woman, and couldn't. Couldn't see her out of control, her legs up in the air, good and sweaty, into some good screwing.

Really getting into it.

Sometimes Hannah just wanted to shock the shit out of her.

"I'm not supposed to think about this?" Hannah said, surprised at how sharp the words came out. "There should be something else on my plate I should be worrying about? Doing something different with my hair? Getting rid of those hard-to-lose ten pounds? Give me a *break.*" Hannah looked away now, back out there in the garden, one of those New York country scenes that would just show up somehow, behind a brownstone in the Village, making you think it was a fairytale cottage in the woods.

"Where's this coming from all of a sudden?" Beth said.

Hannah shifted slightly in her chair, looked back at her.

"I thought this was supposed to be about my destiny? Getting hold of the reins of my life again. Isn't that what you said? I think they were your exact words, as a matter of fact."

Beth bought time, took another note in what Hannah had seen was perfect penmanship. When she finished she looked up and said, "Getting hold of the reins, yes."

"That's not the way this thing is going."

"How did you expect it to go, Hannah?" Crowding her a little by using her name. "We talked about how the lights were going to be turned up, something appropriate to the level of the ballplayers' celebrity. It's been obvious in the past, from the other big cases, the thirst the public has for this sort of . . . episode."

"Episode," Hannah said dryly. "Like from a television series?"

Beth gave her a fake smile.

"We're going to argue about terminology? Frankly, Hannah, I'd like to have more time with you on this. I don't know how you could have come in here initially and kept something like this . . ."

Hannah, the keeper of secrets. She had worked her way into it with Beth the way she had with the police. Maybe she thought of Beth as another form of the police.

Detective Brian Hyland was friendlier, of course.

"I'm sorry I took so long," Hannah said.

Beth started to say something, but Hannah put a hand up.

"It isn't the publicity that's surprised me," she said. "It's the . . . *force* of it. I expected a storm, but not like this. I guess what I'm saying is, I didn't know I was going to end up with a hurricane."

Beth said, "Now your terminology is rather interesting."

"How so?"

"In all these last couple of weeks, before you pressed charges, you talked repeatedly about being lost in a storm. It's always been your most vivid metaphor."

Hannah said, "I was after more control and got less. I just feel like I don't want to be seen in the way I'm being seen. Or not seen. If that makes any sense." She poured some Evian out of the liter bottle Beth always kept on the desk, with two glasses.

"Do you want to be seen?" Beth said.

Hannah got up from her chair and went and sat on the windowsill to her right, leaning against the window frame, able to see a little of the garden, the country scene, from there. Wanting the next part to come out just right.

"I just don't want to be some artist's *version* of me," she said. "Marty Perez? The newspaper columnist?" Beth's face was a blank. She probably only read the *Times*. "Anyway," Hannah said, "he's been very kind so far. Very supportive. Most people have, other than the sportswriters. Those bastards. My mother has been right about very little in her life, but she was right about sportswriters and how low they are on the planet's food chain. They're writing about me, what happened to me, and half the time I don't even know what they're talking about." She crossed a leg, sneaker to knee. Compared to Beth's Keds, Hannah's Reeboks looked like they should be on some homeless woman. "But even when people are being nice, it's as if they're working around me, never actually getting *to* me. Does that make any kind of sense?"

She hated herself because it sounded like she was pleading to be understood. Looking for Beth to give her a pat on the head.

"It makes a lot of sense," Beth said. "Go on."

Hannah said, "I'm not looking to make some kind of speech or statement, say something that might jeopardize my case if we ever get to a trial. I don't need to go on *Oprah*. I just want the chance to stand up and say, 'Hey, everybody, this is who I am. This is what I look like.' I'm not afraid of them anymore. If somebody asks me what I want to say to Adair and Collins, I'll just say something like, 'I was afraid of them for a long time but I'm not afraid of them anymore. So don't anyone be afraid for me.' "

Hannah felt herself smiling. It didn't happen too much in here. Maybe because it was the truth-telling place.

Beth said, "It won't be enough for them, Hannah. You have to understand that."

"Maybe not. But the way it's set up now, it's not enough for me. It's crazy. Maybe it's crazy that Adair's name is out there and Collins's name is out there. But if people are going to talk about me, let them talk about *me*. Let them see who I am."

Beth did the head-tilt, looked quizzical.

"It's important to you, people knowing who you are?"

Looking straight at Hannah, with pale green eyes. It was the way babies looked at you, eyes wide and direct, as if they could somehow see everything.

"I don't want to be famous, if that's what you mean."

"Who said anything about being famous?"

Hannah, feeling a little defensive all of a sudden, off balance, said, "If you're suggesting I'm in this for the publicity, you're wrong. I don't need those things."

"Those things?" Beth said, brightening. "Could you be more specific?"

"The stroke," Hannah said. "The attention. Walking into places for the first time in my life and having people say, 'There she is.' "

"Yet you want to put your picture on the front page of the newspaper and on every news show."

Hannah stood up again.

"I don't want to be the *victim* anymore." She made a brackets motion with her fingers after "victim." "I've done some reading the last couple of days. I don't *want* to be another episode in the series. Patty Bowman Desiree Washington Hannah Carey. I don't want to feel like I'm behind some stupid dot on Court TV."

"You're not on television yet."

Hannah said, "But don't you understand? The dot's already there. In place. It's all supposed to be for my benefit, and it's as humiliating as anything. You know what I was thinking when they chased me at the Vertical Club? I was wondering if the dot *travels.*"

" 'As humiliating as anything,' you said."

"You know what I mean."

"No one knows the Central Park jogger's name to this day, Hannah."

"That's different." She saw her own reflection in the window behind Beth.

"How so?"

"Oh, come on, it just was. That was about some pack of wild animals. She was going to have the public's sympathy. She wasn't up against the happy face from the cereal box and the Fresh Air sneakers commercial."

"You said most of the media has been sympathetic to you. Why would you think people in general wouldn't be?" She wrote something down.

"I think most people are going to take their side. Have you seen what the sportswriters are writing?"

Beth, pursing her lips, frowning, said, "Why in the world would you care what sportswriters think?"

"I believe they speak to the way most men think about something like this. And so many women it would surprise both of us."

"It's not a sports story."

"Yes," Hannah said, "it is."

The clock, a small travel alarm, was facing Beth. It started to make light beeping sounds, one a bit louder than the next. They were out of time.

Beth said, "Will I see you again before you make up your mind? Or was it made up before you came here today?"

"I'm not sure."

"What are you really thinking about doing?"

"Calling a press conference."

There it was.

Beth got up and came around the desk, brushing past her, opening the door, not even five feet tall. "Well then," she said, and Hannah said, "To be continued." They shook hands the way they always did, all business, and then Hannah was out on Eleventh Street, thinking: She doesn't get it.

She started to walk toward Sixth, then started jogging. She had decided this would be her run today, even through city streets, all the way to Jimmy's. If she saw anybody who looked like media, Jimmy had showed her the back way into the building.

Hannah ran and thought to herself, When had anybody gotten it?

Ever?

He was sitting on some steps leading up to a brownstone next to her brother's building, wearing sunglasses and some kind of long-billed baseball cap with no logo on it that Hannah could see, so she didn't get a very good look at his face. Not that she wanted one. He was just this skinny guy in jeans, part of the scene on West Seventy-first, until he got up and started walking toward her, casually, tossing the newspaper in a wire bin behind his back.

Hannah didn't realize it was Richie Collins walking toward her until he took the cap off, pulled the sunglasses away from his eyes.

That was when she dropped the Food Emporium bag, hearing the bottle—apple juice? fruit punch Gatorade?—shattering on the sidewalk, sounding to her as if the bag had been tossed off a roof.

"We need to talk," he said. "Or whatever."

Hannah stood there, not wanting to stoop for the bag at her feet. She looked down there, saw the puddle beginning to form. Red. It had to be the Gatorade.

It's the middle of the day, she told herself. It's the middle of the block, the sun's out, people were all around them.

She didn't know what to do, though.

She couldn't make herself go anyplace.

It was Collins who bent over, cap stuck in the back of his jeans now, sunglasses in the pocket of the T-shirt, surveying the mess on the sidewalk, trying to pick up the bag, hearing the broken glass in there. He held the bag in front of him. The Gatorade was dripping out the bottom.

"Yo, I think you busted something in here," Collins said. Hannah stood there, staring down at the back of his head, which seemed to be shaved almost bald. A Spanish-looking guy in some kind of blue custodian's outfit walked past them, whistling. Then a blond woman, with groceries of her own, and behind her a black kid with a basketball under his arm, the kid wearing a T-shirt that came down all the way to his knees and baggy shorts that showed a little under the T-shirt, not even noticing that it was Richie Collins down there taking things out of the Food Emporium bag: salad in a plastic container, Baggie filled with fresh plums, Newman's Own salad dressing. A blue box of goddamn maxi pads. With the wings.

Collins lined them up on the sidewalk, then walked over to the garbage bin, emptied the broken glass into it, gave the bag a good shake. Hannah stood where she was, in the sun, right here on Seventy-first Street in the middle of the day, wondering why she couldn't make a scream.

Hannah wondered why she couldn't even *say* anything to Richie Collins, right in front of her, chatting with her like they were neighbors.

"I just wanted to talk, you know, before you went ahead and made a mistake," he said. The words came out a couple at a time, like a radio signal breaking up, every time he would take something off the sidewalk and set it back in the white plastic bag. Sometimes he would look up at her.

Hannah: her mouth feeling dry. Finally, she said, "No."

Then: "You get away from me, or I'll scream. I swear to God, I will fucking scream."

Collins stood up, everything back in the bag, holding on to it. She was taller than he was. Hannah hadn't noticed before.

"Relax," he said.

Hannah thought: All you have to do is walk away. Walk right inside the building. That would be the end of it. She looked over. The doorman, Ernesto, smiled at her, gave her a wave.

"You frankly don't need to do anything," Collins said, softly.

He pushed the bag toward her. She backed away from him a step, but took it. Collins reached behind him, and then he was sticking the cap back on his head. He took the *Top Gun* glasses out of the pocket, put them on one-handed.

Back in the disguise?

"How?" Hannah said.

He looked at her, confused. "What?"

"How dare you come near me?" she said, wanting to yell at him, but hearing herself in some kind of rough whisper. "You sonofabitch." She started to cry. "You raped me, you sonofabitch." She put her hand up, to wipe her face, and it was Richie Collins now who backed up a step, as if afraid Hannah might hit him.

She wanted him to be afraid.

He said, "I don't want a scene here. I just wanted . . . I thought we could have a chat or something. Before things got out of hand."

"So you can get to me?"

"You know what happened," he said, almost pleading. "You *know*. You were drunk, oh sure. But you know."

"I know. The police know. Everybody knows about you."

Hannah started to say something more. Collins held up a hand.

"Let me finish, then I'm gone." He took a deep breath, let it out fast. "It wasn't like you said, and you know it wasn't, and I'm just here to tell you, for Ellis and me, before this whole thing gets really fucked-up, for everybody, that if you drop it now, maybe something can be worked out. This isn't from any lawyer. Just Ellis and myself."

"You're offering to pay me?"

"What I said, something could be worked out."

Hannah nodded, as though thinking it over. Collins seemed to relax, until he heard her saying, "Oh, you're going to pay all right. You're going to pay." Now her voice was rising. "You're going to pay for raping me and for coming here today." She was crying again, letting it all go. "You want to pay? You've come to the right place, you piece of shit, you come near me again I'll kill you, you sonofabitch bastard."

Collins stayed calm, not seeming to work at it. "Why are you doing this? You want to tell me that?" Shaking his head. "Shit."

"What?"

"If it's not about money, which I have a lot of and Ellis has a lot more of, what is it about?"

He smiled at her.

Hannah said, "Get away from me."

He put his hands up in front of him, still smiling, like a bad boy, caught.

"Lying bitch."

She had the bag against her with her left hand, and now Hannah tried to swing at him with her right, only Collins was too fast for her, snapping his head back, moving away from her as he did. Collins shook his head sadly and started walking toward Amsterdam. He looked back at her, over his shoulder. Stopped and turned around, the way Columbo always did in those television movies. Ernesto, the doorman, had come out to see if everything vas all right, was standing right next to her by now. Hannah heard him saying something, but she was listening to Richie Collins.

"Who is fucking who here?" Collins said.

13

DiMaggio was in the back of the ballroom at the Plaza Hotel, standing on a folding chair against a wall so he could see everything. Feeling like he did as a kid, trying to see over the parking lot fence behind the bull pen at Shea Stadium. Only this was a press conference at the Plaza, with all the trimmings, for a rape victim nobody knew anything about a week ago. This was New York City. Where shit happened. Late one night when he was with the Yankees, DiMaggio had somehow ended up drinking beer with Willie Nelson at Elaine's and Willie Nelson had said, "You know, you can pretty much turn New York up to any speed you want to."

DiMaggio looked over the cameras and photographers and reporters to where Hannah Carey sat on the stage they'd set up for her. She wore a flowery-type blue dress and a single strand of pearls. The still cameras kept going off, that was the big sound in the room, all the motor drives and shutters. DiMaggio kept watching Hannah Carey, who didn't seem to be blinking very much at any of it. If she was surprised at the turnout—the late-coming overflow was in another ballroom down at the other end of the ornate hall, watching on closed-circuit television—she wasn't showing anybody. She sat there the way a model would between shots, back straight, eyes empty. DiMaggio couldn't help it, he kept trying to picture her with Adair or Richie Collins or both of them, in some kind of pile, and could not. He'd had five minutes in the car with her. Read everything about her there was to read. Now he was watching her get ready to make her statement and still could not put her with them no matter how hard he tried. Couldn't see her in some kind of two-on-one porno scene.

DiMaggio had been talking to people for one week exactly, Wednesday to Wednesday. He had spoken briefly to Brian Hyland, the Fulton cop, on the telephone, and to some of the trainers from the Vertical Club and a couple of the ball boys; he had hit some of the bars in Connecticut. He had tried calling Hannah Carey, without success. He found out who Jimmy Carey's agent was and got an address for him on West Seventy-first; DiMaggio had left messages for Hannah there, heard nothing, started to wonder if she'd really left town the way Marty Perez had written. Now she had turned up at the Plaza.

DiMaggio wondered if there had ever been a coming-out party for a rape before.

The press conference was scheduled for noon. Ted Salter had called DiMaggio at the Sherry to tell him, DiMaggio sitting at the piano, fooling around with Mancini's original arrangement for "Moon River." He had planned to go up to Fulton, to talk to some of the other Knicks. Then Salter called and said, "She's coming out."

"Who's coming out?" DiMaggio had cradled the receiver against his right shoulder, his left hand lightly touching the keys.

Salter said, "The rapee, that's who. Do you believe this shit?" Salter didn't wait for an answer, saying, "I just got a call from the news director at Channel Two. He used to work for our network here. Our girl is holding a goddamn press conference."

Now it was twelve-twenty. Hannah's lawyer stepped to the

microphone, introduced himself as Harvey Kuhn. He was a short bulldog guy looking stupid in a double-breasted suit, but not as stupid in the suit as he did under one of those full curly Burt Reynolds wigs.

Kuhn thanked everybody for coming, trying to be friendly, but barking like he was talking to some prosecution witness. Then he took the voice down to a growl and said, "Ladies and gentlemen, let's keep this simple. A brave woman . . . Hannah Carey."

She got up then, at least a head taller than Kuhn, Kuhn having to give this little jump to kiss her chastely on the cheek. She produced a typewritten piece of paper from somewhere, maybe the shelf inside the podium. She set it down in front of her, smoothing out where it had been folded.

DiMaggio was surprised they didn't have her reading it off a TelePrompTer.

"Thank you all for coming." She smiled weakly, then cleared her throat, the sound barely audible even over the microphone, way down there underneath the motor drives and the shutters. "I'm stepping forward today on behalf of all rape victims. All women somehow made to feel ashamed and forced into hiding by the way rape is handled in this country. Somehow we—all of us, men and women—have gotten it all wrong." She looked up. "The victim's privacy is now violated in the name of privacy."

She was giving it a good, solid read.

"In some people's minds, Ellis Adair and Richie Collins, as professional sports heroes, have already become the victims. It happens all the time this way, and the result is that the real victim becomes an abstraction."

DiMaggio wondered if she had written it herself. He looked over at the brother; Jimmy Carey was staring up at his sister solemnly, almost her twin in his light-blue sports jacket and dark shirt. DiMaggio recognized Marty Perez, not from the picture that ran with his column but from the old days in the Yankee clubhouse, when he used to strut out like the top sportswriting rooster in the bunch. Perez stood at the end of the podium, to Hannah Carey's right, cigar in his hand, not even taking notes. Maybe he wasn't taking notes because he was the one who wrote it for her.

How far into this was he?

Harvey Kuhn stared out at the crowd, maybe trying to read it. Maybe he was one of the jerk-off lawyers who thought he could read juries, too.

Hannah Carey kept going. "I respect the wishes of all women who have come before me. I pass no judgment on the ones who have been victims of any kind of sexual battery in the past and then found themselves put on trial by our society. I share their pain. As I hope they share mine. But I have made the decision not to hide." Hannah Carey took a long look now at the room, doing a slow pan, taking it from wall to wall. DiMaggio thought she saw him in the back, but couldn't be sure. He didn't know who was coaching her, Perez or the actor brother, but whoever it was had done the job.

"I do not choose to hide behind a gray dot, or a blue dot. I was raped last October in Fulton, Connecticut, by Mr. Adair and Mr. Collins. I was afraid to come forward at the time because I was not strong enough. Now I am. Strong enough to face all of you. Strong enough to press charges. Strong enough to see this through, not just for myself, but for all women. I am not afraid any longer, so don't be afraid for me. This will be my last public statement until, hopefully, I will be able to tell my complete story in a court of law. Thank you."

She folded up the paper. Kuhn popped up on one side of her, saying "No questions," but when had that ever stopped anybody? The questions started to come from all over the ballroom, and then a lot of press in the room started to surge toward the stage. Harvey Kuhn was in front of Hannah and Jimmy Carey was behind her, but now they all bumped into each other, like some old slapstick routine from the Three Stooges. Hannah stopped to look at the swarm, not running as she did at the Vertical, but fascinated, wide-eyed, as the Plaza ballroom seemed to tip suddenly, all the press spilling toward her. DiMaggio could hear them cursing, each other mostly, and some of them yelling about publicity stunt, and then this anguished chorus, rising up out of the swarm for Hannah Carey: one question one question one question.

Jimmy Carey finally took one arm, then Kuhn took the other and they got her out of there, walking to the right, where Perez was, waving at them like a traffic cop. Marty Perez waited and let them pass, making sure the rest of the press could see him as part of the entourage, there on the inside, briefly lingering in the doorway, waving at someone, then making a strut exit of his own.

DiMaggio shook his head. Still a rooster.

Hannah kept whipping her head around, trying to keep up with all this guy stuff.

There was a whole roomful of it. They were all talking at once, like she wasn't even there in the suite with the big view of Central Park that Harvey Kuhn, the high-rolling lawyer, had rented for the day.

Kuhn had been Marty Perez's idea. Then Jimmy had joined in. He had always been great at going along. Hannah went along herself this time. She was doing it a lot, she decided. Sometimes she wasn't even sure if the idea about the press conference was hers anymore. Now she sat there by herself on the couch, in this suite that was like some elegant drawing room. She was feeling light, a little dizzy, like she was being carried along, riding on top of something, afraid to look down.

Marty Perez stood there in a cloud of cigar smoke. "I'm telling you, I wrote some of it and I couldn't wait to hear what she was gonna say next." He went over to the bar and poured two Scotches, came back, and handed one to Harvey Kuhn. They clicked glasses and Kuhn said, "This could be the beginning of a beautiful goddamn friendship."

Jimmy Carey, his back to Central Park, outlined against the first small explosions of color out there, said, "A beautiful reading is what it was. When she finished, I wanted to say, 'Send everybody else home, she's got the part.' "

Hannah couldn't decide which one was enjoying himself more. Guy stuff. She wondered if guys got hard even when they were around each other, when they got going on some kind of ball game or something, or telling about some business deal where they'd kicked somebody's ass.

Hannah was thinking she'd have to get out of here soon, starting to feel a little sick, wondering whether it was just Marty Perez's cigar or all the testosterone or both.

It always came down to some kind of guy stuff eventually. Guy *shit,* she thought. Adair and Richie Collins, that was one kind. This was another. She was just along for the ride. She wanted to yell at them, tell them the whole point of the press conference had been for people to see *her.* But that was the kind of thing Hannah always kept inside, even with Beth.

"You think it would be all right if I left now?" she said. "This has taken a lot out of me."

Perez looked at her like she was some room service waitress who was waiting for a tip.

Even her brother seemed surprised that she was still there. Jimmy Carey said, "You want me to show you the way out through the service entrance?"

"I think I can handle it," she said. "You guys seem like you have a lot to talk about. I'd just be in the way." It didn't come out as sarcastic as she wanted.

Kuhn came over and sat down next to her on the couch. As he set his drink down on the coffee table, Hannah stared at his fake hair. It was curly and jet black and came too far down his forehead and even with that, Hannah could see this line of sweat at the edge, even in the cool suite. She imagined the rug like some dam, holding back all this water from spilling down into his eyes and all over his face.

When Kuhn turned back to her, giving her what must have been his courtroom face, she made sure to look him in the eyes.

"Before you go, we need to discuss one more thing," he said.

"What would that be?"

Kuhn said, "Hollywood."

"Hollywood."

From across the room her brother said, "I forgot to mention it maybe."

"Forgot to mention what?"

"We've had some preliminary inquiries from some movie people," Kuhn said.

"They called me," Marty Perez said, "and I put them with Harvey." Perez tried to look humble, Hannah thought, and didn't do much of a job at it. "Just trying to do the right thing," he said.

Jimmy came over and sat on the arm of the couch. "We've got to at least hear them out, Sis. For the option money alone."

Hannah said, "Can we back up for just a second?" She stood up and moved to the center of the room, the way she did sometimes with Beth, when she started to feel cornered by all her questions.

"Let me get something straight," she said. "They're talking about making a movie of this before . . . before there's even an investigation?"

"In a word, yes," Harvey Kuhn said, popping "yes" in there

pretty good. "You want Hollywood? There it is. They don't wait. They wait, somebody cuts the line. You know how they're always saying the deal is everything out there? Forget it. The idea is everything. They like the idea, what can I tell you? Maybe the Tyson story was too black for them, black guy, black girl. This one jazzes them all up: Hannah the beautiful victim and Fresh Adair, the Willie Mays of basketball or whatever the hell he is."

"I'm pleased they're so pleased with me," Hannah said. She turned to her brother, feeling him staring at her, the excitement of all the movie talk making his eyes wide and bright and a little crazy, like he had taken some kind of pill. "Sis," he said, making himself go slow, trying to keep himself down, "I talked about this with Marty and Harvey already. Here's what we decided."

"What *you* decided," she said, getting it in there fast.

"Here's what we talked about," he said. "We all came into this knowing there was a chance the cops might not bring charges against these two bastards. So say that happens. That happens, then we move on, you know we do, and address the possibility of a civil suit. Now play that one out for a second. We could win that, and there still might not be any bucks in it for you."

Hannah said, gently, "Who ever said this was about bucks, Jim?"

"No one did. No one did. It's the one thing we're not supposed to talk about, leastways in front of you. So Marty and Harvey and I, who are looking out for you no matter what you might think sometimes, talk about it. Okay? Say the cops do bring charges. Say we go to trial and lose there, the way the woman lost to the Kennedys in Florida. Didn't just lose, got her hat handed to her. Then what? Where are you then, Sis? It's time to pay Harvey's fee and the bastards are innocent and you've been dragged through the mud and you don't have a nickel to show for your trouble. My question to you is this: Is getting them to trial, just that, going to be enough for you? That and everybody telling you how brave you were to come out the way you did in the first place?"

Hannah didn't say anything because she didn't know the answer to that one yet.

Jimmy said, "So who does it hurt if we just listen to what these movie people have to say? Are people going to say you committed a crime here because you made some money on this?"

"You're saying they would start writing a movie now?" Hannah said. "Who would write a movie like that, not even knowing how it all comes out?" She had this picture all of a sudden of some fat movie mogul with a big cigar running in and tossing a script on the table in front of them.

"They mentioned something to me about writing it," Marty Perez said, offhandedly. "I told them that was a little premature." Perez sipped some Scotch, said, "But I have to tell you, kiddo, your brother's making pretty good sense here. You ought to walk away from this with more than the good wishes of your feminist sisters, if you know what I mean."

Hannah couldn't help it, couldn't even put up a fight, so she just let the smile come. It was for all of them, brother, lawyer, the newspaper guy. It was for them and the whole situation, the turns it was taking, spinning everybody further and further away from the night in Fulton when it all happened.

"What's so funny, Sis?"

Hannah, still smiling, said, "I was just thinking that Richie Collins started telling me the first night that I should be a better sport."

Nobody said anything at first, not wanting to get anywhere near her on that one. Finally, Harvey Kuhn said, "Are you saying we can move forward a little?"

Hannah nodded.

"Bingo!" Kuhn barked.

Marty Perez was back over at the bar—Hannah hadn't even seen him make his move.

"You know what they say?" Perez said. "If you die with money in the bank, you miscalculated."

14

Brian Hyland had been putting him off for a week. The first time DiMaggio called, Hyland said, "Are you calling to help me?"

"I don't know what you mean," DiMaggio said.

"You're a high-priced big-time investigator, you should be able to figure it out. I'm asking you if you're coming up here to help me. Because if you're not, then I just look at you the way I look at everybody else these days."

DiMaggio said, "Which is how?"

"Some asshole in from out of town to get in my way. Call me in a couple of days." And hung up. DiMaggio called him in a couple of days. Hyland didn't return the phone call. Now it was Thursday, the day after Hannah Carey's press conference, a little more than a week since DiMaggio had come up from Jupiter. He had taken a shot about seven in the morning. Hyland was already in his office. When DiMaggio told him who it was, Hyland said, "You don't discourage very easily."

Hyland said, "How much time are we talking about?"

"Half an hour, tops."

"My office, ten o'clock," Hyland said, hung up.

Hyland was waiting for him in the parking lot behind the Fulton police station when DiMaggio got there. They shook hands and Hyland said, "Let's take a walk." They crossed the street in front of the police station and leisurely made their way toward the narrow river that sliced in behind the main street and ran alongside the railroad tracks. Hyland started by telling DiMaggio he had played some minor-league ball.

They always had to tell you if they ever played any ball.

Hyland said, "One year of rookie ball. Blue Jays chain. They had this team in Dunedin, where they train. I was like everybody else: the greatest player ever to come out of someplace. In my case, Fulton, Connecticut. I spent the first half of the year hitting right around a buck-eighty."

DiMaggio thought, Buck-eighty. There wasn't a baseball fan alive who didn't have the language down now. Nobody just talked about baseball anymore; it's as if they were broadcasting it on cable.

"Got hot in August, though," Hyland continued. "You bet. Ended up at .228. I called up the scout who signed me the day after the season ended, told him I was coming home to take the police exam. Went back to the Holiday Inn, packed up my suitcase, and put my Volkswagen on 95 North and didn't get off until the Route 7 exit." He laughed. "If I'd known I was going to end up with the whole world on my ass with a case like this, I might've stuck it out."

"Believe me," DiMaggio said to him, "you're better off."

"You think so?"

"What do you like the best, giving the daily press briefing or dealing with the millionaire assholes?"

Hyland just nodded, as if he couldn't make up his mind. Finally said, "The press briefings win going away. Forget about ball, I was better off in high school. I was sports editor of the paper. Not only did I play the games, I wrote them up afterward."

"The perfect world."

"A lot simpler than the one we got going right now."

DiMaggio walked with him into a parking lot behind the ice-cream parlor Scoops.

"Listen," he said to Hyland, "I came up here because I wanted you to know that I wasn't going to fuck you up. I'm not looking to get in anybody's way. If I find out something that helps Adair and Collins, whatever it is, I give it to the Knicks and I assume they give it to their lawyer. If it goes the other way, I give it to the Knicks and they probably do something bad to Adair and Collins. But I'm not looking to big-time you is all I'm saying."

"Bullshit," Hyland said evenly.

DiMaggio said, "No—"

Hyland didn't even look at him, just put one of his big ballplayer's hands up. Cop as traffic cop.

"Yeah, it is bullshit," he said. "I'm sure you're a swell guy, Mr. DiMaggio. Not much of a hitter, I didn't just look your ass up in the newspaper clippings over at the library, but in the *Encyclopedia*. I don't think there's anybody ever hired you who wouldn't say you're an ace. But just by being here, you're big-timing me. Because what your presence here says to me is that the New York Knicks don't trust me. So if you're up here under the impression that we're going to work together, save it. We're not."

There was a jewelry shop up the hill from Scoops, a little restaurant called Portofino, a dry cleaner, a bank. Now they were finally along the river in a dazzling autumn sun, walking along a jogger's track, the water of the river as clear as it could be, the smooth rocks close to the surface looking like they had somehow been painted there.

"We might be on the same side, has that occurred to you?"

"That happens to be bullshit, too."

"You seem to have made up your mind about me already," DiMaggio said. "Maybe I'm a little more flexible."

"Yippee," Hyland said.

"Maybe I like to wait before I make my mind up about a case like this. Even when I'm in it like a prosecutor."

"I don't give a shit, frankly," Hyland said. "I am trying to make a case against Ellis Adair and Richie Collins. You are here to make a case against Hannah Carey, no matter how noble you try to make yourself. So I'm telling you to your face what I could've told you on the phone: Stay out of my way. Because if you hinder my prosecution your portfolio isn't going to help you out up here."

DiMaggio said, "You've got no case."

"Maybe I don't," Hyland said. "But I'm a very optimistic person. We were going to get to know each other better, which we're not, you could find that out for yourself."

"Even without physical evidence?"

Hyland smiled for the first time. "Thought I had some."

"Her dress."

Hyland said, "It was in all the papers."

DiMaggio said, "You say you thought you had physical evidence."

Hyland said, "Miss Carey thought she was doing right by keeping the dress in a garment bag."

DiMaggio said, "And contaminated whatever samples might have been on it. So you've got no physical evidence and no crime scene."

"You've done a little research," Hyland said. "Oh, I've got a crime scene all right. Their rented house over at Fulton Crest. The same one they've rented the last few years. It's just a crime scene—"

"—alleged crime scene—"

"—one year removed," Hyland said.

"So now you're doing what I'm doing," DiMaggio said. "Talking to people and finding out if someone will back up whatever Hannah Carey told you."

"Consistency of testimony."

"Found any?"

Hyland snorted disdainfully. He stopped and casually scooped up a handful of rocks, began scaling them easily into the river, sidearm. "With all due respect, fuck you, DiMaggio."

They were almost to the train station, in a little wooded area with a couple of benches. Hyland motioned to one of the benches and they both sat down, Hyland making a big throw downriver with his last rock. DiMaggio said to him, "Do you believe her?"

Hyland put the big hands behind his head and stared out at the river. He took a deep breath and kept looking out there as he talked. Way in the distance, DiMaggio could hear a train.

"Yes," he said. "I'm not going to go into it. You're not here to help me, I'm not going to help you. I wish she could remember things better than she does. But do I believe she was raped by these guys? Yeah, I do."

Behind his head, Hyland cracked his knuckles. The sound made DiMaggio wince.

"I keep thinking about the first call from her," Hyland said. "Wouldn't give me her name. Wouldn't even say who the players were. So the cat-and-mouse game was on. A few days go by, I don't hear from her. Then about three weeks ago, she called again. This time she gave me Collins's name, which didn't exactly shock me, from what I've heard about him. I say to her, 'Why can't you come in and at least talk to me?' 'I'm not ready,' she says. Okay. What else am I gonna say? A few days later, she called me and told me she's got proof. 'You'll see,' she says. This time she sounded like she could break down and cry any minute. Finally, one day she called and said, 'I'm coming in.' She's said that before, by the way. But this time she showed. And here we are."

DiMaggio got up, walked over to the riverbank, and put his own hands in the icy water. The water felt fine. He never knew what was going to work, heat or something cold. There just came a point where he had to break up the achy feeling. He looked back at Hyland, said, "There's no way it's a setup. In your opinion?"

Hyland shook his head.

DiMaggio said, "You're convinced she didn't make this up?"

Hyland said, "I am convinced something very lousy happened that night." Now he stood up, came over to DiMaggio. "Your hands okay?"

"Fine." He took them out, wiped them off on the slacks of his blue suit.

"But I'll tell you something, just so you can feel like a big-time hotshot investigator before you get out of my hair," Hyland said.

The train was coming up on them now, the whistle and the engine noise shattering the small-town river quiet. Hyland had to shout to be heard.

"This may not be the politically correct thing to say. But even I wonder what really took her so goddamn long."

15

Ellis and Richie were in the cramped locker room at Fulton, all nice and new and painted this year for the Knicks, but still smaller than someplace like the visitors' locker room at Boston Garden. That rat hole wasn't just small, it was so old and tenement dirty you thought you were back at Booker, going on real rat hunts. When he was little, Ellis used to think of himself as a comic book hero: Ellis the rat hunter.

The other players were already out on the court. Ellis and Richie were the last two in the locker room, like always. It was a game they liked to play with Gary Lenz, who always made a big show out of being a tough guy when they got out there late, or even close to being late. Lenz knew there were different rules for Ellis, which meant different rules for Richie Collins, too.

The Knicks coach knew what everybody knew, that fucking with Richie was the same as fucking with Ellis.

He watched Richie take a new pair of Nike highs out of the box, smiling at them, touching them here and there like he was feeling them up. "Ooh," he said. Ellis had seen this one before, Richie acting as if he were talking for the sneakers. "I want you inside me, Richie."

No matter where he was, what they were talking about, it always came back there.

During the season, Richie would break out a new pair of Nikes for every game. Eighty-two games, eighty-two boxes of Nikes. Ellis didn't think too much of it, he just figured it was Richie's new-money way of making up for when they were kids and had to go to Kmart and buy the knockoff shit. Trax, the sneaks were called. They had to hear it from the boys on the corner, the dealers and the crackheads, who always had the best leather basketball shoes and leather jackets and nice designer jeans.

"Here come the KAY-mart boys," the corner boys would say. "Been saving up their allowance money, here they come in their fifteen-dollar discount values. Buy 'em for fifteen dollars, have 'em last fifteen days." Then they'd chant at Ellis and Richie as they disappeared toward Booker: "KAY-mart! KAY-mart! KAY-mart!"

Making it sound as bad as nigger nigger nigger somehow.

Now Richie frowned at the new highs with the little burst of blue dots around the heel, lacing them, wanting to get the laces just so, all smoothed out. Richie, trying to sound innocent, said, "I've been meaning to ask you something, Fresh."

There was something in his voice, something that bothered Ellis. He just waited.

Richie said, "I been meaning to ask you where you went in the Jeep the other night. When Jenna came over? I thought you'd want to stay around and play."

Before he thought, which was always a mistake, Ellis said, "Playing all the time, whatever comes along, maybe that's what got us into this rape shit in the first place."

Richie stopped lacing and put the new sneakers on the bench, pushing the box to the side, taking his time. Finally, he turned and gave Ellis the slitty-eyed look that always meant trouble.

Shit.

The last thing you wanted to do with Richie Collins, before a game or practice, was get his balls in an uproar by saying the wrong thing.

"It's *me* now, is it?" Richie said.

Ellis didn't say anything at first, he was looking past Richie, like he was trying to see all the way into practice, trying to figure out what that was going to be like. It wasn't too hard to see it, Richie pissed off but not saying anything about it, and then fucking with him every which way he could all day long. Pass too high. Or too hard. Pass just a little bit behind.

Didn't see you, Fresh. Sorry

My fault, Fresh, catch you next time.

Knowing him the way he did, what he liked out there, what he didn't like, Richie could make it feel like two practices, three sometimes. Ellis remembered when they were younger, he'd be on Bobby Hurley's team sometimes. Pickup games in the summer and whatnot. Hurley came from Jersey City, too. Nice kid, great little player, even when he was fourteen, fifteen. His father was coach at St. Anthony High, which won everything once Ellis and Richie were gone from Lincoln. They called Hurley "the nice Richie," just because of the way he carried himself. Like a gentleman. Ellis always liked playing with him because all Hurley did was pass the ball, not try to fuck with his mind.

Ellis, trying to downplay everything with Richie now, said, "You know what I mean."

"Do I?"

"I'm not saying it was your fault or my fault. Don't matter now whose fault it was. I just think from here on, we got to chill. We can't be grabbing on every piece of strange that comes along." Ellis tried to look relaxed, like this was no problem, but feeling in a rush like he always did, wanting to get through this part of the morning.

Wanting to be back on Richie's good side.

Being on Richie's good side, sometimes that seemed like the biggest part of Ellis's day.

"We're in this together, Fresh," Richie said evenly. "Let's not forget that."

"I don't."

"People been trying to come between us for as long as both of us can remember, starting back when the other project boys couldn't understand why you wanted some white boy in the game."

Ellis said, "Nobody is gonna come between us. All I meant—"

"Doesn't matter what you *meant*, Fresh. How it came out sounding was that we did something *wrong* that night, when we didn't do anything wrong."

He had one of the Nikes in his hands now, staring down at the business he was doing with the laces, talking into that, lecturing Ellis without even looking at him.

"I hear you," Ellis said, the words sounding weak, whiny. "But something's going on out there, Rich. Sometimes I feel like they changed the rules and nobody told us."

"I heard this guy on the radio the other day, calling some of these hard women around femi-Nazis," Richie said. "He meant that women nowadays have turned so mean it's like they're Hitler or somebody."

Ellis nodded, letting Richie know he understood about Hitler and Nazis.

"But don't let this one scare you, Fresh. She's trying real hard, coming out the way she has. She wants to try the whole thing in the papers and on television because she knows she doesn't have a case." Now Richie looked up at the clock, nodded himself. Two minutes to ten. They were supposed to be out there by ten.

Richie said, "Don't go soft on me, Fresh. You know I hate it when you go soft." Grinning at him.

It always went back to jumping somebody.

Richie said, "So, you want to tell me where you were last night?"

"Into town is all. Went to Bradley's, listened to some jazz. Wasn't too crowded, was late enough so I didn't have to deal with no 'Hey, Fresh' shit."

"Downtown, huh?" They were on the way up the steps, above ground now, so there was a window letting in the morning light, the sun seeming to brighten up the mood. The atmosphere. Richie said, "You sure you're not holding back strange on me?"

Maybe it was over. You could never tell with Richie, who could be the grudge kind. But maybe he was going to let the original shit pass.

So go with that.

"There might've been a little situation to check into," Ellis said. "Not nothing for last night, but for future considerations." He gave a sideways look at Richie, who nodded, acting happy all of a sudden. Ellis wouldn't know for sure until the first time he got open, though. Then Richie would tell him with the first pass if he was still on the rag. For now, Richie just stuck his nose up in the air and made loud sniffing noises like a hunting dog, some pointer, whatever they were called.

"Know what, Fresh?" he said. "Sometimes I think you're as much a puss hound as I am, you just don't let on, talk it up as much."

"That must be it."

"Life's a bitch," Richie said.

Ellis knew what was coming next.

"And that means we *got* to go through as many bitches as we can."

Richie always cracked himself up with that one for some reason, so he was laughing as he gave the double doors to the gym a big shove. Ellis looked up at the clock over the basket at the other end. Ten on the dot. Gary Lenz was blowing his whistle, staring at Richie and Ellis, giving them his stare. Ellis thought: Goddamn, everybody has an attitude today.

"Bitch, bitch, bitch," he said under his breath to Richie, which was a mistake because now Richie started laughing all over again.

What's so funny? DiMaggio wondered.

Collins and Adair were the last two players on the court, and DiMaggio, aware that practice started at ten, had seen it nagging on Gary Lenz, who seemed to be alternating looking at his watch and at the clock, until they finally came through the doors. DiMaggio had met Lenz the day before, introduced by Frank Crittendon. Crittendon explained that DiMaggio was going to be around, on Ted Salter's orders, and that Lenz needed to know that his normal rules for outsiders—press, fans, family—did not apply. Crittendon surprised DiMaggio with the smooth way he put the hammer to his coach, enjoying himself, even as he was laying most of it off on Salter, the big boss.

If Crittendon couldn't boss players around anymore, he was going to grab every chance to do it with his coach. If you can't smack the one you want, smack the one you can reach.

Sometimes DiMaggio forgot all the locker-room dynamics, how rare it was for things to get handled man-to-man, face-to-face.

"I hope you're not talking about practice, too, Frank," Lenz said.

Lenz made "practice" sound like "Jesus."

"Ted Salter said Mr. DiMaggio has the run of the place. He didn't say, 'Give him the run of the place except for Gary's practices.' "

He was screwing with him a little more and everybody knew

it, Lenz especially, rocking back and forth on his heels, hands locked together behind his back. Not ready to back off yet.

"You know, Frank. I don't know what good it is for me to have these rules if anyfuckingbody"—not looking at DiMaggio, just hip-hopping in place a little faster—"can walk in here like he owns the place."

DiMaggio hadn't said anything except "Nice to meet you."

Crittendon said, "Work it out, Gary. He's going to be around," and walked away. Now it was just the two of them, nobody there to impress except DiMaggio. Lenz decided to drop it. "Just so long as you don't get in the way."

"I promise not to steal the play."

"What's that supposed to mean, *the play?*"

DiMaggio, tired of Gary Lenz all of a sudden, said, "The play where somebody, Richie Collins usually, passes the ball to Adair and he scores and everybody makes a lot of money, including you. That play."

"Let me explain something to you," Gary Lenz said. "You fuck with me, I'll fuck with you. Are we clear?"

DiMaggio said, "I look forward to us reaching that stage of our relationship." Lenz walked away, nodding, like he was talking to himself about his asshole. DiMaggio watched him go. He had known Gary Lenz his whole life, in one form or another, managers or coaches, going all the way back to American Legion ball. They always told you what geniuses they were when you won, then put it all on the players when you lost.

Now DiMaggio sat up in the balcony and watched Lenz go over to Adair and Collins and say something, turning and pointing to the other players, waiting in a half circle at half-court. Adair looked as bored as he had when DiMaggio met him in Frank Crittendon's office. Collins seemed to be doing a yes-coach nod for both of them. How many days of the season would the scene be played the same way, all part of the bullshit theater

of sports? Finally, Lenz walked over to where the other players
and his two assistants were waiting. Collins walked behind him,
briefly making little humping motions. Adair just shook his head,
still bored but grinning now, shoving Collins to make him stop.

High school with money.

DiMaggio thought: What am I doing here?

He could have been back in Jupiter in the cool upstairs room
looking out at the water, the speakers set up, the room sound-
proofed so it didn't matter if the neighbors didn't like his music.
Sitting at the old Chickering, number one prized possession of
his life, practicing old Fats Waller stretches to exercise his right
hand, the worse of the two. No clock in the room, no sense of
time except for what the sun was doing over the water. Sitting
there and imagining he was Ellis Larkins or Shearing or Oscar
Peterson or even Fats himself.

DiMaggio closed his eyes, getting himself out of Jupiter and
back to Gary Lenz's practice. Except it wasn't his practice, no
matter how much he tried to be the feisty drill sergeant as he put
them through the drudge work, walking them through the plays,
making them bust their asses on kick-it-out fast breaks, one after
another, trying to punish them into midseason shape.

The Knicks coach tried to make practice about him when it
was all about Ellis Adair.

DiMaggio had never seen Adair play in person. He had seen
him on television, but only a few times there; he barely watched
sports on television at all anymore.

He liked watching the Dallas Cowboys play football, but the
rest of *that* sport seemed to be three hours of field goals. Baseball, when the bastards weren't out on strike, had become nearly
four hours of beauty-parlor chitchat around maybe ten minutes
of action. DiMaggio remembered turning on a game between the
Knicks and the Bulls when Adair was a rookie out of Seton Hall,
curious to see if all the buzz about him was true. And he had seen

what everybody else saw, a skinny, fluid player who really could jump like Jordan, jumped over him a few times that night, but who had even more flair than Jordan and some old-time Elgin Baylor in him, too.

Up close it was better.

After a few minutes of Gary Lenz's practice, DiMaggio realized he couldn't take his eyes off Adair. It was like the time DiMaggio had been dragged by this dancer he was dating to see the ballet movie *The Turning Point*. DiMaggio sat there through the first part of it, bored, making watch checks about every ten minutes, Shirley MacLaine and Anne Bancroft trying to outshriek each other. Then Baryshnikov danced. DiMaggio didn't know anything more about ballet than when he'd sat down in the theater, but he sure knew this: What Baryshnikov was doing was so different from everybody else it was a laugh.

Ellis Adair was a laugh. DiMaggio thought: This is the way it's all supposed to look. Adair always seemed to have this loopy, lopsided grin on his face, a little crooked, always seemed to be a step faster than everybody else going down the court, a step faster and a foot higher when the ball was in the air, doing things in the air then, almost halfheartedly, offhandedly, making these dips and swoops like gulls did outside the upstairs Jupiter window.

Lenz kept making him stop and start. Do this, do that. Go *there,* goddamnit. But every time he would let them play, really let them play, Adair would make another move or play or shot or drive that would blow the top off the gym. DiMaggio watched him and couldn't help himself, he felt like a kid, the way he had when Tony DiMaggio, on one of his daddy furloughs, had taken him to Shea that first time to see Mays.

DiMaggio sat up there until the end of practice, lost in the sounds of the gym the way he got lost in the music sometimes: the bounce of the ball and the whooshing sound of it going through the net, the slap of one hand on another, Lenz's whistle, the curses and grunts as the big bodies, as graceful as they were, collided underneath the basket. These were the sounds you never heard in the arena or when you watched on television. This was more intimate for DiMaggio somehow. More personal, in some way he could not explain to himself. This was the inside.

And for the first time, he had trouble putting this Ellis Adair, the basketball Ellis, the one they called Fresh, with the sulky one he'd met in Frank Crittendon's office.

For the first time, DiMaggio had a hard time putting Ellis Adair in a pile with Hannah Carey.

It made no sense. There it was, anyway.

16

When practice was over one of the trainers went down to the other end of the gym from where Adair and Collins had come in, unlocked the double doors, and let the press in. They all went straight for Gary Lenz. The other Knick players, in a show of support for Adair and Collins, still weren't talking to reporters. DiMaggio watched Lenz, who started talking before anybody got near him, smiling under his Harpo Marx curls, happy to have the audience all to himself.

A. J. Fine was leaning against the basket support, waiting for a ball boy to bring him a towel. When he spotted DiMaggio, Fine nodded in recognition. "I know who you are."

"Zing," DiMaggio said, "went the strings of my heart."

The kid gave him the towel and Fine walked over, putting out a right hand that was surprisingly small, DiMaggio thought, for a basketball player.

"I'm considered somewhat of an oddball with my teammates," he said. "Not only do I keep up with the news, I actually understand it."

"Wow."

Fine said, "You're impressed, I can tell."

DiMaggio knew that Fine played the role of jock intellectual the way Bill Bradley had played it once. He was six-five and slightly dumpy-looking, thick in the legs; he had red thinning hair and freckles and looked a little like Archie from the comic books. Watching him at practice, DiMaggio thought he could have played with Bradley on the teams DiMaggio remembered from the old days. Fine had one of those time-warp games, setting picks with his elbows way out there, throwing two-hand chest passes, throwing *bounce* passes sometimes, not jumping worth a damn, looking like a plodder thrown in with Ellis Adair and the rest of them to even up the sides, but in perfect rhythm with the game somehow, the beat, a white crooner out there with all the rappers but getting the job done with a minimum of sweat and effort.

"Frank Crittendon said I wouldn't have to beg you to talk to me," DiMaggio said.

"Heck no," Fine said. He deliberately rubbed down both arms, then the back of his neck, then his face, then tossed the towel casually behind him.

DiMaggio said, "You're not worried about alienating your teammates?"

"If I really cared what my teammates thought," Fine said, "I'd have to be on Prozac. How much time are we talking about?"

"Depends on you."

"I'm loose this afternoon. I'll meet you at the Fulton Luncheonette. You know where that is, downtown? Almost across from the library?"

DiMaggio told him he did.

Fine got to the gym doors and turned around. "How many people know?" he said. "We might as well get that out of the way."

The players still left in the gym were shooting free throws at the other end in some contest that was causing a lot of loud jive hilarity with both the black players and the white players, everybody motherfucking everybody else. Gary Lenz seemed to be in midfilibuster with the writers.

"How many people know what?" DiMaggio said.

Fine said, "You know what it means. How many people know that I used to date Hannah Carey?"

He had found it out at Joey Bernstein's public relations office that morning.

Joey was one of DiMaggio's New York heroes, a Damon Runyon character who had started out as a copyboy at the *Daily News* fifty years ago and had done everything, known everybody, ever since. He had covered the Dodgers for the old *Journal-American,* he had been the Dodgers' last PR man before they left Brooklyn for the West Coast, he had been an advance man for Bobby Kennedy in the sixties. He had even gone to work for Steinbrenner for a while, as much as he had always hated the Yankees. His last year was when DiMaggio backed up Thurman Munson. It turned out Joey had also booked big bands in the fifties, and one of them was Ralph Flanagan's. He remembered Tony DiMaggio and so he and Tony DiMaggio's son became friends. They liked the same kind of music. It was Joey who had first taken DiMaggio to hear Ellis Larkins.

Now Joey had his own "store," as he called it. One of his clients was Madison Square Garden. Salter had told him that Joey was at his disposal for as long as he was in New York, but DiMaggio explained that he and Joey went way back, he didn't need any help on that one. Joey had been waiting for him at his office on Eighth Avenue when DiMaggio got there at seven in the morning. Joey was dressed in one of his black gangster suits with wide pinstripes and a red-striped shirt with a white collar and a wide red tie with a huge knot, the color of the tie the same as the silk square in his breast pocket.

Joey thought that if he started later than seven, some public relations flack in some other part of town would get the jump on him.

"I brought a bagel for you," he said. "Garlic."

DiMaggio made a face.

"It's good for you, don't look at me that way," the little man said. "Garlic in your diet, a gallon of water a day, you'll live forever."

"Which is your plan."

"Which is my plan."

"To do everything you say you've done, you're a hundred and fifty years old already."

"And feeling every day of it," he said. "So what can I do for you?"

"I want you to poke around in that computer thing you told me about."

"It is called Genius. They go up against another outfit, known as Nexus Lexus. I happen to represent Genius." He theatrically tightened the knot on his tie. "Which figures."

"You said you can look up everything ever written about everybody," DiMaggio said.

"Not quite. But they pitch themselves—actually, I pitch the bastards—as the most extensive library of clippings in the history of the world. You want me to look up on Hannah Carey? It must be her because if it is the two basketball players, my printer will be printing out all morning."

DiMaggio said, "Can you cross-check?"

"Meaning?"

"Meaning, if two names are in a program like this, can you put in both names, then find out if there's a story someplace with both of them in it?"

Joey said, "I actually followed that."

"Can you do it?"

"I'm pretty sure," Joey said. "If I can, which two names are you looking for?"

DiMaggio said, "I want you to put her name with Adair, then her name with Collins. I'm talking about before she accused them of the rape. Then put her name with the rest of the players on the team. Mays. Riordan. I've got the roster with me."

"Why, if I am not being too nosy, though nosy has always been a career for the great Bernstein?"

"I want to see if she has a prior history with the Knicks. Something that hasn't come out yet, even if it will eventually."

DiMaggio ate his bagel and read the papers and watched Joey Bernstein, who came out of old New York newspapers and all of the wonderful Runyon lies about Broadway, punching away at a state-of-the-art computer program, playing the keyboard like it was a piano. He thought Joey's new hairpiece was more silvery than the last one he had.

After about half an hour, Joey Bernstein said, "Bingo, as they say in the lesser faiths."

"What?"

"A. J. Fine and Hannah Carey. A *New York Newsday* takeout from a couple of years ago. She is buried at the bottom of the story and described as the sister of a Jimmy Carey, starring at the time in *One Life to Live*. A soap opera. They call her Fine's steady. I think I may have placed this story to tell you the truth."

"Can you print it out for me? Everybody else will find out eventually. But maybe I can get a little bit of a jump."

"No task is too menial," Joey Bernstein said. "What does this mean, A. J. Fine and Hannah Carey being an item?"

"I'll let you know."

"I have to know everything," Joey Bernstein said. "Information is power."

DiMaggio smiled. "No shit," he said. "I never heard that one."

* * *

It was after two when Fine came into the Fulton Luncheonette, which was already DiMaggio's favorite place in the whole town, with its dark, pretty Greek girls behind the counter and ten tables and fresh homemade pies and some local station playing DiMaggio's kind of music when he was in there for breakfast. Now in came Hannah Carey's old squeeze, wearing a white long-sleeved shirt, no logo, frayed at the collar, faded tan corduroy slacks, a pair of scuffed tan bucks, white socks. Like he'd just walked across the green in Hanover after his twelve o'clock class, giving you that worn preppy aristocratic look, his Lands' End bag slung over his shoulder. He either wore contact lenses on the court or just went without because he had on these thick black-framed glasses like Woody Allen wore. DiMaggio couldn't decide whether Fine just wanted to dress like the world's tallest grad student or whether this was just another jock pose and he was as full of shit as the rest of them.

Maybe Fine was just better read.

Fine tossed his bag on the next table and turned his chair around so he could stretch his legs out. One of the Greek girls came over and refilled DiMaggio's coffee cup. Fine ordered a tea with lemon.

"So what do you want to know," he said.

"I want to know who she is."

"That it?"

"With as little bullshit as possible, I want you to tell me about her. You and her. After that maybe you can enlighten me on Ellis Adair and a cockroach named Richie Collins."

"You've spent some quality time with Richie then?"

"I've met all three. Accuser and accused. It's been a real thrill."

"What do *you* think about all this?" The waitress came over and brought Fine's tea. He didn't even look up, just started squeezing the lemon in there. So she smiled at DiMaggio. A real smile. She knew him from breakfast. Real smiles, real people. Maybe that was why the ballplayer looked so out of place, that and the size of him, scaling down everything in the small room.

"I don't know what I think yet," DiMaggio said. "I can't read her. I think Richie Collins would have sex with a bowl of oatmeal if he could get it to stay warm long enough. Ellis Adair fascinates me, to tell you the truth. I've been around ballplayers, one way or another, my whole life. So I'm smart enough to know it's a mistake to confuse the way they play with who the hell they are. How they conduct themselves in what you call your real life. I've seen guys who played you an unbelievably beautiful game of baseball blow it all on crack or on little boys. I worked on a case once, a sensitive wide receiver who'd had books of poetry published; he ended up raping an off-duty cop and then beating her half to death. There isn't any connection." DiMaggio sipped some of his coffee. "But I'll tell you the truth, I have a hard time seeing the guy doing what she says he did."

Fine said, "Me, too."

"What about Richie?"

Fine had this habit of widening his eyes before he spoke, as if he were just waking up from a nap.

"He's dangerous, in my opinion. Nothing you could tell me about him would surprise me."

"Dangerous?"

Fine said, "A bully, just without the size to back himself up, if that makes sense to you. One of those guys who'd threaten to kick your ass, then hire somebody to actually do it. It doesn't matter if you're on his team or not. Turning your back on him is a mistake because he *will* get even with you eventually. No matter how long it takes. And with whatever's handy, an elbow, a knee, a trip. Just for the sport of it, as far as I've been able to gather. And for good measure," Fine said, "throw in an almost pathological need for sex."

"Oh yeah."

"You say you've been around sports your whole life," Fine said. "So have I. I don't know how much of a player you were, frankly, whether you were good or just some kind of shit player—"

"—I was a shit player—"

"—but I've always been a star. Not here the way I was in high school, or at Dartmouth, or even in the Olympics. But there has been a constant level of success. Okay? Celebrity. I am familiar after all this time with the standard-issue adulation that comes with being a sports star in this country. Which is to say: Girls and women have always been there with me, from cheerleaders to college professors to, well, Hannah. They have been there, in varying degrees, for me and my teammates. And in all that time, I have never seen anyone to whom sex is more important, in an almost primal way, than Richie Collins."

"Could you see Hannah attracted to someone like that?"

"Maybe."

DiMaggio said, "Richie Collins is her type?"

Fine sipped some of his tea. "I didn't say that. You asked me if I could see Hannah being *attracted*. You say Ellis is fascinating? Shit, so is Richie because of his ability to draw all kinds of women to him. I tell you what, I've always been amazed at the range of his conquests. He feels this need to always bring them back to the hotel bar before they head upstairs. I've been introduced to topless dancers in Chicago and a psychiatrist in Denver. I swear to God, there was an ex-nun in Portland. Somehow he just sucks them in." Fine tried to look embarrassed. "Do I sound like something less than a feminist here?"

"I don't give a shit one way or another."

Fine said, "No, I don't suppose you do."

DiMaggio said, "Why don't you tell me about you and Hannah."

Fine had met her at a Knicks game. One of the trainers at her exercise club trained some vice president of the Garden. "The suite directly below Ted Salter." The trainer would get tickets sometimes and one night he couldn't go so he gave the tickets to Hannah, who went with a girlfriend, Lisa something.

"Lisa Dee, she called herself. I just met her the one time, after this game. I never knew if it was her last name or an initial. But I had seen her around before with a couple of the other guys, I just figured she was on the circuit."

"Circuit?"

"Girls for all seasons. Baseball, football, basketball. Some of them have been out there as long as I've been in New York."

"We used to call them Baseball Annies."

"They're more versatile now. Maybe it's a Deion Sanders thing. They're two- and three-sport girls. They come up to training camp, they even go down to Florida for spring training."

"Any of them hookers?"

"They may be. Nobody ever asked me for money. A lot of them are bored rich girls, with enough money to support their habit."

"Same habit as always."

"Thrill-fucking athletes."

Lisa knew the drill. During warm-ups, women looking to set something up for later on would present themselves under the basket. The security guys and cops would let them stay until just before the horn sounded, announcing the game was about to start. These were the ones on the circuit, the ones looking to get on.

DiMaggio: "Then what?"

"It's pretty interesting. It's all done with eye contact, smiles, nods. It's like this game goes on before the game. If you see somebody you want, all of a sudden there'd be a problem with your sneakers or the tape job on your ankle. You might discover, shit, I need to do a little more stretching. The trainer comes out. You tell him where she is, what she's wearing. He goes under the basket, retrieves balls while we're shooting, makes sure he makes contact with her."

"It sounds like high school."

"It is. Anyway, he'll tell her 'Play-by-Play, forty-five minutes after the game.' It's a bar here they put in when they redid the Garden, built the Paramount theater and all the rest of it. You take a shower, talk to the press, go in there. There she is. There Hannah was. Wearing the blue dress I'd seen her wearing under the basket. Some of them wear hot clothes to make you notice them. Lisa did. Hannah didn't. It was just this elegant-looking blue dress."

"So that's how you met her."

"That's how I met Hannah and Lisa Dee."

"They were both there."

"They sure were."

"Meaning?"

"Meaning it became obvious after a while, as we all got a little high on wine, that they were an entry."

"You're saying—"

"—we all left together."

"—you and Hannah *and* this other woman."

"It's usually not my style. But yes. Just the one time. First time. We never did it again."

"She ever explain it?"

"She said she thought she was supposed to be wild if she wanted to meet athletes."

"Even the Ivy Leaguers?"

"Even them."

She knew a little bit about basketball, a lot more about him. "Like I was some kind of exam she'd been studying for." She said she wanted to meet him because he was different. And so they began their affair.

"The only way to describe Hannah is as a passionate joiner. Everything I liked, she liked."

So they went to art galleries. When the Knicks would get a day off from practice, they would go up to his weekend place in Rhinebeck. She talked a lot about her brother the actor, never about her mother, just that she had been a tennis player and lived in some ritzy part of Connecticut. In nice ways, he would ask her why she wasn't doing more with her life than exercise clubs and waitressing. She said that until she'd met him, it was like she'd hit some Pause button on her life. She was in therapy, she told him that. She said she was just waiting to see what the "next thing" was going to be.

Fine: "After a while, it became obvious that in her mind, the next thing was getting married to me."

"That wasn't in your program."

"It was always a bigger deal to her than to me. I never stopped dating other women."

"That bother her?"

"I didn't think it was any of her business, frankly."

It became her business, as it turned out, when she decided to surprise him one time at a hotel in Landover, Maryland, when the Knicks were playing the Bullets in one of the last games of the regular season. She told the desk clerk she was Mrs. Fine, got a key, went up to his room the afternoon before the game, and found him in bed with one of the flight attendants from the team plane.

He thought it was over right there. She didn't. She called, she sent telegrams. She asked *him* for another chance. She would show up outside practice when the Knicks were getting ready for the play-offs. After a couple of months, Fine assumed she had given up. The season ended with the Knicks losing in the finals of their conference. Fine went to Europe. Hannah Carey was out of his life, out of his mind.

"She wasn't the type for the circuit, so I didn't expect her to keep showing up for games or anything."

"You never saw her again."

"One time. It must have been the week before she said Ellis and Richie raped her. Up here. I went into this place Gates, over in New Canaan, to have a beer and watch *Monday Night Football*. I came down these steps from the street, and there's a door that leads into the bar area. And there she was, sitting at the bar talking to Richie."

"The stories keep saying that she didn't meet Collins and Adair until the night they raped her."

"Hannah always had a rich fantasy life, Mr. DiMaggio. You ought to keep that in mind."

17

Eleven o'clock, Saturday morning. Third Saturday in October. Marty Perez sat in the parking lot in front of the Fulton Sports Shop, at the intersection of Route 7 and Old Ridgefield Road and waited for the guy to come out. Marty hoped he'd be alone when he did.

Marty was in the front seat of his old blue BMW, the tape playing softly. Rubén Blades was almost talking his way through the ballad. Now he found himself going right along with Blades in Spanish, on every word. Marty surprised himself sometimes. Usually it was when he was alone, like this, when he was relaxed, waiting for something to happen. Then there'd be no urge to despic himself, to turn himself back into Marty Peters.

Go back to being Marty the WASP.

Sometimes it was food that did it, the taste of something in a restaurant suddenly making it all vivid, and he would be at his grandmother's table, eating *arroz con gandules,* rice and that kind of pea they could pick off the trees themselves and shuck. *Arroz con gandules* or *asopao,* the stew she would cook up sometimes on Sunday nights, with a side dish of *sorullos,* his favorite of all, cornmeal fritters deep-fried into little sausages.

Sometimes it was music that did it. Like now. This old album from Blades, one of the three he made with the great Willie Colón. Blades was Panamanian, but old Willie was Puerto Rican all the way. Marty knew what part of the island, but had forgotten. Fuck it. He let them both take him home now. Closed his eyes and thought of the spring nights when he would be back sometimes on school vacations, going over, playing some blackjack in the tiny casino at Palmas, like he was gambling in somebody's living room. Then walking out to the beach after that, late, with a bottle of Don Q, and waiting for the little barmaid in there—Elena—to get off. Then she would come through the trees not wanting to have a drink or wait, undressing both of them, whispering, *"Ahora mismo."*

Reaching for his belt buckle and telling him, "Right now . . ."

Blades finished the song and there was a click from the tape player as the thing began to rewind. Marty gave his head a little shake and looked at the front door of the Sports Shop. There was still a line, fathers and sons mostly, waiting to go in and get autographs, the little bastards in their Knicks sweatshirts and cheap blue-and-orange Knicks caps, the fathers looking bored, checking their watches. It probably seemed like a great outing, a way to kill off time with the kid, now they had to stand in this goddamn line. Good, Marty thought. Let them wait, too. He could sit here and listen to the music, try to figure out how he was going to approach this, get into it with him.

Marty smiled. They could call him a bullshitter all they wanted. Call him the *king* of the spic bullshitters. They were *pendejos*. All of them. Worthless shits. *"¡Pendejos!"* he said out loud, spitting it out. The reason he would be back on top, in television this time, bigger than ever, was because he was *here* on a Saturday morning, while the *pendejo* shits were still asleep.

It was Michael Cantor who gave him the idea. Marty knew he took Cantor for granted sometimes, forgot what a great newspaper editor he really was, a great *idea* man. But then Marty would be in the middle of something, not knowing where to go with it, and Cantor would do everything except take his cards and play his hand for him.

They were having lunch the day before, their usual Friday lunch, Chinese, Tommy's Gold Coin, a couple of blocks up Second from the *News* building. They were walking back to the office when Cantor said, "Incidentally, I think we've gone as far as we can with Hannah's side of it. At least for now."

Incidentally. Cantor always used "incidentally" or "by the way" to shift gears. They had been talking about the Giants. Cantor's family had tickets that went all the way back to the Polo Grounds. Sometimes he would get going on them, who the quarterback ought to be, what was wrong with the offense, and Marty would think about maybe putting something in his drink to get him to shut the fuck up.

Then out of the blue, Cantor hit him with this Hannah thing, catching Marty off guard. The editor was good at that. He had a lot of conversational moves, always acting like it was an accident when he made the point he wanted to make all along. Sometimes Cantor didn't act like Marty's editor at all but his therapist.

Or maybe his conscience.

Marty got defensive right away. He couldn't help himself. He was a thin-skinned spic and always had been. He'd write the worst sort of shit about people and expect them to take it, then feel himself going to pieces himself at the hint of criticism.

"You want me off it," he said to Cantor, "just say so."

"No, no, no," Cantor said. "Let me finish here. She's given us a great run, we've been ahead of everybody else in town from the first day. The circulation guys were on the phone again this morning, begging for more. *Squealing.*"

They were waiting for the light at Forty-second.

Cantor said, "Take a look at this." He reached into the pocket of the Brooks Brothers suit and pulled out a crumpled piece of graph paper. He held the paper out in front of him so they both could see it.

Cantor said, "We haven't had a run like this since that judge went nuts and started sending rubbers to his old girlfriend instead of Hallmark cards. Remember that one? Anyway, Hannah gave us a two percent bump when we had her out front last Monday. Four percent on Friday. You don't think *that* gave all the car advertisers hard-ons? And this past Sunday? They figure an extra thirty thousand copies."

They went across Forty-second, Marty just taking it all in, chewing on his cigar.

"All I'm asking you," Cantor said, "is that we see if there's anything for us on the *other* side. Even if it's for one day."

"You want me to do it?" Marty asked.

"It's not like you haven't done it before. Keep coming at them the same way. Hammering away. Like a quarterback throwing short all day, the same pattern. Finally, the cornerback comes up and—badda bing!—the quarterback throws the bomb. It's my opinion that you could give Collins and Adair a day and not lose her. You could finesse them. Cut a deal—"

"A deal?" Marty said incredulously. "We'd be offering them tipping money."

"Not money. Offer them the wood."

After all these years, Cantor was still in love with the lingo. *Wood* meant the front page, from when they used to use wood to set the type out there.

"Tell them it will be the wood in a good way this time," Cantor said. "We'll do it like *Vanity Fair* does. Shit, you see some celebrity out there, you know before you read the article it's going to be a blow job. So bullshit these guys a little. Tell them you'll turn the column over to them and they can write their own defense in the first person."

"Bullshit being a specialty of mine, of course."

Cantor smiled. "You can make a big show out of it. I'm Marty Perez, and I'm big enough to give everybody a chance. Look at me, I'm hammering the shit out of them and they're *still* talking to me."

They were in the lobby now, over by the gigantic globe. Cantor never walked in the entrance on Forty-second and Second, he always liked to walk past the globe.

Marty shook his head slowly. "These guys aren't talking."

"You'll at least give it a try."

It didn't come out as a question from Cantor.

"I'll think about it," Marty said.

Cantor said, "I want to give you a big kiss."

"Maricón," Marty said.

Now here he was, back in Fulton, sitting in the parking lot, waiting for Richie Collins to finish his autograph signing inside.

It was noon when Collins came out a side door, looking like one of the scraggly-assed kids who should have been in the line, wearing a Megadeth T-shirt, faded black jeans, and sneakers that looked so new Marty wondered if he'd bought a pair inside. Marty started to get out of the car, then had to wait because some girl had beaten him to Richie Collins.

Marty instinctively reached into the backseat for the camcorder he kept there. He had started carrying it when he started doing *Chronicle*. You never knew with celebrities. It made Marty feel like a peeper sometimes, one of those celebrity-page photographers hanging around outside the hot clubs, even places like Elaine's, hoping to get some movie star acting like an asshole. Doing some asshole thing.

It was Houghton who had suggested Marty buy the thing and keep it in the car. And then one day Marty was on the side of the

Plaza when a bellhop told him Michael Jackson was coming out.
Long before the shit came down with Jackson and the kids.
Marty had the tape rolling when Jackson came out with his entourage, carrying the seven-year-old. It seemed like nothing at
the time.

Marty filed the tape anyway.

And had it for *Chronicle* the night the kid in California
charged Jackson with molesting him.

Marty held the camera in his lap, shooting through the windshield, the lens just peeking over the top of the dashboard. He
hit Record, making sure to keep himself and the camera still,
watching the whole thing like it was some silent movie.

The girl was almost six feet tall and had long blond hair and
wore black leotards with a long lemon-colored T-shirt that barely
covered her ass. She was standing by a Jeep Cherokee that Marty
assumed belonged to Collins.

Seventeen years old, Marty figured. Eighteen tops. He knew
he was getting to be an old bastard. He'd watch the college
games on television sometimes and the cheerleaders would look
younger and younger to him. When he was a kid, did they ever
look to him like someone's daughter?

This one was sure a baby, though. Daddy's big *chula* girl, sexy
in her black tights, looking for trouble on Saturday morning.

Marty had heard that with Richie Collins, the younger the better. Art Berkowitz, a funny kid who covered the Knicks for the
News, told Marty one time at the Gold Coin, "Richie spends more
time in cars with high school girls than the driver ed instructor."

Collins ducked his head and smiled.

The girl was doing most of the talking.

Collins laughed a couple of times.

She made a slow move of brushing her hair out of her face.

Marty Perez thought to himself: I better get him now or he'll be in the car with her and gone. And his pants are going to be around his ankles before he hits the first stoplight.

He hit Stop on the camcorder, which he placed on the floor in the backseat. Then he got out of the car and walked toward them, tossing his cigar away. "Hey, Richie. Richie Collins."

Collins and the girl both turned around at the same time, a little startled, like Marty was a cop shining a flashlight into the backseat. Marty wasn't paying any attention to the girl now, he was watching Collins.

Collins started shaking his head before Marty got up on him, very casual.

"You've got to be shitting me," Collins told him.

"Okay, Richie?" the girl said in this pleading voice, ignoring Marty. "Is that okay?" She tugged on his arm. *"Okay?"* She seemed nervous at being seen, but she wasn't leaving without an answer from Collins. Whatever the question was.

"Okay," Collins snapped, yanking his arm away, still watching Marty. "I told you it was okay. You've still got the number? Call me in about an hour."

"There's no need to get mad, Richie," she whined.

"I'm not mad." He patted her big hair. "I just have some business I got to take care of all of a sudden. It won't take me long. Now, *good-bye!"* He patted her on her ass, which seemed to make everything all right, as far as Marty could tell. She got into her car, a red Nissan, and drove away.

"Cute girl," Marty said. "Your niece?"

"Just a kid from Fulton High with a runaway crush."

"I noticed."

"Hey, Perez, I'm loved by kids of all ages, what can I tell you."

Marty said, "Tell me what age, give an old man a thrill."

Collins said, "You got big balls, you know that?"

"Qué cojones," Marty said. "As we say back home."

"Where's that, Miami?" Richie Collins said.

"Close enough."

"I have nothing to say to you." He reached into his pocket and got out his car keys. Still not moving, though.

Waiting for Marty to make his pitch.

"I think you do," Marty said. "Have something to say. Even if you think I'm just another newspaper asshole who's got the whole thing wrong. Even if you think Hannah Carey is just in for some kind of big score, and I'm looking to ride it. Even if you probably want to kick my fat Puerto Rican ass all the way back to the city. You and Ellis, you both probably think I sold you out and went with her because she's the one who made a better story."

Collins casually crossed his arms, leaned against the Jeep. Still not making any move to get in. "I told you I have nothing to say to you."

"You're here."

"Only because I'm thinking to myself, Rich, *could* you kick his ass and get away with it? Maybe tell old Marty you're going to give him a story, then take him somewhere private and beat the living shit out of him."

"I'll make you a deal," Marty said.

Collins laughed. "You got nothing I want. You guys never do."

"I got the power, babe. The power of the press."

"You got shit."

"Richie, listen to me one more minute, then you want to go, go. The *News* has been whacking you all over the place for two weeks. If they see your version in there now, maybe enough people slap their heads and think, Maybe we were wrong."

"I don't need you. I don't need the fish-wrap *News*. I don't need good ink. You want to know why? Because there's no case. There's no case, no charges, this thing is gonna get dropped, so see you later, good-bye."

Marty said, "Till she sues."

"She sues? So what she fucking sues?" Richie's voice got louder. "She loses that one, too. Then she's gone and you're back to being a nobody. Fresh and me, we lay low for a while, then we just keep on keepin' on. It's why we don't have to talk to anybody. Not the cops, and especially not you."

Now Richie Collins reached for the door handle.

Marty said, "Let me ask you one more question. Off the record."

"One question. I gotta get some sleep. We got in late, game in fucking Milwaukee last night."

"Marty said, Did it happen the way she says it happened?"

Richie Collins smiled, a broad shit-eating smile, then looked up at the sky. "No."

"Did either one of you fuck her—with or without her consent?"

"You said one question. I answered it. Now I'm out of here." He jerked his head in the direction the girl had gone in her hot little red car. "It's my day off, I've got plans."

"You go ahead," Marty said. "You keep telling yourself you can ride this out. You want to know where you're going to ride it out? In Sacramento. Or whatever shit team they can deal you to when this thing *is* all over. You think the Garden brought in DiMaggio to *help* you, Richie? You seem like a smart guy. If they believe you're innocent, why bring in a hotshot like DiMaggio?"

Collins tried to look bored, but Marty kept going. "I'll tell you why. Because the big boys think you did it, Richie. They *want* you to be the one that did it. Nobody else is going to tell you this, so I'll tell you. If DiMaggio comes up with anything, you're out of here first chance they get."

"Bullshit."

Marty thought: I don't need an editor to play my hand for me, I can play it myself.

Play the trump card.

"You shouldn't have gone to see her the other day, Richie. Dumb play for a smart guy like yourself."

Richie Collins, rigid, said, "Who—"

"You mean, who would tell a nobody like me something? She told her brother and her brother told me and now I'm telling you. You got everything going your way and you go and harass the *victim?*"

Collins, defensive now, said, "I wanted to ask her why she's making this shit up."

Marty said, "Tell that to the Fulton cops. Or the state's attorney over in Norwalk."

"You're going to put it in the paper?"

"I haven't decided."

Collins said, "What are you looking for here, exactly?"

"You don't want to give me a play-by-play on the whole night, don't. You want that we didn't even have this conversation, we didn't have it. I just want something that could cast some doubt on her version of things. Maybe get people thinking she is making some of this up, like you say she is."

"The stuff you've been printing like it's gospel?"

"Work with me, Rich, is all I'm saying. It helps me, it helps you."

Collins smiled. He nodded his head like, yeah, now all of a sudden this makes sense. "You're telling me you're willing to give her up?"

"A man's got to eat, Richie," Marty said, smiling right back.

Richie said, "Follow me."

18

DiMaggio loved it when they would big-guy him.

"Big guy, you better be sitting down when you read the *Daily News*," Ted Salter had said, sounding pretty chipper for seven-thirty in the morning. He sounded like he'd been up since five. He was the type. Guys like Salter wanted to jam up every day, already planning for the day when they got fired. Or had a stroke. Or dropped dead. Didn't anybody in New York sleep late anymore?

"You're awake?" he added almost as an afterthought.

DiMaggio said, "I'm awake. And I've seen the paper." He'd just finished reading the *News*. The front page had the story about how Hannah used to date A. J. Fine and all the details of her first time with him, including the other woman. The front-page headline was SHE'S SO FINE.

Marty Perez wrote it, but not as one of his columns, with his picture. They ran a little box with it that said "News Analysis," whatever that meant.

Salter said, "You think it's true?"

DiMaggio said, "Yes."

"What does it do to the investigation?"

"Nothing," DiMaggio said. "Maybe in court if they ever get

to court. But what she did with Fine has nothing to do with what happened with Adair and Collins. It doesn't mean she deserved to get raped."

"If she did get raped."

"If she did."

"What does it do to you?" Salter said.

"I'm where I've been since I got here," DiMaggio said. "Hyland—he's the Fulton cop, good guy, by the way—he keeps saying he's got no case. Maybe he's right. But I talked to him last night, and he told me the state's attorney over in Norwalk wants to be attorney general next time. I forget when next time is. Next year or the year after. He thinks this can be a big score. So he's turned up the heat on Hyland. He *wants* to make formal charges against your boys. And he wants to make them now. So if I'm going to come up with something to make this go away for you, I better do it."

"From your lips to God's ears," Salter said. "Are you coming up with something for old Uncle Ted?"

"I've been working the bars up there, looking for somebody who remembers seeing anything. Her story is that she was having a drink at this place Gates, then went over to another place, Mulligan's. But no one can remember her, they just generally see players in those places. They also can't place which night of the week it was. It's a year, remember. There were always women around these guys. Hannah's a good-looking blonde, it doesn't exactly narrow things down."

"Listen," Salter said, "I wasn't calling to bust your balls. I'm calling because she's going to be at the Garden today."

"Who?"

"Hannah. She and her brother and her lawyer, what's-his-name with the dead muskrat on his head, are meeting with a couple of our West Coast movie guys at ten o'clock."

"Movie guys?"

"What can I tell you? They don't wait out there. They go. Especially when they find out Fox is interested already, Warner Brothers. Even the guys with the mouse ears."

"Let me get this straight," DiMaggio said. "You, meaning Fukiko, employ the two guys she says raped her."

"Check."

DiMaggio said, "And me."

"Check."

"And now you are talking to *her* about doing a movie."

"Talking. Not doing. You ever been to Hollywood? Big difference between talking and doing. Big difference between making a deal and doing."

DiMaggio, fascinated, said, "You don't see any conflict of interest there?"

"*You* say conflict of interest. *I* say we're just protecting our flanks here. Seeing the big picture, no pun intended. Hey, don't turn this into ethics class, big guy. I just thought you'd want to know. Maybe when she's done, you could accidentally bump into her. You said you were having trouble getting in touch with her."

"I don't think she's going to want to talk anymore. Especially after today."

"She'd be crazy to, if you think about it."

DiMaggio said, "Unless she is crazy."

"What does that mean? You told me they did it."

DiMaggio didn't say anything. He knew that any kind of silence scared the shit out of Salter.

When the silence stretched on too long, Salter said, "You're saying now they *didn't* do it?"

"I'm a very open-minded person."

"Bullshit," Salter said. "What's going on here?"

"What's going on here is it's not as simple as I thought at first. It usually isn't. It means that there's a connection between her and the Knicks before the night with Adair and Collins. Maybe it's important for our purposes, maybe it's not. But the meeting with them becomes a little less random all of a sudden. Maybe Adair and Collins knew who she was. Maybe she was trying to get back at Fine for dumping her."

"The plot thickens."

"I hope it doesn't make the movie boys overheat."

"The paper says she dumped Fine, by the way."

"That's not what Fine says."

"So you really did know about this? How come you didn't tell me?"

"Because I can't do this and hold your hand. When I know where something fits, you'll know."

"Very open-minded of you," Salter said.

"Almost as open-minded as Fukiko."

"You want to come over or not?"

DiMaggio said he did. Salter told him to come to the Thirty-first Street entrance to the Garden, between Seventh and Eighth, and take the elevator to his office. There'd be a guy at the door expecting him. DiMaggio said he'd be there at nine-thirty. He hung up the phone, moved one of the speakers from the CD player next to the bathroom door and turned up the volume on his new Tony Bennett album, the one with all the Astaire songs on it. Then he got into the shower and wondered how Ted Salter figured in a movie about Hannah Carey.

Maybe it was *all* a movie.

Maybe he should approach it that way from now on. With the big guy from the Garden and with everybody else.

It turned out that Salter was full of surprises.

"Want to watch?" he asked DiMaggio. They were in his office at the Garden by then.

"Watch?"

"Her movie meeting. You ever sit in on one? They're a scream. Usually you go in with an idea and have to pitch the moguls. This time it will be the other way around. The moguls pitching our Hannah."

DiMaggio said, "You're getting me excited."

"Act cool all you want. I'm telling you, it'll be a riot. You don't want to watch?"

"You're saying they're going to let us sit in on the meeting?"

"Fuck no. We can watch."

DiMaggio looked at him. A black blazer today with charcoal gray slacks and a black crewneck sweater. A black shirt underneath the sweater, slipper-looking black shoes up on the desk, no socks. Tortoiseshell glasses. He was drinking water out of a plastic bottle, DiMaggio couldn't see the label. DiMaggio said, "Watch?"

"I'm telling you because it might help you. You don't tell anybody else. Only a few security people know. Fukiko guys. They'd do the sword in the tummy before they'd talk." Salter finished his water, casually dropped the bottle into a wastebasket. "Anyway, there are a couple of conference rooms where I can occasionally sneak a peak if I get the urge."

"You watch," DiMaggio said. "And you tape."

"And I keep."

"You and the whole happy corporate family can sit around and watch them like home movies on the holidays."

"I only keep the tape if they say something interesting. Or really fucking mean."

"And if they do?"

"Get out of line? Or if something's going on behind my back?"

"If somebody's trying to screw with you."

"I never bring up something they said on the tape unless there were enough people in the room that any number of them could have given a particular bastard up. I call them in and give them my winning smile and say, 'Oh, one hears things.' "

He was really proud of this shit.

DiMaggio said, "Do you tap the phones, too?"

"What kind of paranoid do you think I am?" Salter dismissed phone tapping with a little wave of the hand. "It's way too expensive, anyway."

"Can I ask you something?"

"Yeah, but make it fast. She's going to be here any minute. And the place where we watch is downstairs."

DiMaggio said, "You brought me in on this, you said, to find out what I could on Adair, Collins, Hannah Carey. If it helps them beat the rap, what I find out, you help them. If it doesn't, and it looks like they did it and this is a problem that does not go away, you find a way to cut your losses."

"Right," Salter said. He reached under his desk and came up with another plastic bottle of water. "What's your point?"

"Why are you even letting your movie people think about going into business with her? If they're in business with her, *you're* in business with her. Say she likes what she hears from them today. We'll be sympathetic, they tell her. You're the hero on this one. And Hannah hears them out and says, 'Okay, I'm in, draw up the contracts, when do we start shooting?' All of a sudden, you've got Adair and Collins on the payroll and you've got her on the payroll." Salter was nodding, uh-huh, uh-huh, like it all made perfect sense to him. His feet were still up on the desk, the suede shoes making soft tapping noises in time with the head bobs.

When he didn't say anything, DiMaggio said, "That doesn't bother you? Even a little?"

Salter sat up now, feet down, elbows propped on the desk. It was some kind of heavy old antique and the surface was clear except for the telephone.

"I never feel bad about good business," he said. The hip-jolly guy was gone. "I never feel bad about covering my ass. Feel bad? All I've done is cornered the market on this rape, whether it happened or not." He stood up. "Now are you coming?"

They used the elevator in his office to go downstairs to the court level. Then they walked past a door that said VISITORS' LOCKER ROOM, took a right, and walked around some security people standing around having coffee. They kept going until there was a door that had STORAGE written in small white letters near the handle. Salter knocked twice and it opened.

As they went in, Salter said, "You're going to love this."

Great, Hannah thought. More guy stuff.

She sat on one side of the room with Jimmy and Harvey Kuhn. On the other side, the Hollywood boys—what else could she call them? they looked like they should have brought nannies with them—sat in two comfy-looking chairs. The boys: The tall skinny one wore a blue blazer and a white T-shirt, baggy denim jeans, and brand-new white canvas tennis sneakers. The short one with curly hair and fat chipmunk cheeks wore a plaid shirt, baggy denim jeans, scuffed saddle shoes, white socks. He looked like he wanted to go right outside to Eighth Avenue and have a game of catch. That was part of guy stuff, too, all of them wanting to be ballplayers.

She felt like she was in a locker room.

The fat one with the baseball was named Kenny, the tall one was Bob. Hannah didn't really get their titles. Both were vice presidents, she was clear on that. One of them had something to do with development. The other one, and she was pretty sure it was Kenny, was vice president of something, something, and finally creative affairs.

Harvey was doing most of the talking so far. Hannah just

sipped hot, orange-tasting tea out of a thick Madison Square Garden mug and waited. She was getting used to being ignored, she decided. Maybe she was born knowing how. She looked over at her brother. He seemed so excited to be in the same room with real movie people that Hannah was afraid he might cry.

Finally, Kenny turned to her and said, "Boring, right?" He dragged the word out. Borrrring. Just the way a kid would.

"I'm fine," Hannah said, smiling. She blew on her tea.

Kenny said, "You're being too polite. The only thing more boring than talking about the industry is talking about mutual friends you have in the industry."

It turned out that a couple of lawyers from Harvey's firm were working in Los Angeles with Fukiko now.

Bob, the calm one, said, "Hannah, maybe the best way to start is for you to ask any questions you might have."

Kenny leaned forward. Hannah saw he was gripping the baseball pretty hard. He had small hands. "Like, do you want to know about other movies Bob and I have green-lighted?"

"Ken," Bob said. Just saying his name not only stopped fat Kenny, Hannah noticed, it snapped him back in his seat. The suddenness of it surprised her. It was like someone jolted his airplane seat into its full upright position. They might both be vice presidents, but quiet, calm Bob, who Hannah thought would be handsome if it weren't for some old acne scars on his neck, was the one in charge.

"I didn't mean that Hannah should ask us to go over our résumé," Bob said evenly. "I just thought she might have some general questions about the whole process."

Now Harvey jumped in. "We all know—"

Bob ignored him and kept going. "Questions about why you should even be in a meeting like this at such a traumatic point in your life. About why we would even be thinking about a movie. Or presume to think we could handle your ordeal with any sensitivity."

"Why me?" Hannah said. "I guess that's as good a place to start as any."

She directed it at Bob, that seemed easiest for her. He actually reminded her a little of A.J. Not the way he looked, necessarily. Just his soothing manner. Not talking down to her or around her. Not being pushy.

He didn't act like it was just all guy stuff. He was *including*— her, maybe that was it. After all the times when she had been Hannah, the invisible girl, quiet as a mouse, afraid to get in anybody's way.

Not wanting to be a problem.

Maybe she was kidding herself, but Bob seemed to want to know what she thought.

What was on *her* mind.

"I'm not even going to suggest that I have any understanding whatsoever of the pain you've been through, not just these last weeks, but over the last year," Bob said.

"What man ever could?" Kenny said. Hannah looked over at him a second. His face almost made her laugh. He was trying to be all grave and serious, but he just looked to her like he was frowning over a real hard math problem.

He was the type who had to be involved in the conversation even when he really wasn't. Bob, who didn't make many fast moves, whipped his head around and stared at him now. The look seemed to say: Play with your ball.

"We think there's an important story to tell here," Bob said. "A story with what I like to call 'bottom.' Not another Year of the Woman Norma Rae Momma Saves the Farm movie." He allowed himself a smile. "Your story, and believe me I make no attempt here to reduce what you've been through to Cliffs Notes, is richer than that. When I first read about you, it occurred to me that you weren't just taking on these two basketball players. You were taking on the *system.*"

Hannah, feeling herself smile back at him, like it was the most natural thing in the world—flattered, really—said, "I did all that?"

Kenny: "We sure think you did."

Hannah was watching Bob. He closed his eyes for just a moment, then said, "Do you like the movies, Hannah?"

She nodded at her brother. "Jim here, he's the big movie expert in the family. He always knows the name of the actor who played the star's best friend."

Bob had one of those fashionable beards, a day's worth, two at most. Maybe he was trying to cover up the scars. He gently rubbed his cheeks. Was he gay? Hannah always found herself wondering, especially with Jimmy's friends. It was silly, just because it was show business, but there it was anyway. There wasn't anything wrong with it. She usually liked Jimmy's gay friends better.

But now she found herself not wanting this Bob to be gay or bi. "I'm not talking about being a movie insider," he said to her now. "We've got enough of those right here." He nodded at Kenny, grinning, but Kenny missed the look. She was starting to like this guy more and more. The two of them, Bob and Hannah, they were the insiders. Everyone else was on the outside. Bob said, "Do you like going to the movies? Do you like *watching* them?"

"Sure. Doesn't everybody?"

"Let me be frank with you then," he said. "What we think we've got here is Anita Hill with a *white* heroine."

"With maybe just a little *Silkwood* in there," Kenny said excitedly, having to get in with that.

Bob sighed. "I came here thinking of this as a two-hour *Movie of the Week.* Now I'm not so sure, as I sit here thinking about it.

With you right here in the room. This could be four hours, over two nights. That's the luxury you have with an MFT."

"MF—?" Hannah said, and Jimmy jumped in, even before Kenny could, to say, "Made for television!" Like he had the answer on a game show.

Hannah said, "I've sort of asked this question before, but now I'll ask it to you." She found herself shaking her head as she said, "How can you even start to write a script or make a movie when none of us . . . when nobody . . . knows how any of this is going to come out?"

Bob stood up, arching his back a little. Not quite as tall as A.J., of course, but the same kind of cute body. Long legs. Pretty flat stomach underneath the T-shirt, as far as she could tell. He had one of those extra-long blazers, so she couldn't get a good look at his butt in his jeans. They looked like 560s, tight at the waist and butt, baggy after that.

"You have to understand," he said, "this script is being written every day in the newspapers. That's why the first O. J. Simpson movie was being shot as he was being *arraigned.*" He came right over to her now, pulled a chair next to her, got right in front of where she was on the couch. Even calm Bob seemed to be getting excited now. It was interesting, Hannah thought, how he had just completely taken over, even shutting Harvey Kuhn up.

"I *see* this story already. It happens for me that way sometimes. Like I'm seeing a map in my head, from the start of the trip to the finish." He drew a line in the air between them, slowly. "They did this to you," he said, "and now you're finally fighting back. Maybe there is a little Norma Rae in there after all. You fight back with a weapon they don't even understand." Nodding. "Your *dignity.* I'm not trying to blow smoke. I've watched you, on television and here this morning. Somebody taped that press conference. I've seen it twenty times by now. I don't know what will happen in court, but they did it." Bob lowered his voice now.

"They . . . did . . . it. They are guilty. There will be no ambiguities in our treatment of this material. Our treatment of you. If we're still shooting when the jury comes in, fine, we'll write the verdict in. But believe me, Hannah, by then we won't need them. Because we'll have made a movie. A great movie. And when the audience sees our movie, the audience will say guilty."

Bob was leaning forward. What color were his eyes? Hannah wanted to call them beige. She could feel Kenny leaning forward, so could Bob, so without looking, he just held out a hand.

"Understand," he said. "We're not telling their story. The hell with Ellis Adair and Richie Collins. We're telling your story."

He put the hand on her arm. "Our only problem is finding a writer who can tell it as eloquently as you did at the Plaza."

Ted Salter said, "What do you think his next move is? Unbuttoning her blouse?"

DiMaggio didn't pay any attention to him, just watched it play out, more interested in Hannah's reaction than in the Hollywood bullshitter. He felt as if he were on the viewing side of some two-way mirror and Hannah and the bullshitter were in a motel room.

Way back at the beginning, Salter had said he thought he was hiring a private eye. Now he felt like one.

DiMaggio, the peeper.

"This kid has sent more TV movies into the toilet than you could count," Salter said. "But you've got to give him high marks on the pitch."

"She likes it," DiMaggio said.

"You sound surprised."

"Listen," DiMaggio said, staring at the screen. In the conference room, Bob said something that got lost because Harvey Kuhn talked over him.

Hannah: "I think so."

Jimmy Carey: "It's called a treatment. Like an outline."

Bob: "We've already got a writer in mind. You might even know of his work. *People* did a big story on him not long ago. He did the story of the breast-cancer doctor last year. Meredith Baxter? Did a huge number during the November sweeps."

Hannah: "When she finally decided to go holistic?"

Ken: "You *did* see it!"

Ken tried to come out of his seat but didn't push forward hard enough and fell back, his feet up in the air.

Jimmy Carey: "The guy who played the young doctor in *Trapper John, M.D.*—"

Ken: "—Gregory Harrison! Great guy. Played the acupuncturist!"

Bob stood up. DiMaggio liked his moves. It was a way of taking the room back from the rest of them.

Bob: "You may hear from Thad—the writer—in a couple of days. One way or the other, we want to make this film happen. Make it *right*. Before you talk to anybody else, we'd at least like you to take a look at our treatment."

Harvey Kuhn: "We'd be under no obligations."

He just needed to get into it.

Bob: "None whatsoever."

Ken: "Of *course* not!"

Ken managed to get out of the chair now and went over and gave Harvey, who was his size, a slap on the back.

DiMaggio went back to watching Hannah. The conversation had moved away from her again, and she didn't like that very much.

Hannah: "I'd—*we'd*—be very interested in seeing the treatment as soon as you have it."

Now she stood up. Bob came over to her. He was smiling. He wasn't the pushy salesman, but he was the relentless one. Bob was the closer. You could see he knew he had her now. He took both of her hands in his.

Next to DiMaggio, Ted Salter said, "Yecch."

Bob: "As I said, let's make this happen."

Giving both hands a tug on "let's."

Hannah: "I don't know—"

Bob: "—and you're not supposed to. That's our job."

In the fifth-floor room, down the hall from the locker rooms at Madison Square Garden, Ted Salter's own private screening room, Salter said, "What are you staring at?"

"Her," DiMaggio said.

"What are you thinking?"

"I'm thinking I might want to try another approach."

19

"You're getting paranoid," Richie said.

They were in the Jeep, coming down the Merritt Parkway from Hartford. They'd played an exhibition game against the Celtics up there, winning by five, six points, something like that, Ellis couldn't even remember. That or how many points he scored. Everybody else always got excited about his stats, how many times he'd done this and that. Not Ellis. All he had ever cared about was two things: Did we win?

And when's the next game?

Richie was driving the Jeep. They were listening to some girl group. Ellis had seen the tape go into the player but couldn't remember now whether it was the Funky Divas singing and the name of the tape was *En Vogue*. Or if it was the other way around and the group was En Vogue.

Shit like this, if he worried on it too much, always gave him a headache.

Richie had been big on girl rock and roll singers since he fucked one—Ellis couldn't remember that group either—in Seattle one time.

"Am not," Ellis said finally, after trying to figure out who was singing. His eyes were closed. He had the seat back as far as it would go. He'd only played the first half against the Celtics. Gary hadn't even wanted to play him that much, but they both knew there'd have been a riot in the Hartford Civic Center if he didn't. They'd cut the number of preseason games down to six, some deal Richie said the union cut. Richie was the only one who seemed pissed about it. He liked traveling before the season started, get his strange lined up for later on, some dump town like Milwaukee.

"Am not what?" Richie said. He'd either forgotten what he'd asked already or was playing with Ellis, looking to start something. It woke Ellis up a little.

That and the fact that Richie was driving real fast all of a sudden, one in the morning on the Merritt with hardly anybody else on the road, just a car passing them every so often. Richie'd told him he'd made a date with this high school girl he'd run into, after some signing he did in Fulton.

"You want to know who it is?" Richie said.

"No," Ellis said. "You know my rule."

Richie said, "You don't want to know what you don't want to know."

Ellis said, "Especially when they're under."

Richie had all sorts of expressions. Over meant they were older than eighteen. Under meant younger. Ellis didn't keep count, but he'd noticed a lot more unders lately. You'd have thought he'd have enough college girls during training camp, the school right there. But Richie liked to prowl the local high schools.

Or have the high school girls prowl him.

He said this one was an under who could pass for an over, no problem.

"Am not paranoid," Ellis said, getting back to what he wanted to talk about, which was the phone. "It's just that every time I'm on the phone I hear this click-click-click shit. I mean, what's up with that?"

"Fresh," Richie said, "you can't even get the CD *in* the machine, now you're some kind of electronic surveillance man?"

Ellis said, "I think it's tapped is all." He reached down and flicked the lever underneath the seat and it popped up into place, like on an airplane. Now he turned the volume down on the music, En Vogue or the Funky Divas or whoever the fuck they were. "And I'll tell you something else: I think someone's been watching the house. Not all the time, but sometimes."

"You're starting to sound like one of those guys, all they want to talk about is the Kennedy assassination," Richie said, then gave him a quick sideways glance and added, "You know, always thinking someone besides Lee Harvey Oswald"—giving him all three names—"was the shooter."

"I know who shot Kennedy," Ellis said. "I'm just telling you, you're never there as much as I am, that two straight days there was the same van across the street."

Richie said, "You mind if I turn this back up?"

"En Vogue . . ." Ellis said it vaguely, so he could go either way with it.

"Are they hot or what?" Richie said.

It was important to Ellis, being right at least once in a while.

Ellis said, "I think somebody might be watching us come in and out, see who we're with, so maybe we should both be a little more careful."

Richie sighed. "Meaning me."

"Goddamn Rich, meaning both of us. Till this shit dies down or whatever."

"Didn't I take the heat off for a couple of days with that dickhead Perez?"

"You mean, giving him A.J. that way? Getting A.J. into it."

Richie said, "Let the Ivy Leaguer talk about all the places *his* dick has been for a while."

"Doesn't get our ass out of traction."

"You got something to say, Fresh, why don't you come right out with it before you drop me." Ellis was supposed to leave him off at Gates in New Canaan. Where the high school girl was waiting for him.

Ellis thought: White girls from the suburbs run around at night like they're from the projects and their mothers are over working a motel near the Lincoln Tunnel.

Ellis said to Richie, "I just don't want one of those *National Enquirer* TV shows getting more into my business than they already *are* in my business. Is all."

Richie turned the radio off with one of his edgy, jittery moves. Ellis saw it on the court all the time, Richie getting a shove he didn't like or fucking up himself but wanting to blame it on somebody else, then he'd be all wired for the next couple of minutes, doing crazy shit, until Gary Lenz finally had to get him out of the game, cool his ass off.

Here we go, Ellis thought.

Ellis tried to go over the whole conversation in his head real fast, trying to remember what part had set him off. It couldn't have been the part about the TV shows, Ellis'd heard Richie say the same thing plenty of times since all this had started.

Richie didn't say anything right away, just gunned the engine a little, like he was passing somebody, except there was nobody else on the road. Ellis tried to see the speedometer and couldn't.

They both knew that Ellis didn't like it when he drove too fast. But then Richie always told him that if you wanted to make a list of all the things that scared Ellis Adair, you'd end up with the Sears catalogue.

Ellis didn't say anything, hoping Richie was just in a hurry to get to his high school girl.

"You know your problem lately, Fresh? I'll tell you what. Your problem is that first you tell *me* how to handle this shit. Then you start talking all over the place and acting like you want to handle it your *own* self."

"That's not—"

"—true? It's not? If the phone was tapped, you don't think I'd know it? You think I wouldn't check it out myself?"

They were going seventy. Ellis felt like he did in a plane sometimes when they'd hit some chop in the night and he couldn't look out the window the way he liked to and see something. See *any* goddamn thing. Just hold on and ride it out in the dark.

Richie said, "The guy in the van is from some tree place. 'Save a Tree' is the name of the outfit. They usually ride around in some station wagon. But it broke down. So one of the Save a Tree guys had to use his own car. Which happens to be a beat-up blue van. Not the *Hard* Fucking *Copy* television show."

Seventy-five now. Richie was back in the right lane. Ellis always worried about getting pulled over, having to go through some song and dance, not knowing if the cop was going to let him off because he was so happy to meet Fresh Adair—"Fresh in the flesh," Richie called situations like that—or fuck with him because he *was* Fresh Adair. Richie never worried about cops, never got pulled over. It was like he had his own radar going, a different kind than he had with women, but just as good.

The Jeep hurtled through these pockets of fog on the Merritt.

Ellis said, "I'm not trying—"

"—to handle things?"

It was never good when he started finishing Ellis's sentences.

" 'Course you are," Richie said. "That's exactly what you're doing, Fresh. You've got all these new things added to the things you're always afraid of. 'Fraid of the dark. 'Fraid of flying—"

Eighty miles an hour now.

"Slow down!" Ellis yelled.

Embarrassed right away at the way it sounded, like some girlie thing. But not able to hold it back.

"Slow the fuck *down!*"

Richie did. Ellis was breathing hard. Thinking: Harder than I ever breathe in a damn game.

"Sometimes I get the feeling that inside your head," Richie said slowly, "you blame me for us being in this . . . situation. And myself, I don't see it that way at all."

Ellis said, "It's me and you, Rich. You know that. Always *has* been me and you. Always will be. I don't want that to ever change. But I just wish you hadn't gone to see her."

Richie was back to the speed limit. Ellis leaned forward in his seat, put his hands on his knees, which were jiggling up and down.

Richie said, "You may be right, Fresh. Maybe I shouldn't've. But it was bothering me, trying to figure out what she told the cops, what she might've told the newspapers, what she might've told this asshole DiMaggio. See, what I'm starting to wonder is just how much of that night the bitch actually *does* remember. Shit, sometimes *I* don't remember it that much. One night out of a million nights." Richie shook his head. "You know I got a great head for details, Fresh. Especially when it comes to strange. But a goddamn year ago? I'm supposed to print out a play-by-play sheet every time I get my dick wet?"

Amazing, Ellis was thinking, this was as close as they'd come to talking about it. Getting it all out in the open. You'd think they'd have talked all about it by now, but this was the way they'd handled things their whole lives. Talked *around* things, never right at them.

"Who knows what she saw, *thinks* she saw, as shit-faced as she was," Richie said. "Point is," he said, "I think if she had any more than has been in the papers, it would've come out by now."

"You think?" Ellis made sure it didn't come out in a pushy way. Just asking a question, letting Richie be the expert.

"Yeah, I do."

Ellis said, "You think she might not? Remember, I mean?"

"Shit, *you* remember how drunk she was when we met her that one time the week before, she was looking for A.J.?"

"Vodka," Ellis said.

"With a slice of orange. I never saw that one before."

"She drank that one down in one shot right before she decided she wanted to start dancing at Mulligan's."

"Which is another thing I'm glad you brought up."

Sometimes Ellis surprised himself and knew where everything was going.

Ellis said, "How come it hasn't come out anywheres that we met her that one time before?"

"I don't know what that's about," Richie said.

Ellis said, happy to let his confusion out, "All that's come out, she hasn't told—"

"—half of it," Richie said, finishing. He turned and smiled at Ellis in the dashboard lights, reminding Ellis of a shark. "The juicy parts."

"I'm sorry, Rich," Ellis said. "I really am sorry."

Where did that come from?

It came from him, that's where it came from. From inside the real him.

"Nothing to be sorry about, Fresh. All part of the game."

Richie leaned forward and hit a button. The tape made that eject sound, came up and out of the player. Then he turned on the radio and Ellis heard the jingle for the sports station, WFAN. All the idiots calling to yell about this and that. Richie liked to listen sometimes to see if they were talking about him. Ellis, even when he'd played in the game, had no idea what they were talking about.

"How about we get some scores before I go off to do my duty?" Richie said.

Ellis said go ahead.

All part of the game. *Don't worry, Fresh. I didn't think nothing of it, Fresh.* Maybe for once Richie meant it. After all this time, Ellis still couldn't tell.

Sometimes Ellis wondered what all *Richie* remembered about that night.

Everything was going too fast. Ellis just did what he did, which was hold on and wait for all of it, every fucked-up part of it, to be over.

20

Salter handed over a tape of the meeting like it was a party favor. DiMaggio watched it again, stretched out on the bed at the Sherry, a big bowl of Epsom salts right next to him. He had come back from the Garden feeling as if somebody had stepped on his right hand. He felt the way he always had after nine innings at the beginning of the season, or the very end, when the weather was too cold for baseball, and he felt like nothing would ever take the stiffness out of that hand, the one without the mitt. The best he could ever do was warm it up and loosen it up enough to go back out the next day.

"Maybe I want to try another approach," he had said to Salter.

But *what* approach?

For all Salter's big talk about getting rid of Adair and Collins if they were guilty, that's not why he had hired DiMaggio. He had hired DiMaggio to find *her* guilty. He wanted DiMaggio to prove that she was the one lying. DiMaggio said he wanted to find out the truth once and for all, and Salter had sat there nodding his head. But the truth Salter wanted was this: Hannah Carey was full of shit.

DiMaggio was a big boy. He knew he had been hired to make

a case against Hannah Carey at the same time Brian Hyland was trying to make his case against Adair and Collins.

There was something about the meeting he hadn't been able to put a finger on until he watched the tape again. Now he knew. It wasn't the way Hollywood Bob had worked her over, like some grifter on the hustle. Watching them from Salter's security room, watching them live, not really analyzing everything, DiMaggio thought it was Hollywood Bob who had run the meeting. Organized the room.

It was her.

She was the one, in her own fragile and understated way, who kept the whole thing coming back to her:

You people are interested in *me?*

DiMaggio thought: Yes. I am. Very interested.

At the first meeting he had told Salter he was sure; now he wasn't so sure. When the thing with the boxer, Tyson, happened, he was sure Tyson had raped the girl. As time passed, again, DiMaggio wasn't so sure. He watched the tape of the girl dancing at the beauty pageant the day after it was supposed to have happened. Smiling. Really selling the bathing suit number. Hi, I'm going to be Miss Black USA, or whatever it was. DiMaggio had the tape of the Barbara Walters special she did—how come they all cried, was it stipulated in some contract?—and waited for something in her story that spoke to him of the violence she was describing. He was smart enough to know he was a man trying to read a woman's mind; he'd read enough in rape books since he'd been in New York to know about denial and all the emotional defense mechanisms; understood that Desiree Washington, Tyson's alleged victim, had already told the story fifty times before she told it to Barbara Walters.

But how could she be so cool, telling the country?

He had talked to Sex Crimes people, one from the Queens D.A., one from Brooklyn. They had both told him the same thing: What a rape victim said the day after it happened or a year after it happened didn't matter. Not one bit.

Every woman dealt with it differently.

The woman from the Brooklyn D.A.'s office, Gail Moore, had looked at him icily across her desk and said, "They didn't look ashamed enough for you?"

"Ashamed has nothing to do with it."

Moore said, "I'm not hitting you with it. I'm just telling you how it is. You're a guy. You're conditioned, up until the last few years anyway, when it's been beat into you finally, to expect women to fall apart at the mention of the thing. Everybody has their own way of dealing with trauma of this kind. By the time a lot of them do come forward, they're cried out."

DiMaggio said, "You think these guys did it?"

"Yes."

"Tyson?"

"Yes."

"The Kennedy kid?"

"Yes."

DiMaggio said, "It's not logical to assume that every time a woman steps forward, she's the one telling the truth. That the guy did it every time. It can't be that way one hundred percent of the time, any more than somebody charged with murder is guilty one hundred percent of the time."

"I didn't say that. You asked me about some of the famous ones. The ones you brought up, I think the guy did it. I think *these* guys did it."

"When that woman stepped forward with the Mets players a few years ago, there was no indictment, no grand jury. No case."

Gail Moore, somewhere in her thirties he guessed, a lovely, light-skinned black woman, said, "You didn't ask me if I thought there should have been an indictment. Or about the merits of the investigation. Or the case. You're asking me if I thought what happened to the women you're talking about fit a classical definition of rape and I'm telling you it did." She said, "You look into this yourself, Mr. DiMaggio. You draw your own conclusions. You, most men really, have no idea what is going on out there. None. I'm not mad. I'm not lecturing you. I'm just telling you. I've been at this for five years, and I frankly don't know how much longer I want to do this job. But here's what I know: When a woman takes it this far, my experience is that she's telling the truth."

"I've got to ask this: You never think, not for a minute, it could be some kind of setup?"

She looked at her watch then. Got up. Done with him.

"I watched Hannah Carey on television. At that press conference. I tried not to look at her as a lawyer, or prosecutor, any of that. Just woman to woman."

"And?"

"And," she said, "I frankly don't think she is smart enough to have made all this up."

He rewound the tape of the press conference again, looked at it one more time, wondering what Gail Moore saw in there that he didn't. Then he watched some of the movie meeting and finally he shut off the television and closed the drapes in the middle of the afternoon and put Ellis Larkins on. He wanted it to feel like night, because Ellis was always a night guy. Now he was again, Ella singing Gershwin the way you were supposed to and Ellis staying right with her because, of all of them, Ellis was the one.

DiMaggio loved Oscar Peterson; George Shearing still was one of the great players. But Ellis Larkins—what was he now? seventy-five?—was his hero. An aristocrat of a performer. The first time DiMaggio had seen him, as a kid, he was playing at the Carnegie Tavern, Fifty-sixth and Seventh. That was his room, the way the Carlyle was Bobby Short's room, and the Algonquin used to belong to Michael Feinstein. And DiMaggio knew right away, before he knew anything, that this was the way his kind of music was supposed to sound, this was the way you commanded a piano, a piece of music, a room. The music came, but you never saw the hands move. There was a book review DiMaggio had read once, he couldn't remember the book, but the guy reviewing it had said there were two kinds of geniuses, the ordinary and the magicians. An ordinary genius, he was a guy you and I would be as good as, if we were just a lot better. Then there were the magicians. DiMaggio remembered the next line exactly: "Even after we understand what they've done, the process by which they have done it is completely dark." That was Ellis Larkins, the bright music coming out of that dark, magical place.

DiMaggio thought: If I could have hit a baseball the way Ellis Larkins played, they would have had to build me my own wing in Cooperstown. Ellis Larkins played piano, he thought, the way Ellis Adair played basketball . . .

The phone rang.

"It's Lisa. Remember me?"

He remembered, actually. He had been leaving cards with his name and number at the Sherry-Netherland at Hannah Carey's gym, her bars, the place where she got her hair cut; he could go into one place on the West Side and they would tell him another place she liked to go. In the last week, he had talked to trainers, waiters, managers, a couple of old boyfriends, women she'd waitressed with, her former modeling agent, finding out random things, none of them big. Sometimes they didn't want to talk at work, so he would hand them a few cards and tell them to get back to him. Sometimes they would. The shit work of any investigation.

Some of his folders were around him on the bed. He opened one he had labeled FRIENDS.

"Lisa Wells," he said. "Twenty-two years old."

"But—"

"—you can do older."

She had asked him out on a date when he'd met her a couple of nights before at a restaurant on the West Side run by Lee Mazzilli, the former ballplayer. DiMaggio said he was a little old for her, and she said, no way, not only could she do older, she had dated a guy in his fifties once. With excitement in her voice.

Making it sound like a field trip.

"I told you I'd give you a call if I came up with anything," she said.

"And you have."

"You bet! I've been following the case a lot closer since I talked to you."

He didn't say anything. He was seeing the girl better now. She didn't need much help to get revved up.

"Boy, was I surprised to find out that Hannah got into a three with her old boyfriend."

"A. J. Fine."

"I mean, I'd seen her in here a couple of times with her friend—"

"—Fine?—"

"No, the girlfriend, plenty of times. And they never looked like the type that would ever, you know, get sweaty together. I mean, what's up with *that?*"

DiMaggio said, "You know this friend of hers? A. J. Fine said he couldn't even remember her name."

Lisa said, "She works in Dakota."

"She moved, you mean?"

She laughed. "No, silly. The new place, Dakota, up on Third."

The only Dakota DiMaggio knew about in New York was the apartment building where John Lennon got shot.

"I don't know it."

"It just opened. That's how I happened to run into Lisa. Lisa the other girl whose name A. J. Fine couldn't remember. We were applying there the same day. I said, 'Hey, I know you.'"

She was starting to make DiMaggio feel dizzy. Trying to stay with her, he said, "Her name is Lisa, too?"

"I mean, is that *wild?*"

DiMaggio said, "You read my mind. Do you know her last name?"

"Lisa Melrose. Like the show."

"The show?"

"Melrose Place. On Fox. Very hot. What's up with that, you don't even know that show?"

He tried again. "So she's working at Dakota?"

"Got the last waitressing job. Bummed me out big-time."

"Thanks," he said. "I'll check her out."

Lisa said DiMaggio should call her sometime. "When I'm a little less jammed up," he told her, then he hung up and called Dakota. It was between Eighty-eighth and Eighty-ninth, on Third. Lisa Melrose worked the eleven-to-five shift. It was two o'clock. DiMaggio asked the guy on the phone, probably the bartender, when lunch quieted down. The guy said after three, all there was left to do was set up for dinner.

"Lisa Melrose," he said in the Sherry. Smiled. "What's up with *that?*"

Jesus, he was getting old.

DiMaggio couldn't decide whether Dakota looked more like a Los Angeles place or a New York place. It was getting harder and harder to tell the difference. He went to Los Angeles and there was a new place called Tribeca, in New York there was a new place called Mulholland Drive. And here was Dakota on Third, which seemed to be all of them. There was one long room with a high ceiling, which probably made Dakota sound louder than a ballpark when it was crowded. There were a half-dozen tables near the front window and then the majority of tables in the back. In between was a bar that seemed long enough to serve as the runway for Miss America.

There was an old guy, looking very natty in a tweed blazer a little warm for the weather and a red ascot, sitting at the end of the bar, sipping a martini and watching a soccer game on the television set above him. The bartender, a big, good-looking kid, who said his name was Ryan. He told DiMaggio that Lisa Melrose was the tall black-haired one serving tea to two women in the back, the only customers back there that DiMaggio could see.

Ryan said, "They're paying up, then she's off. It just depends now how they break the tip down into pennies and nickels."

DiMaggio nodded knowingly. "You know who could fix the deficit? Women who eat out."

"Lisa know you're coming?"

"Not exactly."

"What did you say you did again?"

"I'm doing some work for the Knicks right now."

"Is she gonna want to talk to you? I had to run a guy out of here yesterday. Had his camera crew waiting outside."

DiMaggio said, "I plan to show her my nurturing side."

"Hey," Ryan said, grinning, "not in front of the tea ladies."

Lisa Melrose came over. She was almost as tall as Hannah Carey; they were probably a sight when they were together. The tray with the bill had some cash on it and a lot of change.

"Jeez," she said. "When they got close there at the end with the frigging tip, they both started to sweat, I swear to God."

Ryan took the tray. "Somebody here to see you." He nodded at DiMaggio. "From the Knicks."

DiMaggio stood up and Lisa Melrose said, "Lisa told me you'd probably show up."

"Blew my cover."

"Knowing her, that's probably not all—"

Ryan said, "Now, now."

DiMaggio said, "You got a few minutes?"

"Why not?" Smiling. "Just let me wash up."

DiMaggio took a cup of coffee with him to a table in the corner near where the tea ladies had been. When Lisa Melrose came back, she had washed her face and put a brush through her spiky hair. DiMaggio smelled some kind of perfume. Her makeup was gone. Now she looked older than the other Lisa, but not too much. The spiky hair made her look severe. She had thick black eyebrows, and even with the high cheekbones there was some tomboy part of her that she'd kept. It didn't bother DiMaggio. She was pretty and didn't seem to put too much work into it.

"Lisa, the other one, said you were some kind of investigator. But unofficial?"

"I'm about as unofficial as you can get."

"So stuff I tell you, it doesn't end up with the police or in the newspapers?"

DiMaggio smiled at her. "Can I speak frankly?"

"Sure."

"I wouldn't piss on reporters if they were on fire."

Lisa Melrose gave him a husky kind of laugh and said, "She said you were kind of cute."

"She's young, she doesn't know any better."

"You mind if I have a drink?" Lisa Melrose wanted to know. "Sometimes one or two tables wears you out like a full house." She went to the bar herself and brought back what looked like a rum drink with a lime in it. She drank some and said, "You're here about me and Hannah and A.J., right?"

"Hannah mostly. I talked to A.J."

She was taking another sip of her drink and stopped with the glass near her mouth. Looking at him with big eyes, almost as black as her hair. "Did he say anything about me?"

"He didn't go into much detail about the whole thing. To tell you the truth, for a jock, he actually seemed a little—"

"—embarrassed?" she said. Nodding. "That's A.J,'s game. He wants people to think that between basketball and reading all his big books, he barely has time to get laid."

DiMaggio said, "He's a sensitive guy, and he doesn't care who knows it."

"Well, he's not exactly too sensitive when he gets his clothes off," she said. Now she drank.

"Like I said, I'm really here to talk about Hannah."

Lisa Melrose, loosening up now, said, "Fine. What do you want to know about that bitch?"

DiMaggio told her Fine had referred to her as "Lisa Dee."

"For Diane, my middle name. I don't give these guys my real name until I get a sense of how things are going to shake out."

Lisa Diane Melrose's story: She had met Hannah at the Vertical Club. Hannah was waiting for the machine Lisa was using. She didn't really know how to set the weights so Lisa showed her, they ended up working out together that day. Then they had a sauna afterward. They got to chatting about all the bullshit New York girl things: jobs, the city, meeting men, safe sex, clubs.

Lisa: "She said that meeting men in New York had never been her strong suit. I kind of burst out laughing. We were still in the sauna. Hannah said, like, what's so funny? I told her that if meeting men in New York was an Olympic event, I already had a bunch of medals."

Lisa Melrose proceeded to tell her about all the athletes she had dated. A couple of Mets. Two hockey players, one from the Islanders, one from the Rangers. A couple of Giants, one of the Celtics when the Celtics were in town. Hannah's eyes, according to Lisa, got bigger and bigger. Why athletes? she wanted to know.

Lisa: "I told her, God, why *not* athletes, girl? They're young, they're cute, most times, anyway, they've got great bods, they love to party. And most of them have got a *lot* of money. I'm not looking to settle down yet, neither are they. So what are we talking about? Great sex, fun places. Laughs. Then they go off to Cleveland or San Antonio or someplace. If it's a baseball player, and you get to know him well enough, you can go to Florida or Arizona for spring training. Have a nice vacation and help a guy out."

DiMaggio: "Help him out?"

Lisa: "Give him an alternative to screwing gum-chewing townies with big hair."

Hannah said she'd love to meet athletes. Lisa told her they'd go to a Knicks game the next week, she had tickets. Told Hannah to wear something understated.

Lisa: "I told her I'd be the hot one. It's a variation of good cop, bad cop."

DiMaggio: "A lot has changed."

Lisa: "What does that mean?"

DiMaggio: "I used to play some ball."

Lisa: "I knew there was something about you I liked."

Lisa told Hannah it would be easy, and it was. The first rule of fucking athletes, she told her, was this: Don't play hard to get. If you were good-looking enough, had a nice-enough bod yourself—and Hannah did—it was just a question of having the right moves.

Lisa: "Remember what I said about the Olympics? They should have *named* some of these moves after me."

Before they knew it, they were all back at A. J. Fine's apartment. Lisa said she had always flirted with the idea of a three— DiMaggio thought she made it sound like a three-point goal in basketball—and had come close a couple of times, but had never actually, you know, done it.

This time, she never had a chance to say no.

DiMaggio: "He forced you?"

Lisa shook her head. "She did."

Quiet Hannah, who spent the whole night acting like a schoolteacher in her prim dress, she took over. Lisa couldn't believe it. DiMaggio told her that A. J. Fine, *he* said it was *his* first time with two women. Lisa said that was obvious to everyone concerned, he didn't know where to start, what to do, when to watch. But Hannah made it easy on everybody. Afterward, when Lisa thought about the whole night, she realized that it was Hannah who had selected A. J. Fine, Hannah who had done most of the talking at Play-by-Play, the bar at the Garden.

It was Hannah, the *trainee,* who got everything rolling.

Hannah who had the most fun.

Lisa: "I finally left about six in the morning. Hannah woke up for a minute and smiled and said she was staying. I had the feeling she meant for the rest of the season or something. She said she'd call me later."

Lisa: "I'm still waiting for that phone call. Let me tell you something about Hannah Carey, okay? She used me as well as any guy ever did."

21

Marty Perez was sitting in the shithouse of a dressing room they'd given him at Channel Two, next to the weekend meteorologist—another spic who couldn't decide how white he actually wanted to be—when it moved on the wire, Fulton, Connecticut, dateline, about the DNA test.

It was Randy Houghton who walked in and handed him the printout. Houghton was dressed in some baggy suit that was almost pink. Jesus, it looked like a *goma*. A rubber. What'd he do, go into the store and say, "I'd like something condom-colored in a double-breasted?" Maybe that was what all the other cutting-edge boys were wearing this week. Condom-colored suits and white T-shirts. Houghton handed him the printout like he was handing him a bad report card.

"I thought you'd want to see this right away." He nodded at the printout.

Hyland, the Fulton cop, had simply released a statement saying that the semen samples from the dress Hannah Carey had given to them had turned out to be inconclusive. "Contaminated" was the word Hyland used. She apparently thought she was being careful by keeping the dress zipped up in a garment bag, but the opposite had happened, and the dress turned out to be

worthless. Marty knew enough about the test to get by. He knew
that the DNA molecule was in most cells, including blood and
semen. They tested DNA strips or strands or whatever out of
blood and semen and could provide a fairly conclusive match.
Some states allowed the test as evidence in cases like this. Connecticut was one of them. There was a tiny possibility of error,
but Marty couldn't remember what the percentage was.

Now it didn't matter anyway.

"No Ellis, no Richie, huh?" Marty said to Houghton. He had
been putting the finishing touches on his commentary for that
night's *Chronicle*. Some nights he did it live, and this was one
of them. He was calling for the resignation of the new district
attorney in Queens. Another cutting-edge boy, youngest in the
history of the borough. There'd been another bias case. Four
mopes from Bayside beating some Japanese honor student home
from Stanford within an inch of his fucking life. Even Marty got
mad. Sometimes it still happened for him. *¡Ay coño!* And he
couldn't tell whether that was good or bad for him anymore, getting a hard-on over something like this, still trying to play cru-
sading reporter.

Did Houghton and all the rest of them think they'd heard it all
before?

Randy Houghton said, "You've still got an hour. You want to
do something on this? I know it's not much, but my feeling is,
people eat up any kind of news on this like they're eating
peanuts."

Marty had thought about it the minute he read the bulletin lead
from AP. Only the thought of cranking something out on deadline exhausted him. Marty thought: In the old days, sure. Shit,
in the old days if he couldn't find a place to write he'd call somebody on the desk and dictate if it meant making the edition.

Now . . . what? What was the word they would have used for
him back home? *Pasao.* Said of something old. Worn out.

"Let me make one call," he said to Randy Houghton.

"If you can do it we want it," he said. "We'll go with this at the top of the show and push the Flashdance—"

"Flashdance?"

"—topless dancers to segment three. But we gotta know. Barry will open with the straight news, then throw it to you." He vaguely held up the format he was holding in his hand. "If you don't think you have time . . ."

"Ten minutes," Marty said. Houghton left. Marty got out his wallet and found the number in Fulton Richie Collins had given to him. Were the Knicks still up there? Jesus, he couldn't keep track of anything anymore. He knew they were breaking camp soon, the regular season started either next week or the week after. Marty just couldn't remember.

"Estoy pasao," he said out loud. He could feel himself start to sweat through his blue oxford television shirt. It always happened in here, the closer and closer he got to airtime.

Collins picked up on the first ring. "Fresh?" he said.

"Perez."

"Well, now. My day is fucking complete."

"And I thought we were buddies now. You're not glad to hear from me?"

"Today," Richie Collins said, "is not the day to dick around with me."

"Why? I just got the release on the dress. I thought you'd be throwing yourself a party."

Richie said, "I got the call from the cops about a half hour ago myself. Acting like they were doing me a favor. They ever showed up in Jersey City, the cops over there would look at them like they were wearing tights."

Marty said, "You ought to be looking at the big picture here, if you ask me."

"Who asked you?" Richie said.

"Listen, it could've been your love juice there on the dress."

"Still wouldn't have proved anything."

"It's like fingerprints."

Richie Collins said, "Just stickier."

"Now they can't even prove the two of you had sex with her."

Collins wouldn't bite. "You trying to get me to say something here, Perez? I told you I'm not in the mood."

Marty said, "What's your friend Ellis have to say about all this? I go on the air in a little while, I could use a quote."

"Ellis says nothing."

"You haven't talked about this? You expect me to believe *that?* He doesn't take a leak without clearing it with you first, that's what you told me."

There was a pause, and Marty flashed on the dial tone coming next, thinking Collins had hung up on him. Marty looked at his watch. Six-twenty. If he was going to do something with this he was going to have to do it off the top of his head. Which meant without TelePrompTer.

Marty said, "Hey?" And Richie said, "I'm gonna tell you something."

"If you are, do it now. I'm under a little pressure here."

"Jesus," Richie said. "I love it when you bastards talk about pressure. Or rip us a new asshole for not handling pressure the way you think we should. And you know what? You have no *idea.* You ever had to stand out there in front of everybody and make one free throw? Those big balls of yours you like to talk about? They'd shrivel up the size of cherry pits."

Marty said, "Listen, I didn't mean it that way—"

Richie Collins cut him off. "Fresh is gone, Perez."

"When you say gone—"

"When I say it, I mean it's going to be announced by the team at practice tomorrow. The Knicks're going to say he's left the team for personal reasons. But the truth is, they have no goddamn idea where he is."

"And you don't?"

"I don't," Richie Collins said and then added, "have shit."

There was a makeup mirror in front of Marty, a makeup mirror with white lightbulbs up and down the sides and running across the top, the glare of it so harsh he didn't like looking at himself in it, made him look so old. Marty looked now and saw Randy Houghton behind him in the doorway, trying to get his attention. Pointing to his watch.

Marty smiled. He held up one finger with his free hand and said into the phone, "So what you're basically telling me is that Ellis Adair has disappeared?"

It wasn't for Collins's benefit, it was for Houghton's. The cutting-edge boy who thought he ran Marty's life.

Richie Collins said, "Are you hard of hearing, Perez? Yeah, Sherlock, I'm telling you Ellis is out of here."

Marty said, "Tell me."

"I wrecked my ankle about a half hour before practice ended and was over having it X-rayed. At Fulton College, you have to go next door. When I got back, Ellis was gone. I talked to Boyzie Mays. One of our guards? He said Ellis was all upset about something in the parking lot. Said he heard him talking about the test in the parking lot before he got into his car and got out of there. We usually come together, but today we took separate cars, I was supposed to go to a signing, over in Fairfield."

"When you say test," Perez said, "you mean the DNA test?"

"Got to be."

"But why would that make him go nutso? It was *good* news."

"You're the guy with all the answers," Richie Collins said. "Why don't you tell me something for a change?"

Marty said, "Nobody but me knows he's gone?"

"So far."

"I gotta get this on the air," Marty said. Then, as an afterthought: "Thanks."

"Don't mention it," Collins said.

Marty hung up the phone, took his cigar out of the ashtray in front of him, took his time relighting it, knowing Houghton was still there in the doorway.

The cutting-edge boy couldn't wait anymore. "Did I hear you correctly?" he said. "Ellis Adair is gone?"

Marty said, "He's gone, kid. But *I'm* here."

22

Ted Salter, Frank Crittendon, Richie Collins and DiMaggio sat in the Knicks locker room on the fifth floor of the Garden, court level, the other end of the hall from Salter's private screening room. Salter and Collins looked like they wanted to be anywhere except here, with each other. DiMaggio figured it was just another day at the office for Frank Crittendon, his office being wherever Salter told him it was.

The Knicks had announced in the morning they were breaking camp at Fulton College a day early. Before they did, they issued a release that said Ellis Adair had left the team for personal reasons, even though DiMaggio wondered what the point of that was since Marty Perez had broadcast the whole thing over television the night before. The release said that Adair's absence from the team was unrelated to what were described as "recent off-court developments." Crittendon was quoted as saying he fully expected Adair to be with the team for the start of the regular season in two weeks, the first Saturday in November.

It was all bullshit, DiMaggio knew that. When he got to the Garden he found out that even Richie Collins had no idea where Ellis Adair was.

Collins had been the last to show up, wearing a hooded Knicks sweatshirt and jeans. Only his white sneakers looked new. He hadn't shaved yet, and his eyes were bloodshot. DiMaggio knew the look, from all the clubhouses and locker rooms like this one. A catcher who'd played behind him one time in the low minors, Franklin Roosevelt Jarrett, DiMaggio never forgot him, out of the Robert Taylor projects in Chicago, over near Comiskey Park, used to talk about "misbehavin' situations." Richie Collins had come from a misbehavin' situation, DiMaggio was sure of it.

Maybe he went out and got laid to take the edge off of Ellis making a run for it.

Collins also looked scared. Why not? Ellis was gone. Maybe Donnie Fuchs, agent and lawyer, was on his way, but he sure wasn't there yet. Ted Salter, the one who signed the checks, was into it now. Richie Collins, for the first time, didn't look so project tough.

"Does he have to be here?" Collins said when he saw DiMaggio.

"Sit down, Richie," Salter said. "Next time we throw a party, we'll let you draw up the guest list." He sipped some coffee out of a plastic cup. "Maybe you'll even find a way to show up on time."

Richie Collins, a little whiny, said, "Mr. Salter—"

"Jesus, sit down, will you?"

Collins sat down in front of his own locker. Maybe it was force of habit. He looked like he wanted to get all the way inside, just hide in there until all this was over. Salter was across from him, in front of Adair's locker. Maybe it was for effect. Crittendon was next to him, in a folding chair.

DiMaggio said, "Where's Ellis?"

Collins turned his head toward DiMaggio, as if he wanted to move right in and say something smart. But he stopped himself, making a little calming motion with his hands, like he was telling himself he was in enough trouble already.

"I told Frank first thing. I told Mr. Salter last night, when he called and told me to be here." Collins shook his head and said, "I have no idea where he is."

"Has he ever done anything like this before?" DiMaggio said. "In all the years you've known him?"

Collins said, "You mean disappear during a rape investigation? Shit, yeah. He can't stop himself."

It almost made DiMaggio smile. Collins not being able to stop *him*self.

"Richie," Ted Salter said. "Listen to me because I'm going to tell you this one time, and then we'll all move on here. This situation we have here, this is not a situation where you want to come in with an attitude. I am tired of you. I am tired of your problems. I am tired of *your* problems being *my* problems. When Mr. DiMaggio asks you a question, it is the same as me asking you a question or Frank asking you a question. I cannot force you to talk about what did or did not happen with this woman. Your legal rights are your legal rights. I'm not going to piss all over them, as much as I would like to, believe me. Because I know the minute I do, you tell your lawyer and he calls the Players Association and then I'm up to my eyeballs in grievances." He closed his eyes. "I get a migraine just thinking about it. But Ellis disappearing, that is *not* a legal problem. It is a goddamn fucking *team* problem. Which you are going to help solve in any way you can. Are we clear on that?"

Collins looked down and mumbled something that no one could hear, so Salter repeated, "Are we clear?"

"We're clear," Collins said.

All along, DiMaggio had wondered if anybody had any real juice with these bastards. Crittendon didn't. The curly-haired dude coach, Gary Lenz, clearly didn't. The players seemed to go through all of it, life and ball, like they were bulletproof. But not this afternoon. Not in here. DiMaggio had the feeling that if

Salter told Richie Collins to bark like a dog, Collins would bark like a dog.

Salter said, "I believe Mr. DiMaggio asked if Ellis had ever done anything like this before."

"Ellis isn't the type for something like this. Ellis was never carefree. You understand? Never impulsive. He didn't do anything—how would you put it?—spontaneous. Whether he was feeling fucked-up or not. Even when we were kids. The only place Ellis ever takes any chances is up in the air, when he's got a ball in his hands."

Richie Collins said, "It's why he was made for basketball, and not just 'cause he has such a talent for it. Ellis likes the regularless of it, or whatnot. Practice at this time, playing that time. Bus will be at five-fifteen. Bus leaves forty-five minutes after the game. He's very deep into that shit."

DiMaggio just watched him go, impressed. Whatever else he was, he wasn't stupid.

"Let me tell you something about Fresh Adair," Collins said. "Him alone and the two of us together. If it wasn't me, it would have been somebody else. He likes to be told. He *wants* to be told."

"You're saying you're worried," DiMaggio said.

Collins looked straight at him. "Fuck yes."

Salter said to Collins, "Why'd he go? Frank talked to Boyzie this morning. Why'd the DNA test set him off?"

"He's been acting even more squirrelly than usual the last few days," Collins said. "If it hadn't been for my ankle, I would've been *with* him." He looked around at all of them, as if trying to make them understand how important that was, had always been, Collins being with Ellis Adair. "But I wasn't with him, and he snapped out on us."

DiMaggio watched him, fascinated, not recognizing this

Richie Collins, wondering whether these were real feelings or whether this was another pose to get him over with Salter.

Collins put it to Salter now: "We've got to find him. Maybe nobody outside of me understands this, or could ever, but Ellis Adair hasn't got any talent for fending for himself."

"Where does he have places besides the city?" DiMaggio said. "Weekend homes or whatnot?" Jesus, he was starting to sound like them.

"We got condos, right next door to one another, at the Polo Club in Boca. But he isn't there, I checked already, with the guy takes care of them for us. Ellis couldn't show up there without the guy, Eddie, knowing."

DiMaggio said, "I thought I read that he's got some place out in California, too."

"No, he just stays at La Costa. Out in the desert? I checked there, too. They haven't seen him."

"Ellis likes warm places," DiMaggio said.

"Ellis likes anyplace he can golf," Collins said. "You believe that shit? Ellis Adair, out of the projects?" Collins smiled. "All he wants to do when he goes out there is put on a pair of green slacks and go play goddamn golf. Play golf or go ride that blue bike of his."

DiMaggio said, "A *bike?*" He tried to see the Ellis Adair he'd watched in practice, the one who could fly, riding around on some bicycle.

Collins nodded. "Remember that movie with the kids on the bicycles? *Breaking Away?* Came out a long time ago. Me and Ellis saw it once when we were kids. And one of the kids in it, I forget which one, had this blue bike. Or Ellis decided it was blue, afterward, I can't even remember anymore. He said to me when he came out, 'One of these days, I'm gonna get me a blue bike, and I'm gonna ride until I come to some place like in that movie, with trees and green grass and everybody smiling at

everybody else.' I told him, 'You want to end up in *Indiana?*'
But he didn't care where it was, as long as it wasn't the projects.
Finally, when we were in high school, some guy came over from
the city, wanted Ellis 'n' me to play on his summer team. And
he says to Ellis, 'What's it gonna take?' Meaning money. But
Ellis says, 'A blue bike.' I pulled him aside and said, 'Fresh, we
got a chance to *score* here.' But he didn't want to hear anything
like that. He wanted his blue bike. Which he got." Collins smiled
in this sad way. "Which got fucking stolen about a week later.
Ellis wouldn't talk about it. I said, 'You can get another bike.'
He said, 'Won't be *that* bike.' Then a few months ago, all this
time later, he shows up with one just like it. I went looking for
it last night. I don't know where Ellis went, like I told you, but
wherever he did, he took that goddamn bike with him."

DiMaggio said, "Let me ask you something: Does he have any
relatives left in Jersey City?"

"His Aunt Mary was the last one, but she died a couple of years
ago."

"He ever go back?"

Collins shook his head no. "The last time I can remember us
being over there was Ellis's rookie year. Aunt Mary's birthday.
She was the one who ended up raising him after his mother died.
Ellis'd end up moving her down to Hilton Head, a nice house he
built for her with some of his signing money. But the house
wasn't ready yet, so Ellis rented her this house over on Garfield
Avenue. That's where the party was."

Richie Collins smiled again. "Funny what you remember?
Aunt Mary said she wanted us to stay the night, which we did.
We went to bed. About three o'clock in the morning, you know
what wakes me up? Bounce of a ball. I look out the window.
There's a court down the hill from the back of Aunt Mary's
rented house. And there's Ellis, in his gym shorts and the sneakers he wore over, shooting around, looking happy as happy could

be. I go down there and say, 'What the hell you doing out here in the middle of the night?' Three o'clock in the morning it was. You know what he says? He smiles at me and goes, 'Rich, maybe things wasn't so bad here.' "

DiMaggio said, "I think I want to take a ride over there."

Collins said, "Take the Holland Tunnel."

Maybe it was a reflex, DiMaggio thought, Richie Collins snapping back into being a punk this quickly.

"I want to take a ride over there with *you.*"

"Right."

Salter leaned forward, but DiMaggio held up a hand. "Let *me* explain something to you, Richie," he said. "You're going to help me out on this sooner or later. Because sooner or later you're going to figure out there's no percentage for you in *not* helping me. You're going to figure out, all by yourself, like a big boy, just how shitty this is all starting to look, especially for Ellis. You don't know where he is? Well, okay, then nobody does. But if he's not in Florida and he's not in California, maybe the best place to start is at the beginning."

Collins said, "It's going to be a waste of time is all I'm trying to tell you. Just 'cause Ellis shot some baskets over at Garfield one night doesn't mean he'd go over there to disappear himself."

"Humor me," DiMaggio said. "Wasting time is pretty much all I've been doing since I got to town." He turned to Frank Crittendon. "You said Gary Lenz decided to move practice into the Garden?"

"We didn't tell the press, but they'll go at six."

DiMaggio looked at his watch. "That gives Richie and me about four hours."

"Do what you have to do," Salter said. "Even if he has to miss practice, I'll square it with Gary."

"Now wait a fucking—" Collins tried to stop himself, but it was out there already.

"No," Salter said in his calm voice. *"You* wait, Richie. You don't know where Ellis is, fine, you don't know. But if Mr. DiMaggio thinks there's even a chance that taking a ride over to Jersey might help find him, then you take the ride." Salter smiled and said, "Would that be all right with you?"

"Yes, sir."

Salter said to DiMaggio, "My car's right outside. Where you came in. Call me if you need anything else." He went for the door, saying "Frank?" over his shoulder. The two of them walked out of the locker room.

It was just DiMaggio and Collins now.

DiMaggio said, "You have to wake up here, Richie. You have to understand that you've got no power base left without Ellis. No juice."

He felt like Salter all of a sudden, tired of Richie Collins, tired of his problems. "So let's go get in the car and take a ride. But I have to be honest with you. If you mouth off to me one more time today, I'm going to break your fucking nose."

Collins got up, walked past him as if all DiMaggio had said was "Let's go."

"Follow me," Collins said. "I'll show you the quickest way out of here. We can cut across the court."

DiMaggio followed him, thinking about Ellis Adair.

Trying to see him somewhere on that blue bike.

Salter's driver, Rudy, said to DiMaggio, "We doing any chase scenes this time?" DiMaggio said, "Not unless we end up in the wrong neighborhood in Jersey City."

Richie Collins, next to DiMaggio in the backseat, said, "Isn't anything *but* wrong neighborhoods in Jersey City."

They went through the Holland Tunnel. Richie Collins didn't say anything. DiMaggio let him go. Rudy found a jazz station on the radio after they got through the tunnel; DiMaggio recognized Coltrane, then Paul Desmond, finally David Benoit doing his light, breezy version of "Cast Your Fate to the Wind." When they got to the Jersey City exit off the Jersey Turnpike, Collins, looking out the window, said, "Get off here," and then took over.

"Anything in particular you want to see?"

DiMaggio said, "You decide."

They took a left on Grand Street off the exit and came to an intersection, crossed that, went another block, and made a right on Pacific. "Up on the right here is the Lafayette project, where I grew up," Collins said. DiMaggio looked past him. It could have been any project in any neighborhood like this. This one just happened to be named Lafayette, in Jersey City, New Jersey. It would have another name in Overtown, in Miami, in the South Bronx and Detroit. This was just Richie Collins's geography.

DiMaggio said, "You still have any family here?"

Collins looked straight ahead. "I barely had any to begin with. Ellis had his Aunt Mary. I didn't have that. My mother was pregnant with me when my old man got killed. He was in the navy. Not fighting or anything. Just standing in the engine room one day when it fucking blew up. She was living in Newark when I was born anyway, and then we ended up over here. I was sixteen when she died."

DiMaggio said, "How—?" And Richie Collins cut him off, looking straight ahead on Pacific, Lafayette behind them now, said, "Her pimp cut her throat." There was just a small beat, and Richie Collins said to Rudy in a dead voice, "Take Johnston Avenue here."

"Who raised you after that?" DiMaggio said.

"I raised me after that," Richie Collins said. "I raised me. And me and Ellis's Aunt Mary raised Ellis."

"How did you get by?"

Collins turned around now in his seat. "I did jobs," he said. "And when that wasn't enough, I took."

"Took what?"

"Whatever I could take. After Ellis came along, and everyone knew Ellis 'n' me were a team when it came to playing ball, then I didn't have to take anymore because people started to *give.*"

He showed DiMaggio the court at a playground called Baby Rucker, with its sad, ruined concrete and fenced-in basketball hoops and a tavern across the street. Collins told Rudy to pull up at Baby Rucker and stop. Collins got out and motioned for DiMaggio to do the same. He went through the playground and hooked his fingers through the fence around the court. "Lot of action here in the summer," Richie Collins said. "Drunks coming across the street to make bets, drug deals going on all night long. But ball like you couldn't believe. Ellis doing shit . . ." Collins closed his eyes. "Bad guys and scumbags all around, and Ellis doing things with a basketball that knocked your fucking eyes out."

They got back in Salter's town car, went back to Pacific and made a left, then took a right on Communipaw and finally a left on Garfield. They went past a big car wash, and then out of nowhere was another basketball court. "Look at that," Richie Collins said. "Stop here," he said to Rudy.

"What's the problem?" DiMaggio said.

"They got a net down," Richie Collins said. "Man, nobody wants to play without a net. You have to be from here to understand. One net down at a place like this can fuck up twenty or thirty lives. Twenty or thirty kids who got nowhere else to go except *here.*"

The two of them got out again, went and stood in the middle of the Garfield Avenue court.

"Aunt Mary's was right up there," Collins said, pointing to a white-frame house up the hill. "This is the court where I found Ellis shooting that night, after her party. Damn, he always liked this court, even when we were kids. I shouldn't've been surprised to find him in the middle of the night. There was nights Ellis'd shoot all night long. He was funny that way. Ellis was afraid of everything growing up. Especially of the dark. I told him once, it wasn't the dark he was afraid of, it was the dark at *Booker T.* But he'd get out here, just shooting by the streetlights at that basket right down there, the one that still has the net, and he wouldn't be afraid of nobody."

They got back into the car. Richie said to Rudy, "I'm gonna use that phone. All right?" Rudy said, "Go ahead, Mr. Collins." Collins got information for the Jersey City Police Department. "Emergency?" he said to the operator. "Only sort of." He got the number, punched it out, and said, "I just want to leave a message. This is Richie Collins of the Knicks. Tell somebody there's a net down at the Garfield Avenue court." He handed the phone back to Rudy in the front seat and said, "That shit shouldn't go on over here."

They ended up finally at Booker T. Washington. Collins explained that there were three big projects over on this side of town. Lafayette, Montgomery, and then Booker T. "The other ones have ten-story buildings," Collins said. "Booker T.'s only got two stories. Less floors, higher crime rate."

Collins said to Rudy, "We won't be long. But go ahead and lock the door anyway." He took DiMaggio down a long sidewalk between the low buildings and into the courtyard in back where the basketball court was. "Ellis lived on the second floor, this building to your right," Collins said. "And this court right here, this was where I first met him, where we started playing ball. There's a lot of games, especially in the summer. There's this great game, over at this place White Eagle, a bingo hall over on Newark Avenue. But that's once you're in high school, and college. You ever hear of Bobby Hurley? Slick little guard, even slicker than me? He came out of Jersey City, 'fore he went to Duke and then the pros. His father's the big coach in town, over at St. Anthony High. Coach Hurley always organized the games at White Eagle. But when you were coming up, trying to make a name for yourself, the best game was at Booker T., right here on this court. This was where you found the best runs in town."

"Runs?" DiMaggio said. Collins would lose him sometimes.

"Best games," he said. "Best ball. If you keep winning you can have yourself a run that would last all day and night. More bad guys over here than over at Baby Rucker. But nobody ever messed with Ellis. There's only one kind of royalty in a place like this, and that's basketball royalty. Ellis 'n' me, we were as safe playing games in here as we were playing ball right now at Madison Square Garden. I used to see drug dealers pull their guns out on each other if they thought anybody was messing with Ellis. See, they knew Ellis was going to get *out*. He was going to do what none of them would ever do. Alive, anyway."

In the middle of Booker T. Washington, Collins pointed in the direction of New York City.

"Ellis was going somewhere," he said.

He looked all around him, at the ruins of Booker T. "So, Ellis," Richie Collins said softly. "Where are you?"

23

Hannah would let Jimmy's answering machine pick up the phone. Then she'd listen and decide if she wanted to talk. Her mother had already called three times. The second and third times she started off by saying, "Hannah, I know you're there," so Hannah just turned down the volume.

If there'd only been a volume switch like that my whole life, she thought to herself.

It was seven o'clock. She was going to watch Marty Perez's show, *Chronicle,* and then *Entertainment Tonight.*

Now the phone rang, and when the machine picked up she heard him saying, "This is DiMaggio."

She pictured him leaving his message, serious in his blue suit, with those sort of sleepy-looking brown eyes and black hair with some gray getting into it, ready to smile but not giving in. Harvey and Jimmy had told her to stay away from him. Except that all of a sudden, Hannah didn't care what Harvey and Jimmy said.

DiMaggio was saying something about New Jersey, having spent his afternoon over there when Hannah picked up.

"Mr. Second Opinion," she said.

"Guilty," he told her.

"Somebody has to be," Hannah said, and smiled to herself.

Sometimes she surprised herself, getting off a one-liner right away and not having it come to her later.

"What are you doing right now?"

Hannah said, "Reading." Then, not waiting, she said, "Where are you calling me from? You said you were in New Jersey today?"

"I'm back now. I'll tell you all about it if you have dinner with me."

Hannah tried to picture him in something other than a blue suit, couldn't.

"What do you say?" he said, trying to sound casual about it.

"I'm not even supposed to be talking to you."

"Have dinner with me. We won't talk about anything you don't want to talk about."

Hannah said, "I hear you've been talking to my friends."

"A few."

"The cops talk to them first, then you come along. Or you talk to them first. They don't have time to talk to me anymore. They're too busy talking to you and the cops."

"It's a living," he said, making it sound like a joke somehow.

"They say you know everything about me except what time I walk my dog."

DiMaggio said, "You don't have a dog."

Hannah laughed. It felt good. Maybe he was funny. It seemed like she was surrounded now by people who were never funny, who were always grim these days. A grim brother. A grim lawyer. Even Beth—a grim shrink.

Hannah thought: Who am I kidding? Even me. A grim *me*.

"Can you give me half an hour?"

"I'll meet you downstairs."

"Dress casual?"

"Whatever."

Hannah said, "No lawyering."

"I promise."

She said, "Mr. Second Opinion."

DiMaggio said, "You don't know the half of it."

"I wanted to see where they came from," he was saying to her, "but that wasn't all of it. I wanted to spend some time with Collins, not just see what he was like cut off from Adair, but in a place where he might not be *on* every minute."

They were sitting in the back room at Antolotti's, one of his favorites. On Forty-ninth, between First and Second. DiMaggio had called Sonny Antolotti, the owner, and told him they didn't want to be bothered. So there was nobody else back there.

He sipped a Corona. Hannah Carey had a Diet Coke in front of her with a lime in it. She was wearing a camel blazer. Her turtleneck was either navy or black, DiMaggio couldn't tell in the light.

She didn't do anything with the opening about Richie Collins.

"What's it like?" she said. "Over there, I mean."

"Here's what it's like: I rode around over there and walked around and wondered if I would have been tough enough to get by, much less get out."

"It's bad," she said.

"Don't get me wrong," DiMaggio said. "There's nice places, too, where you can see the city across the river. But the projects where Adair and Collins come from might as well be another country. Or on the goddamn moon."

The waiter brought a plate with bite-sized pizza slices on it and set it between them. "On Sonny," he said. Sonny Antolotti was a big ball fan DiMaggio had met when he was with the Yankees. The season he got those hits on the last day to get over .200, Sonny was hip to the significance of not ending up under .200 and treated it as if DiMaggio had won the batting championship.

He bought DiMaggio and his flight attendant dinner on the house.

"So you spent the day with Richie Collins," Hannah said, bringing it back to him on her own. Surprising him.

"You don't have to talk about him if you don't want to."

"Don't worry, I won't," she said. "Tell me more about Jersey City."

"Why are you so interested?"

She said, "I'm interested in them, too." He studied her hands, palms flat on the table in front of her. Big hands for a big girl, but with slender fingers and nail polish just a slightly darker shade than the pale hands themselves. DiMaggio thought about tracing them on the white tablecloth the way you did when you were a kid. Taking his time.

They were beautiful hands.

Now she said, "I'm just not interested in spending any more time with them." Hannah Carey took the swizzle stick out of her Diet Coke and held it the way you would a cigarette.

DiMaggio said, "The funny thing with him, Collins, was he seemed so *proud* of all the places he was showing me. But then telling me over and over, every few minutes, how happy he was to be away from there."

Hannah Carey said to DiMaggio, "You sound like you might feel a little bit bad for them."

"No," he said. "That's not it."

"Are you sure?"

DiMaggio noticed a tiny scar over her right eye. You could almost miss it. A tiny pockmark. And he noticed that in Antolotti's dim lights, her blue eyes seemed almost gray. She was locked in on him the way she had been on Hollywood Bob.

Like the pretty girl in the front row of class staring up at the professor. She was looking at him that way and getting him to do the talking when DiMaggio wanted it to be the other way around.

DiMaggio said, "I don't feel bad for them because of the projects or Jersey City. You start explaining things away that way, you can explain away every cheap crackhead punk with a gun and an attitude. I just think I understand them a little better is all. I've got a frame of reference now, especially with Richie Collins."

"Why him and not—?"

"Ellis? Because he's black and Richie isn't."

"It matters?"

"In those projects I saw, yeah, it matters. There're other places, lots of places, where I'd say the black guy had to be tougher, not just to survive, but to go on and *do* something. Just not at Lafayette and Booker T." He paused. "Richie Collins is probably every lousy thing people say he is as a human being. But he's tough enough."

"It always comes back to that," she said. "With you guys."

"Which guys?"

She smiled and said, "All guys."

DiMaggio said, "You know, I'd rather talk about you."

"I'll bet."

"Where you came from, I mean."

"It's like Mother always said," Hannah Carey said. "Take a look at the *Official Airlines Guide.*"

He said, "Tell me about it."

Keep her talking.

The best Sheila Carey ever did was Top Ten twice, Hannah said. Ahead of Betty Stove, that big Dutch girl, one time. She made the quarterfinals of Wimbledon once, the quarterfinals of the Open. That was it. Her tennis never made her a celebrity.

It was being on the circuit and having kids that made her a celebrity.

"My mother likes to tell people now that she was the first nineties woman," Hannah said. "Only it was the seventies."

She had started out on the tour as a teenager, decided she wasn't going to make it, dropped out, got herself a teaching job outside Philadelphia, married the head pro at the club. She had Hannah when she was twenty, Jimmy fourteen months later. The head pro died in a car accident. Sheila Carey got herself back in shape and decided to take one more crack at the tour.

"She packed up a dozen Wilson rackets, Jimmy, and me," Hannah said.

So in the winter they traveled the circuit that Billie Jean King built, then it was to Europe for the spring and early summer, then Wimbledon and then to tournaments in Switzerland and Sweden and Austria. Sheila Carey told them they were seeing the world. At Antolotti's Hannah said, "Every once in a while we'd see a castle or a museum even. The rest of the time I got to see the backseat of the courtesy car or the women's locker room. Or Mother's match."

DiMaggio said it didn't sound like much of a way to be a kid, and Hannah said, "I never felt like a kid. I always felt like a spectator with a locker-room pass."

Hannah started playing tennis at thirteen, learning the game from all the big names, taking to it much more easily than Jimmy did; Jimmy's part was being the darling of all the players, the straights and the lesbians both. He was the prettier of the two of them. "He was prettier even then," Hannah said, lifting her shoulders and then letting them drop. They all loved Jimmy. The attention neither of them got from their mother, they got from all the other players. Jimmy, she said, seemed to need it more.

"My pretend game was that I wasn't even there," Hannah said. "Where's Hannah? Oh, there she is."

DiMaggio thought: Ellis Adair wasn't the only one who wanted to be invisible.

Hannah said her mother fell out of the Top Ten after a year. Then she was out of the Top Twenty, and then she was out of the rankings completely and they were living in Roslyn, Long Island. She remarried, a plastic surgeon. "Dad Number Two," Hannah said. Jimmy was packed off to Phillips Exeter. At sixteen, Hannah was a good enough tennis prospect to be the best girl at a place called the Port Washington Tennis Academy.

And she hated it.

"It isn't even probably a surprise, though, that my mother looked at my tennis completely differently than I did," she said. "But then Mother has always looked at everything completely differently than I did."

DiMaggio asked, "Stage mom?"

Hannah said, "It was even more than that. All my life, she didn't know what to do with me. Like she didn't know who I was supposed to be? Now it was easy for her. I was going to be *her.*"

Sheila Carey decided she didn't need some Aussie kid nobody'd ever heard of to teach her kid tennis. Sheila took over, and then when she thought Hannah was ready, she shipped her down to Melbourne, Florida, and now Hannah wasn't just the best girl at the Port Washington Tennis Academy; she felt like she was in the tennis army.

She was seventeen by then, taking a few high school-equivalency courses in the morning and living in a dorm with girls who had come to Melbourne from all over the world.

Hannah hated them all. "Talking backhands." She started sneaking out at night and getting drunk.

"I was seventeen but looked older," Hannah said. "I was as tall as I am now. I didn't have too much trouble getting guys to buy me drinks."

There were a couple of warnings from the guy who owned the tennis academy, Billy Ranieri, and then a trip down to Melbourne by her mother. Hannah would go a few weeks being a good girl, and then finally she borrowed a coach's car and mistimed the automatic gate in front of Billy Ranieri's Tennis Academy and totaled the car and was out of there.

"I came back to Long Island and finished high school and tried college for a couple of years and Europe for one year," Hannah smiled. "I'm running out of gas here. Before long, I was one of a million girls in the big city going from aspiring model to aspiring actress and to waitress and then I had too much to drink again one night and got raped. I'm trying not to drink anymore, or get raped. And that is all the talking I care to do about me tonight."

DiMaggio said, "No follow-up questions?"

Hannah said, "I've already told you more than I should have."

"Not necessarily."

"Why don't you tell me what you found out about me."

"Why don't you let me ask a few questions."

"No." Someone dimmed the lights behind them. Now Hannah's eyes looked blue again. She was smiling again. DiMaggio couldn't tell whether she was playing with him or not. He felt it again, the way he did when he watched her from Ted Salter's secret room at the Garden: The conversation was all over the place, but she was the one moving it around.

"I'd rather talk about you," she said. "What's the matter with your hands? I look at you sometimes and it's like they're hurting you so much you want to scream."

"I have arthritis," he said. "They get a little stiff sometimes, that's all."

She stared at his hands until he slid them off the table and put them in his lap.

"Liar," she said softly.

"Let's order," DiMaggio said.

* * *

It was after ten when DiMaggio paid the check. He had spent most of dinner telling her about his baseball career. She was a good listener. So he told her about Tony DiMaggio and the pink flamingos and learning to play the piano.

It was more than he usually told.

When they got outside to Forty-ninth, Hannah said, "Well."

There was some wind up off the East River. It was as if DiMaggio felt the first breath of winter, even as autumn was just beginning.

"You want to take a walk?" he said.

"I'd like that," Hannah Carey said.

They walked over to First and took a left and started uptown.

"It was different with you and the piano," Hannah said. "I mean, different than tennis was with me."

"How so?"

"I couldn't stand my mother *and* couldn't stand tennis. You don't seem so crazy about your dad, but you love the music."

"I think it was a way of asking him to take me with him," DiMaggio said. "Before I really got to know him."

Hannah said, "You haven't talked about your mother at all."

They were on the west side of First, waiting for the light at Fifty-first.

"You did have a mother, didn't you?" Hannah said, trying to make a joke of it.

"I've talked enough," DiMaggio said.

"Something happened to her, didn't it?" Hannah said. "You don't have to tell me—"

Why not? DiMaggio thought. What the hell.

"She got raped," he said.

His mother always drank, even when Tony DiMaggio was still playing in local bands on Long Island—he actually had his own for a while, "Tony DiMaggio and the Yankee Clippers"—before he hit the road for good.

"I'd come home from school," DiMaggio told Hannah. "I mean when I was eleven, twelve, in there, and my mom would be asleep in front of the television set, watching some soap opera, *The Guiding Light* or *The Edge of Night,* and the ashtray would be full of Viceroy butts, she smoked Viceroys, and there'd be an empty bottle of Four Roses, sometimes tipped over on the rug next to her chair."

She'd wake up crying sometimes when she heard him getting a snack or going out to play ball and beg him not to tell his father. But even as a kid, he remembered wondering why his father would care about his mother's drinking when he didn't care about anything else that happened in the house.

When his father hit the road for good, his mother stepped up the drinking. When DiMaggio was a junior at Commack High School, she started bringing guys home from the saloons.

"They were just guys," he said. "Cops sometimes. Gas station guys. Didn't much matter. She'd try to wait until after she knew I'd gone to bed, but sometimes I'd be out late. The year I got my driver's license, I'd saved up enough in the summer to buy an old Volkswagen convertible, and I'd run into her. Then I'd go to my room. And everything would start the same way. I'd hear the bastards slamming this shitty ice tray we had on the kitchen counter. Then my mother would put a record on. Old stuff. The stuff I like to play now. After a while, I'd hear them moving some of the living room furniture around. My mother loved to dance."

There was one night when she didn't come home. DiMaggio, all this time later couldn't remember why he woke up early the next morning. He'd been a late sleeper as a kid, even alarm clocks couldn't do the job with him, and half the time his mother, hungover but getting herself together enough to fix him breakfast, would have to shake him awake to get him off to school on time.

Except for this morning.

DiMaggio woke up a little after six and his mother was sitting at the kitchen table, smoking, drinking a cup of coffee.

DiMaggio said to Hannah, "Yuban." Thinking to himself as he did: Richie Collins was right, it *was* funny the shit you remembered.

His mother's mascara was all under her eyes. Her stockings were bunched around her knees. It took him a minute to notice that it wasn't just mascara with one of her eyes. She'd been hit. He saw that her best print dress was ripped on one side, down at the bottom, at the hem. He asked her what happened, and that was when she noticed him standing there.

She looked at him for what he remembered as being a long time. She had boiled some water in a soup pan, boiling an egg, and it was still bubbling; before she said anything, he walked over and moved the pan to another burner.

Then she said something and DiMaggio said, "What?" and his mother said to him, "I said, he made me."

"Who made you?" he said, and she named a guy he had met at the house one time, a cop.

DiMaggio said, "She looked up at me, I remember this the best, and I saw how old she'd become. Not thinking about the bruise even. Or her makeup. Just how old and sad she looked. And she just said, 'He made me.' "

She had thought they were coming back to the house to drink and dance. But this time the cop drove to this spot he knew, not too far from one of the Commack exits on the LIE, Long Island Expressway. He was drunk already. He told her he wanted to do it here, like the kids he always had to roust did it.

DiMaggio and Hannah crossed First at Fifty-seventh and walked toward Sutton Place, then crossed the street again. There was a small park there, overlooking the East River. They sat down on a bench.

"You know what my mother told him?" DiMaggio said. " 'It isn't nice.' Imagine that? 'It isn't nice.' Then he raped her. Then there was somebody else getting into the backseat, and she found out that one of his buddies had followed them. He was next."

She wouldn't see a doctor. She wouldn't file charges. They both told her that if she made trouble, they knew she had a son. They knew he drove his little Volkswagen. They *knew* he wanted to be a baseball star.

So DiMaggio waited outside the bar for a week, trying to screw up his courage. He was set to go home one night when the cop who did it, the one she knew, came stumbling out. DiMaggio got out of the Volkswagen, walked up and hit him twice, knocked him down, before he knew what was happening.

DiMaggio said, "Then he got up."

He ended up breaking DiMaggio's nose, and cracking a rib. He was wearing motorcycle boots. He finished him off by stomping on his hands until he broke them.

"Before he left, he knelt down next to me," DiMaggio said. "And he said, 'You got your ass kicked for nothing, kid.' I said, 'What's that supposed to mean?' And this guy says to me, 'It means she wanted it.' "

That was what started it with his hands.

They sat in silence when he finished, both of them staring across the river at Queens. Finally, DiMaggio said, "Listen, I'm sorry."

She said, "For what?"

"If it was too close."

"It was close enough," she said. "But I had the feeling it was harder for you to tell than it was for me to hear it."

"I doubt it."

"No, really." She turned to face him. She had pulled the collar of her blazer up against the night. "Is that why you're here? Why you took this case?"

"I don't know. Maybe."

Hannah Carey stood up. "She wanted it," she calmly said to DiMaggio. "That's what they always say, isn't it?"

24

"Ay bendito," Marty Perez said.

"I know that one," Michael Cantor said. "That's the one you say when you're feeling sorry for yourself. Which is why I know it, because you're feeling sorry for yourself all the time."

Marty bit off the end of his cigar and spit it toward the wastebasket on the side of Cantor's desk, but he missed. When he made no move to get it, Cantor stood up and picked it up carefully, as if it were some dead bug.

"I came in here so you could tell me how I'm going to find Ellis Adair."

Cantor said, "That's the whole game now, at least until they decide to indict or not."

"Ahora mismo," Marty said, joking at Cantor around the cigar.

"Enough of this shit. What is this, Berlitz? What does—?"

Marty told him, "It means I want to find his black ass. Knock on his door like I'm the law and say, 'Okay, boy, come with me.' "

"Boy?" Cantor said.

It was eight-thirty in the morning. Cantor had told him on the phone that if they were going to talk, to do it then; he was up to his eyeballs in bankers the rest of the day. Adair had been missing for forty-eight hours. The Knicks didn't know where he was; Richie Collins still didn't know. Collins had gotten one phone call, the night before. Adair wouldn't say where he was, when he was coming back, just that he was fine.

Marty happened to call Collins a little before midnight, to see if anything had changed.

"He wanted me to know he wasn't dead," Collins said. "Said it wasn't a deal like Michael Jordan's dad, he hadn't got himself shot and dumped someplace. Then before I could ask him anything else, he said, 'I need some time, sort some shit out.' And hung up."

Marty wrote it in thirty-five minutes, and they put it on the front page of the Sports Final, which was the last edition of the *Daily News*.

"I can taste this one," Marty said. "I find him, I write him up big-time, we hold it for the late edition so nobody else gets to rewrite it and act like it's theirs. Then I turn around and put him on television the next day."

Cantor said, "He's going to do all this for Marty Perez of the *News* out of the goodness of his heart?"

"Yes."

"Why?"

"I haven't figured that part out yet."

"You really do have big balls," Cantor said.

Marty said, "Richie Collins told me the same thing. Everybody must know."

Cantor shrugged.

"Qué conjones," Cantor said.

"Now you're getting the hang of it," Marty said. "All I've got to do is find him."

"Where does somebody like Ellis Adair go to disappear?"

Marty said, "I keep thinking it might be the place where we'll least expect to find him."

"And where is that?"

"Maybe here," Marty said.

"You're shitting me," Cantor said, looking at his Cartier watch. It was the move that meant get out. "You think he's in New York?"

Marty said, "Sounds so nice they named it twice. And why not? Where the hell else is he gonna go?"

Marty walked out ahead of Cantor, into the early-morning quiet of the city room.

"Okay, asshole," Marty said out loud. "Come out, come out wherever you are."

It was half an hour later. Marty was already working on his second cigar and fourth cup of coffee and feeling jumpy when the kid, Casseas, who worked reception out by the elevators, buzzed him.

He said there was a woman out there to see him, most definitely. Casseas was black and probably Haitian. Marty could never be sure on the Haitian, but Casseas had picked up all the conversational frills the black kids used. Most definitely. No doubt. They seemed to think it made them sound smarter.

"What's her name?"

"She don't give me a name, mon."

"Then tell her I'm busy."

"I think you want to talk to this one," Casseas said. "No doubt."

"Why is that?"

Marty drummed his fingers on the desk. Shit, how many cups of coffee had he had? He felt like he was having a stroke.

Casseas lowered his voice. "She says that Richie Collins raped her one time and she wants to talk to you about that. Most definitely."

"¿Qué haces?" Marty said.

Teresa Delgado said, "English, please." She smiled.

Marty guessed her to be in her mid-twenties. She was tiny, not much over five feet, had a round face and straight, shiny black hair, looking soft enough to touch. Teresa Delgado was not dark, though. She had creamy white-girl skin. There was a sweetness about her, a calm, that came into Marty Perez's office and seemed to settle his caffeine jitters immediately. There was something about her face, the smallness of her, that gave her a doll quality.

"Can I get you anything?"

"No, thank you."

"Sorry about the condition of this office." He grinned. "It's like Grand Central: We've tried to get the homeless out of here, but they still find a way."

Nothing.

Yeah, you've always been a real champ at loosening things up, Perez. *Qué tipo.* Cantor was right. What a guy.

"I probably should have come forward sooner—"

"It's not an exact science, Miss Delgado—"

"—Teresa—"

"—Teresa. It took Hannah Carey a year."

She had taken her shoulder purse, some kind of expensive-looking leather or a great imitation, and put it in her lap. She was working it over pretty good. Her hands looked even whiter than her face; she sure had some strong white blood in her somewhere from daddy or mommy.

"Ten years for me," she said.

Marty said, "Why now and why me?"

Teresa Delgado looked up at him with her big eyes.

"I read those first things you wrote about Hannah Carey when no one in the newspapers was giving her a chance. I was very impressed by that."

Marty thought: Still the king of the bullshitters. "Thank you," he said, trying to sound humble. Bullshitting her some more.

"I've been following the case ever since," she continued in a voice without accent or inflection, a sad voice that Marty didn't think belonged to a face this pretty, this sweet.

Teresa Delgado said, "They're going to get away with this, aren't they?"

"You can't know that—"

"They are, aren't they?" Pressing him.

"They probably are," Marty admitted. "If she'd only done things differently. Back then, I mean."

"It's like you told me," she said. "This isn't an exact science."

"No."

"Sometimes, though."

"I don't understand."

"Maybe it is, once in a while. I haven't told you my story yet."

Marty watched her. A little girl named Delgado, talking about bad things. Getting ready to, anyway.

"They were both in the room with me, too."

Marty kept his Panasonic tape recorder, the little one, an RQ-311 minicassette recorder with the built-in microphone, next to his phone. He pushed it forward, showing it to her, checked to see if there was a cassette in there, and jabbed at the Play button. Smiling, but making sure to let her know.

"You say both."

"Both Richie Collins and Ellis Adair."

Marty said, "Richie Collins and Ellis Adair were in the room when you were raped."

"By Richie Collins," she said.

Marty said, "What about Adair?"

Teresa Delgado said, "He watched.'

Marty Perez, his heart beating so hard now he thought he really was having a stroke, told her she probably should start at the beginning.

She lived in a frame house on Newark Avenue, Teresa Delgado said, down the hill from a terrible old bingo place, White Eagle Hall, where Richie Collins and his friends used to play ball in the summer. She was two years younger than he was and had a terrible crush on him anyway, so sometimes she would sneak into White Eagle Hall on the summer nights, sometimes with a girlfriend, sometimes alone, and watch the games.

"It was like something you thought should be closed down," she told Marty. "Closed down or condemned. Richie and his friends, though? They treated it like a museum."

There were always other girls around, older girls, and it seemed that, according to her observation, Richie Collins always had two or three he was dating at one time. But she was fifteen years old, she said. Teresa Delgado, daughter of a dead Jersey City policeman and a mother who worked two jobs to support Teresa and three sisters, decided that summer that she was in love with Richie Collins.

"His mother had died the year before," she said. "He was living by himself over in Lafayette."

"How did she die?"

"It was said that she was stabbed by a mugger," said Teresa Delgado. "But you heard things . . ."

"What things?"

"That she was a prostitute," she said. "And that she was killed by the man she worked for."

Marty said, "Her pimp."

"Yes."

"And the kid was allowed to live alone?"

"It was Lafayette, Mr. Perez," she said. "It was the projects." That seemed to explain everything. "He told everyone that he was moving in with Ellis Adair and his Aunt Mary over at Booker T. Washington. But he stayed at Lafayette."

"How did he pay?"

"I don't know," she said. "But he did."

Teresa Delgado came to know what nights there would be games at White Eagle Hall better than the players did. She knew when the biggest crowds of adults would be in the folding chairs on the side, so close to the tiny court they were practically in the game. She came to know the players by name, ones from her neighborhood, all the huge black boys from the projects across town, the part of Jersey City that she had only seen a couple of times in her life, from the back of her Uncle Luis's car. He had been born in the Dominican the way most of her family had, and he had friends over in Montgomery.

To her, it was like provinces in another country. Montgomery. Lafayette. Booker T. Washington.

"I followed the game the way real sports fans follow a season," she said. "I knew which night the college boys would play, which nights they would mix college and high school. But it was all so I could watch him."

Sometimes she would wait outside, so he would have to pass her when the game was over. Teresa Delgado, fifteen years old and in love for the first time, did not even care when he would come out with another girl.

"I knew there would be a night when he would really see me," she said. "And I was certain, Mr. Perez, that when he saw me he would be able to see all the way inside me." She smiled at Marty, as if embarrassed at the picture she drew for him of herself.

At last there was the night when Richie Collins came out alone. And she was there, alone.

"How old are you?" he said. Before asking her her name.

"Eighteen."

"Liar."

"Am not."

"What's your name, little girl?"

She told him.

"Would you like to have a date with me?"

"What kind of date?"

"I could take you for ice cream. Don't all little girls like ice cream?"

She was so brave now. It was happening, not exactly the way she had imagined it, but close enough.

"So brave," she repeated to Marty.

"I drink wine," she told Richie Collins that night.

"You're not old enough to drink."

"Am too."

They really did go for ice cream the first night, a little place on Newark Avenue, down the hill from White Eagle Hall. The next time, they went for pizza. The third time, he told her he was ready to see if she really did drink wine. He said there was nobody home at his friend Ellis's. Did she know Ellis? Everybody knew Ellis by then in Jersey City. They took the Greenville local bus that Richie always took home after the basketball games. Teresa felt wicked and grown-up, going into the world she had only seen from Uncle Luis's car.

Richie Collins took her up to Ellis Adair's apartment. She was surprised to see Ellis there. Richie had told her they would be alone.

And later on, after they had drunk a lot of the wine—"cheap Gallo red"—Richie Collins raped Teresa Delgado, not the eighteen she said she was, fifteen years old and a virgin, on Ellis

Adair's living room couch, with a Mets baseball game on the television in the bedroom and the window open and all the summer-night noises including basketball coming up through the window from the playground down below.

He raped her with Ellis Adair wandering in and out of the room, waiting for Richie Collins to be finished.

"So they could go do something," she said. "Ellis seemed impatient that Richie was taking so long."

Marty said, "Did you scream?"

Teresa Delgado said, "I was too ashamed."

Then she said to him, "Besides, there was this part of me, even when the pain started to come, that thought, all this time, girl, this is what you wanted."

She told him more about it, as much as she could remember, and finally Marty Perez, remembering the sexy young blond girl who'd been hitting on Richie Collins outside the Fulton Sports Shop, said to Teresa, "What happened? When it was over?"

She shrugged and said, "He took me down to the bus and gave me a quarter."

25

Ellis didn't want Dale to go. Didn't understand how somebody could leave now.

But Dale said, "I am *going* to keep working." Working this time meant Europe. First London, then Paris, then Rome. A week in each one. Ellis didn't know why a modeling job in Europe had to take nearly a month, but there it was, and so Ellis had Dale's triplex to himself until he sorted things out.

"I wish there was a way to smuggle you through customs, big boy," Dale said, and kissed him.

Tall beautiful Dale, dark skin, some kind of Hawaiian mix going: Dale, who made being beautiful look as easy as Ellis made basketball. Looking young enough still to do those billboards everybody talked about, wearing that skimpy black underwear.

Dale, looking as sad as Ellis could ever remember, gave Ellis another kiss good-bye. "I wish there was something I could say to make you feel better."

"You want *me* to feel better?" Ellis said.

"Yes, you."

"Nothing to say."

"We'll get through this."

Ellis said, "It isn't fair."

"It's like they say. Life sucks, then you die. Isn't that what they say?"

"Don't," Ellis said.

Really wanting to say, "Don't go."

"I'm sorry," Dale said.

"Ellis said, I was sitting there this morning, looking out at the park. Like I used to sit out on Aunt Mary's terrace and watch guys score rock. And I'm thinking, I did everything they told me to do. You know what I'm saying? I played by the goddamn *rules*. I worked my ass off and didn't do no drugs and I kept making myself better playing ball. And now all *this* happens. All this *shit.*"

He stopped because he didn't want to cry in front of Dale. Because he shouldn't have been the one crying, anyway. "Sometimes I think I should've been one of those Idas I told you about," he said. "Be a playground legend. You understand? But never left Jersey City."

Dale, with those sad eyes still going, said, "How in the world did someone like you get from there to *here?* "

Dale meant the triplex here, on Fifth Avenue, Seventy-ninth and Fifth, with the houseboy who lived downstairs someplace and never talked except to say, "Is there anything else?" The houseboy who seemed to exist only to go get Ellis something when Ellis didn't want to go outside. Nobody knowing he was here in New York, right underneath everybody's nose, in his very own secret and invisible home.

Not even Richie, who Ellis had called just to say he hadn't died.

"You know the way I showed you to get in and out?" Dale said. "If you want to take one of your night walks, all disguised?"

"No doubt," Ellis said.

"Take care of yourself," Dale said.

Ellis said, "How can you say that? Take care of *your*self."

Dale said, "We'll take care of each other," giving a little toss to the long black hair because they both knew how much Ellis liked that one and then pushing the elevator button. The doors closed, then it was just Ellis, as invisible as he could be, way up above the park.

It was the third week of October now. Less than two weeks to go to the opening of the regular season. And Ellis Adair, who was supposed to have more moves than any motherfucker alive, was trying to figure out what his next move should be. For once sorting things out without Richie. At least for the time being.

But not even being able to pray on everything without wanting to cry his eyes out.

From the start, Ellis had worried about that dress, on account of what had happened in the car, on the way back to the house. He had even been thinking about renting the movie *Presumed Innocent*. Ellis couldn't remember exactly, but him and Richie had gone to see it on the road someplace. With Indiana Jones playing the good guy they thought killed his girlfriend. Richie had read the book first, which was always a treat for Ellis because Richie would talk through the whole movie. "Watch this, Fresh." Or: "Pay attention to this part, Fresh." Like he was running Ellis through some set plays, practically telling him which parts of the movie he was supposed to like.

The movies were like everything else in their life then.

Anyway, Ellis remembered that the wife was behind it all in the movie, that was the big surprise ending. It was some sort of thing with the guy's come. She saved it or some such thing. At first trying to set him up because she caught him jumping this other girl. Then feeling bad at the end, even after he got off.

Ellis couldn't remember all of it. He just knew there was a way for them to screw around with those samples and then you could end up guilty, even if you weren't.

He wondered if Hannah Carey even remembered the ride over, drunk as she was. Ellis looked out at Central Park thinking on that. Or maybe she was just acting drunk, though Ellis seemed to recall she was putting those vodkas with the orange slices away as fast as the waitress brought them.

Ron, the house guy, said, "I know you said you don't like to read the papers, but I thought you might want to change your mind." Ron only lived in when Dale was out of town and the apartment was empty. But they all decided he should stay around while Ellis was there, in case Ellis needed something.

The first couple of days after Ellis left Fulton, he didn't read the papers. What was the point? He knew where he was and they were just making it up, which is what they did most of the time, anyway. It was like after he played the games. He didn't need some sportswriter telling him why the Knicks'd won or lost; shit, he knew while it was happening. And sometimes you just lost the game, it was as simple as that. Except sportswriters didn't want it to be simple, so they analyzed the shit out of it. Which is why Ellis stopped reading after a while.

But now Ron handed him the *Daily News* with the headline RICHIE RAPED ME and a smaller one underneath that went like this: "While Ellis Watched."

Of course Ellis remembered her, the little Spanish girl, or whatever she was, no bigger than a doll, from the other side of town. He wasn't sure anymore if he'd stayed there the whole time. It seemed to him she might be making that part up. But what did that matter anymore? People making things up and dragging Ellis into it? That wasn't news anymore, not to him.

Now Teresa Delgado was going to be on with Oprah. Ellis read it all slowly, like Richie always told him to, so he didn't miss something important. And a little bit into the story there was something else, about how *A Current Affair* was offering Hannah Carey $250,000 to do a week's worth of interviews, just tell her life story, but that *Hard Copy,* another show, was up to $400,000.

Ellis laughed. Scared as he was, scared that he was losing it all now—scared to *death,* that was the truth—he couldn't help laughing.

Teresa Delgado on *Oprah,* which the story said she'd picked over *Donahue* and *Geraldo.*

Hannah Carey with two shows fighting over her, maybe more.

He thought: They're being recruited like I was for college.

Ellis thought: Before this is over, they're going to have to hold a *draft* for Richie's girls.

26

"You know what I feel like?" DiMaggio said to Hyland. "I feel like I'm swimming in the dark."

Hyland sipped a beer. "This is why I had to stop on the way home from work, so I could listen to your problems?"

They were sitting in Mulligan's, the bar from which Hannah Carey had left with Ellis Adair and Richie Collins. At least that is what Marty Perez had written and the other newspapers were printing as fact now. The bare bones of the story, at least the story the public knew, hadn't changed: Hannah Carey was on her way up to her mother's home in Litchfield that night; her mother was out of town and she was going to spend the weekend up there. They closed off the Merritt Parkway because of an accident right before Exit 38. Hannah used to know a bartender at Gates, a restaurant in New Canaan. She stopped in there, met Adair and Collins, went with them to Mulligan's, where the Knicks players had congregated after a welcome-back dinner.

Collins asked her for a ride home. She went into the house he had rented with Ellis Adair to use the bathroom before driving to Litchfield. Adair was inside waiting for them.

They raped her.

"I know we've gone over this before," DiMaggio said. "But why do you feel like I'm the enemy here?"

Hyland said, "You're not the enemy. You're just in the way. I go to the city, I try to talk to somebody, some waitress Hannah Carey worked with, and they go, 'I told this to some guy named DiMaggio the other day.' And you know what? They all seem to think you're official."

DiMaggio said, "I never tell them I'm a cop. I tell them I work for the Knicks."

"I have a feeling you don't spend a hell of a lot of time making the distinction."

"So I'm wasting my time here. Or your time."

Hyland said, "Maybe the Knicks'll give you a bonus for trying so hard."

DiMaggio said, "I'm not going to lie to you, Connecticut is starting to wear my ass out."

Hyland smiled. "Your ass probably wore out long before you got here."

"I have no authority," DiMaggio complained. "I've gotten to talk to the accused and the accuser. But they don't have to answer any of my questions. So I end up talking to people who know her or know them. Then I end up talking to you again. Only you don't answer my questions, either."

Hyland said, "Put yourself in my shoes for a minute, if you can stop whining long enough. She came in on her own, said these two guys raped her. But these two guys, they don't have to talk to me. They didn't even have to give me blood and hair samples. But their lawyer convinced them it was bad for their image, not cooperating at *all*. So they throw me a bone and give me the samples, which are worthless because she kept the goddamn dress in a zipped-up bag for a year, and so I've got nothing to match them up *with*."

Hyland waved over the bartender. DiMaggio saw that the bartender, whom Hyland had introduced as Jack, was wearing a white shirt, striped tie, and Bermuda shorts. Hyland said, "You want another Scotch?" DiMaggio said he was fine. Hyland said to Jack, "One more and I'm out of here."

Hyland put an elbow on the bar, turned to face DiMaggio.

"How many nights in a row for you here?"

"Three."

"You find out anything interesting?"

"You don't give me shit, but I'm supposed to help you? Is that how it works?"

"Think of it as being a good citizen."

"I know what you probably know," DiMaggio said, "because you've talked to everybody I've talked to. Some people remember Hannah Carey being here. One of the bartenders working that night, who I tracked down in Australia, said she was drunk, and even got up at one point and sang with the band they had here that night."

" 'Runaround Sue,' " Hyland said. "You see her as the type to get up in a bar and sing oldies?"

"I don't see her as the type to get up and sing at all. She must have been drunk." He sipped some Scotch. "But if she was that drunk, let me ask you this: Why would Richie Collins ask *her* for a ride home?"

Hyland smiled. "Is that a hypothetical question?"

"Will you give me a fucking break?" DiMaggio said.

"You want me to speak hypothetically. Let's just say that hypothetically, her recollections of that evening, the before part and the after part, might not be so sparkling." Jack brought him his beer and Hyland waited until he placed it on top of the napkin.

"Just suppose," Hyland continued, "for the sake of conversation, that when a very good cop might ask her about an inconsistency that might crop up—when I am very definitely looking for the opposite—the woman might have a habit of saying something like, 'Brian, I'm sorry, I just don't remember.' "

DiMaggio said, "I've talked to bartenders, the owner, waitresses, customers, enough people who were there. Whenever the Knicks go out of town to play some exhibition game, I'm here. Everyone agrees that they've never seen Mulligan's more crowded. Everyone agrees that there were always women around Richie Collins. And nobody I've talked to yet can remember seeing them leave together. Either her with Collins or her with both of them."

"I've got an idea," Brian Hyland said. "Why don't you give up and go home?" He blew on the head of his beer, leaned over, and sipped some without taking it off the bar. It was five-thirty, and people were starting to come in for a drink after work. Jack hit a switch on the wall and DiMaggio heard Sinatra and Anita Baker singing "Witchcraft" from his *Duets* album. He looked around at the framed *Sports Illustrated* covers lining the walls, all of them with golfers on the front, the covers going all the way back to Ben Hogan and Sam Snead. DiMaggio had been at Mulligan's enough lately, he was starting to have dreams about golfers and Hannah Carey, not basketball players.

"Tell you what," Hyland said. He clapped DiMaggio on the back. "You find Ellis and deliver him to me, I'll be your friend."

"A reason to live," DiMaggio said.

Hyland finished his beer and left. Mulligan's got louder, busier. Jack turned up the sound system. DiMaggio liked Hyland. He had turned out to be a hard case, but he was a pro. DiMaggio knew that if they switched roles, he'd play it the same way Hyland was playing it. He'd tease DiMaggio once in a while, with the dress, with the gaps in Hannah Carey's story, but wouldn't give away anything. Because he wasn't interested in impressing DiMaggio. Because he was a good cop, and he was doing the best he could with Hannah Carey.

Where the hell *was* Ellis Adair? What had made him snap? Adair wasn't the smartest guy in the world, you didn't have to be around him five minutes to figure that out. But what had made him do something this dumb?

If he didn't leave when Hannah Carey first came forward, why leave now?

Find Ellis, DiMaggio thought. Maybe he'll tell you.

He slid some money across the bar and walked outside. He wasn't ready to go back to New York yet. He was up here again, do something with the time. He decided to drive over to Fulton. He had never been inside the house Adair and Collins rented, the one where Hannah Carey said they'd raped her. They'd been living there during training camp, so there was no way for DiMaggio to get a look at the crime scene, or alleged crime scene, even from the outside.

Maybe he'd be inspired.

Maybe he'd drive up, see a light in the window. Go knock on the door and have Ellis answer it. DiMaggio could give him a big smile and say, "Hi, honey, I'm home."

He took Route 106 into Fulton, took a left before he got to Route 7, then a right into the main driveway of the development called Fulton Crest: chalet-type condominiums set up above the Norwalk River, the main road going over a little bridge and then winding up into the woods, branching off into smaller roads as you went along. The bigger structures, real houses with more privacy, were all the way in the back of the Fulton Crest property. Without having been there, just reading about the layout, DiMaggio knew Adair and Collins had taken the last house, all the way in the back. They had their own garage, he remembered that, too. When DiMaggio got there, he saw the garage next to the house and a sidewalk that took you from the front door, across a narrow driveway, then down some stairs to what looked to be a guest parking lot.

It was far enough from everything else that no one would have heard any screams.

He drove past the house and came back around, then parked in the guest lot. He walked up the stairs. He had only been back in New York for a few weeks, but already the noise was getting to him again; the old shout. Fulton in the night was Jupiter in the night, without the muted crash of the ocean out the window. He stood there in the street, in front of the place where it all had started. It was a red brick house, made to look older than it probably was. There was a small terrace outside one of the bedrooms on the second floor.

He thought: What really happened that night after Mulligan's, when they were all inside and the door was closed?

DiMaggio walked around to the left side, saw that there was no backyard to speak of, just a small area out the back door and then the woods. From somewhere in the woods, he heard the rustling of some small animal. Or maybe it was just the wind. Now DiMaggio walked around to the other side. Still waiting for inspiration. He thought about looking in, but the shades were drawn over here, the same as they were on the other side.

Except that they hadn't been pulled all the way, and so some light escaped from inside.

DiMaggio went over, crouched down, tried to look inside. There wasn't enough room under the shade. He could make out the bottom of a bed, the bottom of the nightstand next to it, a thick rug of some ornate design. But there was a light on.

DiMaggio walked around to the front door. What did he have to lose? There was an old-fashioned knocker on the door. DiMaggio used it. Nothing. He rapped it harder against the elaborate design carved into the heavy front door of 75 Fulton Crest. He tried the handle now, just to see.

The door was unlocked.

DiMaggio walked in. There was a wide foyer in front of him, a living room area to his left. He found the light switch to his left, turned the lights on in the foyer.

"Hello," he said, his own voice startling him.

"Hey," he said. "Anybody here?"

He walked slowly down the hall, past the kitchen, also on his left, toward the first-floor bedroom where he figured the light must have been coming from.

"Honey," DiMaggio said. "I'm home."

He heard music coming from the end of the hall. A song ending, then the disc jockey giving call letters, saying, "Cool oldies."

The music was coming from the bedroom. The door was slightly ajar. DiMaggio could feel his heart and did not know why. He was probably crazy to come here in the first place. Maybe it was all crazy from the start. From Salter's first phone call.

DiMaggio pushed the door open and there was Richie Collins on the bed, naked and dead and on his back, the handle of the knife or icepick or whatever it was sticking straight out of his chest.

27

Hannah had put on the new cable channel, NY 1, when they came on with the news about Richie Collins.

". . . the center of a shocking sex charge scandal" was the first thing she heard from the kitchen. She had gone in there for a Snapple iced tea. She grabbed the bottle out of the refrigerator. When she got back into the living room, there was a reporter on the screen, standing in front of a sign that said NORWALK HOSPITAL.

The reporter was finishing up, saying, "Again, New York Knicks guard Richie Collins, dead at the age of twenty-eight. This is . . ."

Then they were back at the studio in New York, the studio looking pretty chintzy, Hannah thought, and they were showing some footage of Collins making a high pass to Ellis Adair and Adair, looking like some dark bird flying out of nowhere, above all the rest of the players, catching the ball and dropping it through the basket with such a fast motion Hannah thought the whole thing had been some kind of optical illusion.

Then they were cutting away down to Madison Square Garden, and some other cable news guy was putting a microphone in the face of some blond guy, yelling, "Mr. Salter!"

Hannah shut the television off and drank the Snapple out of the bottle.

So how do I feel?

Was that the question?

No, that wasn't the question at all, Hannah decided.

The question was about whether it was over now.

The question was: Is this enough?

And maybe, Hannah thought, trying to be so smart about herself, so analytical, one more question:

If it really *was* over, how did she feel about that?

Ellis had told the house guy to go ahead and shut the phones off, take the rest of the night off. That was about five in the afternoon, when Ellis liked to take his nap.

He thought he might watch some of the World Series later, it was still going because of some rainouts. Ellis always needed a nap when he wanted to go the distance on a baseball game. He could never understand those boys wanting to play baseball, frankly, even the top boys like Barry Bonds and the Griffey kid, out there until the end of October, if they were good enough to last that long, freezing their asses off, standing around most of the time, getting to be on offense four times a night, maybe five times if they were lucky.

Most of the time, the whole sport was one guy staring at another guy. The pitcher holding the ball, like he never wanted to throw it. The batter always stepping away from the plate, like he didn't want to hit it, even if the fucking pitcher gave him a chance.

Ellis had said to Richie one time, "This isn't a sport. It's a stakeout with bats and balls."

Ellis couldn't remember what he was dreaming about when he woke up. He wasn't good at remembering his dreams. Richie was. Richie would want to give you a play-by-play if he had a good one. But mostly they were about girls. They all sounded the same to Ellis after a while. Ellis woke up, he couldn't remember shit. Somebody had asked him one time, wanting to do a book on Ellis, did he ever dream about basketball. And Ellis'd said, "I never dream." Everybody had made a big to-do about that one quote, though for the life of him he couldn't understand why.

Everything was dark when he woke up. The television was still on. He looked at the clock. Two-thirty in the morning. Sonofabitch, I already had my eight hours, Ellis thought, and reached around on the couch for the remote. There was just some rerun of the news. A blond guy and a serious-looking sister sitting next to him, wearing these big glasses.

Maybe they'd tell who won the ball game.

"Again," the blond guy was saying in a deep voice, "in case you missed it earlier, Richie Collins, the Knicks guard involved in recent rape allegations along with his friend and teammate Ellis Adair—"

Goddamn, it never goes away, Ellis thought.

"—was found murdered earlier this evening at the rented home he shared in Fulton, Connecticut, during the preseason with Ellis Adair."

Ellis shook his head.

"No," he said.

The blond guy was saying something else to the woman. Ellis couldn't hear.

"No," Ellis said.

The remote in his hand, he felt himself start to rock on the couch, staring at the screen as they started to roll the credits.

"Noooo," Ellis Adair moaned.

Ellis started to cry now, rocking hard, his finger on the button switching the channel, the other channels flying by, Ellis not even noticing.

"Noooooooooo!" he screamed in Dale's apartment and got up and started putting the lights on. Ellis ran through the first floor, turning them all on, then ran up the spiral staircase and turned more lights on.

Then up the last staircase, to the bedroom, turning on the overheads and the floor lamps, even the ones in the bathroom. Ellis in his secret place. Dale's place. Ellis in the place even Richie didn't know about.

Ellis all alone.

28

DiMaggio did everything by the numbers, knowing that if he didn't, Brian Hyland would want to do him the way somebody did Richie Collins. Dial 911, tell them what he found at Fulton Crest, tell them to call Hyland right away. Wait for everybody to show up. He knew enough not to tamper with the crime scene. He waited out front. Collins wasn't going anywhere.

The first black Taurus, FULTON POLICE written in white on both sides, pulled up in eight minutes. DiMaggio timed them. Hyland was there seven minutes later. He walked right past DiMaggio, just pausing long enough to say, "You won't get out of the way, will you?"

DiMaggio let him go. Hyland got to the front door, turned around. "And not one fucking interview," he said, all business. "To anyone." He went inside 75 Fulton Crest.

When Hyland and his Crime Scene guys were finished, they drove back to the station, DiMaggio gave them a statement, read it, signed it, drove home. He heard the first bulletin about ten o'clock, on WCBS, the all-news channel. He switched over to WFAN, the sports station, and it sounded like the end of the world. He listened to jazz the rest of the way back to the city. There were four messages from Ted Salter. DiMaggio stuffed the message slips inside his pocket, told the guy at the front desk no calls, and went upstairs and went to bed.

And dreamed, finally, about Richie Collins, not dead in his own bed in Fulton but on some court over in Jersey City, hanging dead from a rim without a net, the kind that could ruin things for a whole neighborhood.

"What was he doing in Fulton?" Salter said in the morning.

"No one knows."

"Is Ellis a suspect?"

"Hyland—the cop up there—says if he runs into me one more time, *I'm* a goddamn suspect."

"So where do we go from here?"

"I'm going back up to Fulton this morning, then I plan to be at practice this afternoon. The team's still going to practice, right?"

Salter said, "As far as I know."

"I want to talk to Boyzie Mays. Of all the players I've talked to, he seemed to know Ellis as well as anybody besides Richie."

"I don't want to tell you how to do your job," Salter said.

DiMaggio said, "There's a relief."

"But your job right now is to find Ellis."

"Don't worry," DiMaggio said. "I don't do murder."

He had no real plan in Fulton. But going up there felt like real action, at least until the Knicks players showed up at the Garden later. Maybe DiMaggio was turning into one of the media flies and just wanted to see what the homicide carnival was like when it came to a place like Fulton.

He got to the intersection of Route 7 and Old Ridgefield Road at ten o'clock; it was as close as he could get to town, that's how much the traffic was backed up. He finally parked at the Fulton Sports Shop and walked up Old Ridgefield Road and left onto

Main Street, where there were so many people, so much action, DiMaggio imagined this was what Fulton got like on Memorial Day or the Fourth of July, one of those parade holidays that made small towns like this go wild with patriotic fervor. Most of the news vans, from the city and from the Connecticut stations, had set up in the park near the police station, across from the Fulton Library. He counted eight television boys and girls doing their earnest stand-ups, looking right into the minicams, as some carpenters did some work on the bandstand at the end of the park closest to the police station.

Already the crowd of locals was forming, ringing the park, three deep on the sidewalk across the street from the Fulton Luncheonette. Behind DiMaggio, the car horns kept blaring. He slowly made his way to the front of the crowd and saw Marty Perez, with a television crew, doing a stand-up, oblivious to the pounding of the hammers. He held a microphone in one hand and an unlit cigar in the other. He wore a wrinkled gray suit and a blue shirt with the tie yanked down from the collar. The sunlight, DiMaggio noted, was unkind to Perez, less forgiving than the ballroom lights of the Plaza had been the day Hannah Carey held her press conference there.

There was a notebook sticking out of one of the side pockets of the gray sports jacket. DiMaggio had heard Marty Perez did some television now, but had never seen him. Perez seemed to be having some difficulty with whatever he was trying to say, DiMaggio couldn't hear over the racket the workers were still making as they tried to finish the bandstand. Whenever Perez would stop, he seemed self-conscious about his thinning gray hair, patting it to keep it in place.

When he seemed satisfied, he handed the mike to his cameraman. Now Perez pulled the notebook out and tried to work the crowd. But every few minutes, one of the other television reporters would come over and Perez would nod, and then there would be the scene of one reporter interviewing the other.

DiMaggio watched, amazed: Maybe he had missed some important changing of the guard all these years living in Florida. Maybe people like Perez really did run the whole fucking world now.

DiMaggio looked behind him, toward the street, and saw more television crews now, maybe twenty in all, and saw a van from one of the local radio stations had set up with a loudspeaker and was covering the whole scene in the park live.

He felt a tap on his shoulder and turned around and there was Marty Perez.

"DiMaggio," he said.

"What a memory," DiMaggio said.

Neither one of them made any move to shake hands.

Perez tossed the cigar away, pulled his notebook out. "Mind if I ask you a few questions?"

"No comment," DiMaggio said evenly.

"I heard you're the one who found Collins's body."

"No comment."

Perez made a big show of stuffing the notebook back in his pocket. "How about we go off the record?"

DiMaggio smiled. "Because I trust you so much."

Perez said, "Maybe we could help each other out here."

"I doubt that."

"You think there's a connection between Adair's disappearance and Richie Collins getting stuck?"

DiMaggio put his hands out, plaintively. "I'm stuck."

Marty Perez shrugged. "I'll tell you something, DiMaggio," he said. "You haven't changed at all. You've still got a lousy fucking attitude."

"You want a quote, Marty, here's a quote: I agree with you.

Now you better get back to talking to people who think you're somebody."

Go talk to people who think you're somebody.

Like *he* was somebody.

Like DiMaggio, the big-time investigator, came up here and broke the case wide open.

Fuck him.

Marty got into his car and drove over to Fulton High School. He sat out in front now and felt like some *maricón* pervert, watching the kids get out of school at lunch, staring at the girls. Marty had the radio on, listening to the all-news channels, WCBS and WINS, jumping around, edgy, worried that somebody might have something new on Collins. He ended up listening to the same shit over and over again. There was a cut from Ted Salter. Then Frank Crittendon, the Knicks general manager, blubbering like a baby, trying to run that jive on everybody, as though anybody in his right mind would shed a single tear over the passing of Richie Collins.

Then Gary Lenz, the Knicks coach: "Richie was a bit of an outlaw, I'm not going to tell you he wasn't. But he was my kind of outlaw, like Butch Cassidy to Ellis's Sundance Kid."

Basura, Marty thought.

Basura and *basura* and more garbage on top of that, so much garbage he wanted to roll the window down, the stench inside the BMW was getting so bad. It was all the *basura* rhetoric of the death. Somebody takes out this *goma* and immediately everybody starts talking about him, talking about the whole thing, like it was the murder of some hero cop. Before long they'd convince themselves Collins was trying to perform CPR on Hannah Carey that night last year instead of raping her.

And everyone still speculating on what Ellis's disappearance had to do with any of this. Trying to analyze *that* without having any idea where Ellis was, why he left.

It made Marty Perez want to laugh. He thought: People who don't trust the media ought to take a look at everything from the *inside* sometime.

He listened to the idiots on the sports station for a while. Some of them called up and wanted to pay tribute to Richie Collins, as if the bastard were still listening to WFAN. One guy called while Marty was listening and blamed the whole thing on him.

"Remember something," the guy said to the host. "Remember how all this started, with that columnist in the *News* writing up the rape in the first place. You guys in the media, you don't care who you hurt, do you? No wonder they all hate your guts."

The host dumped out of the call, chuckling, and then the next caller wanted to know how the host thought Boyzie Mays would do now that he was the starting guard.

Marty jabbed at the button, turned the thing off.

Where was the girl?

Marty didn't have much of a plan beyond finding the girl he'd seen with Collins that day at the Fulton Sports Shop. Once he found her, *if* he found her, he'd see if she was still going out with Collins, see if he could scare her into telling him something. *Anything.* If Collins hadn't come up here to see the girl, maybe she knew who he had come to see. It was a long shot: Marty knew that when he got into the car for the ride up. Maybe the time Marty saw her with Collins, maybe that was the one and only time she *did* Collins. Maybe Richie Collins was trying to go through the whole senior class at Fulton High. Or junior class. Maybe that's what the *títere* did every September in Fulton.

School was back in and so was Richie.

"A kid from Fulton High," Collins had said that day. Then said he was loved by kids of all ages. Maybe he was bullshitting about the high school. Maybe she'd come walking out with the rest of the lunch crowd. And maybe he'd have to wait all goddamn day. Which he couldn't do with a goddamn column to write, and a *Chronicle* commentary.

Maybe if the kid saw Marty, *she'd* remember *him* from the Sports Shop, run like hell. Grab the first teacher she saw and say there was some old fuck outside, bothering her.

"¡Coño!" Marty said out loud.

It was a long shot, but the girl was all that Marty had that the rest of them didn't have. Only Marty Perez and maybe Ellis Adair, wherever he was, knew that Richie Collins had something going with a six-foot high school girl who kissed him good-bye on Saturday morning, looking pouty, and then rode off in her little car.

What the hell kind of car was it?

What make?

Marty leaned back, closed his eyes, tried to make himself relax. They were all out of school now, he wasn't going to miss anything if he stopped watching the front door. Jesus, he used to be able to remember everything. That was before he got so tired. In the old days, he could interview somebody at a fire, or at a murder scene, outside some courtroom, and get back to the office with an hour to make the last edition or blow the night and the story entirely, and Marty would never even have to open his notebook. He'd just close his eyes, the way he was doing it in front of Fulton High School, and hear whole conversations verbatim, as if he had a tape going inside his head.

That was before the inside of his head started feeling like a *zafacón* sometimes.

Wastebasket.

A red car!

You bet it was.

A sporty little red car for the big blond girl. He could see her clearly now, getting that look on her face when Collins brushed her off a little, made it clear that she would have to wait. She had obviously been pinning him down on some date for later. Could this baby girl have done it? Stuck him right through the fucking heart?

If she could *find* Richie Collins's heart, Marty thought.

Now he had it in his head, like a photograph: Collins giving her that come-to-daddy look before he saw Marty was watching.

It was nothing more than a hunch. An old-time feeling Marty felt in his stomach. But a million hunches like it had paid off in the past. Maybe Richie Collins had gone out with a million girls. Only Marty had seem him with this one, in Fulton, a few weeks before somebody stabbed him to death in Fulton. It wasn't much, but Marty knew he had run down the field with a lot less in his life.

"A red car," he said out loud.

He closed his eyes again, leaning forward now in the front seat, head resting against the steering wheel, not even worried about what the high school boys and girls might think if they came out and saw him, some weird guy asleep at the wheel of the old BMW.

"A red *Nissan,* " Marty said, sure he was right, and then rode around to the parking lot he knew was in back of Fulton High School until he found what sure looked like the hot *joven* girl's hot red car.

DiMaggio had first talked to Boyzie Mays the day he met with A. J. Fine at the Fulton Luncheonette. DiMaggio didn't do much talking. He found out right away that with Mays you listened. He was eight months out of rehab and wanted to tell DiMaggio all about it: Do the whole recovery rap.

"People think you just want to get back to playing ball, making money," he told DiMaggio. "Shit, that ain't half of it. It's getting so motherfucking tired of talking about yourself, your addiction to rock, the first time you tried rock and when you knew you couldn't leave it alone. You end up sounding like the most boring-assed nigger in the world. But they keep telling you, You got to talk, Boyd, which is my real name, you got to talk it *out,* Boyd, or you'll never get better. You got to get in touch with your feelings, Boyd. And maybe it does get your ass better, but not for the reason they think. You just finally figure out if you don't do no more dope, then you don't have to talk about it no more."

Then, DiMaggio remembered, Mays seemed to tell his whole life story in about ten minutes. Number one draft choice out of Maryland, backup to Richie Collins, All-Rookie Team even averaging fifteen minutes a game, getting on dope after that, getting traded to Dallas, ending up in rehab. He came back this summer, earned a job in the Knicks camp for rookies and free agents.

Now Collins was dead and Mays had the job. DiMaggio didn't want to talk about that. He had been looking at the notes he'd taken after talking to Mays the first time. There was a throwaway line in there about how Mays used to run with Ellis Adair when he was a rookie, some "wild-assed parties" Adair used to take him to.

"Fresh didn't always look the part, coming on like some happy sitcom nigger," Mays said. "But that boy would take a walk on the wild side now and again."

DiMaggio was waiting by the side of the court at the Garden, the narrow runway leading back to the locker rooms, when the Knicks finished practice; he was alone. Gary Lenz had called off practice the day before, then closed this one to the media. Lenz was the first one off when practice was over; he slowed down when he saw DiMaggio, looked like he might want to say something smart, then kept going. Mays was one of the last Knicks off the court. DiMaggio could see A. J. Fine still out there, playing one-on-one with Danny Riordan, the rookie who had replaced Ellis Adair in the starting lineup, at least for now.

Mays said he remembered DiMaggio. "From Mr. Slater," he said, and smiled. "You the man."

"That's me," DiMaggio said. "The man."

Boyzie Mays said, "This ain't about Richie, is it? They told me not to talk to nobody about that."

"It's about Ellis."

"He come back?"

DiMaggio shook his head. "I want to talk about those wild-assed parties you told me about."

"I told you that?" Mays smiled. "Damn, I'm a big-mouthed nigger sometimes." He snorted. "Not sometimes, all the time. All the rock I did, I can't remember which shit I've talked and which shit I've just *thought*. You do as much dope I did, all you end up with is rocks in your head."

"Give me about fifteen minutes," he said to DiMaggio, then walked away shaking his head, looking smaller than the six-one the program said he was, reminding DiMaggio a little of Spike Lee without the glasses. His number 20 gray practice jersey was stuck to his sweat. DiMaggio could hear him still talking to himself, saying, "Big-mouthed nigger" as he took a right in the hall on his way to the Knicks locker room. DiMaggio felt like it was only twenty minutes ago that he'd been in there watching Salter work Richie Collins over, treating him like a dink.

Now DiMaggio just tried to imagine what Boyzie Mays must have been like on cocaine if he talked this much straight.

Mays said he was too tired to go anywhere, they could just go sit high up in the Garden seats. Not even the cleaning people would bother them up there.

So they went way up, up there with the retired uniforms from the old Knick teams, white uniforms hanging up there like ghosts, belonging to Walt Frazier and Willis Reed and Bill Bradley, who went from basketball to being the senator from New Jersey. DiMaggio watched Bradley give the keynote speech at the Garden when Clinton got nominated and remembered thinking Bradley was used to working the room with a much better class of people.

Now DiMaggio looked at Bradley's number 24 and wondered how he would have handled a punk like Richie Collins, not just playing with him but riding the buses and the airplanes and dressing with him every night, even watching him work the bars like some pimp working a bus station.

Mays had brought coffee with him from the locker room for both of them. DiMaggio was starting to feel as suspicious as a sportswriter. Did this guy really want to talk or was he looking for something? Christ. He had only been back in New York for a month, been around these people for that short a time, and already he was looking at everybody like a cheap hustler, even when they tried to be friendly.

"Nice up here," Mays said, and DiMaggio had to agree. There were still a couple of lights shining on the basketball court. The rest of the Garden was in semidarkness, so the lights on the court felt like spotlights and seemed to turn the place into a museum, highlighting the fiberglass backboards and one basketball, left behind somehow, sitting there at midcourt. DiMaggio had always liked ballparks and arenas better when they were empty. From high up, where he remembered the cheap seats used to be at the Garden, when you still had cheap seats in sports, the setting had a simple, quiet playground elegance.

DiMaggio's hands were starting to ache. Maybe there was a connection since sometimes they started to ache when his head did, the way it was now, working Boyzie Mays, wondering if this was just another dead end. But he was noticing them now and had to stop talking for a minute, hope the pain would pass, wanting to kick himself for not soaking in the morning and not having any Advil with him. Not that he'd take it in front of Mays. Everybody had his macho front, including him, he thought, even when the pain made him want to scream. He never knew when a day would turn into a bad day, but there it was all of a sudden, and DiMaggio was flinching, like a fighter anticipating a punch, when someone would reach to shake his hand.

DiMaggio picked up his plastic coffee cup from the seat next to him and sipped his cold coffee just to have something to do with his goddamn hands.

"I've been thinking, maybe I shouldn't be talking about Fresh neither," Mays started.

DiMaggio said, "You're not hurting him by helping me."

"Is Fresh in more trouble, on account Richie's dead now?"

"There's a point where perception becomes fact," DiMaggio said.

"Meaning that after a while if you look guilty you start to *be* guilty. Ellis needs to come back now. The longer he stays away, especially with Richie dead, the more people start to wonder. Did he do the rape? Did he even have something to do with Richie's death?"

"Shit. If Ellis did Richie, be like a wife doing her husband."

"It happens all the time," DiMaggio said.

Mays looked around, as if to make sure they were really alone up there. They were.

DiMaggio said, "The thing I wanted to talk to you about, getting back to that, was those parties you mentioned."

Mays nodded, smiling, happy with the memory. DiMaggio figured that he was probably happy to have any memories.

"Big-ass parties," Mays said. "Was like I told you before. They was *wild*-assed parties. Uptown and downtown. When Ellis first asked me to go it was, like, okay, but why me? Then

I just figured he got tired of Richie bossing his ass all the time, maybe he just wanted to get away from the *sound* of the boy. Or maybe he wanted to talk brother to brother once in a while, even if Fresh was never too big on conversation. So we'd go to some of these parties, and it was like we'd like to have left the motherfucking *planet*. Like we was on the starship *Enterprise*. There'd be rock and high-class for-hire babes and men dressed up like women. Women dressed up like men, too. Queers all over the place, but cool queers, you know? They'd make their pass on you and you could give them an I-don't-fuckin'-think-so look, and they'd move on, no hassle. I said to Fresh one time, 'Boy, you a *long* way from Jersey City.' And Fresh said, 'You know what, Boyz? I can be invisible here. There's too much shit going on for everybody to care about every move I make.' "

Mays stopped to take a breath.

It was like he was reloading. DiMaggio was starting to wonder if he ever ran out of saliva.

"When you'd go to these parties, you ever go to the same place more than once? Was there a regular circuit?" DiMaggio asked.

Boyzie Mays leaned back, put his feet up on the back of the seat in front of him. He was wearing a purple silk shirt, matching purple slacks, and no socks to go with purple shoes that looked more like bedroom slippers. And even in the bad light, DiMaggio could see some little design Mays had razored into his hairdo, above the ear.

DiMaggio thought: Who was the first black guy to do it? Go into the barber's, sit down, and say to the guy, "A little off the top, and could you also write in my nickname over my ear?"

Out loud, Mays went through his list of famous names: a tennis player; a rock star DiMaggio was vaguely aware of; then another tennis player, French, who'd opened the best restaurant in Tribeca, at least according to Boyzie Mays, who finally said, "But I tell you who threw the best parties. Not only threw the best parties, but even started to show up at games after a while, sit in those rich-boy seats 'cross from our bench. You know the big model named Dale? Dale the bitch from the billboards a couple of years ago? In that black underwear?"

DiMaggio just waited, not wanting to throw him off while he sorted through the rocks in his head.

Mays clapped his hands. "Dale Larson!" he said, all excited. "Dale Larson threw the best parties, oh fuck yeah."

DiMaggio took out a small spiral notebook and wrote down Dale Larson, which was another cutting-edge name he was supposed to know and didn't. The last model he'd paid any attention to was Twiggy.

He'd call Joey Bernstein for an address or a phone number. Joey knew everybody.

He and Boyzie Mays took the elevator down to the street, the Thirty-third Street side, came out the employees' entrance, right next to a saloon called Charley O's. Boyzie Mays took off the wirerimmed glasses he'd been wearing and put on some big shades, like he was getting back into character. Boyzie in his cool shades and cool pose, in his purple outfit, his initials diagrammed into his hair, DiMaggio able to see the writing now. Boyzie looking bigger outside, in real life, than he had inside.

They all did.

DiMaggio said, "You think Ellis Adair raped that girl, Boyzie?"

"No."

"How come?"

"Because everybody has a line they won't cross. Real simple for some, too: Live or die. Me, I went to rehab. And when I look back, it really don't matter what got me there. *Staying,* now, that was a different matter. Once I *stayed,* that was Boyzie Mays saying, Fuck, I ain't *ready* to die yet. I look at Ellis, and look at what I know about him, and, my opinion? I don't think he crosses over the rape line. Maybe I'm full of shit. I can't really explain it. But if you're asking me, put it on the line, did he rape that girl, no, I don't think he did."

DiMaggio said, "Then how come he ran?"

Boyzie Mays looked at him over the top of his shades and said, "Maybe the boy decided the rest of the world finally crossed over the line with him."

Mays walked over to the corner of Thirty-third and Eighth, hailed a cab. DiMaggio watched the cab disappear into the uptown traffic. He was deciding whether or not to walk back to the Sherry when Donnie Fuchs, Adair and Collins's agent, came out of the employees' entrance.

The clothes were as sharp as the first time DiMaggio had met him, up in Fulton, but it was as if Donnie Fuchs, who had been such a tough guy that day in Frank Crittendon's office, had shrunk in the weeks since. His color was bad. Now the clothes, a shapeless blazer, gray T-shirt, white slacks, looked even baggier on him than they were probably supposed to.

"DiMaggio," he said, making no move to shake hands.

"Sorry about Richie, Donnie."

Fuchs said, "I was just upstairs with some of the Knicks PR people making funeral arrangements. We'd do it faster, but with a homicide and all . . ." He shrugged. It seemed to take so much out of him. DiMaggio was waiting for Fuchs to sit down on the sidewalk until he got his strength back.

DiMaggio said, "Where's the funeral going to be? Over in Jersey City someplace?"

"Saint Patrick's," Donnie Fuchs said, and managed a grin. "No disrespect intended, but do you believe that shit? Richie Collins in Saint Patrick's? There goes the neighborhood."

"Where's Ellis, Donnie?"

"I told Salter, I told the cops, I'll tell you." He sounded whiny now. "I swear, I haven't heard from the guy."

"Not even since—"

"Not even since his buddy got himself stabbed to death up in Fulton, though for the life of me I don't know what he was doing up in Fulton." There was no one around them. Fuchs lowered his voice anyway. "It true you found him?"

"No comment."

"I'm not the press."

"You're also not my friend, Donnie. No disrespect intended."

Fuchs started to go. DiMaggio put both hands on his shoulders. "Where's Ellis, Donnie?"

"Let me ask you something, DiMaggio. Whether we're friends or not. You think I want this? You think I want him away so that they can start to turn him into a fucking *suspect* here? I may not be one of nature's noblemen, but I did not get to where I am by being stupid. If I knew where he was, I would go get him with the *army.*"

"You're his agent."

Donnie Fuchs casually reached up, took DiMaggio's hands off him.

"No," he said. "I'm not. I'm like everybody except Richie, and I wasn't always so sure about Richie." Fuchs shook his head. "I'm just another butt boy," he said.

29

She had just hung up on Brian Hyland when Jimmy came into the living room. Hyland had said he wanted to take a ride over and have another chat with her.

Hyland had been in to see her that afternoon, acting very nice the whole time, but wanting to know if she had an alibi for Monday night, when Richie Collins had been murdered. Hannah told him then and told him again on the phone, she had been at her mother's house in Litchfield, with her mother's housekeeper, who house-sat when the house was empty. Sheila Carey was in Palm Beach for a couple of weeks, visiting friends. Hannah just wanted to get away from New York for a day. The tabloid shows were in a bidding war, trying to get her to do an exclusive interview. *A Current Affair* and *Inside Edition* had gone to $500,000, according to Harvey Kuhn; *Hard Copy* had decided to bypass Harvey, they just kept leaving messages on Jimmy's machine, saying they would top any bid by any other show.

It was like *The Price Is Right* a little bit, Hannah thought. Or maybe that old show—which one was it? with Door Number One and Door Number Two and Door Number Three?—where you guessed where the big prize was.

It was one of those times when she started thinking about

A.J., what he'd done to her. She loved him, of course. She was sure that he still loved her, but if he hadn't treated her that way, hadn't left her . . .

She didn't tell Brian Hyland about A.J. because she didn't talk about him anymore, even with Beth. She just told him that she watched the news shows up in Litchfield, watched *Entertainment Tonight,* said good night to Imparo, the housekeeper, a sweet woman from Colombia, slept fourteen hours, then drove back to New York the next morning and found out about Richie Collins watching television.

"Hey, I believe you, I believe you," Hyland had said just now on the phone. "I just want to ask you a few more questions on the other."

He meant the rape.

"Nothing big, nothing to worry about," Hyland said. "Could I come back in tomorrow morning? Say ten o'clock?"

Hannah knew he wasn't asking her, he was telling her.

"Whatever you say," she said.

Thinking: Even the good guys bullshitted you when they wanted something.

"Okay then," Hyland said. "I'm writing it down. Thursday at ten, Hannah Carey. And if you see your brother, tell him I'd like to ask him a few questions, too. Like I said, no big deal."

"We'll be expecting you then," Hannah said, and hung up as Jimmy came walking into the living room, fresh out of the shower, a red towel in his hand, a white one wrapped around his perfect waist. Hannah noticed he didn't just have his usual perfect bod, but a perfect tan, too. He had been out in Hollywood with Bob and Ken and the two writers they had put on her movie, standing in for Hannah. "The first half of the movie is back story, Sis," Jimmy had told her before he left. "They tell your life story, they tell the story of the players. Setting up, you know, *that* night at the end of the first two hours."

Hannah knew her life was going to be condensed to four whole hours now, instead of two.

Jimmy had jumped at the chance to go out there for a couple of weeks, round-trip first-class fare, what he said was a junior suite at the Four Seasons Hotel. "On Doheny," Jimmy'd said one night on the phone, as if that meant something to her.

Now he was back, back on Monday morning after taking the redeye, on his way out at ten o'clock at night, meeting some friends at some new hot place on Second Avenue. Hannah didn't get the name when Jimmy told her. She wondered if it ever got confusing for Jimmy, knowing all the hot new places all the time.

Maybe there was some hot button you could press on the phone to get up-to-the-minute information on hot new places.

Hot button. Hot places. That was a good one, Hannah thought. For me. She thought about running it past Jimmy, but he'd probably just give her that look like she was hopelessly square. Or hopeless.

Or just dumb.

"Hey," Jimmy said. He'd said something, Hannah hadn't heard him. "We'll be expecting who?"

"Detective Hyland."

"You talked to him already."

Hannah shrugged. "He wants to talk to me again."

"Maybe he doesn't buy your alibi."

"I don't like that word. Alibi."

"Why not? You think he came in today 'cause he missed you?"

"He doesn't think I'm a suspect for God's sake. He's just doing his job."

"Right."

"What does that mean?" she said, starting to wonder where he was going with this. "Right?"

Jimmy grinned, playing with her.

"Where'd Imparo sleep?"

"In the guest room where she always sleeps. You know Mom. If she thought she slept in her bed, she'd have to call those people that deliver mattresses right to the house, get a new one."

"The guest room in the back? You could have lit firecrackers in the front of the house, you wouldn't wake Imparo up. Remember the party we threw that time a few years ago when Mom was in West Palm? If she slept through that, she could sleep through anything."

"What's 'anything' supposed to mean?"

"You could have gone out."

Hannah got up, went into the kitchen for a Snapple. From in there she said, "If you think you're being funny, you're not."

Jimmy waited until she came back. "Sorry," he said.

"Mean it," she said, just like when they were kids.

"Mean it," he said, holding his hand up, like taking a Scout's oath. "Cross my heart and hope to have looks to die for." He started for his bedroom and Hannah said to him, "And what about you, Jim?"

He turned around, hair shiny and mussed, looking more like a teenager than ever. Grinning his cocky grin, what he liked to tell Hannah was his babe grin.

"What about me?"

"What about an alibi for you? Brian Hyland said he'd like to ask you a few questions tomorrow, too. After he talks to me. What kind of alibi do you have for Monday night?"

His face held the grin, but he stopped with his eyes. "Why would I need an alibi?" Jimmy said. "Which I have, by the way. It's one of the benefits of knowing every single bartender in town. What'd they used to say on *Cheers?* Everybody knows my name, they're always glad I came."

"You're the one who tried to beat him up on national TV

practically," she said. "Defending your sister's honor. Maybe you'd take it one step farther."

"Now who's not funny?" Jimmy Carey said.

"Me," Hannah said. "But then, I haven't been funny in a long time."

Jimmy stared at her. "Let me do the jokes around here," he said, and went to get dressed for the new hot place.

Hannah slept late, until about nine-thirty, and went to knock on Jimmy's door. But there was no need, it was still open, the red towel on the bed, the other one on the floor, the way he'd left them. Maybe he'd gotten lucky. Or maybe he'd just crashed at a friend's apartment. He'd been doing that the last month if he was out too late, not wanting to scare Hannah in the middle of the night; knowing how easy it was to give her the jumps now.

He probably had forgotten already that Brian Hyland wanted to talk to him, too.

The doormen were the same way about not giving her the jumps, even buzzing her to tell her if Jimmy was on his way up. So when the buzzer went off now, she figured it was either Jimmy coming home or Brian Hyland showing up early.

Hannah went over to the speaker near the front door and imagined Ernesto, the tiny guy from Ecuador, not much bigger than a midget, down there with Brian Hyland, if it was Brian. She wondered if Brian had to show him a badge. It would probably give Ernesto a real thrill, make him feel like he was in a movie or something.

Did everybody think of things that way?

How everything that was happening would look up on the screen?

Did everybody step back sometimes and imagine the whole thing was a movie?

Ernesto's voice, crackling over the cheap intercom system, said, "I got two women to see you here."

He stopped and she could hear him talking to them.

"One's name is Kelly."

He started to say something else, but Hannah pressed her own talk button now, cutting him off.

"I don't know anybody named Kelly."

She released her finger just as Ernesto was saying, "—Teresa Delgado."

Hannah Carey thought: Her I know.

"Send them up," she said.

"I got this address from Mr. Perez," Teresa Delgado said, giving Hannah a firm handshake, like she was practicing to be a guy. "I hope you don't mind."

Hannah said, "Come in. Please."

She was starting to feel like some kind of professional hostess. Come in. Please. To my *life*.

Teresa Delgado wore a white linen dress, and her hands, no rings, held a small white leather purse. The girl Kelly, that's how Teresa Delgado introduced her, without giving a last name, not that Hannah really cared, sat next to Teresa on the couch. The girl wore a denim skirt that showed off a lot of leg and a black tank top. Hannah didn't meet a lot of girls her size, but this one sure was.

She reminded Hannah a little bit of herself at that age, which had to be seventeen or eighteen, tops.

"I apologize again for just showing up," Teresa Delgado said, "but I felt it was time we all met. So I just came. I have a habit of doing this lately. First with Mr. Marty Perez, now with you."

"You could have called," Hannah said, not in a mean way, just telling her it would have been all right. "After reading the papers the other day, I almost called *you.*"

The girl didn't say anything.

Hannah said, "I wouldn't have turned you away is what I'm saying."

"I am not a very confident person, even if some people think I am," Teresa said. "I am better than I used to be. But still not so much, really, in the confidence department. I come from a culture where men are treated as gods by the women. These are tough habits to break. So I try to reduce my chances of rejection wherever possible."

"Even with another woman who was—"

"Yes," Teresa said, smiling at her, the smile making her pretty. "Even with such a woman as that."

Hannah looked at the Seth Thomas wall clock behind the couch. If Brian Hyland was on time, and Hannah figured he'd be the type, whenever he said he was going to call at a certain time, he called on the dot, she had about half an hour for somebody to get to the point.

Hannah said, "You said we should talk."

Teresa turned to the girl on the couch, the girl's blond hair parted in the middle in that sixties style they all were starting to wear again. "Kelly is sixteen years old," she said. "Just sixteen. She is a junior at Fulton High School." She put a hand on the girl's arm and said, "Why don't you tell Hannah the rest."

Sometimes you had to draw Hannah Carey a picture, but not now. Even Hannah, who was always a little slow on the uptake, knew what was coming next. She said to the girl, Kelly, "He raped you, too, didn't he?"

Without making a sound, without moving or changing expression, the girl started to cry, the tears just coming. Like it was a movie. What did they call them? Some kind of fake tears? Like somebody just applied them to Kelly's cheeks.

"Yes," the girl said.

Teresa said, "She read about me in the newspaper. It did not make as big an impression as when I was with Oprah the other day. She went back to the newspaper." Teresa Delgado smiled. "They had not been recycled yet. She read the story again to find out that I am from Jersey City and got my number from information. I almost changed it, all the other television shows calling me up and offering me money."

Teresa Delgado brought her small right hand up, made a fake slapping motion against her cheek. "Why am I telling you about television people? And these vulgar people from the movies?"

Vulgar? Hannah thought.

Kelly said, "I watch *Oprah* every day. You can find out some very cool things. I heard her start talking, and it was so awesome, and a little weird. She was talking about *exactly* what I wanted someone to be talking about. It's like when you turn on QVC, you know? The shopping network? And you've been thinking about buying this one necklace or whatever, and there it *is!*"

"Anyway," Teresa said, continuing, "I decided we should come here this morning. I thought it would be appropriate to form our own support group."

"Support group," Hannah echoed.

"It will be explained when you hear," Teresa said.

"Why not the police?" Hannah said, and felt stupid as soon as she did.

"She is a girl," Teresa Delgado said, taking a Kleenex from out of her purse and handing it to Kelly. "You are a woman. I am a woman. It took you a year to come forward, and it took me all these years."

"I'm sorry," Hannah said, comfortable with that one, as always.

"Don't be," Teresa said. "Don't be sorry. They always want

us to be sorry. For something. For everything." Softly she said, "Don't they?"

Hannah said, "Yes."

Teresa said, "When they don't want us to be afraid anymore and they don't want us to be guilty, they want us to be sorry. Are you a Catholic, Hannah?"

"No."

"But you know of the Holy Trinity?"

"Father, Son, Holy Ghost," Hannah said quickly. Was it still the Holy Ghost? Or was it the Holy Spirit? Hannah seemed to remember there had been some kind of change, she noticed it at a wedding one time.

"Well, there is a different Trinity for women like us, maybe all women," Teresa said. "When we bless ourselves, genuflecting before men, it should be in the name of fear and then in the name of the guilt and finally in the name of being sorry. I was raped and you were raped and she was raped."

Teresa Delgado was small, but she was a tough little bird.

"We are the ones violated," Teresa said, picking up a little steam, "but as soon as that is over, we begin to violate ourselves. Violate our confidence. Our dignity. Our self-worth."

Hannah couldn't help thinking she should have had Teresa Delgado around when it was time to write her little speech at the Plaza. It was crazy, getting a thought like that. But there it was, once again like it was up on the screen. Hannah could see herself really bowling them over with words like Teresa's.

Maybe when this was all over, she could have Teresa sit down with the screenwriter. Or meet Bob and Ken. Especially Bob. Just to show her they weren't all vulgar . . .

She heard Teresa saying, "Hannah? I feel like I lost you there. Maybe it sounded like I was making a speech?"

"No," Hannah said, "no, that's not it at all. I was just thinking that you were saying things that are inside me, I just can't ever find the right words for."

"So you understand why Kelly did not go to her mother or her father or the police?"

Hannah said, "I don't want to rush you, but there's a Fulton policeman coming here in a few minutes to talk about Richie Collins."

Kelly turned to Teresa, eyes wide.

"No!" she said, a gasp, really. "My father knows every policeman in that town. They'll *tell!*"

Teresa Delgado said, "We will be gone before he comes, do not worry. But since I think we are going to be friends here, maybe you should tell Hannah who your father is."

The girl said, "Frank Crittendon. You know who he is, right?"

Hannah, trying not to act floored, said, "The general manager of the Knicks."

"As you can see, it is a problem," Teresa Delgado said. "But not as big as the other."

Now Hannah felt like someone had to draw her a picture.

Kelly Crittendon sighed. "Teresa says I can tell. So here goes." She looked at Teresa, who smiled and nodded, like, go ahead. "Richie raped me Monday afternoon."

Hannah said, "This Monday—?"

"This Monday," Teresa Delgado said.

"Jesus Christ," Hannah Carey said.

"Pray for us," Teresa Delgado said.

Teresa told Kelly to tell it the same way she had at breakfast.

Kelly Crittendon said she felt like she had known Richie Collins her whole life. "Even if it was only half."

She had always looked older than her real age. Been bigger than the other girls. The first to get a chest. She was a tomboy, ball-girling for the Knicks in training camp from the time she was twelve.

Richie noticed her even then.

The guys at school, they never noticed her.

Kelly said, "We all knew my dad wanted a boy. I mean, Mom she's, like, even taller than me, when you put her next to Dad, they look sillier together than Billy Joel and Christie looked before, you know, they split up. She jokes all the time that Dad only married her so they could breed a shooting guard. So it's like I was always expected to not just do boy things, but like them. You know? But my secret was, I only did the stuff to be *around* boys. Like: I was noticing them way before they were noticing me. Wanting them to notice me in the worst way. But nobody did. Till Richie."

By the time she was in her teens, he flirted with her constantly. The October before this one—my October with the Knicks, Hannah thought—he had her start calling him "Uncle Rich." That was for her father's benefit.

It had reached the point, though, where both Richie and Kelly knew he wanted to be more than her uncle. And she wanted the same thing.

She started thinking about him all the time, all during that season. She couldn't go to all the games; they finished up too late and her father usually had something to do afterward, some meeting with the coach or a late dinner in the city that wouldn't even start until around midnight. Sometimes he'd even stay over at the Regency Hotel on Park Avenue, where the team rested up in the afternoons before home games.

So she didn't come too much, but when she did, it wasn't about seeing the games. Just Richie Collins. After the game, she'd wait an hour in the hall, like she was waiting for Frank Crittendon to collect her. But she was waiting to say hello to "Uncle

Rich," have him give her a little kiss on the cheek, nobody noticing the squeeze he'd sometimes give her, too.

On game nights, she said, then laughed and said most of the time her father was in a world of his own, so he didn't notice the clothes she'd wear to the games, clothes that didn't just get looks from Richie Collins, but all the players after a while.

Only Richie, though, looked at her the way you look at something you can *have,* Kelly Crittendon said.

She said, " 'One of these days, little girl,' he'd say. And I'd go, 'One of these days *what?*' And he'd go, 'One of these days, you're going to have to fight me off.' "

Out of nowhere, she started to cry again. Hannah just sat there, not knowing what to do for her. Teresa Delgado took out another Kleenex, wiped Kelly Crittendon's tears herself this time, saying, "He never changed."

Then she added, "Until he died."

Six months before, in the spring, before the Knicks' last regular season game, Kelly had told her father she would meet him at the game, just leave her ticket for her; she'd take the train in from Fulton, where Frank Crittendon had bought his dream house. It was a Saturday. Kelly took the train, got a cab at Grand Central, and took it to the Regency, arriving there right after the Knicks' morning practice. Getting his room number had been easy. Her father was a meticulous man, "a real fuddy-duddy about detail stuff." There was always an itinerary in his briefcase.

She wore what she would wear to the game: this cool hot-yellow shirt over black tights. Heels.

She had waited as long as she could.

She had convinced herself that Richie Collins—ten years older? more? so what, ten years was nothing—wanted her as much as she wanted him. She was sure that he sensed this thing that had been growing between them. So Kelly did what she had been dreaming about doing for more than a year, a year that seemed like fifteen lifetimes to a fifteen-year-old: She knocked on Richie Collins's door.

Kelly: "I was on the pill. I wasn't a virgin anymore. I'd, well, like I'd practiced doing it with this guy Kenny, the best player on the Fulton basketball team. All my life, I'd heard Daddy and everybody else make *practicing* something sound like a sacrament. I figured I'd better practice sex, too, if I didn't want to look like a jerk."

Looking at Hannah and Teresa for approval.

Teresa Delgado said, "We are willing to do anything for them."

Hannah jumped in for the first time, surprising herself. She said, "Anything and everything," not thinking about Teresa or this girl, knowing she was talking about herself.

Teresa said, "We want to make them happy and *so* proud."

Richie wasn't even surprised to see her, Kelly said. Or if he was surprised, he was too cool, too grown-up, to show it.

He had a suite.

Kelly: "We didn't even make it to the living room. I could see this big fruit basket in there, the biggest I'd ever seen. But we did it right there. Standing up."

Her eyes got very big, and Hannah thought she might cry again.

Kelly: "It wasn't . . . I had thought about how it would be all different from this. But I didn't even get a chance to take my blouse off. Richie just kept saying we'd waited long enough. He said he *needed* me. Need you, baby. Need you, baby. I think back, and that's all I can remember him saying."

After that first time, they decided it was too risky to meet at the hotel, especially with the play-offs coming up and the whole city turning up the lights on the Knicks. So they began meeting at his apartment.

Then, way too soon for Kelly, so soon she couldn't believe it, the season was over. The whole rest of her life, she said, the season seemed to go on forever.

Now she would have done anything to get another month.

Frank Crittendon, after taking care of the NBA draft, took his family to their summer home on Cape Cod. Richie Collins, because of his sneaker contract, went off to conduct basketball clinics in Europe and Asia. Promising to see Kelly in September.

Kelly: "He asked me if I'd ever heard of that song 'See You in September.' He said it was like him. I asked him what he meant and he said, 'An oldie but a goodie.' He said the song was from way back there in the fifties."

Teresa gave out this little gasp. "He told me the same thing that summer," she said. "About that same song." Hannah noticed it was the first time she had heard an accent from her, *told* sounding like *toll,* like she was talking about paying a toll.

When training camp started, Richie and Kelly started up again. It still seemed so reckless to her, so wicked, sneaking around right under her father's nose. She knew he would kill her if he found out. "Kill me and then kill Richie," she said.

But she couldn't help herself.

Kelly: "It's like something Miss . . . like *Teresa* said in the papers, about how the heart knows what the heart knows. I read that and it was like, wow. I mean, I had only read the story the first time, going, like, Oh, here's somebody Richie fucked over the way he fucked me over."

Hannah couldn't help but notice how easily the word came out of the girl's mouth, the girl just sixteen, this girl who had given up her virginity, practiced, just to make herself ready for Richie Collins.

It was right after training camp started that he started asking about her girlfriends.

Kelly would bring friends to watch practice with her. He'd stop sometimes and make faces at them, make them giggle. Then later, when they were together, he'd say to Kelly, "Who was *that?*" When Kelly would pout, he'd laugh it off, saying, "What's this, my baby girl is jealous?" And then drop it for a couple of days.

It became obvious to her that Richie Collins wanted to have sex with Kelly and another girl.

Kelly: "He said we could get all dressed up first, like a prom. He'd get some champagne. He said it would be the most fun I'd ever have. If we could just find the right girl to fill out the ménage à trois. When he said it the first time, I acted like I knew exactly what he was talking about. Then I had to go look it up."

She said no. He kept at her, making fun of her, saying maybe he was wrong about her. Maybe she was too young. Making it sound like being too young was being too fat or something. But the thought of getting naked, *doing it,* with another girl, a friend, was dirty. Gross.

Even after some of the things Richie had already made her do in bed. And in his car. One time in the locker room after everybody was gone.

On the *court.*

She couldn't make herself do it with another girl.

He told her he didn't want to see her anymore if she didn't want to be a good sport.

One Saturday morning, though, she knew he was doing an autograph session at a sports shop in Fulton. She went over there and waited and made up with him. That was the day the reporter showed up, Kelly said. Richie told her about it after.

Hannah perked up on that one.

"Do you happen to remember the reporter's name?"

"Sure. The same one Teresa talked to. Mr. Perez."

Hannah said, "He was waiting for Richie outside that sports shop?" She looked at Teresa Delgado. "I'm sorry, but I didn't know he and Richie were so close."

"You don't trust him?" Teresa said.

"I sort of did," Hannah said. "But now I'm not so sure." She'd have to talk about this one with Jimmy, if he could ever find his way home. "He certainly does seem to get around, though."

Teresa said, "I'm not sure I follow," and Hannah said, "I just thought he was on my side more than their side is all."

"I'm sorry," Hannah said now to Kelly. "Please go ahead. I've gotten used to everything being about *me* all the time."

Richie and Kelly were together that Saturday in Fulton, once Richie had his meeting with Marty Perez. It was their last time, she said. Right after the Knicks broke training camp and went back to New York to get ready for the start of the season "Right after you," she said to Hannah, she found out that Richie Collins had been calling one of her friends behind her back.

Kelly: "She's a sophomore. Richie kept telling her I was too *old* for him. After he'd kept telling me I was too young to do it with him and another girl. Nice, huh?"

Kelly's girlfriend, Emma, finally told Richie that if he called her again, she was going to tell her parents; Emma said she would have done it the first time he called, except that she was afraid it would get Kelly in trouble.

When Kelly found out, she called Richie in New York. He said he didn't have time to talk to her, but maybe they could get together when he came up to clean out his condominium in Fulton.

They agreed to meet after school. Her last class was Computers, she got out at two-thirty. It left her enough time to go home and change out of her school clothes. Even after the way he had hurt her, she said, and the way he had tried to use her and tried to two-time her, Kelly Crittendon still wanted to look nice for him.

She put on a summer dress she'd bought for him but never got a chance to wear.

She parked where he always had her park, in this guest lot down the hill from his house, the area secluded by trees and some tennis courts. She remembered checking herself in the mirror one last time. She had even borrowed this neat headband from Emma, she said, not telling Emma why she needed it.

Kelly: "He was smiling when he answered the door. Like, saying, I'm the old Richie. He looked at me the way he did the first time, at the hotel. And then he grabbed me the same way he did that day. I thought he was just kidding around at first, giving me a fooling-around hug, just to let me know he wasn't really mad. Like, not even thinking that *I* was the one who was supposed to be pissed at *him*. Then he wouldn't let go. So I start to go, 'No, no, no, we have to talk.' And Richie goes, 'If it's about that bitch Emma, you've got it all wrong, she was the one chasing after me.' So I go, 'Emma isn't like that.' Trying to get him *off* me for a second. But then Richie goes, 'You're *all* like that.' Still running his hands all over me. I asked him what *that* was supposed to mean and he goes, 'You all want it.' Now he had his hands, like, under my dress, trying to see if I had panties on."

Kelly stopped, not looking at either one of them, just fixed on her hands, clenched there in her lap.

Kelly: "He liked me not to, you know, wear any. So when he found out I was, he gave me this creepy look. Scaring me. He went, 'Oh, we're going to play Miss Hard to Get all of a sudden?' I was crying by then, saying, 'I want to *talk,* please, can't we talk?' And he just goes, 'Later.' And then . . . then . . . he was just *on* me, crazylike, crazier than he ever was when we'd done it, on the living room floor. There was some game show on the TV. I don't even know why I know that. A game show."

Teresa Delgado said to Hannah, "Was a ball game for me. What about you?" Hannah said she didn't remember the TV being on when they got there, just later, when they were both through with her and Richie was jerking off watching the porno movie.

Hannah was proud of herself, using the guy language to tell Teresa Delgado about it. "The jerk-off jerking off," she said. Maybe she could get off good ones when it was just women around.

Richie Collins raped her there in the living room. Kelly said she never screamed. "I was still more afraid of somebody finding me with him than I was of him doing what he did to me." When it was over, he left her there on the floor and went to take a shower, saying, "Let's face it, kid, breaking up is hard to do."

He stood over her, naked, grinning, saying, "Think of it as one more oldie but goodie."

Kelly Crittendon, when she got there in her story, stood up, went to use Jimmy's bathroom. When she came back, her eyes were red and she'd applied fresh lipstick. Hannah thought the lipstick made her look like a little girl playing grown-up. But she was grown-up enough to finish telling what she had come there to tell.

Kelly: "As soon as he left the room, I ran. I remembered that Mom was in the city. I figured my dad wouldn't be home. I took a shower and stuffed my dress in a garbage bag and took it down to the garage. I don't know, I thought if the dress was gone, if I didn't have it anymore, then maybe it didn't happen. Or wasn't as bad as I thought. Then I took another shower and went to my room and went to sleep. When I woke up, nobody was home yet. That was when I decided I wanted to hurt him back."

She decided she would wait until dark and bust up his car. Windows. Windshield. Anything, she said, that would break.

She waited until ten o'clock. When they had agreed to meet, Richie said it had to be in the afternoon, he had to meet with somebody later on.

Hannah asked, "Did he say who?" Kelly shook her head. "He just told me he was going to stay overnight and drive back into the city in the morning for practice."

When she went back to the house—"It's in this development or whatever called Fulton Crest," she said—she parked in the same place and started up the steps to where his garage was, about fifty yards from the front door. You had to go past the front door to get there.

She never got to the garage. The front door opened suddenly. Kelly was sure it was him, sure if he saw her he would chase her and catch her and bring her back and rape her again.

She hid in the bushes.

Kelly said, "But it wasn't Richie who came out."

Hannah said, "Another woman?"

Kelly Crittendon gave her a funny look.

"It was my father."

"Your father was there the night Richie was . . . ?" Hannah stopped.

Teresa Delgado nodded slowly and said, "Yes."

Kelly waited in the bushes until she heard her father's car pull away. Then, confused, she forgot about Richie's car and drove around for a couple of hours before going home. Her parents were asleep when she got there. She didn't hear about Richie's death until later in the day, in the car on her way home from school. Her father had not mentioned anything about the night before. She had not asked him about it.

Hannah said, "So you don't know if your father is the one."

Kelly looked at her, then shook her head.

"We don't any of us know," Teresa Delgado said.

Somehow, the thought comforted Hannah. She wasn't the only one who needed an alibi all of a sudden. She couldn't wait to see Jimmy's face.

He thought he knew everything, but he was barely watching the same movie.

30

His father said it to him one day when they were waiting at the Commack station, so Tony DiMaggio could take the train to another bus, start another tour with Ralph Flanagan. His father always waited until a few minutes before he left so he didn't have to really wear himself out with a father-son chat.

"Rule number one of life," Tony DiMaggio said. "You can't make this shit up."

DiMaggio started to ask him, Make *what* up, but his father wasn't through.

"Just remember what I'm telling you," his father said, acting as if he were passing on the secret of life. "Don't go out in the world looking for logic, kid. For things to *follow.* You follow? This isn't the movies or a good book. Life doesn't *follow.*"

DiMaggio thought about that when it was all over, how they had all gone along, gone along, then everything happened at the end. Like basketball. People saying everything happened in the last two minutes.

He thought about that and how he never thought to ask anybody the right question.

Not even knowing there was one.

DiMaggio: star investigator.

He just picked up the phone and took a shot, dialed the number that Joey gave him, just saying, "I'd like to speak to Dale please," when the guy answered.

"Out of the country."

"When do you expect her back?"

"Out of the country indefinitely. You're some kind of smart guy, right?"

He thought the guy was just copping an attitude.

"How about if I just leave a message?"

The guy said, "Suit yourself."

DiMaggio left his name, the phone number at the Sherry, his room number. Before the house guy hung up, DiMaggio had a flash. "Hey, since Dale isn't there, can I speak to Ellis, please?"

As a joke.

The house guy hung up on him.

DiMaggio thought you could look at it two ways. The guy just had an attitude and got tired of talking to him. DiMaggio could have that effect on people. And besides, the guy had no intention of giving Dale Larson the message anyway.

Or he got nervous.

Look on the bright side.

Maybe in the morning he would take a walk over to the address on Fifth, somewhere up in the seventies, Joey had given him.

For fun.

He spread out all his notes, all his research, on the floor, the way he used to do with Dowd. After doing this kind of work all this time, DiMaggio was always surprised at how random an investigation could feel, like he was all over the lot. Even with that, he always kept his research and notes organized: notebooks, newspaper clippings, files, his yellow legal pads, videocassettes, phone records. And on top of every item was a synopsis, with the most interesting stuff highlighted. It was looking through one of his Boyzie Mays notebooks that he had remembered about the wild-assed parties.

DiMaggio even carried a blackboard with him, making diagrams sometimes, like he was making some kind of presentation to the goddamn board of directors.

He usually got efficient like this when he felt the whole thing getting away from him. Which is the way he had felt since they found Richie Collins.

He sat in the middle of all this shit and wondered if there was an answer for him somewhere. Or better questions.

He read and reread Marty Perez's column about Teresa Delgado, trying to match up details of her story with what he knew about Hannah Carey's. And reread the notes from his dinner with Hannah.

And went over what he had from Salter and Crittendon and Boyzie Mays and A. J. Fine.

And all the Lisas.

He would stop sometimes to soak his hands, bowls on each side of him, one for each hand, listening to David Benoit play. DiMaggio tried to keep his mind on the case, stay on the rape, not worry so much about Richie Collins all the time. But he saw Benoit and wondered if he ever woke up with any pain. What he would do the first time it happened to him, the way it happened every morning to DiMaggio.

Every morning of his goddamn life, starting with Advil.

He dried his hands, emptied the bowl, poured himself a glass of Scotch. He allowed himself one sometimes, when he was working at night. He told himself it was strictly medicinal, just to take the edge off.

DiMaggio went back to the Hyland notes from the other night, right before he found Richie Collins.

There it was again.

" 'Runaround Sue,' " DiMaggio said in the suite, like he was making a request to himself. He went over to the piano, knowing the best thing was to give his fingers a rest, but playing around, trying to come up with some kind of rocking start that would have pleased Dion and the boys.

" 'Here's the moral of the story from a guy who knows,' " he sang, smiling, knowing how awful he sounded. But trying to picture Hannah Carey, drunk, singing it at Mulligan's in New Canaan, the way Hyland said she had, before she got herself raped that night.

Would she remember if he asked her? She said she didn't have blackouts, but she also said she didn't remember singing, another part of the evening she'd conveniently forgotten. She was either lying about the blackouts or lying about the blanks in her memory. If she was lying there, DiMaggio thought, where else?

" 'Sue goooooes out with other guys—' "

He knew they could probably hear him in the hall. Fuck it, it was his suite.

Didn't they understand how a star investigator worked?

It was nine o'clock when he finished cleaning up the room. He called down to the concierge and told him to have the rental car brought up from the garage around the corner.

It was Friday night at Mulligan's: the restaurant to the right, and bright, as you came in the front door; the saloon part, much darker and louder, to the left, with its golf decor; high tables filled with people and the bar jammed; beyond the bar, another small eating area, and right before that, the small bandstand area, empty, at least for now. It had been a Saturday night for Hannah and Richie and Ellis a year ago.

How many nights had he now spent in this place? And in other places like it?

How many nights looking for somebody who would remember that night better than Hannah did?

He sat at the end of the bar near the kitchen, the only seat he could find, and ordered a beer from a good-looking kid, hair slicked back, wearing a white shirt and flowery tie. No Bermuda shorts. DiMaggio figured he would wait for the place to think a little, quiet down, and ask for the thousandth time if anybody had been around that night.

Hyland said it had been like pulling teeth, even for him, and he seemed to know everybody in the whole area. It wasn't that they didn't want to cooperate, he said, it was that none of these places wanted the publicity. Everybody had gotten a thrill at the start, but now they didn't want the cops around anymore, the press, the TV cameras, asking questions about a rape that happened a year ago.

"Why they think a rape investigation is bad for business is beyond me," Hyland had said.

DiMaggio had told him, "People can be so funny."

Now he sat and drank his beer, feeling out of place as usual, as if they knew he was an outsider, sitting there at the end of the bar in his blue suit. Or maybe the suit wasn't the problem. Maybe it was just a prop and the real problem was that DiMaggio was permanently out of place.

Somebody had taken the rock and roll off the sound system and snuck Garland in there, in a duet with Streisand, Garland singing "Get Happy" while Streisand belted out "Happy Days Are Here Again." DiMaggio was old enough to remember them doing it on Garland's old Sunday-night television show on CBS, the one show he watched with his mother.

She loved Judy Garland.

DiMaggio's mother would say, "She's had a very hard life, you know."

He didn't know whether it was the song taking him back there or just the memory of the Sunday nights in the living room in Commack, watching with his mother before she would pass out on the couch and he could take the lit cigarette out of her hand and shut the set off and cover her and go to bed himself.

She used to sing in bars.

One of the cops from the neighborhood told him. Not somebody who hit on her, but somebody DiMaggio liked, a guy named Tommy Duggan, who'd coached him one season in Little League.

DiMaggio was waiting for the train one day. He'd ride it into the city when he was a teenager, she wouldn't even notice he was gone, going into Manhattan like Boyzie Mays coming up from Maryland, hitting some of the jazz clubs, already looking older than he really was, acting older. He was sitting there at the Commack station waiting, always good at waiting, trying to make his voice sound like Louis Armstrong singing "All of Me" on one of his father's albums, not knowing anyone was there.

DiMaggio was always so good at being alone, it was like he practiced.

And from behind him, he heard a voice, Duggan's as it turned out, say, "You sure didn't get it from your mother, kid."

He saw himself as a kid, startled, turning around and then relaxing when he saw it was Duggan.

"Didn't get what?"

"Your voice."

"What's that got to do with Mom?"

Duggan was surprised.

"You never heard your mother sing? Around the house or anything?"

"Mom doesn't sing around the house."

Which was true. She drank around the house and looked sad around the house. She smoked all the time, from the time she woke up until he took the cigarette out of her hand. He heard her crying.

She never sang for him.

Duggan said, "Hey, kid, I didn't mean anything by it. I was just talkin'. But nothin' for nothin', she gets up sometimes over to the Elms, sings 'Over the Rainbow' and makes half the joint start cryin'."

Duggan gave him another look. "She really never sang for you?"

The kid shook his head, and then the train came and in Mulligan's now, a million years later, he tried to remember if it was before or after he found her that morning, after the rape. If she ever sang after that . . .

He wondered if his mother sang that night. Hannah Carey sang "Runaround Sue." What song would his mother have chosen . . .

At the bar, a woman's voice said, "That's some conversation you're having there, fella."

DiMaggio turned. She had auburn hair, cut short. Maybe it was lighter than auburn, it was hard to tell at Mulligan's. She also had a lot of freckles and a great smile.

DiMaggio smiled back and felt like he was off the case all of a sudden.

"I didn't know I was having a conversation," he said.

"Oh yeah, you were." She put a hand out. "I'm Ellen."

He hesitated out of habit, because of his hands. It was long enough to stop her smile. DiMaggio shook her hand.

Not too bad.

"DiMaggio."

"You're kidding."

"Sometimes," he said, "I wish."

"You have a first name maybe?"

He told her.

"Ellen Harper," she said. The smile was back. "You better watch it, before long I'll be spilling my guts and telling you what I do for a living."

"So what do you do for a living?"

"I'm a teacher. High school."

"Around here?"

"Fulton High. What about you?"

"You got a few minutes?"

Ellen Harper said, "Until the tour bus leaves."

He noticed a couple of empty tables behind her in the back of Mulligan's. "Would you like to go sit down?"

She stood up. She was wearing a white T-shirt with some kind of short-sleeved denim vest over it and tight jeans. He watched her hands as she reached for her beer and the change in front of her on the bar. No rings.

"Single," she said casually.

"Single teacher Ellen Harper," DiMaggio said. "Pretty."

"Pretty worn out," she said. "I have just spent an entire evening of my life grading blue books. It was a spot quiz. I asked them to give me a report on the last book or magazine they read that had nothing to do with schoolwork. You want to know how many *Spin* magazine reviews I got?"

DiMaggio said, "How old am I if I don't know what *Spin* is?"

"Old enough to officially buy me a drink. A beer would be nice. Nice quiet beer. The Knicks have once again departed from Fairfield County. Rapists and nonrapists alike. Now I'm going to sit down with you, but you have to promise to talk."

"I'll talk," he said. "I'll talk."

They sat in the corner, DiMaggio in a big leather chair that looked like it belonged in somebody's living room. He took off his jacket, ordered another beer, and told Ellen Harper what he did for a living, what he was working on, what he was doing in Mulligan's.

"Nothing like this has ever happened around here," she said. "It's only supposed to happen on Court TV."

She said, "I mean, we expect the usual training-camp craziness and the high school girls getting hysterical over some of the players. I mean, you try to warn them every year, and it's still like they've just been let out of the convent or something. But this year, what's the woman's name?"

"Hannah Carey."

"But with her yelling rape, even after the fact, and now the murder, I officially feel like we're not in Kansas anymore, Toto." She sipped some beer. Her hands were small, he saw, and didn't seem to go with the rest of her, the long elegant length of her, built like a high school girl herself in her T-shirt and tight jeans. There was a white line where her wedding ring could have gone once, ring finger, left hand.

"You mind if I do a little work?" DiMaggio said.

"A little."

"Last year, were you around when the Knicks were around?"

"Oh sure. I'm a townie lifer. Grew up in New Canaan, went to the Congregational Church as a kid. Country Club of New Canaan. New Canaan High. The whole deal. I was married here. I was divorced here, and don't even bother asking."

"What I shouldn't bother asking, what was that going to be exactly?"

"I got the dog, he got the intern from Duke. There, you've got all the important details." Ellen Harper reached inside the vest and came out with a pack of Marlboro Lights. "You mind if I smoke? I still give myself a couple a day so I don't turn into a serial killer."

He smiled at her again. He was surprised how easy that was. "In that case, be my guest."

She blew some smoke toward the ceiling and said, "I've tried to leave a few times. But somehow I always come back. I just spent most of the summer in California, as a matter of fact. Trying to finish a *novel.*" She leaned on *novel* and made it sound like the most solemn work imaginable, as a way of mocking herself.

DiMaggio liked her already, even if she did move the conversation around so much he wanted to put her up against Boyzie Mays for the title.

"Anyway," she said, "I guess this is sort of the long way around—"

DiMaggio said, "Really?"

"Very funny. The bottom line is, I'm used to seeing this whole area make an ass of its collective self, but never ever the way it does over these basketball players."

"You used to see them in here?"

"All the time. In fact, I was here the night of all the allegedness. I mean, I was here early. It felt like the whole team was here that night, as a matter of fact. I watched some of the mating rituals, I saw the fight with A. J. Fine—"

DiMaggio said, "The fight?"

"In the parking lot. Between Hannah and A. J. Fine. I just happened to be walking in."

DiMaggio, trying not to be too eager, said, "Why don't you tell me about the fight."

She said that when the main lot at Mulligan's was full, there was this parking garage right next door, maybe he'd noticed it? And when *that* was full, when the place was really jumping, there was a parking garage across the street, down from the Baptist Church. She had to use that one that night. She usually didn't even lock the car—"Do you care about this?"—but she locked it when she parked across the street. She had gone back to do that, and when she came across the street the second time, she saw A. J. Fine and Hannah Carey at the bottom of the hill, at the entrance to the other parking garage.

"You knew who Fine was?"

"Remember where you are," she said. "I'm surprised that when these guys came in, they didn't introduce them over some PA system, like they do for the real games."

"You hear what they were arguing about?"

"No," she said. "But it all looked pretty dramatic. She seemed real upset. And she was crying, I could tell that from the front door. I felt kind of lousy even stopping to watch, you know? Like I was one of the local swivelheads. But it was hard not to notice them. They're a couple of pretty impressive specimens."

DiMaggio signaled for a couple more beers.

Ellen Harper said, "Fine eventually got her settled down, and the next thing I know they drove off."

"But she was back later, right?"

"Singing. It was one of those nights when everybody got into a big golden oldies thing. I'm trying to remember what she sang exactly because it brought the house down—"

DiMaggio said, " 'Runaround Sue.' "

She said, "How'd you know?"

"I'm a trained investigator."

"Cheers," she said, and picked up her fresh bottle of beer, not even bothering with a glass.

"You never told any of this to the police."

"I told you, I just got back from California. I didn't really follow the case out there, but isn't the big deal now the Collins murder?"

"It's a big deal," he said. "But I'm still working on the other."

"You said the Knicks hired you. But it's more than that with you, isn't it?"

"I want to know," he said.

Ellen Harper said, "Let me get this straight: I'm the only person who saw them leave together?"

"Correct."

"You talked to Fine?"

"He failed to mention it."

"He lied."

"That's another way of putting it."

"Hannah Carey?"

"She's said from the start there are gaps in her memory."

"Oh," Ellen Harper said.

He thought about Fine, sitting there at the Fulton Luncheonette like the Ivy League absentminded professor, acting like he was above the crowd.

Bullshitting him.

Ellen said, "You're having another one of those conversations with yourself." She was leaning forward, her pretty face cupped by the tiny little-girl hands, looking at him with big solemn gray eyes.

She said, "What I told you, it's important, isn't it?"

"It might be."

"You're out of here?"

"After we finish our beers."

"How would you like to buy a girl dinner sometime?"

Where was she a month ago?

He said, "How about two dinners?"

"Two?"

"I believe in long-term contracts."

"See how much better this works when you're not just talking to yourself all the time?" He took his notebook out and she gave him her phone numbers, home and at work. They went outside. Her car was right by the front door. "Call me tomorrow?" she said.

"Twice."

She backed out. Single pretty teacher Ellen Harper. The car was out front, on the street. His old Orvis duffel bag with his address book was in the backseat. He looked up A. J. Fine. He had an apartment at the Westchester Country Club. DiMaggio remembered him saying he liked it there because it was halfway between Fulton and the city.

It was right on his way home. Why not? DiMaggio thought. Just go ring the doorbell and wake the bastard up.

31

Marty looked at the fax, not believing it.

It was the registration of the red Nissan, the one his friend at the Seventeenth Precinct had gotten him from the Department of Motor Vehicles in Norwalk, the closest one to Fulton. The cop owed Marty a favor. He was married, but he had this Hunter College girl on the side. The guy had called him about six months ago, desperate, thinking he was losing his *chula* girl, telling Marty he needed Streisand tickets at the Garden.

Marty had covered it for him; it was how you did business, or stayed in business, especially in New York, everybody being on the take, one way or another.

"No tengo chavos," Marty said now in his apartment.

Who needed money when people all over town still owed him favors? Who needed money when you still had the juice? Now he had the girl's registration on the coffee table and the clippings on her family.

Still not believing it. He had waited until four o'clock that day at Fulton High, waiting for her to come collect the car. When he couldn't wait anymore, because of all the goddamn typing waiting for him in the city, he'd copied down the license plate and left. Maybe she was at cheerleading practice. Or getting into the

kind of field-hockey outfit that would have made Richie Collins
faint. Then the cop ran the plate for him, and Marty finally remembered that he had the girl on tape.

He walked over to the television set and hit Play. He'd almost
forgotten he had the cassette, because he forgot even important
shit now. But it was in a stack on his desk. He must have taken
it out of the camcorder when he got back from Fulton that Saturday afternoon. The angle was a little off, and the focus, which
always happened when he had to shoot through a window, especially a car window. There they were anyway, Richie Collins
and the girl, at the Fulton Sports Shop.

The young girl, the *joven,* making that pouty face.

Richie doing come-to-daddy.

Then the girl driving off, happy, knowing Richie would have
something for her later.

Kelly Crittendon.

Frank Crittendon's daughter.

¿Qué haces?

Now what?

He had that nervous feeling, good nervous, like he did in the
old days when he knew he had something first. Solid didn't matter the way it used to, just being first. In the old days, Marty
knew, he would have called Cantor, would have called around
until he found him, used the beeper number if he had to. And
when the phone rang, Cantor calling back right away, he was so
fucking neurotic, Marty would have played it cute with him, even
though both of them knew that even Marty Perez, the king of the
bullshitters, never beeped the editor of the paper unless it was
important. Unless he had something. Then they would have
arranged to meet at the office no matter what time it was—what
was it now? a few minutes past midnight?—and decided whether
it was worth it to take a run at the last edition. Or hold the last
edition. And decided it was worth it, you bet your ass it was

worth it, Cantor calmly orchestrating everything like the day was just starting, redoing the front page. Cantor would have gotten the Knicks guy out of bed, or out of the bar, had him track down Crittendon and the girl, and he would have gotten the production guys in to see how the video would reproduce for the front page.

The two of them would have turned Cantor's office into the war room, everything happening in there, Marty banging away at Cantor's computer, his back to the room, Cantor interrupting him only occasionally, only if it was important, the rest of the time just saying, "Type, Type" every time Marty would ask him how it was going.

Or saying, "How close?"

Marty started to get hot, just thinking about it.

So how come he hadn't called Cantor yet?

Marty Perez knew the answer.

It was a television piece. It was one of his lucky-shot television pieces, the kind of shot the spic kids called a *chivo* on the playgrounds. *"¡Quiero chivo!"* they would yell when you would pull some shot out of your ass and make it. Ellis Adair and Richie Collins, they probably called it a prayer. Now Marty had the *chivo* prayer shot right in front of him, on tape, not just some high school girl coming on to Richie Collins, but the general manager's daughter. Jesus, he could see the promos already, the little teases all day on Channel 2, with Kelly Crittendon, sixteen years old, brushing up against Collins, nearly humping him against the side of the Jeep.

Marty thought: I've got my own little Amy Fisher for *Chronicle*.

Not solid, but definitely first.

The kid with Collins didn't prove anything, Marty knew that. It didn't solve anything. But solving shit, maybe that was for the old days, too. The tabloids fighting for the smallest piece of dirt, rooting around like little mongrel dogs, *sato* dogs, through garbage cans, had changed everything. Loosened everything up. Be first, and be loudest. Everybody just assumed that the headline, the come-on, was supposed to be bigger than the story. Let the little clerks over at the *Times* worry about doing it the way they were taught in journalism school. The guys who lasted, the big-balls guys, knew how to sell the story.

Knew how to make it be about *them*.

Geraldo, when he was running around for Channel 7, even breaking stories, he couldn't carry Marty's notebook. But it didn't matter, because of television. Now he had one of those Oprah shows, syndication money out the ass.

Marty sat there and couldn't get Amy Fisher out of his mind.

He kept adding it all up, adding the high school girl into everything that started with the rape and now included a murder. So what if his little tape didn't prove anything except Richie Collins was probably doing the boss's daughter? Marty was the one putting the Lolita angle into it.

People would eat it up.

He picked up the phone, but not to call Michael Cantor. Marty punched out the number he had for Frank Crittendon in Fulton, got his machine, saying he'd be in the city until the Knicks opener on Saturday night.

That meant the Regency.

It was twelve-fifteen Saturday morning.

Marty went over to the liquor cabinet, got out the Don Q, fixed himself a good dark one, just a splash of tonic, no fruit, a little ice. He looked at the plaques and certificates over the bar, thinking that was a good place for them. Over a bar. Associated Press awards. The National Headliners Association. The certificate he got when he won the Meyer Berger Award. Even from the Associated Press sports editors, for the story on that girl jockey overdosing that time.

The old days.

He drank some rum and called Randy Houghton. You could call the little bastard at any time of the day or night, he was always up watching something, afraid he might miss something, even in the middle of the night.

One of the television boys and girls who ran the fucking world now.

"Houghton."

"Perez."

"Hey, babe, you're not going to believe this, but I was just thinking about you."

Houghton always said that.

"Listen," Marty said, not wanting to play, and just laid it all out for him, laying it out down and dirty so that even Randy Houghton, who liked to finish everybody's sentences, couldn't find a place to interrupt.

"Okay, I'm hard," Houghton said. "Now what do we do?"

"I want a crew to meet me at the Regency."

"In the morning?"

Marty said, "Now."

"You're going to ambush Crittendon?" Houghton's voice was high-pitched, almost squeaky, the way it got when he was excited.

"I want to surprise him is all. Just go over and call him from the lobby, tell him I'm on my way up."

"What if he says he won't talk?"

Marty drank the last of the rum and thought about having another, just to settle himself down.

"I tell him I understand his position, but if he doesn't, I've got to run a tape I've got of his daughter hanging all over Richie Collins."

"What if he still won't talk?"

"We run the tape tomorrow night."

Houghton told him he'd call Channel 2, it'd probably take half an hour to get a crew over to the Regency. If they weren't there by one, to call him back. If not, assume everything was a go. Marty hung up and went back over to the bar. He reached for the rum. He'd figure out what to tell Cantor later.

He was the king of the bullshitters, he'd think of something. Are you kidding?

32

DiMaggio said, "Are you alone?" to Fine, not really caring if he was or not.

"I'm alone," A. J. Fine said. He had on a faded green Dartmouth T-shirt and Knick sweatpants, black, and he had a book in his hands, marking his place with a finger, the fat paperback of the Truman biography that came out a few years ago. DiMaggio remembered that it won a bunch of big awards, which meant somebody must have read the sonofabitch.

Now he wondered if the book was a prop for the Ivy Leaguer, even at this hour, not knowing who was going to be at the door.

"I might be a little grumpy," Fine said, "even when a good friend like DiMaggio shows up unannounced in the middle of the night. But I am very much alone." He gave DiMaggio that quizzical eyebrow. "Not that it would have mattered, right?"

"There you go." DiMaggio waited for Fine to get out of his way, let him in, though he didn't mind the surroundings. Even the hallways were elegant at the Westchester Country Club. DiMaggio didn't even know people could live here, he just vaguely had heard the name, knew they played some big golf tournament here every year. But it turned out the main building was like some fancy old apartment hotel and Fine had the penthouse suite. The guy at the desk, when DiMaggio gave him his name, said, "You know, Ralph Branca, his wife, used to live here. You remember Branca, right?"

DiMaggio said, "Hey, who doesn't remember Ralph?" Then he told him it was all right to ring A.J., they were old friends, it was going to be one hell of a surprise.

"A.J.'s going to love this," DiMaggio said to the guy at the desk.

Now Fine was leaning against the door frame, ducking his head a little, casual, still not making any kind of move to let DiMaggio in. "This must be important," he said.

"You bet."

"How'd you get up here, by the way?"

"I lied," DiMaggio said. "But you know about lying, right?"

Fine said, "Maybe this could wait."

DiMaggio said, "And maybe I could call Ted Salter right now. Or the papers. Or Marty Perez. Tell everybody how I've at least cracked some of the Hannah Carey case."

"What part would that be exactly?"

Jesus, they were all starting to wear him out. DiMaggio pushed past A. J. Fine, startling him, knocking Harry Truman out of his hands.

Give 'em hell.

Over his shoulder, he said to Fine, "The part about the person who drove off in a car with Hannah Carey before Richie and Ellis even got their hands on her."

Fine wanted to cute it out all the way. "Who might that be?"

DiMaggio could hear classical music coming from somewhere. "You," he said. "Now are we going to keep fucking around with this or are you going to tell me about it?"

*　*　*

"Any break in Richie's murder, by the way?" Fine said.

Without asking, he had stopped in the kitchen, come out with two cups of hot coffee. Now they were in the living room, on matching sofas with Navajo designs on the upholstery, facing each other against some coffee table that looked like it had been made out of old fence posts. The rest of the room was all Santa Fe, or whatever they were calling it, as well. DiMaggio didn't even question it anymore, he just walked into these rooms when the people had money and expected the southwestern shit to be all over the place.

"It's one in the goddamn morning," DiMaggio said, "so let's get right to it. Why'd you lie to me?"

Fine had both hands on his mug, blowing on the coffee, his hands making it look as if he was drinking out of a thimble.

"Why did I lie?" he said. "Because I don't belong in this. Because I never belonged in it in the first place." His voice was rising, sounding girlish almost, the Ivy Leaguer not so cool now. Trapped a little bit and knowing that and acting petulant. "I lied because fucking Hannah Carey in the first place was an incredibly stupid mistake. Sonofabitch. At least the clap goes away. She never does."

DiMaggio sat there, watching him try to calm himself down, DiMaggio's aching hands on his own mug, feeling the heat, not wanting to drink.

Just hold on to the mug.

Fine looked at him, his glasses crooked on his face, hair spiky and a little wild-looking.

Fine said, "I figured I was safe with Hannah. Once it didn't come out in the original newspaper stories, it was just a question of whether she'd told the cops. But when that Fulton detective—"

"—Hyland—"

"—right, Hyland, questioned me, he never brought it up. Which means that Hannah didn't talk."

DiMaggio said, "Protecting you?"

Fine said, "Protecting her*self.* If it comes out that she was up there chasing after one player, it makes her a little less of a victim with the others. I figured I was in the clear anyway."

DiMaggio said, "I got a witness."

"I'm aware of that," Fine said. "But a witness to what? The crime of omission? I didn't lie to the police. They asked me if I saw Hannah at Mulligan's. I told them yes, I saw her at the bar. They asked me if I talked to her at the bar. I said no. Technically, it was true. I talked to her outside, when she followed me out. They asked me when I stopped seeing her. I told them. The only person I lied to was you."

DiMaggio said, "Where'd you go after you left Mulligan's?"

"Does it really matter?" Fine said, sounding irritated again.

"Humor me."

Fine looked away, said, "There's a little duck pond just down the road. Down by Route 123. We went there."

"And did what?"

"Talked."

"What else?"

"We just *talked,* goddamnit!" Fine snapped.

"I don't think so," DiMaggio said. "You had sex with her, didn't you?"

Fine looked at him.

DiMaggio kept going. "She goes for a ride with an old boyfriend and just talked, so what? She can tell the cops that. But she can't tell them she went off and got laid in an old boyfriend's car the night she says she got herself raped. She either tells Hyland all of it or none of it. Because if she tells him about going for a ride, he asks you. And you might tell him that a couple of hours before she alleges that she got raped, she's all sweaty with you down by the goddamn duck pond."

DiMaggio made a little motion with his coffee cup. Cheers. "Isn't that what happened?"

"Yes!" It came out in a hiss.

They sat there glaring at each other across the fence-post coffee table.

"So why? Here's this woman you're doing everything to get away from, who won't admit it's over, who keeps chasing. Now you run into her, and the two of you go off for a quick hump? Why?"

Fine stood up. There was a basketball lying in the corner. He reached down and scooped it up and now was twirling it absently in his hands, not even looking at it. Pacifiers for big boys.

Cops liked to touch their guns.

"Does this leave the room?"

"It goes where it goes," DiMaggio said. "As far as I'm concerned, you're still a sideman in all this, even if you couldn't keep your own dick in your pants. But you get no promises from me. You've got no rights anymore. You lied to me, fuck you."

"People don't usually talk to me that way."

DiMaggio said, "Probably not even in junior high school, when they first put your name in the paper. It's part of the problem here."

Fine put his hands on the ball like he was going to shoot it, like he was going to toss it out the window and into the night, clean as a whistle, to great cheers that only he would be able to hear because everything he'd ever done with a basketball in his hands had always been cheered.

"Why did I do it?" he said. "You want the truth? Because she was *there,* DiMaggio. Because she was a lot drunk and I was a little drunk and we were both feeling a little loose and horny, and because we'd always humped like champions."

Not even trying to be the Rhodes scholar anymore, what was the point?

Fine said, "It was training camp and it was New Canaan, Connecticut, and I was in the mood, and I didn't feel like going through a lot of conversation with some coed, or some lawyer, or some bored Fairfield County housewife babe, out on a toot and willing to go down on me in the back parking lot, if that's what it would take to be able to say she did it with A. J. Fine. You want to know why, DiMaggio? That's why. Because Hannah Carey was *there*. And available. And willing. Because there's always a Hannah around, and it just happened to be her turn again. Jesus Christ, do I have to draw you a picture? You were an athlete once. You were in the big leagues. It's always *there*. It doesn't matter who they are, where they come from. I don't even try to analyze it anymore. I even tried to fight it as a kid. But why? It doesn't matter how aloof they seem at first, how unavailable they seem. Two years ago, I went home with a minister's wife just to see what that would be like and she offered to pay me to tie her up. Why Hannah that night? Because I didn't feel like working for it, that's why."

Fine stopped then, took a deep breath, like he was catching his breath. Like coming clean had taken everything out of him all of a sudden. DiMaggio could still hear the music; he was sure it was that tape of Pavarotti and Domingo and Carrers. Now they were singing a medley from *West Side Story*. Fine took more deep breaths as he walked around the room, the ball still in his hands. He had wanted to be different from the animals. Better. Superior. Now his cover was blown. Here he was in front of DiMaggio, looking like the rest of them.

A little like Richie Collins, even.

If they thought it could save their ass, sometimes they even told you the truth.

"What was the fight about?" DiMaggio said.

"What the fight was always about," Fine said. "Why did we have to break up? Why don't you take me back? I loved you. I *love* you. Please take me back."

"She was there looking for you that night?"

"Oh sure. I don't know how she knew, but she did. She *always* did. She found out about the welcome-home dinner. Somebody told her a bunch of us were going over to New Canaan so we could drink. She could always track me down. If I had gone home, she would have been waiting for me here. She wanted to play the injured party a little more. It's her best part. She happens to be playing the hell out of it right now, you might have noticed." He shook his head, disgusted. "Anyway, I tried to leave as soon as I saw her. But she followed me out to the garage, which is where your witness must have seen us. I didn't think there was anyone around. I told her for the millionth time it was over. She got hysterical. As usual. She was like that when she was drunk, giddy one minute, into some huge crying jag the next. And always horny. She wanted to do it right there in the garage at Mulligan's."

The three tenors had stopped singing.

Fine said, "I finally gave up. We got into the car. And I drove down to the pond and settled her down the way I always used to settle her down."

"Then what?"

"I drove her back to Mulligan's." Fine tossed the basketball up in the air, grabbed it hard with both hands. "Told her to wait there while I went and parked the car."

DiMaggio finished it for him. "And you left her there."

Fine, not looking at him, studying the ball, nodded.

DiMaggio said, "And she waited. And waited a little more. Then a lot. And finally went in and ended up at the table with Richie and Ellis Adair."

"It could have happened like that. I just couldn't deal with her anymore."

DiMaggio said, "Poor baby."

"Hey, fuck *you,* DiMaggio."

DiMaggio was over on him before Fine really understood what was happening. He took the ball out of his hands, and then he shoved it as hard as he could into Fine's stomach, shoving him back into the couch at the same time, feeling the air come out of him.

"Watch your mouth," DiMaggio said.

Fine started to say something, but now DiMaggio leaned close to him, got in his face like they were always telling you to do in sports, close enough to smell the coffee on his breath.

"I know, I know. Nobody talks to you like that."

Fine said he drove straight home from Mulligan's after he left Hannah and went to bed. In the middle of the night, he heard Hannah's voice talking to his answering machine. He kept changing his number, trying to stay ahead of her. But she always had the new number. He had shut the ringer off, but the volume was too high on the machine.

Hannah's voice woke him up.

"You could barely understand her, she sounded so hysterical. I just figured she'd gone back inside Mulligan's and gotten drunker. It was only near the end that I could make out any of what she was saying."

"Which was?" DiMaggio said.

"She said she'd been raped."

"She say who did it?"

"Not before she ran out of time on the tape."

"You didn't pick up the phone?" DiMaggio said. "With her telling you she'd been raped?"

Fine leaned back now, hands shaking a little as he put them underneath his glasses and rubbed his eyes.

"Nothing I'm going to say anymore is going to change your mind about me," Fine said. "But, no, I didn't pick up. Because it wasn't anything I hadn't heard from Hannah before."

"She used to cry rape?"

A. J. Fine said, "All the time. Well, not all the time. Sometimes she'd tell me she'd been getting hang-ups. Or that someone tried to get into her apartment. Or that she thought she was being followed. Hannah the victim. You don't want to believe me, that's up to you. Maybe she's played the part convincingly enough for you, and you're convinced I'm the asshole. But it reached the point, with me anyway, where I didn't know what was real for her and what wasn't." Fine stood up. "I'm not sure if Hannah can make that distinction or not herself anymore."

DiMaggio stood up, too, tired, not even able to think if there was something else he should be asking. Fine said he'd walk him downstairs. "It's not more suck-up," he said. "I want to take a walk, work off some of the caffeine."

When they got downstairs, the desk guy said to DiMaggio, "Was he surprised?" Nodding at Fine.

"Oh boy," DiMaggio said. "Was he."

Fine walked him over to his car. "Who finds out about this conversation?"

No use bullshitting him. "Salter does," DiMaggio said. "And Hyland, the Fulton cop. I owe him that."

Fine said, "Does it get in the papers?"

In the end, it was all that mattered. To all of them. How they looked. It was unbelievable, DiMaggio thought, the power they gave these pissants like Marty Perez, guys who would never have their money. Their fame. They let the papers run their goddamn lives. They picked up the paper in the morning and it was like they were looking in the mirror. How do I look, how do I look, how do I look. . . .

"Does it?" Fine said.

"Hyland doesn't talk, I guarantee you that. Maybe you should talk to Salter yourself." Maybe it was talking about Salter that made him flash on Ellis all of a sudden. He'd meant to ask before. Now he said to Fine, just throwing it out there, "Who'd know where Ellis is?"

Fine put a hand up, rubbed his forehead hard. "No one I can really think of. I mean, Ellis had acquaintances, people he had his picture taken with. But not friends, at least the way he was friends with Richie." He shrugged. "I mean, Dale Larson started to come to some games last season, and some of the guys made some jokes. But I didn't think of him as any more than another photo op. You know who he is, right? The model?"

"Who is?"

"Dale Larson. You must have seen him on billboards and shit."

DiMaggio just sat there. He said to Fine, "Dale Larson is a guy."

Not even making it into a question.

Not even sounding surprised.

Fine smiled for the first time all night.

"Depends on your definition. But, yeah."

33

The funny thing, leastwise Ellis thought so, was that part of him was happy Richie was gone. It made him feel guilty, admitting that. Made him feel light, like the boys said now. There it was, anyway. He'd picture Richie there, dead, and no matter how hard Ellis tried, he couldn't make himself feel as bad about that as he knew he should.

If you added it all up, Ellis decided, good in with the bad, Richie had been more like a warden to him than a friend.

Ellis could feel that way even knowing that the rape charge was still out there, soon as he went back. But he wasn't going back, at least not right away. Fuck 'em, let them wait, people ought to be used to waiting for Fresh Adair by now. Let them wonder when he was coming back. People wondering now more than ever with Richie dead.

Not understanding.

Not really knowing.

But when did they?

Ellis missed ball, though.

Even now, in the middle of the night, before it got light over the park, that gray-pink light coming up out of there all of a sudden, Ellis would think about ball. How he should be getting back to sleep, there was Gary Lenz's shoot-around in the morning, the season ready to start tomorrow night. The whole world looking for him, and Ellis here, right under everybody's nose.

It'd always been a problem, Ellis wanting to be alone, but knowing on the other hand he was no damn good at being alone.

He sat on the terrace, the night air cold, but feeling good, thinking about what the Garden would be like tomorrow night. How the Garden got for openings, whether it was the season or the play-offs. The whole thing feeling like the Broadway opening Richie made him go to that one time. About the Phantom, Ellis at first thinking it was the one used to be in the comics. Ellis loved that guy, a superhero just wearing a mask, no name.

Ellis didn't care so much for the *Phantom* music, but he remembered how big the night felt to him, everybody being into it. After that, when there'd be a big game at the Garden, he'd look up sometimes, expecting the scoreboard over the court, up there in the spokes, to come crashing down the way that chandelier did in *Phantom,* right there at halftime.

Ellis needed somebody to tell him whether he should go back now or not.

Somebody like Richie.

How fucked-up was that?

He couldn't count on Dale on this one. Dale was so happy to have Ellis all to himself. Even with everything else going on, all the bad, Dale was happy just to know he could call at any time, day or night, and know Ellis would be there. If Ron, the house guy, was gone for the day, Dale would use that code they'd worked out, and it'd be all right for Ellis to pick up.

Dale wanted this to feel like Ellis's *home.*

"Home for the homeless homey," Ellis had said the other night, and Dale had laughed and said he loved him. Then Ellis had said, "Me too," because it made him feel funny still, saying the actual words himself.

Richie always said it a different way. Not meaning it the way Dale did. But meaning it, in his own pushy way.

"Love you, Fresh," Richie'd say. "You know I love you, man."

Or Richie'd say, "When the rest of them are all gone, Fresh, who's gonna be there for you?"

Only now Richie wasn't there for him. Now Richie was gone.

Ellis sat here in the middle of the night, four o'clock, wanting Richie to be around just for a little while longer, figure one last thing out for him. Four o'clock, invisible the way he said he always wanted to be, but trying to figure out how to make himself uninvisible.

Ellis needed to move.

He went inside and got his cheap-looking Yankee hat, the kind they gave away to kids. Put on the funny sunglasses Dale had given him, ones that took up half his face but really weren't sunglasses at all, they actually made things brighter. And the fake beard Dale had gotten him. And the baggy windbreaker and the bicycle shorts.

Ellis's disguise, when he worked up the nerve to take the blue bike out in the night.

Ellis went and got the bike, Dale's birthday present to him, out of the maid's room and then went down the back stairs, the secret way out you could have when you had a place like this, Dale's kind of money, coming out the little alleyway on Seventy-ninth Street.

Thinking on things himself, shit, it was harder than he thought it would be.

It always came back to waiting.

When he didn't know what else to do, DiMaggio waited.

So he sat in the backseat, listening to the overnight show on WQEW, which he was pretty sure used to be WNEW, but had moved up the dial, changed call letters, for some reason DiMaggio didn't know about. But then he was often behind the curve on things. Like who the hell Dale Larson was. Now he listened to Rosie Clooney on a station that didn't even exist when he was in New York last, in the town car across Seventy-ninth Street from Dale Larson's building, watching the front door.

He had driven straight here from Westchester, not even bothering to stop at the Sherry-Netherland. He had gotten here a little after two, and now it was after four o'clock.

It was only a hunch that Ellis Adair was in there, that Dale Larson the guy had taken in his ... what? Lover? Special friend? DiMaggio had a hunch. A feeling. Nothing more. He knew he could be wasting his time.

But then, what was new about that?

What did he have to go on? Boyzie Mays running his jive mouth about Ellis? A. J. Fine? He had nothing is what he had, except a feeling that this was where Ellis had been hiding out all along. Maybe he'd had it ever since the house guy hung up on him, just something about the way the guy did it, like DiMaggio had spooked him even asking to talk to Ellis.

What if Ellis had managed to get himself lost right in the middle of New York?

There were a million ways to get in there. Or at least take a shot. He could wait until eight o'clock or something, fake his way in, use the same moves on the doorman he'd used up at Fine's place in Westchester. Or give Ted Salter the number, have him talk to the house guy, tell him he was Ellis's boss and put him on the phone or else.

Or call Hyland, get him in on it, have him bluff his way in with a badge.

Except Hyland had his own problems, trying to find out who stuck Richie.

Rosie Clooney sang "Mack the Knife," putting some scats in

Mike Lupica

there the way Ella did. The disc jockey then introduced a record by a singer DiMaggio didn't know, Nancy LaMott. She sang "Moon River." DiMaggio had never heard it sung better in his life, by anyone. Here he was, behind the curve again. Where did Nancy LaMott come from?

A cab pulled up to Larson's building. A young stud in a tuxedo got out with his date, looking drunk in her bare feet, holding her high heels in her right hand, laughing like a fool, DiMaggio could hear it from across the street. The doorman came out, held the door for them, they went right in.

DiMaggio knew he could get in sooner or later.

But then what?

Ask Ellis *what?*

Hey, Fresh, don't answer if you think I'm prying, but are you gay?

What'd it mean if he was? That he couldn't have raped her?

The books said a lot of gay guys raped.

All along, even before Teresa Delgado showed up to say all Ellis did was watch when Richie Collins raped her in high school, DiMaggio had felt Ellis Adair wasn't the one here. That maybe he was as much a victim as Hannah, in some way he couldn't even explain to himself or figure out.

DiMaggio had heard about other big athletes being gay before, the way you heard the stories about movie stars, even before Rock Hudson got AIDS. DiMaggio would hear a name and think, Okay, that guy has made it, he's a real A-list celebrity now, they were saying he was homosexual. Or she was homosexual.

DiMaggio never cared one way or the other.

He wasn't looking to out Adair. He just wanted him to talk, once and for all. Maybe if Ellis and Dale Larson were lovers, if Ellis could see DiMaggio had him there, he could get him to tell the truth about Hannah . . .

It almost made him laugh. Jesus, he was no better than the rest of them. I give you this, you give me *that*. I've got something on you. You take care of me. Or else.

He was tired of being here, tired of this case. Tired of these people. Especially tired of waiting. He just wanted to find out what happened that night. Maybe it was tied into Richie Collins's murder, maybe not. DiMaggio wanted to be back in Jupiter, sitting on the beach, when Hyland cracked that one. If he ever did.

Find Ellis, Salter had said.

So DiMaggio waited.

The overnight disc jockey, a woman, said it was four-fifteen in New York City.

The big guy came out of the alley then across the street, a big black guy, DiMaggio saw, Yankee cap turned around on his head so the mesh was in front. Dressed like one of those psycho bicycle messengers.

Except he was too tall.

And who made deliveries at four-fifteen, even in New York?

The guy checked the traffic on Seventy-ninth and put out his arm, signaling for a left turn even though there wasn't a car in sight, then made the left onto Fifth, on the park side, pedaling slowly as he went past the town car.

A guy on his blue bike.

DiMaggio saw the weird-looking sunglasses, the beard. Saw how long the guy's legs were, almost too long for the sleek bike.

DiMaggio put the car into gear, looking at himself in the rearview mirror. Grinning at himself.

Follow that bike.

34

Marty's cameraman, José Pedroza, was also out of San Juan, a pretty little suburb called Río Piedras. The sound guy was named Andy Forst. Pedroza and Forst waited around the corner with the equipment so as not to draw the attention of the doorman. Marty waited near the hotel entrance for Frank Crittendon to come back from dinner, or wherever he'd been. Pedroza and Forst spotted Crittendon first, walking uptown on Park, west side of the street. They whistled to get Marty's attention, and Marty stepped out in front of Crittendon before he could walk into the Regency.

Crittendon didn't even act surprised to see him.

"I've been waiting for you to show up," he said, taking the little pipe he'd been smoking out of his mouth.

Marty said, "Me specifically?"

"Somebody like you."

"There's some things I need to talk to you about."

"I know," Frank Crittendon said. "I know." He stuck the pipe in his mouth and said, "I'm in 804."

* * *

When they were finished with Crittendon, Marty told Pedroza and Forst he'd take the cassette. He'd worked with both of them before and trusted them not to screw with him.

"Randy said I should drop it by his apartment," Pedroza said. He looked like a wiry lightweight boxer, maybe about five-five, with curly hair and a thick mustache. He always wore one of those khaki bush jackets, no matter what the weather. Lots of pockets. And one of those Indiana Jones fedoras. Marty told him all the time he looked like the spic who'd rolled the great white hunter.

Pedroza said, "He said I should drop it by his apartment, he'd be up."

"I'll do it," Marty lied. "I just want to go over to the *News,* transcribe it first. I figure we have to run this tonight on one of the regular newscasts. I just want to follow it up with a column for the Sunday paper."

Pedroza said, "Houghton even said something about maybe a special Saturday *Chronicle.*"

They were standing at the corner of Sixty-first and Park. Marty said, "I'll work it out with Houghton. You guys go to bed. And don't tell anybody what you heard in there."

"Eh viejo," Pedroza said. He knew Marty hated being called old, but it was a joke with them now. "Don't lose that tape, or the next job I get will be back with the *jíbaros* in P.R."

"You remember Juan Bobo?" he said to Pedroza.

"From the storybooks? Sure."

"Well, I may be old, but I'm not Juan Bobo," Marty said. *"No me jodas."*

He just wanted them to go, leave him alone, so he could go get a little bit drunk before he did anything.

Marty was feeling so sick he wanted to throw up.

"Cuidado," Pedroza said.

"*¡Basta!*" Marty said, faking a smile for both of them, then starting down Park, the tape in his briefcase. Trying to think about the tape, what was on it.

Frank Crittendon sitting there crying . . .

You got the story, Marty told himself. Wait until Houghton, who deep down thought he really was an old man, not joking about it all the time the way Pedroza did, sees this. He'd have to convince Houghton to wait until the eleven o'clock newscast, the more Marty thought about it. That way, it would be impossible for the other stations to catch up and Marty could still make a clean newspaper hit in the Sunday paper, a million copies.

"*¡Qué tipo!*" Marty said out loud. This was why he got into television in the first place, not just for the money, though the money was a big part of it. But to get them all coming and going.

What a guy.

So why did he feel sick?

He had crossed over to Third at Fifty-fifth. He found himself in front of P. J. Clarke's. Marty looked at his watch. Three o'clock. But there were still a few people sitting at the bar. Marty opened up his briefcase and got his old New York Giants baseball cap, the one his father had given him, out of there and pulled it down over his eyes. Just in case. He didn't feel like fucking talking. Playing Marty Perez tonight. He just wanted a couple of drinks. The people at the bar, some old guy in the middle, a drunk couple down at the end, didn't even look up when he came in the Third Avenue door in front. Maybe there were more people in the backroom. That was the way it used to be in the old days, when Clarke's was the place, before the newspaper boys and girls started to go to Ryan McFadden's and Macguire's.

He didn't even know the bartender, some kid, who gave him time for two rums and then said, "Mister, I don't want to rush you, but I got to close it down."

He walked down Third, taking his time, not even feeling the

rum. He kept walking, hoping he could make Frank Crittendon go away, stop thinking about Crittendon breaking down the way he did, Crittendon begging him to keep his daughter out of it, Crittendon swearing to Marty, when Marty hit him with his visit to Richie Collins's house that night, that he didn't kill the bastard. . . .

Marty waited for the light and then crossed Forty-second at Third. Halfway across, he heard the car coming, turned his head just in time, the car right on him, running the light. He dove out of the way at the last second, stumbled, ended up on his ass, back to the street, sitting on the curb, briefcase lying in a puddle. Marty wheeled around just in time to see the car, one of those Mad Max gypsy cabs with LIVERY in the back window, probably some crazed spic behind the wheel, flying toward Second Avenue. Let him drive right into the river, Marty thought. He started to throw his arm into the air at the guy's taillights, give him the finger, scream some curse at him in the night as he did.

Then Marty caught himself, *looked* at himself, sitting here like he was sitting in the gutter, four o'clock in the morning. Maybe you nearly got what you deserved, Marty Perez thought.

Maybe the fucking cab just tried to blindside you the way you just blindsided Frank Crittendon.

Marty started to laugh.

Like a *viejo* fool. Maybe he was Juan Bobo after all.

It was a very fast bike.

Ellis made a right into Central Park at Sixty-sixth Street, and that was the first time DiMaggio passed him, slowing down then to make sure he missed the light when he came out on Central Park West. Wasn't this the way he took Hannah when he rescued her from the media horde chasing her from the Vertical Club? It wasn't even a month ago and already seemed like a year.

Ellis was on him when the light changed, passing DiMaggio in his rental, going south, downtown, then making a left when he got to Fifty-seventh. Then a right on Fifth. By then DiMaggio had developed a good rhythm following him, gradually changing sides of the street, missing some lights as long as he kept Ellis in sight, falling in behind the traffic when there was traffic on Fifth, even pulling ahead a couple of times.

They went past all the expensive places on Fifth, Cartier and Bijan and Gucci, Ellis with the bike wide-open now, Ellis hunched down low, not even seeing the windows and names flying past him on his right and left, Dunhill now, Mark Cross, Ellis so low to the bike it was as if he and the blue bike were one piece.

He took a left at Forty-second.

Went past Grand Central Station now, and the Grand Hyatt. Then a Gap store with a huge window that seemed to take up a whole block. Then Ellis crossed Third, went past some nut in a baseball cap sitting on the curb laughing like a hyena, reaching for a briefcase, and then there was the *Daily News* building on his right, on the south side of Forty-second.

DiMaggio studied Ellis, half a block ahead, pumping his legs hard sometimes, bending them out a little from the bike, gliding when he'd come to a downhill stretch, not ever noticing the town car that had been with him all along, alone with the speed of the bike and the street in front of him, alone, DiMaggio thought, with being alone, a big canvas bag stuffed into the basket behind his seat.

He took a left on First, going uptown again.

Ellis stayed to the left of the tunnel that opened up at Forty-ninth Street, going past bookstores and delis and a rib place, another bookstore, passing a church, St. John of Something at Fifty-fifth, then crossing Fifty-seventh again, then checking the traffic, mostly cabs, as he went diagonally across First, then suddenly taking a right at Sixty-second, heading toward F.D.R.

Drive and the East River. DiMaggio made the right with him.
Ellis crossed York, and now DiMaggio wondered if Ellis was
crazy enough to put the bike on the F.D.R.?

But then, maybe they were all crazy.

Ellis made a right now on the east side of the street and sped
down to Sixty-first, went up on the sidewalk, got off, and leaned
the bike against a chain-link fence there. He stretched for a
minute, shaking his legs loose, twisting his back around.

Finally, he pulled the canvas bag out from behind the seat,
shook it, and the basketball bounced out.

When Ellis had stopped, DiMaggio made a quick right. Now
he eased down the block a little, away from Ellis. Just enough
to keep him in sight. DiMaggio had been so busy watching Ellis
he didn't realize he was watching him through a playground for
kids, with swing sets and slides and seesaws, with a basketball
court next to the playground, cut in underneath F.D.R. Drive. If
you weren't looking for it, you had no chance of seeing the court
from the street. DiMaggio smiled, remembering his ride through
Jersey City with Richie Collins. Thinking it was like Ellis had
found his own little corner of Jersey City now, his own Baby
Rucker on the East Side of Manhattan.

Playground to playground.

Ellis got just enough help from the streetlights. And there was
plenty of traffic noise from the F.D.R. even at four in the morning, to mute the bounce of the ball, the sound of it hitting the old
metal backboard.

And right away, as soon as he started to play, the setting didn't
matter. Even in the hat, the stupid glasses, the fake beard, it was
unmistakably Fresh Adair.

He started out shooting from the outside, DiMaggio able to
hear the rattling sound it made as it went through the wire-mesh
net. Then Ellis would retrieve the ball quickly, sometimes almost
on it before it hit the ground, sometimes dunking absently, be-

fore he could go back outside and make another jump shot, then be moving toward the basket again, lost now in his own elegant choreography.

Even when a car would stop at the light on Sixty-first, maybe fifty yards from him, there was no reason to see Ellis in there, at the far end of the court.

See the amazing show that was going on.

Left-handed hook. Right-handed hook. Fakes, stutter steps, pullup jumpers. Stopping every so often to look behind him. Then back to the game, back into the night, like the thousand nights like this he must have had back in Jersey City.

DiMaggio got out of the car, careful not to slam the door, trying to walk quietly toward the court, past where the blue bike rested against the fence. Ellis Adair had his back to him, underneath the basket now, bouncing the ball off the backboard, catching it, dunking in the same motion. Doing it again.

"Ellis."

He turned around, startled, not picking DiMaggio up at first on the other side of the fence.

"Say what?"

DiMaggio stepped onto the court. "It's me. DiMaggio."

"Ain't no Ellis here. Don't know no DiMaggio." He tilted his head to the side. "Get away from my bike."

"You do know me," DiMaggio said, taking a couple of steps closer, wondering what he would do if Ellis just made a run for it. He smiled. "I'm the asshole Ted Salter hired to investigate you and Richie." Spell it out so he understood.

They stood there on the court, fifty feet apart, Ellis with the ball on his hip. DiMaggio said, "I need to talk to you."

"You alone?"

"Yes."

Ellis said, "How'd you—"

DiMaggio said, "Doesn't matter. Point is, I found you. I found Dale's place. I found you and Dale."

Ellis said, "You found. You found. You found *shit* with me and Dale."

"Listen," DiMaggio said. "I don't *give* a shit about you and Dale. I don't." He was talking fast, wanting to get it all out there, right now, not wanting to lose him.

Trying to make it sound as if he was on Ellis's side.

Which maybe he was.

DiMaggio said, "I know stuff I didn't know before."

"Know who killed Rich?"

"No." He took a couple of more steps closer, his arms stretched out wide, feeling silly, feeling like he was showing Ellis he was unarmed. "Listen, you mind if we sit down someplace?"

DiMaggio got a few feet away and stopped.

Ellis said, "I don't know that we got anything to talk about."

"Just hear me out. I found out A.J. had Hannah before she went off with you guys that night. I believe she's lied to me. Now I need to find out how much lying she's done." DiMaggio took a deep breath, let it out. "It's just you and me. I don't have a tape recorder." He opened his jacket. "You can pat me down if you want. I'm not wearing a wire. I just want you to tell me the rest of it."

"I don't have to tell you nothing, Richie said."

"Richie's fucking *dead.*"

Ellis didn't say anything, just stood there with the basketball on his hip.

DiMaggio said, "You've got to come back, Ellis. You look guiltier every day you don't."

"Guilty of what? Takin' out Rich? You're standing here telling me I'm a suspect?"

DiMaggio said, "You think you're not? Let me explain something to you, Ellis. When somebody's wife gets killed, you know who the number one suspect is, before the cops know anything? It's the husband. It's the one closest to her. You saw what happened with O.J., right from the start. So who was closer to Richie Collins than anybody in the whole world? *You* were."

Ellis shook his head. He said, "Doesn't prove one goddamn thing."

"You're absolutely right. It doesn't. But it's a place for them to start. And they don't have to prove anything at the start. There's a reason they're called *suspects,* Ellis. Maybe they think you're pissed at Richie because he got you into this mess with Hannah Carey in the first place. Hey, the cops say, maybe Ellis is innocent, after all. Maybe it was Richie who raped her and Ellis got fed up with being called some dirty rapist, too. Maybe Ellis got tired of taking the fall."

Ellis Adair stared at him, ball still on the hip, frowning at DiMaggio, as if trying to keep up. Like he was listening to him as hard as he could.

DiMaggio said, "And who's missing? You are. The season's starting, your best friend is dead, and nobody can find you. You know what the cops say to that one? What's Ellis Adair got to hide? They're starting to think it was you Richie went to meet that night at the house. There's enough people who will tell them how Richie's been bossing you around all these years. Maybe the cops are starting to think you got fed up with his bullshit and you're the one who killed him."

Ellis said, "That what you think?"

DiMaggio said, "It doesn't matter what I think. It's what the cops think, that's what I'm trying to tell you. It's how things *look.*"

Not even thinking about what he was doing, DiMaggio took a step closer to him and took off Ellis's sunglasses, pulled off the fake beard. Then took the Yankee cap off his head. Ellis stood

there and let him do it, like a kid allowing himself to be un-
dressed.

"I didn't kill him," Ellis said softly.

"Then go tell the police that yourself. Or call Ted Salter and
have him arrange for you to tell the police."

"I didn't kill Richie, and I didn't rape her," Ellis said evenly.
Just like that.

DiMaggio didn't give him any time, any room. "What about
Richie? Did Richie rape her?"

"I don't know."

"Come on, Ellis."

"I think he did. I just didn't see him do it."

DiMaggio said, "Give me ten more minutes. Let me finish this
job and get back to Florida." He took a deep breath. "It's time
to turn yourself in, Ellis. You're going to walk on this rape thing,
I'm sure Donnie Fuchs has been telling you that from the start.
You don't want to go from there to being a suspect in Richie's
murder." Ellis turned away, toward F.D.R. Drive. DiMaggio
grabbed his arms, surprised at how skinny they felt, and reposi-
tioned him so they were facing each other. "You got an alibi for
Richie?"

"Yes."

"Dale?"

"Somebody at Dale's. I was there all night."

DiMaggio tried to read his face in light that kept changing because of the traffic on the F.D.R. but couldn't decide if he was
telling the truth or not, even with his kid's face no longer hidden by a disguise. "Tell the cops that. Tomorrow. But tell me
about you and Richie and Hannah Carey right now."

"Maybe I'll just go off again, somewhere you can't find my
ass this time."

DiMaggio said, "I found you once. It's always easier the second time, once you know the other guy's moves."

"Not my moves."

DiMaggio said, "Why'd you take off, anyway? The DNA test on the dress, it made you look innocent, not guilty."

Ellis nodded his head slowly, like he wanted to explain, but all he said was, "I'll tell you about it someday."

"Just tell me about that night."

"You got no leverage to make me tell."

"I got Dale."

"Like I said, you got what you *think* you got."

"You say."

"God*damn!*" Ellis shouted all of a sudden. "God*damn!* Always somethin', isn't it? Always somebody wanting something. You come on like you want to be my friend. Like Ellis and DiMaggio, we're on the same *team*. Talk to me, Ellis. *Work* with me, babe. But you got your own angle. You *gots* to know. You gots to know and I *gots* to help you."

DiMaggio said, "You're right. I've got to know."

"Why is it so fucking important to you?"

"Because I'm starting to think maybe the wrong people ended up victims here."

"You mean Rich?"

"I mean you."

Ellis nodded to the playground. There was a bench next to the seesaw. They went over and sat down and Ellis told him what he did know.

Ellis's story:
Richie knew Hannah from when she was A.J.'s girl. He'd even run into her the week before, at Gates over in New Canaan, Ellis said. Got her drunk. Thought about maybe getting her into a scene with this high school girl he was meeting there later. But Hannah only wanted to talk about A.J., wanting to know if A.J.

might be coming in. Richie told her come back next week after the welcome-home dinner, everybody would probably be around, the team had decided to party after the boring welcome-home party.

Finally, the high school girl showed up and Hannah blew Richie off.

Ellis: "It only made Richie want her more. Richie didn't take too much to turndowns, even if he was trying all the time. So right away that night at Mulligan's, when he realized Hannah and A.J. was in the same place, Richie said, 'The Dartmouth boy's going to get some shit big-time from his ex.' Then he told me he might hang around, give the bitch a second chance."

The place got more and more crowded and before long most of the Knicks were there. Richie and Ellis got separated. The next time Ellis noticed Hannah Carey was later. A. J. Fine was gone, and all of a sudden Richie had his arm around Hannah and was bringing her over to where Ellis was sitting. Ellis couldn't tell at first whether she was drunk or high, but she wasn't at the table five minutes when she jumped up and wanted to sing with the band.

Ellis: "Some old song Richie knew the name of. Said it was a golden oldie."

About eleven o'clock, Richie said they should all go someplace more quiet. Hannah said something like, Why leave a great party, right, Ellis?

Ellis: "Rich acted mad because she didn't want to leave, but I knew better. She was making it pretty *damn* clear she wanted to be with me. That's why he was mad."

He said that no matter how hard he didn't try sometimes, even as Richie Collins was trying his ass off, it didn't matter, they wanted to be with Ellis. Always.

Ellis: "I never knew what way to go. If I got up and left, and the girl left, too, Rich'd get all mad at *me*. Or he'd get all mad if I stayed and he couldn't get nowhere with the girl. The best thing was, when there'd be two of them, even if they didn't want to get in one of Rich's piles."

DiMaggio asked him why.

Ellis: " 'Cause if I took one of them home, did my deal right in front of him, it would get him offa me for a while, not be asking me where I was last night, where'd I go? Asking me if I had some strange I hadn't told him about. It was like I had this clock inside my head. The kind they always said I had on the court? Okay, Fresh, been a while since you made Richie happy by jumping some strange, better get out there tonight. Be the Ellis he wanted me to be. The Ellis he never wondered if I *wasn't*, he was so wrapped up in his own head about the way *he* wanted things to be. How they was supposed to *look*. He knew I wasn't pussy-crazy like him. But, hell, no one was. He wanted me to be Ellis the stud. So I was, at least enough to get him off my back."

Ellis finally suggested he and Hannah go back to the house so they didn't have to sit in Mulligan's all night. Maybe Hannah would change her mind back there. Or do them both. Ellis drove her car, Richie drove the Jeep, following them.

Hannah never asked where Richie was, and Ellis didn't say.

Ellis: "She was real drunk by then. She started to fool around with me, trying to get me all turned on. Then she started crying, telling me all about A.J., how she knew he loved her, he'd always loved her, how could he fuck her over this way. How maybe he'd get all jealous when he found out she'd gone off with me. I just wanted to get her back to the house and turn her over to Richie and get her out of my face."

Richie was standing in the living room when they walked in. Hannah said something like, "What're you doing here?"

Ellis: "She still didn't seem too happy to see Richie there. But then Richie made her a drink and put some music on. I went into the kitchen and got a glass of water. Richie came in and said,

'You done with her?' Thinking something had happened in the car. I told him I couldn't get another hard-on if I tried. Richie said, 'Okay, but if you change your mind, you know where to find us.' "

Ellis went to bed. He said the next thing he heard was Hannah Carey screaming from the living room.

Ellis: "I got up and put my sweats on, got my bike, let myself out the back way, decided to go for a ride. I knew I wasn't gonna be able to sleep until she was gone. See, there was always a lot of yelling with Richie and it'd got to where I couldn't tell the difference, whether they was having a good time or not."

When he got back, Richie was asleep in front of the television, some porno movie playing, and Hannah Carey was gone.

DiMaggio said to Ellis, "So he did rape her, and then she got out of there like she said."

Ellis said, "Or they had theirselves a real nice time and Richie fell asleep and she went home. Don't give me no she-said. I read some of those stories, too. About how she tried to leave and I jumped out of the front-hall closet on her, raped her in the hallway. She told the police or somebody a lot of lies. Jump on her out of a closet. Shit."

"All this time, you never asked Richie?"

"We talked all around it till this one night. And alls he said was, 'Fresh, wasn't no big deal.' Then he gave me a look he'd give me sometimes, and said, 'Fresh, you think your man Rich, he ever has to force these bitches?' Then I asked him about that yell I heard out of her, even knowing what he was gonna say."

"Which was?"

"Which was, 'Aren't they s'posed to yell?' "

Ellis said he never thought about Hannah Carey again until Frank Crittendon came to the gym that day at Fulton College and told him that he and Richie were being accused of rape. Right from the start, Donnie Fuchs told them not to sweat, there wasn't going to be a case. Richie would tell Ellis the same thing, all the time, saying most people were just going to think she was copy-catting all the other bitches, the one with Mike Tyson and the one who cried rape that time with the Mets in Florida.

Ride it out, Richie kept telling Ellis.

DiMaggio said, "And it didn't bother you that she charged both of you, not just Richie, even though you were innocent?"

"I just figured it was part of it," Ellis said. "Part of being Fresh Adair. You don't get it? All just part of being *me*. People are always threatening to sue me, or all the ones like me. She just went ahead and followed through. You know Joe Montana, right? The quarterback? I was at a dinner with him one time? Joe Montana told me he was in training camp this time, backing out of the lot in his car, and then he hears yelling and stops because this guy, he's lying behind the back wheels. *Wanting to get fucking run over.* So he can sue. Just part of the deal. It don't matter whether you like it, don't like it. I can't remember a time when somebody didn't want a piece of me. Starting with Rich."

Ellis turned to DiMaggio now, looking like some young, handsome high school kid in his ratty thrift-shop clothes. Maybe looking like the scared project kid Richie Collins had always described to DiMaggio.

"Now you tell me, DiMaggio," he said. "You tell me something. Where you goin' with all this, even if it's my word against yours when we get way down to it? You gonna sell this to the papers? Or to *Inside Affair* or whatever the fuck that show is? What's your angle? What piece of Ellis Adair are *you* looking for?"

"I'm almost there," DiMaggio said.

"Where?"

"To that other room with Richie and Hannah." DiMaggio

stood and stretched and shook his hands loose as he did. He'd been squeezing them, trying to quiet them down, while Ellis had been talking about the night a year ago in Fulton, and that was a bad idea, always.

Ellis said, "How you gonna get her to tell?"

"I don't know yet."

"And what do *I* do?" Ellis said.

DiMaggio looked down at him in the hazy light, night being filtered through this hour into morning, morning coming fast now, like it was coming across the river from Queens, the first commuter of the day. It was there in his face, in his tone.

Ellis really wanted to know what to do.

He had always wanted somebody to tell him, Richie or a coach or an agent.

Dale Larson.

"Go back to Dale's," DiMaggio said. "Wait for me to call. But you know what I really think you should do? Think about showing up tomorrow night and playing some ball."

"How come you didn't ask about Dale and me?" Ellis Adair said.

"I'm a little unusual, even for this line of work. I still think there's stuff that's your own business."

Ellis got up and stuffed the basketball back in his bag, then walked over with DiMaggio to the blue bike. DiMaggio said, "Who do you think killed Richie?"

"I been thinking a lot on that. Thinking on it until my head hurts, and then I stop. Wondering whether it was some husband. Or boyfriend who found out about Richie and his girl. Or some young girl's old man. Or some girl herself." He threw a long leg gracefully over the seat. "You know what I decided? It was just somebody Richie fucked once too often. Or fucked *with.*"

Ellis Adair, looking like a kid, said, "I don't have much time here, on account of the city'll be waking up soon." He smiled. "You want to shoot around a little? Play winners-out. I'll spot you six baskets, game of seven."

DiMaggio said, "Another time." He said to Ellis, "It really could be anybody with Richie."

Ellis said, "All the way back to Jersey City."

35

DiMaggio and Ted Salter were at a coffee shop on Fifty-eighth, around the corner from the Sherry and right across the street from FAO Schwarz. Salter had said to beep him if it was ever an emergency. DiMaggio beeped him at six-thirty Saturday morning, told him he'd found Ellis. Salter wanted to know where he was, and DiMaggio told him it wasn't important. "Excuse me?" Salter had said, "It isn't goddamn important?"

"Trust me," DiMaggio had said on the phone.

Now it was nine o'clock. Salter wore some flashy warm-ups, mostly navy-blue but with a lot of green-and-white lightning bolts slashing all over the place and a rooster where DiMaggio expected to find the polo pony. Salter's hair was slicked back, wetter-looking than usual, DiMaggio couldn't tell anymore whether guys had just gotten out of the shower, or just wanted it to look that way.

All Salter really wanted to know was if Ellis was going to play the opening game that night, tip-off at seven-thirty at the Garden.

DiMaggio told him Ellis would be there.

"Where's he been?"

"Shacked up."

"No kidding. Well, it's always a great settler-down in times of turmoil, right?"

Then DiMaggio told him everything he knew so far about what happened that night with Hannah, Ellis, Richie, and A. J. Fine.

"So you're telling me he's innocent?" Salter said. "Yessss!" he said, smiling, making a fist and throwing a short punch into the space between them.

"No," DiMaggio said. "That's not what I'm telling you." It was like DiMaggio had thrown a punch right back at him. He saw Salter slump, shrinking back into the expensive warm-ups.

"Could you please tell me what you *are* telling me then?"

DiMaggio said, "I think Ellis could pass a lie detector test that everything happened the way he says it did. I think he's convinced himself. But that doesn't mean he's innocent." DiMaggio leaned closer to Salter, lowered his voice. "Because I think Richie Collins *did* rape her. And Ellis was there. And Ellis didn't do a thing to help her. And if *that* comes out, Ellis doesn't look much better than if he had done it himself."

Salter rubbed his eyes as if they were on fire. "But that doesn't have to come out?"

"No, it doesn't."

"Because we still don't think they can make the rape charges stick?"

"I told you from the start that I didn't think they could. I told you I thought they did it, and it wouldn't matter in the end, at least in the eyes of the law, because I thought the case was impossible to make. You wanted me on this anyway. You wanted to know everything. And I feel like I'm almost there. When I'm all done, you want to ask me about guilty and innocent and who the real victims are, ask me then."

"You have no idea how unhappy my Japanese bosses are with this," he said. "With *me.*"

"Explain to me how this is your fault, exactly."

"Because it goddamn well has to be *somebody's* fault, that's why. Because, as you might imagine, they got into the sports business for the good*fuckingwill* of it all. And now, in less than a month, they get a rape charge against a couple of their basketball players. Then one of the players, the most famous player in the goddamn world, disappears. And the other one gets himself killed."

"But you get Ellis back now."

"It's a start," Salter said. "That's why I need him in uniform tonight."

"After he talks to the cops," DiMaggio said.

"Fine, fine, after he talks to the cops. But I need him in uniform. I need an emotional scene at the Garden. I need for him to do the moment-of-silence deal for Richie. I had to have some time alone, he can say. I couldn't cope with everything that has been happening. I felt wounded. But I'm still the same Fresh Adair you've always known. And I know Richie would have wanted me to be here." Salter waved a hand and said, "Etcetera, etcetera."

Salter said, "It doesn't get me out of the woods, but it does get the Japs, and the public relations police, off my ass for a couple of days."

"I'm sorry I won't be there to witness all this honest and heartfelt emotion," DiMaggio said.

"Hey," Salter said, "you want to come? I could put you at courtside next to Spike and his wife."

The idea of fixing everything with a couple of comp tickets seemed to brighten Salter's whole mood.

DiMaggio said, "I'm still working until you tell me otherwise. Ellis only got me into the house. I'm still not in that room with Richie and Hannah. That's why you called me in the first place, remember? I thought *you* wanted to know."

"You're right," Salter said. "I did. But you want to know what I've decided? I've got enough problems with these assholes when they're *alive* to start worrying about them dead."

The coffee shop, even on a Saturday, was starting to fill up. Outside the window, a homeless guy, black, baseball cap turned around on his head, looked in. For a moment, DiMaggio thought it was Ellis, hunched over, still wearing his disguise.

Still trying to be invisible.

Out for one more ride, or walk, before he had to go back to being Fresh Adair tonight.

Salter said, "So you're going to stick around?"

"I want to take one more run at Hannah Carey."

Salter's beeper went off then. He slapped at his pocket like he was slapping at a bug, and went outside to the pay phone on the street. Smiling as he punched out the number.

Starting to feel like he might be in charge again.

Then Salter sagged suddenly at the phone, like someone had hit him behind the knees. He reached up with his free hand to grab one of the glass walls shielding the phone, trying to steady himself.

DiMaggio threw money on the table and went out in time to hear Salter say, "I'm only a few blocks, I'll be right over."

He tried to hang up the phone with a shaking hand, missed, then slammed it in. Salter turned around, jumped when he saw DiMaggio right behind him.

"Frank Crittendon killed himself," Salter said.

They'd found Crittendon in his room at the Regency. When DiMaggio and Salter got there, they were already behind the first wave of media. There were vans from Channel 2 and Channel 7; a kid carrying a minicam that had NY 1 on the side was making a broken-field run across Park Avenue, dodging cars, horns blasting at him from both sides of the divider. DiMaggio was used to it by now, no gap between the event and the coverage, as if it had all become one smooth merge.

There were print guys on the sidewalk, too, DiMaggio was starting to recognize the bastards from some of the other scenes. The car horns kept going because the vans already had traffic starting to back up in front of the Regency. And pedestrians, regular people out for a walk on Saturday morning, were starting to form a crowd on both sides of the hotel's revolving-door entrance.

The people didn't know what the action was, just that there was action.

Part of the scene.

Salter grabbed DiMaggio and pulled him through the crowd. "If we don't put our heads down, we'll never get in there." A cop was in front of the revolving door with the doorman, asking people to show their room keys. But Len Boyle, one of Salter's PR guys from the Garden, was with them. "This is Mr. Salter," Boyle said to the cop, like he was announcing that the cavalry had arrived.

Boyle walked with them toward the bank of elevators on the left side of the front lobby.

Salter said, "Does the team know?"

"Gary's been calling them in their rooms," Boyle said.

"They're still here then?"

Boyle, a big, handsome kid with red hair and a lot of freckles, said, "The shootaround at the Garden isn't till ten."

Salter jabbed at the elevator button. Without looking at Boyle, not raising his voice, he said, "Tell Gary to cancel the shootaround. And tell him no interviews now, or before the game. Anybody I see on the news tonight, before I talk to them, is a fucking dead man." The elevator doors opened, and Salter said, "You stay here and work the press as best you can." The doors started to close, and Salter stuck a hand out. "Where is he by the way?"

Boyle said, "Eight-o-four."

The cop in charge was named Stanton. He had a crew cut and sleepy eyes and looked too young to be homicide. He looked like he could have been one of the reporters from downstairs, wearing a blazer and blue jeans and cowboy boots, sucking hard on a cigarette in the hall.

Salter introduced himself to Stanton.

Stanton shook his hand, said, "I've been expecting you." Then nodded at DiMaggio and said, "Who's he?"

DiMaggio said, "I'm with the band."

Stanton, deadpan, said, "Crime-scene wise guys. My favorite."

Salter said, "His name is DiMaggio. He's been working on the rape investigation for the Garden."

Stanton was the wise guy. "How's that going so far?" he said to DiMaggio.

Over Stanton's shoulder, the door to 804 was open and the crime-scene people seemed to be finishing up, and Stanton said, "I'll bumper-sticker this for you?"

Salter said, "Fine."

Crittendon had left a six o'clock wake-up call. Then a backup for six-fifteen and a third for six-thirty. Salter nodded. "Frank was careful," he said. The switchboard got no answer on any of them. The assistant manager, a Brit named Whitaker, knew Crittendon, knew he liked to have an early breakfast by himself in the Regency's restaurant, a big power-breakfast place, alone with the papers. Whitaker sent a bellman up to knock on the door. Still no answer. Whitaker went up and let himself into Room 804 and found him in bed, the bottle of Seconal on the nightstand next to him, empty.

"Note?" Salter said.

Stanton shook his head.

"Family?"

"Notified. On their way. And I put in a call to the Fulton cops. I don't know if this has anything to do with the Richie Collins case up there. But they got a right."

Stanton said, "Whitaker, the assistant manager, he says Crittendon was a good guy."

In a dead voice Salter said, "Yes."

A short guy, a little overweight, came past them carrying what looked to be an old-fashioned black doctor's bag. DiMaggio figured it must be the medical examiner. He reminded DiMaggio, the way he was built, of Frank Crittendon.

DiMaggio walked down the hall, away from 804, and flashed on his first conversation with Crittendon, up in Fulton.

They look at me like I'm garbage, he'd said.

Salter finished with the cops and came down to where DiMaggio leaned against a wall. He didn't look like the corporate tiger anymore, clapping his hands in the coffee shop, ready to go out and bite the world in the ass.

"Jesus Christ," he said, leaning back himself, taking a spot next to DiMaggio. "Jesus Christ."

"Was he sick?"

"I have no idea."

"When did you talk to him last?"

"Yesterday. He was asking how you were doing on your deal, wondering if there was any chance Ellis might turn up before the game."

"He seemed fine?"

"He seemed like Frank. A little tired. A little worried about everything. A little scared that because everything had gotten so out of hand I might blame him. Or the Fukiko guys might tell me to blame him."

Salter said, "I didn't tell you this at the coffee shop, not in so many words. But I don't care anymore about Hannah Carey. I don't *care* what happened with her and Collins because it's starting to sound to me like they deserved each other. I mean, sonofa*bitch,* she's turned this into a career, hasn't she?"

DiMaggio said, "And your company was going to be in business with her before I told you what I told you this morning."

"This all started because I was looking out for the company, pal."

"Is that your defense? Pal."

"Go fuck yourself."

"I'm asking," DiMaggio said.

Salter started back toward 804, turned around. "See the thing is, this wasn't ever supposed to be about somebody like Frank. It was supposed to be about *them.* Even when Collins got it, it was still about them, whatever had happened with the three of *them.* But not Frank. Frank Crittendon was decent. I forgot that myself sometimes. I wasn't very nice to him sometimes. I'm a bad boy. Bad shit happens to me I say, Okay, that comes with the territory, let's play two. But not Frank, goddamnit!" He was shouting at the end. *"Goddamnit!"*

"Let's get out of here," DiMaggio said.

They waited for the elevator, and DiMaggio said to him, "You don't know this had anything to do with the rape or Richie."

"Then why do I have that feeling?"

There was no answer for that one because DiMaggio had the same feeling about Frank Crittendon, not picking up on his three wake-up calls.

They look at me like I'm nothing, he'd said.

What was it about this investigation? What was it about all these invisible people?

The Brit manager took them out the service entrance. DiMaggio wanted to wait around, see if Hyland showed up, but he was afraid Salter was going to snap, so he stayed with him. They came out between Park and Madison on Sixtieth, away from the press.

"I need to talk to Ellis. If we play the game, I want to tell him how to play it tonight," Salter said.

"You might not?"

"I need to talk to my Japs before I talk to Ellis."

"Here's the number, call him." DiMaggio took his notebook out, wrote Dale Larson's number. Salter said, "Where is this?" And DiMaggio said, "Where he is."

Salter said, "What are you doing right now?"

"Waiting for the Fulton cops to show up. They're going to want to talk to Ellis, too."

They had started walking toward Madison. Salter stopped suddenly and said, "What'd I do with the car?" Panicking like somebody who'd lost his car keys or his wallet.

"You told him to wait where he dropped us off, on Sixty-second."

"I'll circle around, call Ellis from the car. Maybe the cops can wait, talk to him tomorrow, after the game."

"Today."

Salter said, "And why is that?"

DiMaggio said, "Because everything you say you don't care about anymore, they don't have that luxury."

DiMaggio left him there, walked back toward the Regency. He came around on Park and saw that the crowd had gotten even bigger. More vans. More reporters. More onlookers.

He thought, They should sell tickets.

DiMaggio saw Marty Perez maybe a few seconds before Perez, standing in the street, at the back of the crowd, turned his head and saw him. He had some kind of old briefcase in his hand and was wearing an old New York Giants baseball cap.

Perez came walking over. "I was looking for you," he said. "I called the hotel, you weren't there, I figured you'd be here."

DiMaggio said to Perez, "I found out something early in my career with guys like you, Marty. You're never looking for me to help me."

"Today's different, maybe."

"How so?"

"I couldn't decide who I should tell. And then I decided on you. All the people who are in this, from the start, you're the only one without an angle."

"There's the financial angle, Marty. I'm very expensive."

"It's always more than money with you, even when you played ball. You always wanted to know."

"Know what?"

"Whatever."

"So what is it that you want to tell me and not anybody else?"

"I know who killed that poor bastard."

"Richie Collins?"

Perez jerked a thumb back over his shoulder at the scene in front of the Regency. "Crittendon," he said.

"Somebody killed him?"

"Me," Marty Perez said.

Back at the Sherry, Perez asked DiMaggio if there was any rum.

DiMaggio went over to the bar; other than Scotch, he never paid much attention to how they stocked it. Now he saw that they had just about everything, including a new bottle of Bacardi. Marty said that would do him fine. DiMaggio poured some over ice and brought it over to where Perez was sitting with his brief-case, an old satchel, really, in his lap. Perez had taken the Giants cap off, set it on the coffee table. "You hate guys like me more than you ever did, don't you?" Perez said. "It's gotten worse since you played ball."

DiMaggio said, "To tell you the truth, Marty, hate would make you more important in my life than you are. Hate requires some effort."

"But if you didn't have to—?"

"I'd never talk to you." It came out impatient. DiMaggio looked at him and said, "You said you killed Frank Crittendon, what the hell is that supposed to mean exactly?"

Perez took a big hit of the Bacardi, kept the glass right there, took another, and emptied the glass. Then he held the glass out to DiMaggio, meaning another. When DiMaggio came back, Perez told him about Richie and the high school girl and finding out it was Crittendon's daughter and how he decided to go for the old man instead of the girl.

"Why not the kid?" DiMaggio said.

"Because she's a kid."

"And you have standards."

"You're being sarcastic," Marty Perez said dully, "but, yeah, even I have lines I won't cross, whether you want to believe that or not." He drank more rum. DiMaggio wondered when the last time was he'd slept or if he just looked this old and used up all the time. When Perez put his glass down, DiMaggio saw he had the shakes. "Or so I like to tell myself," he said.

He told DiMaggio about waiting for Crittendon in front of the Regency, how Crittendon hadn't even acted surprised. In the elevator going up to Room 804, Marty told Crittendon this was about Kelly and Crittendon had answered, "I know, I know," just as he had on the street.

DiMaggio said, "Doing this to a high school girl's father, this was on the acceptable side of your line, though."

"What do you want from me?" Perez said. "It's a big story. Big stories are what I do. I had this part of it to myself. That's the game." The old Marty Perez looked at DiMaggio for a moment and said, "But what you do is pure."

"It was his daughter, Marty."

Perez said, "They're always somebody's daughter." He squeezed the sides of the satchel and said, "I needed it, okay?" Nearly whispering, Marty Perez said, "I *needed* it."

They went up to Crittendon's room and the crew set up. Maybe if Crittendon had thought it through, Marty Perez said, he would have told them all to get lost, just to buy himself some time. Get his story straight. Or come up with the one that worked. But Crittendon just sat there, very calm, while they set up. Perez said he almost seemed relieved. Crittendon asked how he got proof about Kelly Crittendon's affair with Collins. Perez said all that mattered was he had it.

They did the interview.

DiMaggio said, "You've got the tape, of course."

Perez patted the bag and said, "With me."

"Are we going to look at it?"

"In a minute. I've cued it up to the part you need to see."

Crittendon admitted that his daughter had had a relationship with Richie Collins. Perez asked him if it was a sexual relationship and Crittendon just repeated that it was a relationship. He said he found out about it. The family was considering filing statutory rape charges against Collins when Collins was murdered.

Perez said, "Then Crittendon broke down."

"And now you think it was you who pushed him over the edge?"

"No," Perez said. "Just listen to me, will you? It was what came next. After I told him what else I knew."

He reached into his bag and took out the cassette and went over and put it in the VCR sitting on top of DiMaggio's television. Then hit Play with one of his stubby fingers.

There was Frank Crittendon's face.

Same face, DiMaggio thought. But it was as if something had happened to every part of it, as if Frank Crittendon had been in a fight, a bad fight, and the eyes were wrong and the mouth was set wrong. DiMaggio looked at the picture and couldn't tell where Perez was sitting, so he couldn't tell whether Crittendon's eyes were unfocused or if he just didn't know where to look.

He heard Perez's voice, trying to be helpful.

"There's a little bit more to it, though, isn't there, Frank?"

Crittendon shifted in his chair. They were shooting him from the waist up here. Same preppy clothes. Blue shirt with the roll to the collar. Bow tie. Hair brushed straight forward, like he was some sad, pasty-faced Napoleon.

Christ, DiMaggio thought.

Crittendon: "What do you mean? I told you everything. Haven't I told you enough—?"

"Everything, Frank?"

The camera guy closed in. Crittendon's eyes were all over the place now.

Crittendon: "Richie. My Kelly . . ."

He started to get jammed up. Perez had said he broke down once. DiMaggio thought he was ready to go again.

Crittendon: "Jesus, she's just a kid."

Looking off to the side, pleading.

Crittendon: "Is it all right if I say 'Jesus'?"

Frank Crittendon trying to be a gentleman to the end.

You could hear Perez say, "Sure."

Crittendon: "Where were we?"

Perez hadn't moved from the television set. He just stood there, dead eyes watching what DiMaggio was watching, listening to himself say, "You were at Richie Collins's house in

Fulton the night he was murdered, weren't you, Frank? Isn't that the part you left out?"

Crittendon (smiling now): "No, I was not. That's crazy."

He looked around again, as if his eyes were on scan, looking for a way out.

For help.

Looking for help with none coming.

Crittendon: "Why would I go over there?"

On the tape, Perez, trying to be friendly, said, "You tell me."

Crittendon: "I wasn't there."

"I've got a witness, Frank. Got a real good one."

Crittendon's face smiled suddenly, the mouth going crooked, the whole puffy face turning into a grotesque clown's mask.

Crittendon: "NO!"

Next to the set, Marty Perez spilled some of his drink, as if the whole room had suddenly shifted underneath him.

Crittendon: "I did not kill him."

The camera stayed tight.

Crittendon (almost whispering): "He was already dead when I got there."

Perez started to say something on the tape, DiMaggio couldn't make it out, but Crittendon didn't seem to notice.

Crittendon: "I was nothing to people like Richie Collins. You have to know that. You know that, don't you? They think *you're* nothing, too. His coach, he had to at least listen to him, whether he liked him or not. Ted Salter, he's the big boss, the money man. But me? Collins . . . all of them . . . looked at me like I was some old *errand* boy. Looked at me with such *contempt.* And all these years, all these punks . . . I had put up with it, with this shit from these shit people . . . thinking they run the goddamn world . . ."

Not worrying about language anymore.

Language or anything.

Crittendon: "Basketball had been my whole life. It was a sport of precision. It had belonged to gentlemen once, to civilized people who didn't think the money was an *entitlement*. Not these smug, sneering punks. And now one of them had . . . *had* my daughter. And I knew. So I went there. Yes. I went there because I wanted to tell him to his face what scum he was. I wanted to know why he had singled *me* out, my family . . . my Kelly. This *scum*. I knew he was up there. He'd said something to the coach at practice. About a date in Fulton. Bragging. Saying they all came back to him sooner or later . . . so I went there. The door was open. I had rung the bell, I was going to leave, then the door blew open a little. I went in. I called out, asking if anybody was there . . . and then I heard the voices from the bedroom and I went in, and there was this vile movie, this dirty movie . . . and there he was . . . blood everywhere . . . the knife still in him . . . I touched him . . . he was dead. He was dead, and I *still* wanted to hurt him. I was crazy in that moment with wanting to hurt him . . . so I grabbed the knife by the handle . . . not even think-ing . . . about putting my hands on it . . . and I *twisted* it into him . . . like I was screwing *him* . . . giving it to *him* . . ."

Crittendon was nodding eagerly, looking right into the cam-era now. Earnest. As if to say, Doesn't it all make perfect sense?

Pleased with himself.

Crittendon: "I thought to myself, Frank, you really know how to hurt a guy. Isn't that funny?"

Frank Crittendon started to laugh.

Marty Perez, crying, reached over and hit Stop.

36

She came out of the Vertical Club when she said she'd come out, about five-thirty in the afternoon. Not wading into the media sharks this time. Just a clear Saturday in New York, the sun emptied out of the afternoon, New York looking like some hazy black-and-white photograph.

Hannah Carey had a purple nylon bag slung over her shoulder. She wore faded jeans with one knee ripped out, a baggy hooded sweatshirt, a black baseball cap with *?!@ sewn over the bill. DiMaggio had seen the caps in the city and up at Fulton College and had no idea if there was some hidden message or a cutting-edge reference.

Or if this was just kids putting FUCK on a baseball hat, the word right out there for the world like a headlight.

One way or the other, he was behind the curve again.

"Hey," he said.

"Mr. Second Opinion," Hannah Carey said. "I was glad you called."

DiMaggio said, "I wanted to say good-bye in person."

"Good-bye?" Hannah smiled. "We just barely said hello."

DiMaggio jerked a head toward First Avenue.

"You're not too tired to take a walk?"

"I'm all showered and tingly and ready to go."

"The last time I was that way was minor-league ball," he said. "You want me to carry your bag?"

She shook her head. "The tingly one should carry."

They walked toward First Avenue.

"You're really leaving, even with the—"

"Richie Collins's murder?"

"Yes."

"Yes," he said. At the corner, he turned south on First and she turned with him. "We could go over and sit there on Sutton, where we went after Antolotti's."

She said fine. He could see where her hair was still wet under the baseball cap. DiMaggio said, "You're sure you're not cold?"

"Like 'em and leave 'em DiMaggio," she said. "I'm fine, really."

If they walked a block east, he could show her the basketball court where he caught up with Ellis. He said, "My job is pretty much done here. The murder investigation, yeah, I'd like to know how it comes out, but that's the cops' business. The Knicks asked me to find out what happened last October with you and Richie and Ellis Adair. And now I feel like I pretty much have, and so I'm on my way back to Florida. Tomorrow probably."

They went underneath the Fifty-ninth Street Bridge, got to Fifty-eighth, and Hannah Carey said, "You sound pretty sure of yourself."

"About?"

"About last year."

"Pretty sure," DiMaggio said. "I just want to tie up a few loose ends before I go. See what happened, it's a little different from the way it came out." DiMaggio took her arm as they crossed First at Fifty-seventh and said, "Here and there."

Hannah took her arm back without making a big show of it. "The police know what happened. It took me a long time to remember."

They walked in silence toward Sutton on the long avenue block, DiMaggio aware of the silence between them, of the traffic noises behind them on First, and off in the distance somewhere, way off to the west, the sound of a fire engine.

"It's so terrible about Frank Crittendon," he said.

Having waited as long as he could.

"Frank?"

"Crittendon. General manager of the Knicks. You haven't heard?"

"No."

"He killed himself this morning at the Regency Hotel. Sleeping pills. It turns out he was at Richie Collins's house in Fulton the night he was murdered. He says he didn't kill him, but the cops already did a check on his fingerprints, and it turns out they're his prints on the knife that killed Richie."

DiMaggio turned and saw that Hannah had stopped. She had a hand over her mouth. If she was acting now, she should never have gotten out of the business. She slowly pulled the hand away from her mouth. He had noticed at Antolotti's that night, sometimes Hannah Carey looked past you, a little to the right or a little to the left. He had taken this course once, at Palm Beach Junior College, on neurolinguistics, all about interviewing techniques and how people, visualizing things, would actually look in one direction when they were telling the truth, another direction when they were lying.

Maybe he should have paid closer attention.

"I didn't know," she said. "No. I never met him. . . ." She shook her head. "I'm a little confused. Did he kill him or not?"

DiMaggio said, "Kill Richie? Before he died, he told Marty Perez that Collins was already dead and he just gave one more turn to the screw, so to speak. It turns out he had motive to go along with opportunity. Frank had found out that Richie had had sex with his daughter. Sixteen years old."

DiMaggio said gently to Hannah, "But you know that, don't you?"

Hannah said, "I'm a little confused—"

"You know that because Kelly Crittendon told you. She came to see you with Teresa Delgado, and she told you that not only did she have sex with Richie, but he raped her, too. And Kelly Crittendon also told you she saw her father coming out of Collins's house the night he was stabbed to death."

"Maybe I don't want to talk to you anymore," Hannah said.

DiMaggio said, "Just a few more minutes. I'm not looking for a confession. I've been on your side all along, and I still am. Trust me," he said to her.

They had walked to the corner of Fifty-seventh and Sutton. He took her arm again. Hannah didn't move.

"Hear me out," he said. "You can at least do that. I already told you, I'm out of your life tomorrow."

"You sound relieved."

"You know what?" DiMaggio said. "I don't know what I feel anymore."

They walked across the street, past a beat-up blue van, and sat down on the same bench they'd used after Antolotti's. They were the only ones there. The day was getting colder. Out on the river, going pretty good, was a single powerboat, its wake looking clean and white in the dirty gray water.

"I didn't even know Frank Crittendon," she said, turning to face DiMaggio. "I certainly didn't know that if I told Marty what I did, Frank Crittendon would kill himself."

"He was a very good guy."

DiMaggio took his hands out of his pockets, cupped them in front of his mouth, and blew warm air into them, then deliberately folded them in his lap.

"Your hands," she said.

"Not too bad today. Blowing on them is a habit. Like people with good hands cracking their knuckles."

"I mean it," she said. "I wasn't trying to hurt anybody. I was trying to repay a favor, that's all. He's been very generous with my side—"

"That's what Marty thought, too. But then the more he got to think about it, the more he felt bad for sandbagging Crittendon the way he did. See, I watched the interview and saw Crittendon going to pieces and when it was over, I said, 'How'd you know that last part, Marty?' And he said, 'Hannah Carey told me.' "

"I told you—"

"I just want you to tell me one more thing before I go."

He reached over and took her cap off and set it between them on the bench. She looked down, confused, but let it sit there.

DiMaggio said, "I know you were with A.J. that night."

She started to say something. DiMaggio just held up a hand and stopped her.

"Let me finish. Ellis Adair says he didn't do anything, and I believe him because I don't think he was particularly interested. What I want to know is if Richie really did rape you that night and *that's* why you killed him or if there was another reason why you killed him I don't know about."

Hannah reached down for her baseball cap and DiMaggio got to it first and put it out of her reach at his end of the bench.

"Could I have my hat, please?"

"No."

"Why not?"

"Because if you don't tell me the truth, I might have to give this hat to Brian Hyland. And when I do that—*if* I do that—Hyland is going to check the hair that's in here against the hair he found on Richie Collins's body. And I have a feeling—because I get these feelings sometimes—that it's going to be the kind of DNA match he *didn't* get off your dress."

Hannah Carey's eyes seemed to follow the powerboat, disappearing now, toward the Triborough Bridge. She said, "I thought only guys—"

"The test goes both ways," DiMaggio said. "It's kind of ironic, if you think about it."

Hannah said, "I don't understand." Just that, looking right at him now. Like she wanted him to explain where he was going with all this.

DiMaggio thought, She looks like Ellis. Having to think things out for himself now with Richie gone.

"Maybe I should go?" It came out of her a question.

"Don't leave now," he said, smiling, trying to relax her. Keep her sitting there. "Not when I'm going good. Besides, what're the cops really going to do with the goddamn hat? All the hair does is prove you were there. Which means you probably lied to them. But even with that, they've still got Frank's prints, they've got Frank admitting to Perez he was there, even if he said he didn't do it. You're in the clear." He smiled at her. "And that is fine with me. Richie Collins *deserved* to die. You did the world a favor."

"I didn't kill him," she said.

"Sure you did."

"What do you *want* from me!"

"The truth."

"About *what?*"

"This really was about A. J. Fine, wasn't it? He dumped you and then he didn't want you back and then when you thought you had him back that night, he left you there on the sidewalk. Isn't that right?"

Hannah Carey made this little rocking motion on the bench.

"Isn't that right, Hannah?"

"No."

"Yes."

She kept rocking, staring out at the river now, rocking and finally saying to DiMaggio, *"Yes!"* Rocking. "He treated me like the *rest* of them. After everything . . ." Rocking harder. "I was like the rest of them, and so was he."

DiMaggio said, "So you were going to show him, weren't you? You were going to make him jealous, walk out with a couple of his teammates right in front of him. Which you did. Except it went wrong then, didn't it? You got in over your head with Richie and Ellis. And now here you are a year later. I don't know why it took a year. Maybe you don't, either. But it did. So here you are, with a story that they both raped you. And all I'm asking is this, Hannah: Did at least *one* of them rape you?"

"I told what happened. I told Brian."

"Ellis heard you scream. Ellis left. Then it was you and Richie."

"I don't want to do this anymore." Hannah shook her head.

"Nobody's forcing you."

"Men always say that, don't they?"

Hannah was still now. She said, "I didn't kill him."

DiMaggio gently turned her, so she was facing him. "Richie raped you. He had it coming. I don't give a shit whether you killed him or not. But Ellis didn't rape you. Before I go I just want to hear *you* tell *me* that Richie Collins did."

He had been afraid she was going to cry before, cry or get hysterical or run away and blow the whole thing. But when she turned from him now, turned all the way around so she was facing him on the bench, she was calm.

"Yes," she said. "Yes, he raped me. That *animal.* I woke up, and he had tied me to the *sofa.* And he raped me. And then he cleaned himself off and left me there and came back. And then he raped me again."

"Why Ellis—"

"Because he *let* him, that's why. You know what the last thing was? That I remembered? You want to know, Mr. Second Opinion, just doing your job? I remember that fucking door slamming while I screamed for him to come help me."

She drank in air in big gulps, blew it out, DiMaggio feeling her breath on his face, they were that close now.

"Ellis didn't do what the other one did?" Hannah said. "Fuck him, okay? He did enough. He *let* him." She stared past him now. "You wanted the truth? There it is. Nobody was going to ignore me if Ellis Adair was in it. And he was. He was an accomplice. He was there, and he *let* him."

DiMaggio stared out at the East River. What did Ellis and the rest of them say? Whoomp, there it is.

All of it, finally.

Nearly all of it.

"Why did you kill him?" he said softly. "Was it that he was going to get off? Did he tell you he was going to do it again? Frank Crittendon said it to Perez. Richie'd told his coach, they all came back around sooner or later."

DiMaggio said to her, "Even you. That's what he meant, didn't he? Even somebody he'd raped. Isn't that right?"

"Frank Crittendon killed him."

"I don't think so," DiMaggio said.

She reached down into her bag and came out with a cigarette and a Bic lighter. She took a drag of the cigarette. "I allow myself one a day."

"Why did you go up there?"

She smoked and stared out at the East River again. "It was such a dumb idea," she said casually, like she was telling him what a dope she'd been to leave the car lights on or the water running. "I realized it when I got up there. I had called him and told him I'd had a change of heart, that I wanted to see him. To talk things over. I was going to see if I could get him into bed and then pull out a gun and scare him. Not a knife." Hannah turned to DiMaggio. "Don't you see? I wanted him to see how it felt for once. Being helpless. I thought I deserved that much satisfaction."

"You have a gun?"

"Had. I bought it after the rape, permit and everything. You can check it out if you want. But when I got back that night, I threw it in the river. I'm not really the gun type."

"You were going to scare him, that was all?"

Hannah nodded. "Exactly. I was going to get him into bed and then stick the gun in his mouth and tell him to scream a little bit."

"But you didn't do that."

"I got scared all over again." She blew some smoke out the side of her mouth. "This time I ran out of there before things got out of hand." Hannah said, "He thought he was *so* irresistible."

"You got him into bed, though?"

She looked at him. "Obviously," she said. "If they found my hair when they found him."

"Where?"

"In his bed."

"How'd you know they found him in bed?" DiMaggio said.

"What?"

"I was wondering how you knew Richie Collins was in bed. Hyland never said they found him in bed. He just said they found him at the house. The newspapers never said they found him in bed. How'd you know he was in bed?"

DiMaggio handed her back the cap. "They didn't find any hair," he said.

"You lied," Hannah said.

Beautiful hands, beautiful fingers.

"I lied, you lied," he said. "And you killed him."

She didn't answer, just pulled up her knees in front of her, pulled them close to her.

"You killed him and poor old Frank Crittendon will take the rap. Richie got away with rape, you get away with murder."

Hannah Carey got up, dropped the cigarette, and stubbed it out with the toe of her sneaker. "Good-bye, Mr. Second Opinion."

"Say good-bye to everybody," DiMaggio said.

He opened the jacket to the blue suit to show her the microphone Hyland had hooked up.

"I'm sorry," he said into the microphone to the Fulton cop. "We're getting nowhere here."

He reached up with his own right hand, touched her cheek, surprised at how cold she felt, turned her face toward the street so she could see Brian Hyland when he opened the side door to the blue van. Hyland sat there with the receiving equipment, cramped in the back with another cop who was working the camera.

"You don't even have to wait," DiMaggio said to Hannah Carey. "You're in the movies already."

What did that mean?

Now you're in the movies?

Why did he have that disappointed look on his face? Why had men *always* looked at her like that? Like she'd let them down?

Like she didn't measure up?

Her mother started looking at her that way when she didn't measure up in tennis, and then it was like the rest of the world took over.

Stop looking at me that way.

Like I don't get it.

Why wouldn't Brian Hyland come over and talk to her?

He just stood there next to the blue van. Giving her the same look. Not the friendly Brian she'd talked to on the telephone. Not the one she finally met. Now he had that disappointed look. Like Hannah had let *him* down.

DiMaggio got up and walked toward the van.

Now you're in the movies?

They were the ones who didn't get it, Hannah thought. It was all a movie, at least once she got it straight in her head. She couldn't make anybody understand, of course. God, she couldn't even make Beth understand.

A.J. never understood.

Sometimes she thought about killing A.J.

Boy, how many times had she pictured *that!*

He had been too rough with her that night down by that stupid duck pond, almost as rough as Richie was later. She hadn't wanted to, she wanted to talk to him, make him understand once and for all that they belonged together. That she was the best thing that had ever happened to him.

But he didn't want to talk. Oh no. He didn't care that she didn't want to. He didn't care what *she* wanted . . .

But she loved him. When they were together, he was the only one who didn't treat her like she was some dumb blonde.

A.J. *listened.*

A.J. was *interested.*

She couldn't kill A.J. She hadn't kept the dress for evidence. She kept it because it was A.J.'s favorite. It was only later, when she could remember everything, she thought there might be some of that DNA stuff on it. After she had seen some of the other cases, realized you could do something.

You didn't just have to lie there, even afterward, and take it.

What were the two of them *talking* about over there?

Wasn't that the way it always went, though? Guy stuff? Like they got what they wanted from Hannah and now she wasn't even here?

Didn't they understand that Richie *had* to die?

That it didn't matter who did it?

God, she was supposed to be the dumb one and it was so *obvious*. At least once it became clear that he was going to get off.

Get off, Hannah thought.

That's a good one. I'll have to remember that one to tell Jimmy.

Not just that he was going to get off. It was more than that. She knew when he came to see her in front of Jimmy's apartment. Scaring her that way.

She started thinking about it that day.

He was *so* happy when she called. So sure she still wanted him. She had been so careful, wearing the body stocking, not sure how you could leave prints. That sexy white body stocking.

Richie thinking it was some kind of sex game. Telling her it was like she was wearing a body condom.

The *safest* sex, she had purred at him once she was down to the stocking.

Like you won't believe, Richie.

He looked so happy. Not disappointed at all.

What were Brian and DiMaggio *waiting* for?

For her to tell them the good parts?

Close your eyes, Richie.

I want to watch.

In a minute.

He was so happy.

I've got a little toy I want to show you, she said.

I love toys, he said.

The knife was in her purse . . .

Who knew Frank Crittendon would make it so easy for her?

Hannah laughed.

Men.

She wondered why more of them didn't end up like Richie Collins.

That was the amazing thing, if you really thought about it.

37

"How many times have you said you're leaving tomorrow?" Ellen Harper said.

"I'll figure it out and tell you tomorrow," DiMaggio said.

They were lying in the big bed at the Sherry, in the back of the suite, in the back of the dignified old New York hotel, after doing undignified things. They had eaten dinner at a place she picked out on Twenty-ninth Street called Tempo. It was when they were having brandy after dinner that she said, "I'm not going back to Connecticut tonight, am I?" DiMaggio smiled at her. He did it all the time, going slow with her, too old not to. He signaled for the check, and they rode uptown in the cab, holding hands, and he played the piano for her.

Then they did something else, finally.

Now they were in bed listening to another Nancy LaMott tape he'd found. Maybe New York hadn't been a total loss, everything going bad. He met Ellen Harper because he came to New York. And he found out about Nancy LaMott, who sang his kind of music the way it was supposed to be sung.

He'd been threatening to go back to Jupiter for two weeks, the two weeks since he found Ellis Adair.

"Sometimes I get the feeling it's not over for you," Ellen Harper said.

"It's as over as it's going to be."

He rested a hand lightly on her hip.

"You're still convinced she did it?"

"Oh, sure."

"And she's going to get away with it, even with what she said on the tape?"

"We just thought that if I could get her to panic and confess on the tape, she might give it all up for Hyland. Other than that, the tape doesn't do him any good. She doesn't even have to talk to him about it, as a matter of fact. Hyland walked over to her from the van when I finished with her and said, 'What about this?' And I've got to hand it to her, she was smart enough to say, 'I'm confused, talk to my lawyer.' Then she got into a cab and went home. Hyland called Harvey Kuhn—her lawyer—and Kuhn said what I would've said: 'You want to try and arrest my client off what she said to a third party on some inadmissible videotape, be my guest. Other than that, we have nothing to say.' "

"You're kidding," Ellen said. "She doesn't have to talk to the cops if she doesn't feel like it?"

"Nope. Hyland's just left with an open investigation on Richie's murder. But he knows it's an investigation going nowhere."

She gently took his hand and kissed it.

Ellen said, "But Hannah lied about having an alibi."

"Hannah turned out to be a rather unreliable narrator, let's face it. And lying about her alibi doesn't prove anything. It doesn't give them probable cause, it doesn't give them sufficient reason to arrest her, or even issue a warrant. They had no physical evidence with her, any more than they had physical evidence with the rape. She got crazy and killed Richie, I'm convinced of that.

Then she got lucky with Frank Crittendon. He got crazy and killed himself."

Ellen said, "I can't believe she doesn't have to talk to the cops."

"Hyland was talking about the O. J. Simpson thing one day, and how that first day after they found the bodies, O.J. went in and voluntarily talked to the cops without a lawyer present. Hyland said, 'You know how many times in the history of the world that has helped a suspect? Never.' Only idiots talk to the cops when they don't have to."

DiMaggio sighed. "This thing began with the basketball players not talking to the cops about rape and ends with the rape victim not talking to the cops about killing one of the players."

"How do you feel about all this?" she said.

"Which?"

"That she gets away with it."

"I don't know." He got out of bed. "You want one more brandy? I think I might have one. At my age, you need help getting to sleep."

She winked at him, said, "After the brandy helps you, I'll help the brandy."

He came back with one glass for both of them.

"Why did you have to know?" she said.

"Because I did. Marty Perez was right about something. I have to know."

He sipped the brandy, handed it to her. "I don't think I ever asked you," Ellen said, "but why do you think Marty Perez helped you?"

"He really felt like he killed Frank Crittendon. And he wanted to work off some of the guilt. If somebody deserved to be a victim here, it was Richie Collins, not Frank."

"All you ended up with are victims."

"I know," DiMaggio said.

"Hannah was just the first one."

"Now she gets away with murder."

Ellen said, "And you want to feel worse about that than you do."

DiMaggio said, "Remember what I told you about my mother?"

The sheets had fallen off her. Ellen was one of those people who were perfectly relaxed naked. She had her head propped up on one elbow. She said, "Yes."

"I told you how I went after the guy?"

She nodded.

"I could've killed that guy."

Ellen Harper took the glass out of his hand then and helped the brandy, and they slept until two o'clock in the morning, when there was one last phone call, this one from Ellis Adair.

The cab dropped him off at the corner of Sixty-first and First. DiMaggio walked over from there to wake up a little more. When he got to the playground, the blue bike was where it had been the first time, leaning against the fence.

Ellis Adair was on the court, wearing most of his disguise, just not the beard this time, shooting layups, one after another, in a light rain. DiMaggio, dressed in sweats himself because Ellis had told him to, walked over to him and said, "Hey."

Adair flipped him the ball, not too hard. DiMaggio caught it. Maybe it was Ellen. Or the brandy. Or still being half asleep. The ball didn't hurt. He flipped a little set shot at the basket and missed everything. Ellis laughed and then sang "Air balllllllll" in a deep voice, the way they did in an arena when somebody shot one.

DiMaggio said, "I'm out of practice." Ellis gave him the ball again, and DiMaggio shot another one up there, this one bouncing off the back rim. He said, "Didn't you guys have a game tonight?"

Ellis Adair said, "Boston. We won. Then we flew right out after the game, our private plane. Landed at La Guardia about one. I needed to get out. I played in worse conditions than this."

DiMaggio said, "Dale back?"

"Tomorrow. I wasn't even sure you'd still be in town."

"I keep saying I'm going to leave, but I don't leave. I met someone."

Ellis nodded at the bench, and they went over and sat down. He still had the ball. He spun it on the tip of his fingers the way the Globetrotters did, smiling as he did, making it look ridiculously easy.

Looking ridiculously young and happy doing it.

"She did it, didn't she? That's what Mr. Salter said anyhow."

"She did it."

"And she's gonna walk."

"Yes."

DiMaggio said, "Let me ask you something somebody just asked me: Does that bother you?"

Ellis gave the spinning ball a little punch, and it bounced away toward the basket. "Not as much as I thought it would, even as much as Rich meant to me. You know what I was thinking on the plane? I was thinking that she just convicted Richie her own self. That one woman down in Virginia, she cut the guy's deal off. Hannah Carey just didn't stop there."

DiMaggio said, "Is that why you brought me over here, to talk about her?"

"No," Ellis said.

He stood and walked over to get the ball. He dribbled it a few times and made a spin move, then fell away from the basket and shot a soft jumper that whooshed through the net. He retrieved the ball and came over and stood in front of DiMaggio but did not sit down this time. A car made a right on Sixty-first, then backed up, and went up to Sixty-second and got on the F.D.R. going north there. Ellis said, "Remember the other time? When I told you I'd explain to you sometime why I left that day?"

Ellis said, "It wasn't the test on the damn dress. That was just a damn coincidence." He took a deep breath and said in a soft voice, "It was the day Dale found out he tested positive for the virus."

DiMaggio sat there, the rain coming harder now. Not having to ask what virus.

"I just couldn't deal with all of it no more. I couldn't tell Richie, I couldn't tell anybody. All the assholes in the world, it had to happen to Dale, who never hurt anybody . . ."

Ellis Adair's face wet with the rain, DiMaggio not being able to tell if he was crying.

"I finally worked up the nerve, got tested myself. After all these years."

DiMaggio knowing what was coming next.

Wanting to be wrong.

"I found out today," Ellis Adair said.

DiMaggio leaned back, put his head back, let the rain hit his face.

Finally, DiMaggio said, "What do you do now?"

"Quit," Ellis said. "Quit like Magic did, so they can't run me out the way they done with him. I was thinking about playing one more game at the Garden, but what's the point. You know? I made a real nice play tonight, down near the end? Went down the middle, and they all come up on me, and I stayed up there. Like I can? And finally I switched hands and spun it in left-handed, off the top of the board. I was thinking on that on the plane. Maybe that was as good a good-bye shot as any."

"Anyway," he said to DiMaggio. "You were decent to me when you found out about Dale 'n' me. Not looking to score off me or whatever. Not wanting nothing. So I wanted you to know. Tell you myself."

"Jesus, Ellis—"

"I'll be all right. I knew I'd have to stop ball someday. Just never figured it'd be like this."

DiMaggio thinking, There's always one last victim.

Ellis said, "What do they always tell you? You play, you pay, right? You play, you pay. We just don't none of us ever think it's gonna apply to *us*. Do we?"

DiMaggio said, "Something like that."

Ellis Adair tossed him the ball again. Smiling this sweet smile. "You want to play?" he said to DiMaggio.

About the Author

Mike Lupica is one of the best-known and widely read sports columnists in the United States. His career began at the *New York Post,* where, at twenty-three, he covered the New York Knicks. After working at the *New York Daily News, New York Newsday,* and *The National,* he now writes a syndicated column four days a week with the *Daily News.* He's also written for *Esquire, Sport, World Tennis, Tennis, Golf Digest, Playboy, Sports Illustrated,* and *Parade.* He appears on ESPN's "The Sports Reporters."

Lupica is the author or co-author of these non-fiction books: *Reggie,* Reggie Jackson's autobiography; *Parcells,* the autobiography of Bill Parcells, ex-coach of the New York Giants and New England Patriots; *Wait 'Till Next Year,* with William Goldman; *Shooting from The Lip,* an anthology of past columns; *Mad as Hell,* an examination of various controversial issues in the sports world; *Summer of '98,* a look at that year's baseball season; and *Bump and Run,* a satirical look at pro football. His other novels include *Dead Air,* which he adapted for the television movie "Money, Power, Murder," *Extra Credits, Limited Partner,* and most recently, *Full Court Press.*

Lupica, his wife, Taylor, and their three sons reside in New Canaan, Connecticut.

"Book 'em!"
Legal Thrillers from Kensington

Scare Up One of These
Pinnacle Horrors

A World of Eerie Suspense
Awaits in Novels by Noel Hynd

Western Adventures From Pinnacle

__Requiem At Dawn
by Sheldon Russell   0-7860-1103-3 $5.99US/$7.99CAN

They called it Fort Supply, the last outpost of the U.S. Army on the boundary of Oklahoma Territory—home to the damned, the disgraced, and the dispirited. Now, Doc McReynolds has been ordered to establish a redoubt at Cimarron Crossing. But while McReynolds leads his company to Deep Hole Creek, a past he'd like to forget dogs his every step.

__Apache Ambush
by Austin Olsen   0-7860-1148-3 $5.99US/$7.99CAN

For a military man it was the farthest you could fall: the command of a troop of Buffalo Soldiers in the Ninth Colored Cavalry Regiment. For Lieutenant William Northey, managing misfits was all that he was good for. Amidst the dying and the valor, a bitter, defeated army man would find a woman to love, soldiers to be proud of, and the warrior that still lived in his heart. . . .